SERAFINA
and the
TWISTED STAFF

SERAFINA
and the
TWISTED STAFF

ROBERT BEATTY

DISNEP·HYPERION

LOS ANGELES   NEW YORK

Copyright © 2016 by Robert Beatty

All rights reserved. Published by Disney Hyperion, an imprint of
Disney Book Group. No part of this book may be reproduced or transmitted
in any form or by any means, electronic or mechanical, including photocopying,
recording, or by any information storage and retrieval system, without
written permission from the publisher. For information address
Disney Hyperion, 125 West End Avenue, New York, New York 10023.

First Hardcover Edition, July 2016
First Paperback Edition, July 2017
1 3 5 7 9 10 8 6 4 2
FAC-020093-17139

Printed in the United States of America

This book is set in 11.16-pt Adobe Garamond Pro/Fontspring;
Minister Std/Monotype, Liam, Qilin/Fontspring
Designed by Maria Elias

Library of Congress Control Number for the Hardcover Edition: 2016006654
ISBN 978-1-4847-7806-7

Visit www.DisneyBooks.com

This book is dedicated to you, the readers who helped spread the word about *Serafina and the Black Cloak* and, in so doing, made this second book possible.

And to Jennifer, Camille, Genevieve, and Elizabeth: my co-conspirators, co-creators, and the loves of my life.

Biltmore Estate
Asheville, North Carolina
1899

**Three weeks after defeating
the Man in the Black Cloak**

Serafina stalked through the underbrush of the moonlit forest, slinking low to the ground, her eyes fixed on her prey. Just a few feet in front of her, a large wood rat gnawed on a beetle he'd dug up. Her heart beat strong and steady in her chest, marking her slow and quiet creep toward the rat. Her muscles buzzed, ready to pounce. But she did not rush. Swiveling her shoulders back and forth to fine-tune the angle of her attack, she waited for just the right moment. When the rat bent down to pick up another beetle, she leapt.

The rat caught a glimpse of her out of the corner of his eye just as she sprang. It was beyond her ken why so many animals of the forest froze in terror when she pounced. If death by tooth and claw came leaping at *her* out of the darkness, she'd fight.

Or she'd run. She'd do *something*. Little woodland creatures like rats and rabbits and chipmunks weren't known for their boldness of heart, but what was freezing in sheer terror going to do?

As she dropped onto the rat, she snatched him up quicker than a whiskerblink and clutched him in her hand. And now that it was well past too late, he started squirming, biting, and scratching, his furry little body becoming a wriggling snake, his tiny heart racing at a terrific pace. *There it is,* she thought, feeling the *thumpty-thumpty* of his heartbeat in her bare hand. *There's the fight.* It quickened her pulse and stirred her senses. Suddenly, she could detect everything in the forest around her—the sound of a tree frog moving on a branch thirty feet behind her, the reedy buzz of a lonely timberdoodle in the distance, and the glimpse of a bat swishing through the starlit sky above the broken canopy of the trees.

It was all for practice, of course, the prowling and the pouncing, the stalking of prey and the snatching hold. She didn't kill the wild things she hunted, didn't need to, but they didn't know that, darn it! She was terror! She was death! So why at the last moment of her attack did they freeze? Why didn't they flee?

Serafina sat down on the forest floor with her back against an old, gnarled, lichen-covered oak tree and held the rat in her clenched fist on her lap.

Then she slowly opened her hand.

The rat darted away as fast as he could, but she snatched him up and brought him back to her lap again.

She held the rat tight for several seconds and then opened her hand once more.

This time, the rat did not run. He sat on her hand, trembling and panting, too confused and exhausted to move.

She lifted the terrified rodent a little closer on her open hand, tilted her head, and studied him. The wood rat didn't look like the nasty gray sewer varmints she was used to catching in the basement of Biltmore Estate. This particular rat had a scarred tear in his left ear. He'd encountered some trouble before. And with his dark little eyes and the tremulous whiskers of his long, pointy nose, he seemed more like a cute, chubby brown mouse than the proper vermin on which she had earned her title. She could almost imagine a little hat on his head and a buttoned vest. She felt a pang of guilt that she'd caught him, but she also knew that if he tried to run again, her hand would snatch him up before she even thought about it. It wasn't a decision. It was a reflex.

As the little rat tried to catch his breath, his eyes darted to and fro for a way out. But he didn't dare. He knew that as soon as he tried to run, she'd grab him again, that it was the nature of her kind to play with him, to paw him, to claw him, until he was finally dead.

But she looked at the rat and then set him on the forest floor. "Sorry, little fellow—just practicing my skills."

The rat gazed up at her in confusion.

"Go ahead," she said gently.

The rat glanced toward the thistle thicket.

"There ain't no trick in it," she said.

3

The rat didn't seem to believe her.

"You go on home, now," she told him. "Just move slowly away at first, not too fast—that's the way of it. And keep your eyes and ears open next time, even if you got a beetle to chew on, you hear? There are far meaner things in these woods than me."

Astonished, the torn-eared wood rat rubbed his little hands over his face repeatedly and bobbed his head, almost as if he was bowing. She snorted a little laugh through her nose, which finally startled the rat into action. He quickly got his wits about him and scampered into the thicket.

"Have a good evenin', now," she said. She reckoned he'd bolster his memory of his courage the farther he got away from her and have a good story to tell his wife and little ones by the time he got home for supper. She smiled as she imagined him telling a great and twisty tale with his family gathered around, how he was in the forest just minding his own business, gnawing on a beetle, when a vicious predator pounced upon him and he had to fight for his every breath. She wondered if she'd be a beast of ferocious power in the story. Or just a girl.

At that moment, she heard a sound from above like an autumn breeze flowing through the tops of the trees. But there wasn't a breeze. The midnight air was chilled and quiet and perfectly still, like God was holding his breath.

She heard a delicate, almost gossamer, whisper-like murmur. She looked up, but all she could see were the branches of the trees. Rising to her feet, she brushed off the simple green work dress that Mrs. Vanderbilt had given her the day before

4

and walked through the forest, listening for the sound. She tried to determine the direction it was coming from. She tilted her head left and then right, but the sound seemed to have no position. She made her way over to a rocky outcropping, where the ground fell steeply away into a forested valley. From here she could see a great distance, miles yonder across the mist to the silhouettes of the Blue Ridge Mountains on the other side. A thin layer of silvery white clouds glowing with light passed slowly in front of the moon. The brightness of the moon cast a wide-arcing halo in the feathery clouds, shone through them, and threw a long, jagged shadow onto the ground behind her.

She stood on the rocky ledge and scanned the valley in front of her. In the distance, the pointed towers and slate-covered rooftops of the grand Biltmore Estate rose from the darkness of the surrounding forest. The pale gray limestone walls were adorned with gargoyles of mythical beasts and fine sculptures of the warriors of old. The stars reflected in the slanting windowpanes, and the mansion's gold- and copper-trimmed roofline glinted in the moonlight. There in the great house, Mr. and Mrs. Vanderbilt slept on the second floor, along with their nephew, her friend, Braeden Vanderbilt. The Vanderbilts' guests—family members from out of town, businessmen, dignitaries, famous artists—slept on the third floor, each in their own luxuriously appointed room.

Serafina's pa maintained the steam heating system, the electric dynamo, the laundry machines powered by spinning leather straps, and all the other newfangled devices on the estate. She and her pa lived in the workshop in the basement down the corridor from the kitchens, laundry rooms, and storerooms. But while all the people she knew and loved slept through the night, Serafina did not. She napped on and off during the day, curled up in a window or hidden in some dark nook in the basement. At night she prowled the corridors of Biltmore, both upstairs and down, a silent, unseen watcher. She explored the winding paths of the estate's vast gardens and the darkened dells of the surrounding forest, and she hunted.

She was a twelve-year-old girl, but she had never lived what anyone other than herself would call a normal life. She had spent her time creeping through the estate's vast basement catching rats. Her pa, half joking when he'd said it, had dubbed her the C.R.C.: the Chief Rat Catcher. But she'd taken on the title with pride.

Her pa had always loved her and did the best he could to raise her, in his own rough-hewn way. She certainly hadn't been unhappy eating supper with her pa each evening and sneaking through the darkness at night ridding the great house of rodents. Who would be? But deep down, she'd been a fair bit lonely and mighty confused. She had never been able to square why most folk carried a lantern in the dark, or why they made so much noise when they walked, or what compelled them to sleep through the night just when all manner of things were at their most beautiful. She'd spied on enough of the estate's children from a distance to know she wasn't one of them. When she gazed into a mirror, she saw a girl with large amber eyes, deeply angled cheekbones, and a shaggy mane of streaked brown hair.

No, she wasn't a normal, everyday child. She wasn't an *any* day child. She was a creature of the night.

As she stood at the edge of the valley, she heard again the sound that had brought her there, a gentle fluttering, like a river of whispers traveling on the currents of wind that flowed high above her. The stars and planets hung in the blackened sky, scintillating as if they were alive with the spirits of ten thousand souls, but they offered no answers to the mystery.

A small, dark shape crossed in front of the moon and disappeared. Her heart skipped a beat. What was it?

She watched. Another shape passed the moon, and then another. At first, she thought they must be bats, but bats didn't fly in straight lines like these.

She frowned, confused and fascinated.

Tiny shape after tiny shape crossed in front of the moon. She looked up high into the sky and saw the stars disappearing. Her eyes widened in alarm. But then the realization of what she was seeing slowly crept into her. Squinting her eyes just right, she could see great flocks of songbirds flying over the valley. Not just one or two, or a dozen, but long, seemingly endless streams of them—clouds of them. The birds filled the sky. The sound she was hearing was the soft murmur of thousands of tiny wings of sparrows, wrens, and waxwings making their fall journey. They were like jewels, green and gold, yellow and black, striped and spotted, thousands upon thousands of them. It seemed far too late in the year for them to be migrating, but here they were. They hurried across the sky, their little wings fluttering, heading southward for the winter, traveling secretly at night to avoid the hawks that hunted in the day, using the ridges of the mountains below and the alignment of the glinting stars above to find their way.

The flighty, twitching movement of birds had always tantalized her, had always quickened her pulse, but this was different. Tonight the boldness and beauty of these little birds' trek down the mountainous spine of the continent flowed through her heart. It felt as if she was seeing a once-in-a-lifetime event, but then she realized that the birds were following the path that their parents and grandparents had taught them, that they'd been flying this path for millions of years. The only thing "once in a lifetime" about this was *her*, that she was here, that she was seeing it. And it amazed her.

Seeing the birds made her think of Braeden. He loved birds and other animals of all kinds.

"I wish you could see this," she whispered, as if he was lying awake in his bed and could hear her across the miles of distance between them. She longed to share the moment with her friend. She wished he was standing beside her, gazing up at the stars and the birds and the silver-edged clouds and the shining moon in all its glory. She knew she'd tell him all about it the next time she saw him. But daytime words could never capture the beauty of the night.

A few weeks before, she and Braeden had defeated the Man in the Black Cloak and had torn the Black Cloak asunder. She and Braeden had been allies, and good friends, but it sank in once again, this time even deeper than before, that she hadn't seen him in several nights. With every passing night, she expected a visit at the workshop. But every morning she went to bed disappointed, and it left her with biting doubts. What was he doing? Was something keeping him from her? Was he purposefully avoiding her? She'd been so happy to finally have a friend to talk to. It made her burn inside to think that maybe she was just a novelty to him that had worn off, and now she was left to return to her lonely nights of prowling on her own. They were friends. She was sure of it. But she worried that she didn't fit in upstairs in the daylight, that she didn't belong there. Could he have forgotten about her so quickly?

As the birds thinned out and the moment passed, she looked out across the valley and wondered. After defeating the Man in the Black Cloak, she reckoned herself one of the Guardians, the marble lions that stood on either side of Biltmore's front doors, protecting the house from demons and evil spirits. She imagined herself the C.R.C. of not just the small, four-legged vermin, but of intruders of all kinds. Her pa had always warned her about the world, of the dangers that could ensnare her soul, and after everything that had happened, she was sure there were more demons out there.

For weeks now, she'd been watching and waiting, like a guard on a watchtower, but she had no idea when or in what shape the demons would come. Her darkest worry, deep down, when she faced it true, was whether she'd be strong enough, smart enough—whether she'd end up the predator or the prey. Maybe the little animals like the wood rat and the chipmunk knew that death was just a pounce away. Did they think of themselves as prey? Maybe they were almost expecting to die, ready to die. But she sure wasn't. She had things to do.

Her friendship with Braeden had just begun, and she wasn't going to give up on it just because they'd hit a snag. And she had only just started to understand her connection to the forest, to figure out who and what she was. And now that she'd met the Vanderbilts face-to-face, her pa had been pressuring her to start acting like a proper daytime girl. Mrs. V was taking her in, always talking to her with a gentle word. Now she had the basement and the forest and the upstairs—she'd gone from having too few kin to having too many, getting pulled in three directions at once. But after years of living without any family besides her pa, it felt good to be getting started with her new life.

All that was fine and good. When danger came, she wanted to fight, she wanted to live. Who didn't? But what if the danger came so fast she never saw it coming? What if, like an owl attacking a mouse, the claws dropped from the sky and killed her before she even knew they were there? What if the real danger wasn't just whether she could fight whatever threat that came, but whether she even recognized it before it was too late?

The more she thought about the flocks of birds she'd seen, the more it rankled her peace of mind. It was plenty warm, but she couldn't stop thinking that December seemed far too late in the year for birds to be coming and going. She frowned and searched the sky for the North Star. When she found it, she realized that the birds hadn't even been flying in the right direction. She wasn't even sure they were the kinds of birds that flew south for the winter.

As she stood on the rocky edge of the high ground, the dark ooze of dread seeped into her bones.

She looked up at where the birds had been flying, and then she looked in the direction they came from. She gazed out across the top of the darkened forest. Her mind tried to work it through. And then she realized what was happening.

The birds weren't migrating.

They were *fleeing*.

She pulled in a long, deep breath as her body readied itself. Her heart began to pound. The muscles of her arms and legs tightened.

Whatever it was, it was coming.

And it was coming now.

A moment later, a sound in the distance tickled Serafina's ear. It wasn't sparrow wings, like she'd heard before, but something earthbound. She tilted her head and listened for it again. It seemed to be coming from down in the valley.

She stood, faced the sound, and cupped her hands around the back of her ears, a trick she'd learned from mimicking a bat.

She heard the faint jangle of harnesses and the clip-clop of hooves. Her stomach tightened. It was a strange sound to encounter in the middle of the night. A team of horses pulling a carriage was making its way up the three-mile-long winding road toward the house. In the daytime, there would be nothing unusual about that. But no one ever came to Biltmore at night. Something was wrong. Was it a messenger bearing bad news? Had someone died? Was the North going to war with the South again? What calamity had befallen the world?

Pulling back from the rocky ledge, she hurried down into the valley and made her way through the forest to one of the arched brick bridges where the road crossed over the stream. She watched from the concealing leaves of the mountain laurel as an old, road-beaten carriage passed by. Most carriages had one or two horses, but this carriage was pulled by four dark brown stallions with powerful, bulging muscles, their hides glistening with sweat in the moonlight and their nostrils flaring.

She swallowed hard. *That isn't a messenger.*

Braeden had told her that stallions were wild and notoriously difficult to deal with—they kicked their handlers and bit people, and especially hated other stallions—but here were four of them pulling a carriage in unison.

When she looked at who was driving the carriage, the hairs on the back of her neck stood on end. The carriage bench was empty. The horses were all cantering together in a forceful rhythm, as if by the rein of a master, but there was no driver to be seen.

Serafina clenched her teeth. This was all wrong. She could feel it in her core. The carriage was heading straight for Biltmore, where everyone was fast asleep and had no idea it was coming.

As the carriage rounded a bend and went out of sight, Serafina broke into a run and followed.

She ran through the forest, tracking the carriage as it traveled down the winding road. The cotton dress Mrs. Vanderbilt had given her wasn't too long, so it was easy to run in, but keeping pace with the horses was surprisingly difficult. She tore through the forest, leaping over fallen logs and bounding over ferns. She jumped gullies and climbed hills. She took short-cuts, taking advantage of the road's meandering path. Her chest began to heave as she pulled in great gulps of air. Despite the trepidation she had felt moments before, the challenge of keeping up with the horses made her smile and then made her laugh, which made it all the more difficult to breathe when she was trying to run. Leaping and darting, she loved the thrill of the chase.

Then, all of a sudden, the horses slowed.

She pulled herself short and hunkered down.

The horses came to a stop.

She ducked behind a clump of rhododendrons a stone's throw from the carriage and concealed herself as she tried to catch her breath.

Why is the carriage stopping?

The horses anxiously shifted their hooves, and steam poured from their nostrils.

Her heart pounded as she watched the carriage.

The handle of the carriage door turned.

She crouched low to the ground.

The carriage door swung slowly open.

She thought she could see two figures inside, but then there was a roil of darkness like she'd never seen before—a shadow so black and fleeting that it was impossible for even *her* eyes to make it out.

A tall and sinewy man in a wide-brimmed leather hat and a dark, weather-beaten coat emerged from the carriage. He had long, knotty gray hair and a gray mustache and beard that reminded her of moss hanging from a craggy tree. As he climbed down from the carriage and stood on the road, he held a gnarled walking stick and gazed out into the forest.

Behind him, a vicious-looking wolfhound slunk down from the carriage onto the ground. Then another followed. The hounds had large, lanky bodies, massive heads with black eyes, and ratty, thick blackish-gray fur. Five dogs in all came forth from the carriage and stood together, scanning the forest for something to kill.

Afraid to make even the slightest sound, Serafina took in a slow, ragged breath as carefully and quietly as she possibly could. The beat of her heart pounded in her chest. She wanted to run. *Just stay still,* she ordered herself. *Stay very still.* She was sure that as long as she didn't break cover, they wouldn't see her.

She wasn't certain what it was—maybe his long, frayed coat and the worn state of his carriage—but the man seemed as if he'd traveled a long distance. It surprised her when he shut the carriage door, stepped away, and looked at the horses. The stallions immediately broke into a run like they had been whipped. The carriage soon disappeared down the road, taking whoever remained inside onward toward Biltmore but leaving the bearded man and his dogs behind in the forest. The man did not appear to be dismayed or upset by this, but acted as though this forest was exactly where he wanted to be.

Saying words Serafina could not understand, the man gathered his pack of dogs around him. They were foul beasts with massive paws and thick claws. They didn't seem like normal dogs that sniffed the ground and explored the forest. They all looked up at their master, as if waiting for his instructions.

The man's face was shrouded by the bent brim of his hat. But when he tilted his head upward toward the moon, Serafina sucked in a breath. The man's silvery eyes glinted with power, peering out from his weathered, craggy face. His mouth came slowly open like he was trying to suck in the moonlight. Just when she thought he was going to utter words, he let out the most terrifying hissing scream she had ever heard. It was a long, raspy screech. And right at that moment, a ghostly white barn owl appeared out of the trees, flying overhead, the beat of its wings utterly silent, but then it answered the man's call with a bloodcurdling scream in return. The sound sent a terrible burst of shivers down Serafina's spine. And as the owl flew by her, its eerie, flat-faced head pivoted toward her, as if searching, hunting. She ducked to the ground like a frightened mouse.

As the owl disappeared into the midnight gloom, Serafina peeked back toward the road. Her heart stopped cold. The bearded man and his five hounds were now looking out into the forest in her direction, the man's eyes still gleaming with an unnatural light despite the fact that he had turned away from the moon. She tried to convince herself that it was impossible for the man and his dogs to see her concealed in the leaves. But she couldn't shake the horrible fear that they knew exactly where she was. The ground beneath her seemed to become slippery with some unknown dampness. The ivy on the forest floor seemed to be moving. She heard a *tick-tick-ticking* sound, followed by a long, raspy hiss. Suddenly, she felt the touch of the man's breath on the back of her neck, and she spun around, cringing violently, but there was nothing there but blackness.

The man reached into his pocket with one of his knobby, leathery-skinned hands and took out what appeared to be a scrap of torn, dark-colored cloth.

"Breathe it in," he ordered his dogs, his voice low and sinister. There was something about the stranger's rugged face and beard, his rustic clothing, and the way he said his words that made her think he was an Appalachian man, born and raised in the rocky ravines and thorny coves of these very mountains.

The first wolfhound pushed its muzzle into the folds of the dark cloth. When it drew its nose out again, its mouth gaped open, its teeth bared and chattering, dripping with saliva. The dog began to growl. Then the second dog and the third nosed the dark cloth, until all five had taken the scent. The wicked, snarling malevolence of the hounds stabbed her stomach with fear. Her only hope was that the trail of the cloth's scent would take them in the opposite direction.

The man looked down at his pack of hounds. "Our quarry is near," he told them, his voice filled with menacing command. "Follow the scent! Find the Black One!"

Suddenly, the dogs howled, savage like wolves. All five of them burst from their haunches and lunged into the forest. Serafina jumped despite herself. Her legs wanted to run so bad that she could barely keep herself still. But she had to stay hidden. It was her only chance to survive. But to her horror, the hounds were running straight toward her.

She couldn't understand it. Should she keep hiding? Should she fight? Should she run? The dogs were going to tear her to pieces.

Just when she knew she had to run, she realized it was too late. She didn't have a chance. Her chest seized. Her legs locked. She froze in terror.

No! No! No! Don't do it! You're not a rat! You're not a chipmunk! You've got to move!

Faced with certain death, she did what any sensible creature of the forest would do: She leapt ten feet straight up into a tree. She landed on a branch, then scurried along its length and hurled herself like a flying squirrel in a desperate leap to the next tree. From there, she bounded to the ground and ran like the dickens.

With howls of outrage, the hounds gave chase, running and snapping at her. They coursed her like a pack of wolves on a deer. But they were *wolfhounds,* so they weren't born and bred to chase down and kill anything as small as a deer. They were born and bred to chase down and kill *wolves.*

As she ran, Serafina glanced back over her shoulder toward the road. The craggy-faced man looked up at the owl as the haunting creature came circling back around. Then, to Serafina's astonishment, he threw his walking stick up into the sky. It tumbled end over end toward the owl. But it did not strike the bird. It seemed to blur and then disappear into the darkness, just as the owl flew into the cover of the trees. Serafina had no idea who the man was or what she had seen, but it didn't matter now. She had to run for her life.

Fighting off a single jumping, biting, snapping, snarling wolfhound was bad enough, but fighting five was impossible. She sprinted through the forest as fast as she could, her muscles punched with the power of fear. She wasn't going to let these growling beasts defeat her. The cold forest air shot into her pumping lungs, every sense in her body exploding with a lightning bolt of panic. Coming up behind her, the first hound reached out its ragged neck, opened its toothy maw, and bit the back of her leg. She spun and struck the dog, screaming in anger and searing pain as the dog's fangs punctured her flesh. The smell of the blood excited the other hounds into even more of a frenzy. The second dog leapt upon her and bit her shoulder, tearing into her with growling determination as she slammed her fist into its face. The third clamped its teeth onto her wrist as she tried to pull it away. The three of them pulled her down and dragged her across the ground. Then the other two dogs came in for the kill, their fangs bared as they lunged straight for her throat.

As the wolfhound charged in, Serafina threw her arm across her neck. Instead of tearing through her throat, the dog's fangs chomped down on her forearm, shooting spikes of pain through her bone as she screamed. The second dog pressed in for the killing bite, but a fist-size stone slammed into its head, knocking it back. Then another stone hit one of the other dogs, and it whirled to defend itself.

"Haaaa!" came a violent shout out of the darkness as a boy with long, wild hair leapt into the fray, striking and punching and clawing, flailing his arms in a spinning, growling attack.

Fierce with pain, Serafina slammed the heel of her hand into the nose of the dog clamped on her arm, pushing the dog away.

"Get up! Stay bold! Run!" the boy shouted at her as he attacked two of the dogs and cleared the way for her.

Serafina scrambled up onto her feet, ready to flee. But just when she thought she and the boy were gaining the advantage and might actually be able to escape, one of the dogs came leaping out of darkness, slammed into the boy's chest, and knocked him off his feet. The boy and the dog rolled to the ground in a somersault of snarling, biting ferocity.

The next dog lunged at Serafina. She dodged it, but another dog came at her from the other side.

"You can't outrun these things for long," the boy shouted. "You've got to get to cover!"

She dodged a lunging bite, and then a second and a third, but the snapping mouths kept coming at her. She slammed a dog in the head and punched one in the shoulder, but the dogs just kept biting, biting, biting.

She ran backward, defending herself from the incoming bites, but then she slammed into a face of sheer rock wall and could retreat no farther. She crouched into an attack position, hissing like an animal caught in a trap.

Just as a dog leapt at her, the boy tackled it to the ground.

"Now!" he shouted. "Climb!"

Serafina turned and tried to scramble up the craggy rock face, but the rock was dripping with water and too slippery to climb. Emboldened by her attempt to escape, two of the dogs immediately charged. She kicked their heads away repeatedly with her feet. She swatted and punched with her fists.

"Don't fight, you fool! Climb!" the boy shouted. "You've got to run!"

Just as she turned to climb, another dog lunged at her, but the boy leapt onto its back, biting and scratching like a wild animal. The hound howled in vicious indignation and twisted around, snapping furiously at the boy. They went tumbling onto the ground in a fierce ball of battle. Two more dogs dove fang-first into the melee.

Seeing her chance, she jumped up and grabbed the branch of a rhododendron, then hoisted herself up the face of the rock. She quickly found a foothold and another branch. Using the rhododendron bushes as a ladder, she climbed as fast as she could up the cliff. *Try that, you handless mutts!*

When she had climbed out of reach of the dogs, she looked back. Two of the dogs ran back and forth at the base of the cliff, growling as they tried to find a way up. The braver and stupider of the two tried repeatedly to run up the sheer wall, only to fall back down again. "Go on back to your master, you nasty dogs!" she spat at them, remembering the dark and shadowy figure.

But as she looked out across the woods, it wasn't their master she was looking for. She couldn't see the other three dogs or the boy. The last time she saw him, he'd been consumed in a terrible battle. She hadn't been able to tell who was winning and who was losing, but it seemed impossible that he could fight off all three of them at once.

She waited and listened out into the forest, but there was nothing. The two dogs that had been on her had disappeared.

They were running along the base of the cliff. *Those mongrels are looking for another way up,* she thought.

She had to keep moving before it was too late. She climbed another fifteen feet until she reached the top edge of the cliff.

Panting and exhausted, and bleeding from her head, arms, and calves, she crumpled to the ground. She scanned the trees below her, searching for the boy.

She looked and looked, but there was nothing moving out there, nothing making a sound. How had they moved away from her so quickly? Was the boy all right? Did he get away? Or was he hurt?

She'd never laid eyes on the boy before, never seen anything like him, the way he moved and fought. He had brownish skin, a lithe, muscled body, and long, shaggy dark brown hair, but it was his speed and his ferocity that struck her most. She reckoned he must be one of the local mountain folk, like her pa, who were well known for being tough as nails and twice as sharp, but the boy had fought as hard as a rabid bobcat. There was something almost *feral* about him, like he'd lived in these woods all his life.

She stood and scanned the terrain behind her—flat, rocky ground and a thicket of shrublike vegetation leading down into a larger ravine. She was pretty sure she knew where she was and how to get home, but she turned and looked out over the cliff again. The feral boy had saved her life. How could she just leave him?

The pain of the bites and scratches she'd suffered in the

battle burned something fierce, like sharp, twisting barbed wire puncturing her flesh. Blood dripped down into her eyes from the wound to her head. She needed to get home.

She looked out across the tops of the trees in the direction she had last seen the boy. She waited and listened, thinking she'd hear signs of battle or maybe see him looking up at her. Or, God forbid, she would see his bloody, torn body lying lifeless on the ground.

Don't fight, you fool! Climb! His words came ringing in her ears like he was still there. *Run!* he'd shouted.

Should she flee like he'd told her to, or should she look for him like she wanted to?

She hated making noise, making herself known to whatever lurked in the forest around her, but she couldn't think of anything else to do: She cupped her hands around her mouth and whispered "Hello! Can you hear me?" over the tops of the trees.

And then she waited.

There was nothing but the crickets and frogs and the other sounds of the night forest.

She could feel the battle-pound of her heart slowing down, her breaths getting weaker, and her arms and legs getting heavier. If she was going to make it home, she had to go soon.

She didn't want to just leave him out there fighting on his own. She wasn't the leaving kind—or the forgetting kind, either.

She wanted to talk to him, find out his name and where he

lived, or at least know he was safe. Who was he? Why was he in the forest in the middle of the night? And why was he willing to leap into a pack of vicious dogs to defend her?

She whispered once more out into the trees, "Are you out there?"

Serafina knew she'd waited for the feral boy too long when she heard the two wolfhounds coming toward her from the north. They had found a way up and around the cliff.

She looked around her. She glanced up at a tree, wondering if she could climb high enough. Then she thought about scaling back down the cliff again to confuse them. But she knew she couldn't survive out here all night on her own. *Get out of here!* the feral boy had told her.

Finally, she gathered herself up.

Whoever the boy was, she hoped he'd be all right. *Stay strong, my friend.*

She ducked into a dense boscage of spruce and fir, the evergreens packed so tightly together that it was like swimming through an ocean of green foliage. As she pushed her way through the thicket, she found her strength giving way to confusion. Her knees kept buckling beneath her, and she couldn't focus on the terrain in front of her. She raised her hand to her head and realized that she was bleeding badly from a tear in her scalp. The blood was dripping down her forehead and into her eyes.

She stumbled through the sea of trees, knowing there was no way to elude the dogs now. Spasms of pain radiated from the puncture wounds in her arms and legs. She had to wipe the blood out of her eyes to see where she was going. The needled branches of the trees were so thick and high that she could no longer see the moon and stars. Her racing feet cracked sticks on the ground, making noise that she wouldn't normally make, but it didn't matter now. She had to run like she'd never run before. But even as she ducked and darted between the trees, she kept hearing the feral boy's voice: *You can't outrun these things for long!* She wanted to turn and fight them, but if they caught her here in the thicket of trees, it'd be impossible to see their attacks. They'd kill her for sure. She had to keep running.

Suddenly, the trees opened up and she nearly fell headlong over a cliff edge into a rocky crash of whitewater rapids below. She pulled herself back from the edge with a gasp and grabbed onto the branches of a tree.

Looking over the edge of the cliff, she could see there was no way to cross the river here. The cliff was too high, the rapids too dangerous. *There ain't nothin' but bad choices,* she thought.

She knew she had to get to cover, but right now, the cover she needed was to conceal her scent.

Pushing herself on, she ran along the cliff as it led down toward the river.

When she came to the stretch below the rapids, she tried to wade quickly across what looked like the safest and shallowest point. She'd never been in deep water before and didn't know how to swim. She pushed hard through the drag of the rushing, knee-deep water, desperate to reach the other side and escape the wolfhounds. The mountain river was so cold that her legs ached. The current ran swift and strong. As she placed each step against the tearing force of the current, she felt the round, algae-covered rocks turning and slipping beneath her searching feet.

She reached the center of the river. The water ripped around her thighs, making it more and more difficult to push against it. She was making headway. But just when she thought she was going to make it across, she felt the current lifting her body away from the rocks beneath her feet. She lost her balance and crashed down into the icy-cold water. She flailed wildly, desperately kicking her legs in search of footing, but the bottom of the river disappeared as the current swept her into deep water. Coughing and spitting, she thrashed and leapt and gasped frantically for air as the river carried her downstream toward the next set of rapids.

The current sucked her into a rifling chute between two giant boulders, then shot her out the other side, tumbling end over end underwater through a dark green pool. As her head broke the surface, she managed to steal another gasp of air before the river grabbed hold of her again, heaving her and yanking her through a spiral of rushing water. She found herself spinning submerged in a whirlpool so deep that she said good-bye to her pa. But then her body hit a jagged rock. She tried to cling to it, but the rushing flow immediately pulled her away again. She'd always thought she was strong, but compared to the force of the river, she was nothing more than a kitten tossed into the water. When the rapids finally spat her out into the calm water downstream, she crawled from the river, wet and bedraggled, and collapsed onto the rocky shore, exhausted.

She had made it across.

She knew that if the dogs followed her downstream and saw her across the river, then they would pursue her. She had to get up, had to keep running, but she couldn't get her arms and legs to move. She couldn't even lift her head. The freezing-cold water and pounding force of the river had sapped all the remaining strength from her muscles. Her limbs were shaking. As she lay on the watery stones at the edge of the river, the protection of Biltmore seemed impossibly far away, beyond her reach. Her body was so tired she could barely get a few *feet*, let alone the miles she needed to go. The small puddles of water among the stones where she lay began to turn dark one by one. She felt so cold.

She wondered if the feral boy was lying mortally wounded in the forest back where she'd left him, or still fighting the wolfhounds. Or maybe he had escaped them. She could hear his voice in her mind. *Run!* he had shouted to her. *Run!* But she could not run. She could not move.

A wave of black calm passed through her, inviting her to simply shut her eyes and let everything go. A cloud of sickening colors veiled her eyes. She could feel herself passing out. How easy it would be to simply drift away. But a fierceness boiled in her heart. *Get up!* she told herself. *Run! Get home!* She struggled to rouse herself, to get onto her feet, to at least raise her head.

She opened her eyes and squinted through the blood. The terrain on this side of the river was low and gentle, dotted with ferns and birch trees, so different from the rocky cliffs that she had left behind on the other side. She saw a light coming toward her in the darkness. At first she thought it must be a twinkling star, for the sky was clear, but it wasn't one light. It was many lights.

She felt her chest trying helplessly to suck in air in anticipation of an attack, but even in the haze of her fear, she hoped that it might be a torch or lantern, her pa coming in search of her like he did once before.

But then she saw that the lights weren't the flickering flames of a lantern, but the scintillating dance of living creatures floating in the air and coming toward her down the river.

Are they fireflies? she wondered as they came closer.

But these were much larger and bright green in color, their wings slowly flashing white and green, white and green, as they flew, like the wings of luminescent butterflies.

But they're not butterflies, either, she thought with a smile. *They're luna moths.*

It was an entire eclipse of moths, each one pale green in color and glowing in the moonlight, hundreds of them flying together down the length of the river, their long tails streaming behind their silent, gently fluttering wings.

She had found her first luna moth in Biltmore's gardens one midsummer's night when she was a little girl. She remembered the luna moth's almost magical glow in the starlit darkness as she held it in her open hand, its wings moving gently up and down. But it was so strange to see so many of them traveling together. Was she imagining this? Was this how death came? A distant memory from the midnights of her past?

But as she watched the luna moths flying over the water, it struck her again that they weren't just hovering. They were traveling down the length of the stream, as if they would follow this river to the one that it flowed into, and then onward to the next river, and the next, through the mountains, and all the way to the sea. They were leaving this place. Just like the birds.

She heard the wolfhounds barking and howling to each other on the cliff on the other side of the river. They were coming.

As the last of the luna moths disappeared, she tried to push herself up onto her weakened arms, but she didn't have the strength. She tried to get her legs underneath her, but she couldn't.

But she'd seen the luna moths for a reason. She was sure of it.

She looked around for a place to take cover and noticed a grove of birch trees just a few feet away. As she tried to figure out how she was going to reach the trees, she saw a pair of eyes glinting in the darkness.

The eyes were keeping their distance, studying her.

Serafina held the eyes in her gaze and breathed as steadily as she could.

At first, she thought she had misjudged the position of the wolfhounds, that they had already crossed the river and were now surrounding her. But they weren't the searing black eyes of the wolfhounds. The eyes were golden brown.

A flood of relief flowed into her.

She knew who it must be.

"I need your help," she whispered.

But what emerged from the forest jolted her with a shock of fear. A mountain lion she had never seen before came straight at her. He was a young lion, with dark fur, but he looked strong, unafraid, and hungry. He was not at all the creature she was expecting.

Serafina tried to get up to defend herself, but it was no use. The beast could easily kill her.

But even as she tried to figure out how she was going to fight this unknown lion, a second lion emerged from the trees.

She breathed a sigh of relief. It was a lioness, full grown and full of power, a lioness she knew well.

When her mother was in her lion form, she was more beautiful than ever, with a thick tan coat, huge paws, and the muscles of many hunts. Her striking face and golden eyes glowed with intelligence.

"I'm so glad it's you, Momma," Serafina said, surprised by the tearful desperation in her own voice.

But in that moment, before Serafina could make out any

sort of answer in her mother's eyes, the lioness suddenly turned her head and looked across the river.

Then Serafina heard it, too. The wolfhounds were upon them. And it wasn't just two anymore. The five were united again, growling and barking and snarling. They would be here in seconds.

Serafina's mother moved quickly toward her and flattened herself beside her. Serafina didn't understand what she was doing. Then the darker lion came and nudged Serafina's body with his head. At first, she thought the lions were trying to rub against her and disguise her scent with theirs, but then she realized their true intention.

Serafina climbed onto her mother's back, clutching her neck and shoulders. With the lioness carrying her and the dark lion close at her side, the three of them moved into the trees, slowly at first, and then more quickly. Serafina felt her mother's fur against her face, and the force of her mother's lungs, and the power of her muscles. The lioness began to move more swiftly through the forest. Soon they were running.

It was the most incredible feeling, streaming through the

night at high speed, propelled by the undulating rhythm of the lioness's bounding stride, so strong and quiet and fast, the dark lion running beside her. Serafina had dreamed of running like this many times, but she had never moved this fast in her entire life. What amazed her was how smooth it was, how agile her mother's movements, how quickly she could change direction and speed, with both grace and power at her command.

When they reached a prominence of high ground, the two lions paused and looked down toward the river. They watched as the five wolfhounds followed Serafina's scent to the edge of the river, then crossed it. But they went straight across, not realizing she had been swept far downstream by the powerful current. At the time, it had felt like a catastrophe that the river had pulled her off her feet and carried her downstream, but now she realized that it had saved her. The wolfhounds sniffed the ground, circling in confusion. They'd lost her scent. And when they ran up and down the edge of the river looking to find her trail, their confusion mounted.

They can't find me, Serafina thought with a smile as she clung to her mother's back. *All they can smell is mountain lion.*

Suddenly, the lions were moving again, running through the forest at high speed, leaping small ravines and creeks, dashing through ferns. The branches and trunks of the trees flashed by. The whistle of the wind filled her ears.

They ran for so long through the night that Serafina's eyes closed, and all she could feel was the movement of the running, the coolness of the air above her, and the warmth of her mother beneath her.

$\mathcal{S}$erafina awoke a short time later on a bed of soft bright-green grass glowing in the moonlight. She felt the warmth of nuzzling fur and the deep and gentle vibration of purring. Her mother's two cubs snuggled up against her, kneading her back with their tiny paws, so happy to see her that they were giving her a back rub. She couldn't help but smile. She could feel their little noses pressing against her shoulders and their whiskers tickling her neck. Over the last few weeks that she'd been visiting the cubs at her mother's den, she had come to love her half brother and half sister, and she knew they had come to love her.

She reached up to feel the cut on her head. It had been dressed with a leafy compress that had stopped the bleeding and numbed the pain. The wounds on her arms and legs had been treated with poultices of forest herbs. She didn't want to, but she was pretty sure she could move if she needed to. She had noticed in the past that pain didn't slow her down like it did many other people. She had surprised her pa in this regard more than once. Cold weather didn't affect her either. Like her kin, she seemed to have been born with a natural toughness, the ability to keep going even when she had been battered and bloodied. But even so, the medicine on her cuts and punctures was a welcome relief.

Feeling a gentle hand on her shoulder, she looked up. Her mother was in her human form—with her golden feline eyes, strikingly angled cheekbones, and long light brown hair. But the most striking feature was that whenever Serafina looked into her mother's face, she knew that her mother loved her with all her heart.

"You're safe, Serafina," her mother said as she checked the dressing on her head.

"Momma," she said, her voice weak and ragged.

Looking around her, Serafina saw that her mother had brought her deep into the forest, to the angel's glade at the edge of the old, overgrown cemetery. Beneath the cemetery's dark cloak of twisted and gnarled trees, thick vines strangled the cracked, lichen-covered gravestones. Straggly moss hung down from the dead branches of the trees, and the darkened earth oozed with a ghostly mist. But the mist did not seep into the angel's glade itself, and a small circle of lush grass always remained perfect and green, even in winter. In the center of the glade stood a stone monument, a sculpture of a beautiful winged angel with a glinting steel sword. It was as if the angel protected the glade in a cusp of time, making it a place of eternal spring.

Her mother had been raising her two new cubs in a den beneath the roots of a large willow tree at the edge of the glade. And on a very different night than tonight, it had been the battleground on which Serafina and her allies had defeated Mr. Thorne, the Man in the Black Cloak.

Find the Black One! the bearded man with the wolfhounds had said earlier that night. She could not help but gaze around the glade for signs of the Black Cloak that she had torn to pieces on the razor-sharp edge of the angel's sword. She'd been sure that she had destroyed it, but she should have smashed its silver clasp and burned the leftover scraps of cloth. She looked toward the graveyard, with its tilting headstones and its broken coffins, and wondered what might have happened to the last remnants of the cloak.

For as long as she could remember, she had prowled through Biltmore's darkened corridors on her own. All her life, she'd hunted. It had been her instinct. She had never known why she had a long, curving spine, detached collarbones, and four toes on each foot. She had never known why she could see in the dark and others could not. But when she finally met her mother, she understood. Her mother was a *catamount,* a shape-shifting cat of the mountains. Serafina had come to understand that she wasn't just a child. She was a *cub.*

Desperate to learn more, she had hunted with her mother in the forest every night for the last several weeks, not just learning the lore of the forest, but what it meant to be a catamount. She had listened diligently to her mother's teachings and studied her mother when she was in her lion form. She had concentrated with all her mind and all her heart just like her mother had taught her. She had tried countless times to envision what she would look like, what it would feel like, but nothing ever happened. She was never able to change. She stayed just who she was. She wanted so badly to ask her mother to help her try again right now, but she had a sick feeling in her stomach that her mother wouldn't do it.

As the cubs trundled around in front of Serafina and nuzzled her face, she petted them and snuggled them, pressing their little ears back with her hands. The cubs were pure mountain lions, not shape-shifters, but they had accepted her from the beginning, never seeming to notice or care that her teeth were short and her tail was missing.

She wondered where the dark lion had gone. He was too young to be the father of her mother's cubs, so why had he been with her?

"Who was that other lion, Momma?" she asked. "The young one—"

"Never mind about him," her mother snarled. "I've told him to keep his distance from all of us, especially you. This isn't his territory and he knows it. He's only passing through with the others."

Serafina looked up at her in quick surprise. "What others?"

Her mother touched her cheek. "You need to rest, little one," she said, and then began to pull away.

"Please, tell me what's happening," Serafina pleaded, grabbing her mother's arm. "What others are you talking about? Why are the animals leaving? Who was that man in the forest? Why has he come?"

Her mother turned and looked into her eyes. "Never let yourself be seen or heard in the forest, Serafina. Always stay low and quiet. You must keep yourself safe."

"But I don't want to be *safe*. I want to know what's happening," she said before she could stop herself, realizing how childish she sounded.

"I understand your curiosity. Believe me, I do," her mother said gently as she reached out and touched her arm. "But how many lives do you think you have, little one? The forest is too dangerous for you. One of these nights I might not be there in time to save you."

"I want to be able to change like you, Momma."

"I know you do, kitten. I'm sorry," her mother said, wiping Serafina's cheek.

"Tell me what I need to do," Serafina begged. "I'll keep practicing."

Her mother shook her head. "Catamount kittens change with their mothers when they are very young, before they walk or run or speak. It becomes so much a part of how they envision themselves that they cannot even remember it being any other way. They see themselves as a catamount, and a catamount they become. I'm so sorry that I wasn't there to teach you when you were young."

"Teach me now, Momma."

"We've been trying every night—you know we have," her

mother said. "But I'm afraid it's too late for you. You won't ever be able to change."

Serafina shook her head fiercely, almost growling at her mother, she was so frustrated and hurt by her words. "I *know* I can do it. Don't give up on me."

"The forest is too dangerous for you to be here," her mother said, her eyes filled with sadness.

"You can come back with me to Biltmore in your human form," Serafina said excitedly. "We can be together."

"Serafina," her mother said, her tone both soft and firm at the same time, like she knew the loneliness and confusion that Serafina must be feeling. "I was trapped in my lion form for twelve years. I can't even imagine going back into the world of humans again, not yet. You have to understand. My soul was cleaved. I need time to heal, to understand what I am. I'm so sorry, but right now I belong in the forest, and I need to take care of the cubs."

"But—" Serafina tried to say.

"Wait," her mother said softly. "Let me finish what I was saying. I need to tell you this." Her mother paused, filled with emotion. "During those same twelve years that I was a lion, you were as trapped as I was. You were trapped in your human form." Her mother wiped a tear from her own eye. "That is what you are now. That is what you've grown up to be. You're a human. And I'm a catamount." Her mother looked down at the ground and pulled in a long, ragged breath. And then she lifted her eyes and looked at Serafina again. "I am so thankful that we had this time together, that I got to know you and see what a wonderful girl you've grown up to be. I love you with all my heart, Serafina, but I can't be your mother the way I know I should be."

"Momma, please don't say that. . . ." Serafina said.

"No, Serafina," her mother said, holding her with trembling hands. "Listen to me. You almost died tonight. I should have never let you wander the forest alone. I almost lost you." Her mother's voice cracked. "You have no idea how much you mean to me . . . and you have no idea how dark a force has been stirred. I want you to go back to Biltmore and stay there. That is your home. You're safe inside those walls. Things are changing here. I must take the cubs and go. The forest is far too dangerous for you, especially now."

Serafina looked up at her. "You're going? What do you mean, 'especially now'? Tell me what's happening, Momma. Why are all the animals leaving?"

"This is not your battle to fight, Serafina. With your two legs, you can't run fast enough to escape this danger. And you can't claw hard enough to fight against it. Once you've rested, I want you to go home. Be very careful. Stay clear of everything you see. Go straight back to Biltmore."

Serafina tried to keep from crying. "Momma, I want to be here with you in the forest. Please."

"Serafina, you don't be—"

"Don't say that!"

"You have to listen to what I'm saying," her mother said more forcefully. "You don't belong here, Serafina."

Serafina rubbed the tears out of her eyes in fury. She

wanted to belong. She wanted to belong more than anything. Her mother's words were splitting her heart in two. She wanted to keep arguing, but her mother would say no more.

Her mother laid Serafina's head down in the grass. "I've given you something to help you sleep. You'll feel better when you wake."

Serafina lay quietly as her mother told her to, but it was all so confusing. Whether house or forest, she just wanted to find a place to be. She seemed to have friends who weren't her friends, kin who weren't her kin. It felt like a dark force was gathering in the forest and seeping into her heart, like the Black Cloak slowly wrapping itself around her soul.

Lying at the base of the angel, she felt herself drifting into a deep and blackened sleep, as if she was falling into a bottomless pit, and there was nothing she could do to stop it.

When she woke a few hours later, she was no longer lying in the grass. She found herself in total darkness. She felt dirt all around her—below her, above her, and on all sides.

It took Serafina several seconds to realize that she was lying in her mother's earthen den. Her mother must have picked her up and carried her into the den when she was sleeping.

She felt warmer and stronger than she had before. She got herself up onto her hands and knees and crawled out of the den, then stood in the moonlight of the angel's glade. Looking up at the stars, it felt like a few hours had passed.

Her bleeding had stopped and her wounds did not hurt as badly as they did before. But as she looked around her, her heart sank, for her mother and the cubs and the dark lion were gone. They had left her here alone.

She found words traced into the dirt.

IF YOU NEED ME, WINTER, SPRING, OR FALL,

COME WHERE WHAT YOU CLIMBED IS FLOOR AND RAIN

IS WALL.

Serafina frowned. She didn't know what the words meant or even if they had been left for her.

She gazed around the angel's glade and then out into the trees. The forest was utter stillness, nothing but a mist drifting through the wet and glistening branches, and she could not hear a single living thing. It was as if the entire world outside the glade had disappeared.

She thought about her mother, and the cubs, and the dark lion, and what her mother had said: *You don't belong here, Serafina!* Of all the wounds she'd suffered, that one hurt the most.

Then she thought about Braeden, and her pa, and Mr. and Mrs. Vanderbilt, and everyone at Biltmore living their daytime lives so separate from her own.

You don't belong there, either.

Standing in the center of the angel's glade, she came to a slow and aching realization.

She was once again alone.

Just alone.

When she thought about what her mother had told her she would never be able to do, an aching, broken, throbbing part of her just wanted to kneel down and cry. She didn't understand. She had been so hopeful with all the changes that were happening in her life, but now she felt like she was caught in between, like she didn't belong anywhere. She was neither forest nor house, neither night nor day.

After a long time, she turned and looked at the beautiful, silent stone angel, with her graceful and powerful wings and her long steel sword. Serafina read the inscription on the pedestal.

OUR CHARACTER ISN'T DEFINED

BY THE BATTLES WE WIN OR LOSE,

BUT BY THE BATTLES WE DARE TO FIGHT.

Then she looked back out into the forest once more. She decided that no matter what she could or couldn't do, no matter who did or didn't want her, she was still the C.R.C. That much she knew for sure. And she'd seen things in the forest tonight that she couldn't account for. She didn't know who the bearded man was, except that he was something so dark that the animals fled before him, something so dangerous that even her mother believed that he could not be fought. Her mother was sure the darkest dangers lurked in the forest, and no doubt they did, but Serafina knew from experience that sometimes they crept into the house. She remembered the driverless carriage and the four stallions going onward up the road toward Biltmore. She could swear there had been someone else in that carriage. In what guise would this new stranger arrive and slither his way into Mr. and Mrs. Vanderbilt's home? Into *her* home. And what had he come for? Was he a thief? Was he a spy?

Standing there in the angel's glade, Serafina came to a decision. If there was a rat in the house, she was going to find it.

$\mathcal{S}$erafina stopped at the edge of Biltmore's lagoon, crouched down in the undergrowth, and scanned the horizon for danger.

She waited and she watched.

From her current vantage point, she didn't see any signs of trouble. Everything looked peaceful and serene.

The mirrorlike surface of the lagoon reflected the last of the shimmering stars that would soon give way to dawn. A family of swans flew low over the smooth water, then circled around and came in for a landing, shattering the reflection of the starlit sky.

In the distance, Biltmore House sat majestically atop a great hill, seeming to rise up out of the trees of the parkland that surrounded it. The windows glinted as the first light of the rising sun touched its walls. With its slate-blue roof, elegant arches, and spired towers, it looked like a fairy-tale castle of old, the kind she had read about in the mansion's library when everyone else was asleep.

As she gazed upon the house, a gentle warmth filled her heart. She was glad to be coming home. She decided that she would try to rekindle her friendship with Braeden, and she'd make sure she thanked Mrs. Vanderbilt again for the dress she'd given her. And she would do her best to mind her pa. But the first thing she had to do was to make sure she watched out for any strangers who had arrived at Biltmore during the night. The pain of her wounds had lessened, but the frightening images of the bearded man in the forest and the other figure in the carriage blazed in her mind. And she kept wondering what had happened to the feral boy who had helped her and then disappeared.

She headed toward the house, making her way up the slope through an area of open grassland dotted with large trees. She slinked from tree to tree, careful to stay hidden.

When she spotted two men and a dog in the distance walking toward the edge of the forest, she crouched low and took cover. She immediately recognized the lean, dark-haired figure of Mr. Vanderbilt, the master of Biltmore Estate, in his calf-high boots, woodsman jacket, and fedora hat. Like most gentlemen, he often carried a stylish cane when he was out and about on formal occasions, but today he had equipped himself with his usual chestnut hiking stave with its spiked metal ferrule and leather wrist strap. Cedric, his huge white-and-brown Saint Bernard, walked loyally beside him. Over the last few weeks, she'd gotten to know Mr. Vanderbilt better than she had before. There was much about the quiet man that was still a mystery to her, but she'd come to appreciate him, and hoped he felt the same about her. She was relieved to see him safe and out for what looked like an early-morning walk. This was surely a good sign that all was well at Biltmore.

But then she saw the man walking with him.

He wore a long tannish-brown coat over his light gray gentleman's suit, and carried a walking stick with a brass knob that glinted in the sun as he moved. He had an old face, a balding head, and a thick gray beard. Serafina narrowed her eyes suspiciously. She immediately thought of the terrifying man she'd seen in the forest, with his silvery glinting eyes and his craggy face. They were disturbingly similar figures. But as she watched, she decided that this wasn't him.

The man walking with Mr. Vanderbilt was older, slower in movement, more bent of frame. She could not see his face well enough to know who he was, but he seemed familiar. And she remembered that the man with the dogs had exited the carriage and sent it on toward Biltmore. Was this the second occupant of the carriage? Maybe it was one of the bearded man's servants sent ahead to spy. Or was he a demon like the Man in the Black Cloak? She knew that someone had come to Biltmore during the night. She just needed to find out who it was.

She slipped behind a large black walnut tree and watched the two men. As they walked slowly into the forest, the stranger poked a hole in the ground with the tip of his cane. Then he took something out of his leather shoulder satchel, knelt down, and seemed to bury it in the dirt. Serafina thought that this was very peculiar behavior.

The two men and the dog finally disappeared into the foliage, leaving Serafina with nothing but lingering doubt about who this stranger was and how he was connected to the man she'd seen the night before.

As she puzzled through what she'd seen, she continued up the slope toward the house. Her heart leapt when she saw Braeden by the stables saddling one of his horses.

Seeing her friend safe and sound, Serafina smiled and felt her muscles relaxing. She could see now that whoever or whatever had come to Biltmore in the carriage during the night hadn't hurt her friend. But the first thing she was going to do was tell Braeden what happened to her in the forest and warn him about what she saw.

Braeden was wearing his usual brown tweed hacking jacket and vest, with a white shirt and beige cravat. He moved around easily in his leather riding boots. His tussle of brown hair was blowing in the breeze a little bit. It did not surprise her to see Gidean, his Doberman, at his side. Braeden seemed to make a lasting bond with whatever animal he met. He had befriended the unusual, pointed-eared black dog while traveling in Germany with his family a few years ago. After the tragic death of his family in a house fire, the boy and his dog had become inseparable. In some ways, Gidean was the last remaining member of Braeden's family before he came to Biltmore to live with his uncle, and he had found few other friends.

Serafina knew that Braeden rode every day. He'd gallop

across the fields like the wind, his horse running so fast that it was like they weren't even attached to the earth. It was good to see him here.

She broke from her cover and ran toward him, thinking that she'd pounce on him and knock him to the ground in fun. She was just about to shout *Hey, Braeden!* when a second figure stepped out from behind the horse. Serafina dropped quickly into the tall grass.

When she didn't hear anyone shout *Hey, there's a peculiar girl in the grass over there!* she crawled over to the base of a nearby tree and peeked out.

A tall girl about fourteen years old with long, curly red hair stood waiting for Braeden to adjust the stirrup on her horse's sidesaddle. She wore a fitted emerald-green velvet riding jacket with an upturned collar, triangular lapels, and turn-back cuffs. The jacket's gold buttons glinted in the sunlight whenever she turned her body or lifted her wrist. Her trim green-and-white-striped waistcoat and long skirt matched her jacket in every detail.

Serafina frowned in irritation. Braeden normally rode alone. His aunt and uncle must have asked him to entertain this young guest. But what should she do now? Should she brush off her ripped, dirtied, bloodstained, fang-shredded dress, and walk over to Braeden and the girl and introduce herself? She imagined an exaggerated, backwoods version of herself coming out of the brush toward them. *Mornin', y'all. I'm just back from catchin' some wood rats and nearly gettin' eaten up by a pack of wolfhounds. How you two doin' this mornin'?*

She thought about approaching them, but maybe interrupting Braeden and the girl would be a rude, unwelcome imposition.

She had no idea.

Out of instinct more than anything else, she stayed hidden where she was and watched.

The girl allowed Braeden to help her up into the saddle, then rearranged her legs and the long folds of her riding skirt to drape over the left side of the horse. That was when Serafina noticed that she was wearing beautiful dove-gray suede, laced-up, flower-embroidered ankle boots. They were completely ridiculous for horseback riding, and Serafina couldn't even imagine running through the forest in such delicate things, but they sure were pretty.

Along with her fancy attire, the girl carried a finely made riding cane with a silver topper and a leather whip end. Serafina smirked a little. It seemed like all the fancy folk liked to carry some sort of cane or walking stick or other accoutrement whenever they went outside, but she preferred to have her hands free at all times.

Seeing the whip, Braeden said, "You won't need anything like that."

"But it goes with my outfit!" the girl insisted.

"If you say so," Braeden said. "But please don't touch the horse with it."

"Very well," the girl agreed. She spoke in a grand and mannerly tone, as if she'd been raised in the way of a proper lady and she wanted people to know it. And Serafina noticed that she had an accent like Mrs. King, Biltmore's head housekeeper, who was from England.

"So, do tell," the girl said. "How do I stop this beast if it runs away with me?"

Serafina chuckled at the thought of the horse bolting with the screaming, frilly-dressed girl, jumping a few fences in wild abandon, and then landing in a mud pit with a glorious splat.

"You just need to pull back on the reins a little bit," Braeden said politely. It was clear that he didn't know this girl too well, which further reinforced Serafina's theory that Braeden's aunt and uncle were putting him up to this.

Beyond all the girl's fanciness and airs, there was something that bothered Serafina about her. A highfalutin fashion plate like her would certainly know how to ride a horse, but she seemed to be pretending that she didn't. Why would she do that? Why would she feign helplessness? Was that what a girl did to attract a boy's attention?

Seemingly unmoved by the girl's ploy, Braeden walked over to his horse without further comment. He slipped effortlessly onto his horse's bare back. A week ago, he had explained to Serafina that he didn't use a bridle and reins to control his horse but signaled the speed and direction he wanted to go by adjusting the pressure and angle of his legs.

"Now, we mustn't go too fast," the girl said daintily as the two young riders rode their horses at a walk out onto the grounds of the estate. Serafina could tell she wasn't scared of the horse but simply pretending to be a delicate soul.

"Actually, I thought we might do a bit of high-speed racing," Braeden said facetiously.

Seeming to realize that Braeden wasn't falling for her precious-princess routine, the English girl changed her tone as fast as a rattlesnake changes the direction of its wind.

"I would race you," she replied haughtily, "but I might get a speck of mud on my skirt from my horse kicking up dirt into your face as I passed you."

Braeden laughed, and Serafina couldn't help but smile as well. The girl had a bit of spunk in her after all!

As Braeden and the girl rode away down the path, Serafina could hear them talking pleasantly to each other, Braeden telling her about his horses and his dog, Gidean, and the girl listing the particulars of the gown she'd be wearing to dinner that evening.

Serafina noticed that as Braeden and the girl entered the trees, the girl looked warily around her. The wilds of North Carolina must seem a dark and foreboding place to a civilized girl like her. She urged her horse forward to move closer to Braeden.

Braeden looked at the girl as she came up alongside him. Serafina could no longer tell if Braeden was simply being polite or if he actually wanted to be this girl's friend, but as they rode out into the trees, she felt a strange queasiness in her stomach that she'd never felt before.

Serafina could have easily followed them without their knowing it, but she didn't. She had a job to do.

Last night she'd seen the man in the forest send the carriage to Biltmore. She reckoned that the sensible place to look for signs that the intruder had arrived was the stables.

She crept in through the back door, wary of Mr. Rinaldi, the fiery-tempered Italian stable boss who didn't take kindly to sneakers-about who might spook his horses. It was easy for her to move quietly on the perfectly clean redbrick floor, and even in the daytime there were plenty of shadows in the stables to take advantage of. The horse stalls consisted of lacquered oak boards trimmed in black railing with curving black grills along the top. She began checking each of the stalls. Along with the Vanderbilts' several dozen horses, she found a dozen others that belonged to the guests.

Ga-bang!

Serafina hit the floor. Her heart pounded. It sounded like a sledgehammer had hit the side of a stall. Having no idea what she was going to see, she peered down the stable's central aisle. Disturbed dust floated from the ceiling down toward the floor, as if the earth itself had shaken, but otherwise the aisle was empty. She could see that four of the stalls at the end had been boarded up all the way to the ceiling. They were completely closed in, as if to make sure that whatever they held had no possibility of escape.

She gathered herself up onto her feet and moved slowly down the aisle toward the boarded stalls. She could feel the sweat on her palms.

The oak boards blocked her view of what was inside the stalls, so she crept up close, put her face to the boards, and peered through the cracks.

A massive beast hurled itself at the boards of the stall. The flexing wood struck Serafina in the head. The surprise of it sent her tripping backward in fear. The beast kicked the stall boards and slammed them with its shoulders, snorting and thrashing. The boards bent and creaked under the pressure of the pounding animal.

When she heard the stable boss and a gang of stablemen running toward the disturbance she'd caused, she scrambled into an empty stall, ducked down, and hid in a shadow.

She gasped for breath, trying to figure out what she'd just seen—a massive dark shape, black eyes, flaring nostrils, and pounding hooves.

A storm of questions flooded her mind as Mr. Rinaldi and

his men came charging down the aisle. The beast continued its terrible pounding and thrashing. The stable boss shouted instructions to his men to reinforce the boards. Serafina quickly climbed out the back of the stall and darted from the stables before they caught sight of her.

Those were the stallions! There was no question now. Whoever he was, the second occupant of the carriage was here.

She scurried along the stone foundation at the rear of the house, pushed her body through the air shaft, crawled through the passage, pushed aside the wire mesh, and entered the basement. Her presence at the estate had become known to the Vanderbilts a few weeks before, so she could theoretically use the doors like normal people, but she seldom did.

She went down the basement corridor, through a door, and then down another passageway. As she stepped into the workshop, her pa turned toward her.

"Good mornin'," he began to say in a pleased, casual fashion, but when he got a look at her bedraggled state, he lurched back in surprise. "Eh, law! What happened to you, child?" His hands guided her gently to a stool for her to sit. "Aw, Sera," he said as he looked at her wounds. "I said you could go out into the forest at night to spend time with your mother, but you're breakin' my heart, comin' home lookin' like this. What've you been doin' out there in them woods?"

Her pa had found her in the forest the night she was born, so she reckoned he must have had an inkling of what she was, but he didn't like dark talk of demons and shifters and things that go bump in the night. It was as if he thought that as long as they didn't talk about those things, they would not be real or come into their lives. She had told herself many times that she wouldn't bother her pa with the details of what happened at night when she went out, and normally she kept that promise, but the moment her pa asked, it all just started gushing out of her before she could stop it.

"I had a terrible run-in with a pack of dogs, Pa!" she said, choking up.

"It's all right, Sera, you're safe here," her pa said as he took her into his thick arms and huge chest and held her. "But what dogs are you talking about? It wasn't the young master's dog, was it?"

"No, Pa. Gideon would never hurt me. There was a strange man in the forest with a pack of wolfhounds. He sicced 'em on me somethin' fierce!"

"But where did he come from?" her pa asked. "Was he a bear hunter?"

She shook her head. "I don't know. After he got out of the carriage, he sent the carriage on toward Biltmore. I think I saw the horses in the stables. And I saw a strange man with Mr. Vanderbilt this morning. Did anyone unusual arrive at the house last night?"

"The servants have been jabbering on about all the folk comin' in for Christmastime, but I doubt the man you saw was one of the Vanderbilts' guests. I'll wager it was one of those poachers from Mills Gap that we ran off the estate two years ago."

Serafina could hear the anger seething in her pa's voice. He was riled up that someone had done his little girl harm. He kept talking as he examined the crusted blood on her head. "I'll go speak with Superintendent McNamee first thing. We'll take a party out there to confront this fella, whoever he is. But first off, let's get you patched up. Then you rest a spell. Your lesson can wait."

"My lesson?" she asked, confused.

"For them table manners of yourn."

"Not again, Pa, please. I've got to figure out who's come to Biltmore."

"I told ya. We're fixing to hammer that nail till it's sunk in deep."

"Sunk in my head, you mean."

"Yeah, in your head. Where else do ya learn things? Now that you and the young master are gettin' on, you need to behave proper."

"I know how to behave just fine, Pa."

"You're 'bout as civilized as a weasel, girl. I shoulda been schoolin' ya more about the folk upstairs and how they go 'bout things, 'cause it hain't like us."

"Braeden is my friend, Pa. He likes me just fine the way I am, if that's what you're pokin' at," she said. Although, as she heard herself defending Braeden's opinion of her, it felt suspiciously like she was lying not just to her pa but to herself. Truth was, she didn't know if she was or wasn't Braeden's friend anymore, and she was becoming increasingly less certain of it every day.

"It's not directly the young master I'm concerned about,"

her pa continued as he got a clean, wet cloth and started looking after her wounds. "It's the master and the mistress, and
especially their guests come city way. You can't sit at their table
if you don't know the difference between the napkin and the
tablecloth."

"Why would I need to know the difference between—"

"The butler told me that Mr. Vanderbilt was going to
be looking for you upstairs later today. And everyone in the
kitchen is fixin' for a big supper tonight."

"A supper? What kind of supper? Is the stranger going to be
there? Is that what this is all about? And what about Braeden—
is he going to be there?"

"That's a bushel more questions than I got answers for,"
her pa said. "I don't know anything about it, truth be told. But
other than the young master, I can't figure any other reason
why the Vanderbilts would be a-looking for you. I just know
there's a big shindig tonight, and the master sent word, and it
didn't sound so much like an invitation as an instruction, if ya
get my meaning."

"Did they say it was a supper or a shindig, Pa?" Serafina
said, getting confused, and realizing as she said it that the
Vanderbilts didn't have events by either of those names.

"It's all the same up there, hain't it?" her pa said.

Serafina knew that she had to go to the event her pa was
telling her about. For one thing, it'd be the best way to see all
the new people who had arrived at the house. But the obstacles
immediately sprang into her mind. "How can I go up there,

Pa?" she said in alarm, looking at the bite marks and scratches all over her arms and legs. They didn't hurt too badly, but they looked something awful.

"We'll clean the mud off ya, get the sticks and blood outten your hair, and you'll be fine. Your dress will cover them there scratches."

"My dress has more holes in it than me," she protested as she examined the bloodstained, tattered pieces of the dress Mrs. V had given her. She couldn't show up in that.

"Them toothy mongrels sure did a number on you," he said as he examined the tear in her lower ear. "Don't that hurt?"

"Naw, not no more," she said, her mind on other things. "Where's that old work shirt of yours that I used to wear?"

"I threw that thing out as soon as I saw that Mrs. Vanderbilt gave you something nice to wear."

"Aw, Pa, now I ain't got nothin' at all!"

"Don't fuss. I'll make ya somethin' outta what we got up in here."

Serafina shook her head in dismay. "What we got around here is mostly sackcloth and sandpaper!"

"Look," her pa said, taking her by the shoulders and looking into her eyes. "You're alive, ain't ya? So toughen up. Bless the Lord and get on with things. In your entire life, has the master of the house ever demanded your presence upstairs? No, he has not. So, yes, ma'am, if the master wants you there, you're gonna be there. With bells on."

"Bells?" she asked in horror. "Why do I have to wear bells?"

How could she sneak and hide if she was wearing noisy bells around her neck? Or did they go on her feet?

"It's just an expression, girl," her pa said, shaking his head. Then, after a moment, he muttered to himself, "At least I think it is."

10

Serafina sat, mad and miserable, on the cot while her pa did his level best to clean and bandage her wounds. As usual, she and her pa were surrounded by the workshop's supply shelves, tool racks, and workbenches. But her pa seemed to have forgotten the work he was supposed to be doing that morning. His mind had become consumed with her.

Some of the copper piping and brass fittings from the kitchen's cold box sat in a twisted clump on the bench. The previous day, her pa had explained something about an ammonia-gas brine system, intake pipes, and cooling coils, but none of it took. He'd raised her in his workshop, but she had no talent with machines. She couldn't remember anything about the contraption other than it was complicated, kept food cold, and was one of the few refrigeration systems in the country. The mountain folk kept their food cold by sticking it in a cold spring tumbling down into a creek, which seemed far more sensible to her.

As soon as her pa was done fussing with her, she slipped off the bed, hoping he'd forget his threat to make her rest. "I've gotta go, Pa," she said. "I'm gonna sneak upstairs and see if I can spot the intruder."

"Now, listen here," he said, holding her arm. "I don't want you confrontin' anybody up there."

She nodded. "I'm with ya, Pa. No confrontin'. I just want to see who's up there and make sure everyone is all right. No one will ever see me."

"I'm needin' your word on this," he said.

"You got my word, Pa."

Off she went to the main floor. She spotted a few guests strolling this way and that or lounging in the parlors, but nobody suspicious. She moved up to the second floor next, but she didn't see anything out of the ordinary there, either. She scoured the house from top to bottom, but there was no sign of the stranger she'd seen with Mr. Vanderbilt or anyone else who seemed like they might have been the second passenger in the carriage. She listened for scuttlebutt from the servants as they prepared for the event in the Banquet Hall that evening, but she didn't pick up anything other than how many cucumbers the cook wanted the scullery maid to fetch and how many silver platters the butler needed for his footmen.

She tried to think through everything she had seen the night before, wondering if she'd missed any clues. What had she actually seen when the bearded man threw his walking stick up into the air toward the owl? And who was the second passenger who remained in the shadows of the carriage? Was it the stranger she'd seen walking with Mr. Vanderbilt? And who was the feral boy who had helped her? Was he still alive? How could she find him again?

Another bushel of questions I don't have answers to, she thought in frustration, remembering her pa's words.

Later that afternoon, when she walked back into the workshop, her pa asked, "What did you find out?"

"A whole lot of nothin'," she grumbled. "No sign of anyone suspicious at all."

"I spoke to Superintendent McNamee. He's sendin' out a group of his best horsemen to hunt down the poachers." As he spoke, her pa wiped his grease-smeared hands with a rag.

"Elevator actin' up again, Pa?" she asked.

Her pa had often boasted that Biltmore had the first and finest electric elevator in the South, but he seemed a mite less keen on the machine today.

"The gears in the basement keep gettin' all gaumed up when it hits the fourth floor," he said. "Everwho installed the thing got them shafts all sigogglin, this way and that. I swear it ain't gonna work proper till I tear out the whole thing and start again." He waved her over to him. "But take a look at this. This is interestin'." He showed her a thin piece of sheet metal that looked like it hadn't just broken, but had been torn. It was odd to see metal torn like that. She didn't even know how that was possible.

"What is that, Pa?" she asked.

"This here little bracket was supposed to be a-holdin' the main gear in place, but whenever the elevator ran, it kept flexing back and forth, you see?" As he spoke, he showed her the flexing motion by bending the sheet metal with his fingers. "The metal is plenty strong at first. Seems unbreakable, don't it? But when ya bend it back and forth over and over again like this, watch what happens. It gets weaker and weaker, these little cracks start, and then it finally breaks." Just as he said the words, the metal snapped in his fingers. "You see that?"

Serafina looked up at her pa and smiled. Some days, he had a special kind of magic about him.

Then she looked over at the other workbench. Somewhere between mending the elevator, fixing the cold box, and tending to his other duties, her pa had cobbled together a dress for her made out of a burlap tow sack and discarded scraps of leather.

"Pa . . ." she said, horrified by the sight of it.

"Try it on," he said. He seemed rather proud of the stitching he'd done with fibrous twine and the leather-working needle he sometimes used to patch holes in the leather apron he wore. Her pa liked the idea that he could make or mend just about anything.

Serafina walked glumly behind the supply racks, took off her tattered green dress, and put on the thing her pa had made.

"Looks as fine as a Sunday mornin'," her pa said cheerfully

as she stepped out from behind the racks, but she could tell he was lying through his teeth. Even he knew it was the most god-awful, ugly thing that ever done walked the earth. But it worked. And to her pa, that's what counted. It was functional. It clothed her body. The dress had longish sleeves that covered most of the punctures and scratches on her arms, and a close-fitting collar that hid at least part of the gruesome cut on her throat. So at least the fancy ladies at the shindig or the supper, or whatever it was, wouldn't swoon at the corpsy sight of her.

"Now, sit down here," her pa said. "I'll show you how to behave proper at the table."

She sat reluctantly on the stool he placed in front of an old work board that was meant to represent the forty-foot-long formal dining table in Mr. and Mrs. Vanderbilt's grand Banquet Hall.

"Sit up straight, girl, not all curvy-spined like that," her pa said.

Serafina straightened her back.

"Get your head up, not hunched all over your food like you gotta fight for it."

Serafina leaned back in the way he instructed.

"Get them elbows offen the table," he said.

"I ain't no banjo, Pa, so quit pickin' on me."

"I ain't pickin' on you. I'm tryin' to teach ya somethin', but you're too stubborn-born to learn it."

"Ain't as stubborn as you," she grumbled.

"Don't get briggity with the sass, girl. Now, listen. When you eat your supper, you need to use your forks. You see here?

These screwdrivers are your forks. The mortar trowel there is your spoon. And my whittlin' blade is your dinner knife. From what I've heard, you gotta use the right fork for the job."

"What job?" she asked in confusion.

"For what you're eatin'. Understand?"

"No, I don't understand," she admitted.

"Now, look straight ahead," he said, "not all shifty-eyed like you're gonna pounce on somethin' and kill it at any second. The salad fork here is on the outside. The dinner fork is on the inside. Sera, you hearin' me?"

She didn't normally enjoy her pa's etiquette lessons, but it felt kind of good to be home, safe and sound, suffering through yet another one.

"You got it?" he asked when he finished explaining about the various utensils.

"Got it. Dinner fork on the inside. Salad fork on the outside. I just have one question."

"Yes?"

"What's a salad?"

"Botheration, Serafina!"

"I'm askin' a question!"

"It's a bowl of, ya know . . . greenery. Lettuce, cabbage, carrots, that sort of thing."

"So it's rabbit food."

"No, ma'am, it is not," her pa said firmly.

"It's poke sallet."

"No, it ain't."

"It's food that prey eats."

"I don't want to hear no talk like that, and you know it."

As her pa schooled her in the fineries of supper etiquette, she got the notion that he'd never actually sat at the table with the Vanderbilts. She could see that he was going more on what he imagined than live experience, and she was particularly suspicious of his understanding of salads.

"Why would rich and proper folk like the Vanderbilts eat leaves when they could afford to eat something good? Why don't they eat chicken all day? If I was them, I'd eat so much chicken I'd get fat and slow."

"Sera, you need to take this seriously."

"I am!" she said.

"Look, you've got a friend in the young master now, and that's a good'n. But if you're gonna be his friend for long, you need to learn the rudiments."

"The rudiments?"

"How to behave like a daytime girl."

"I ain't no Vanderbilt, Pa. He knows that."

"I know. It's just that when you're up there, I don't want you to—"

"To what? Horrify them?"

"Well, now, Sera, you know you ain't the daintiest flower in the garden, is all. I love ya heaps, but there ain't no denying it—you're a sight feral, talkin' about prey and hunting rats. With me, that's all fine and good, but—"

"I understand, Pa," she said glumly, wanting him to stop. "I'll be on my best behavior when I'm up there."

When she heard someone coming down the corridor, she

flinched and almost darted. After years of hiding, it still made her scurry when she heard the sound of footsteps approaching.

"Someone's comin', Pa," she whispered.

"Naw, hain't nobody a-comin'. Just pay attention to what I'm tellin' ya. We've got to—"

"Pardon me, sir," a young maid said as she stepped into the workshop.

"Lordy, girl," Serafina's pa said as he turned around and looked at the maid. "Don't sneak up on a man like that."

"Sorry, sir," the maid said, curtsying.

The maid was a young girl, a couple of years older than Serafina, with a pleasant face and strands of dark hair curling out from beneath her white cap. Like the other maids, she wore a black cotton dress with a starched white collar, white cuffs, and a long white lace apron. But from the look of her and the sound of her words, it seemed like she was one of the local mountain folk.

"Well, spit it out, girl," Serafina's pa told her.

"Yes, sir," she said, and glanced at Serafina self-consciously. "I have a note from the young master for the little miss."

As the maid said these words, she eyed Serafina. Serafina could see the girl trying to make sense of the weird angles of her face and the amber color of her eyes. Or maybe she was noticing the bloody wounds peeking out from beneath the edges of the burlap gunnysack she was wearing. Whatever it was, there was apparently plenty to stare at, and the girl couldn't quite resist availing herself of the opportunity.

"Ah, ya see, Sera," her pa said. "I told ya. Good thing we've been a-practicin'. The young master is sending you a proper invitation to the supper this evening."

"Here you go, miss," the maid said as she stretched out her hand with the note toward Serafina as if she didn't want to get any closer to her.

"Thank you," Serafina said quietly. She took the note from the maid slowly so as not to startle the girl with too quick a movement.

"Thank you, miss," the maid said, but instead of then leaving, she froze, transfixed, as she studied Serafina's streaked hair and odd clothing.

"Was there something else?" Serafina's pa said to the maid.

"Oh no, I'm sorry, pardon me," the maid said as she pulled herself out of her stare, curtsied in embarrassment to Serafina, and then quickly excused herself from the room.

"Well, what's it say, then?" Serafina's pa said, gesturing toward the note.

As Serafina carefully opened the small piece of paper, her hands trembled. Whatever it was, it felt important. As she read Braeden's words, the first thing she understood was that her pa had been wrong. She wasn't receiving an invitation to a dancing party or a formal dinner. The note dealt with a far darker subject. Just the first sentence tightened her chest with fear. Suddenly, she remembered seeing the black-cloaked Mr. Thorne falling dead to the ground, killed by her and her companions. Then another image flashed through her mind: her and Braeden at the gallows, hanging by their necks for the crime of murder. But as she read the frightening note, there was another emotion as well. She glowed with the knowledge that it was Braeden who was telling her these words. At long last, it was her old friend and ally.

S,

A murder investigator has arrived at Biltmore. He's the strangest man I have ever seen. You and I have been summoned at 6:00 p.m. for questioning about the disappearance of Mr. Thorne. Be careful.

—B.

11

Serafina suspected that the murder investigator was the second man in the carriage. It appeared that she didn't need to look for him, because he was looking for her. She thought, too, that he must have been the stranger she'd seen with Mr. Vanderbilt earlier that morning. But no matter who he was, getting interrogated by the police couldn't be a good thing. What was she going to say when he asked about Mr. Thorne's disappearance? "Oh, him? Yes, I remember him. I led him into a trap by my mother's den, and my allies killed him. Do you want me to show you where it all happened?"

As she headed up the narrow, unlit back stairway toward the main floor, it felt like her head was filled with more thoughts than her mind could hold.

It was half past five in the afternoon. She had half an hour to spy on the house and gather clues before she had to report for the interrogation. But she ran into an immediate problem.

The young maid who had stared at her earlier was waiting for her at the top of the stairs, blocking her path.

Serafina stopped and narrowed her eyes at her. "What do you want?"

When the girl stepped toward her, Serafina stepped back warily.

"I need to talk to you, miss. . . ."

Serafina did not reply.

"Beggin' your pardon, miss," the maid said, "but you don't want to go up there lookin' like that."

"This is the way I look," Serafina said fiercely as she gazed steadily at the girl.

"I mean your dress, miss," the girl said.

"It's the only one I have," Serafina said.

The maid nodded, seeming to understand. "Then let me lend you something. My day-off dress or my Sunday dress, anything. But not . . ."

"But not this," Serafina said, gesturing toward the burlap sack she was wearing.

"I ain't heard nothin' but good things about your pa," the maid said sheepishly. "People say he can fix just about anything round here. But, beggin' your pardon, miss, I think we can agree that he ain't no dress designer."

Serafina smiled. She was absolutely right about that. "And you're going to help me?" she asked tentatively.

"If you want me to," the girl said, smiling a little.

"What's your name?" Serafina asked.

"I'm Essie Walker."

"I'm Serafina."

"The girl who brought the children back," Essie said, nodding. She already knew who she was and seemed pleased to meet her.

Serafina smiled and nodded in return. T.G.W.B.T.C.B. wasn't quite as catchy as C.R.C., but she liked it.

As she looked at Essie more closely, it seemed to her that she had a gentle face, without any deceit or guile, and a warm, friendly smile.

"Where do your people bury, Essie?" Serafina asked, which was how she'd heard her pa ask other mountain folk where they were from.

"I don't rightly know," Essie said. "My ma and pa passed away when I was but one or two. My nanny and papaw raised me for a while, out on a farm up Madison County way, pert nigh Walnut, but when they passed, I didn't have nowhere to go. Mrs. Vanderbilt heard about me and took me in and gave me a bed to sleep in. I told her I wanted to make myself useful."

"You're pretty young for being a maid at Biltmore," Serafina said.

"Youngest maid ever," Essie said, smiling proudly. "Come on, let's go. We'll get ya sorted out." Essie reached for Serafina's hand, but Serafina reflexively pulled away, snapping her whole body back before Essie was even close to touching her.

Essie caught her breath, startled by Serafina's quick movement.

"You're a mite skittish, aren't ya?" Essie said.

"I'm sorry," Serafina said, embarrassed.

"It's all right," Essie said. "We've all got somethin' that spooks us, right? But come on. Time's a-tickin'."

Essie turned and bolted up the stairs. Serafina followed easily right behind her. The two of them ran up three flights, then darted through a small doorway that led to a back corridor, then up another stairway to the fourth floor. Essie led them down a tight passage that ran beneath the North Tower, past a cluster of maids' rooms, around a corner, down six steps, and through the main Servant Hall, where three maids and a house girl were gathered around the fireplace on their break.

"Don't pay us no mind," Essie called as she and Serafina ran through the room. They dashed down a long, narrow corridor with a Gothic arched ceiling wedged beneath the steep angle of the mansion's slanted rooftop. There were twenty-one rooms on the fourth floor for the maids and other female servants. And Essie's room was the third on the right.

"We'll duck in here, miss," Essie said as Serafina followed her in.

During her nightly prowls, Serafina had sometimes snuck into one of the maids' rooms when the maid went down the hall to the water closet, so she had seen the clean, plainly finished rooms before. But Essie had made up her room's simple white metal bed with soft pillows and an autumn quilt. To Serafina, it looked like a perfect warm spot for curling up in the late-afternoon sun. But she had a feeling Essie didn't get much time for napping. A clump of wrinkled clothing lay across the splint-reed chair, two of the drawers on the chestnut dresser were pulled out, and there was water left over in the basin on the washstand.

"Pardon the mess, miss," Essie said, quickly picking up the underclothing from the floor and pushing the dresser drawers shut. "Lord protect me if Mrs. King comes up for an inspection this afternoon, but five o'clock comes awful early some mornin's. Wasn't thinkin' on company when I left."

"It's all right," Serafina said. "You should see where I sleep."

"I was all blurry-eyed this mornin' on account of I stayed up with that awful Mr. Scrooge," Essie said as she moved the clothes off the chair. Hearing these words, Serafina's ears perked right up. Who was this evil Mr. Scrooge? But then she saw a copy of *A Christmas Carol* by Charles Dickens on Essie's nightstand, piled with some Asheville newspapers, a Bible, and a scrap of what looked like Mrs. King's weekly work schedule. Serafina realized with a bit of a shock that Christmas was only a week away. The tan leather-bound book with gold-leaf lettering on the front looked suspiciously like the same edition of *A Christmas Carol* that Serafina had "borrowed" from Mr. Vanderbilt's collection the year before. *So I'm not the only one who steals Mr. Vanderbilt's books,* Serafina thought with a smile.

Across Essie's dresser lay all manner of feminine accoutrements: hairbrushes, hairpins, little tins of ointment, and a glass bottle of Essie's lemon scent, which Serafina could smell from a country mile. The room's cream-colored walls were cluttered with scraps of Essie's sketches of flowers and fall leaves. Serafina knew that she should be doing her job, creeping through the shadows, and spying on Biltmore's guests, or at least worrying about the interrogation that was minutes away, but she could not resist the temptation of seeing a little bit of Biltmore up close in a way she never had before.

In the center of one of the room's walls was mounted a single Edison lightbulb. Serafina's pa had told her with a swell in his chest that Mr. V was friends with Mr. Thomas Edison and liked using all the latest scientific advancements.

Seeing all this amazed Serafina. Essie had her own lightbulb! Serafina knew from her pa that many of the mountain folk of western North Carolina were living in clapboard shacks and log cabins without electricity, central heating, or indoor plumbing. Many of them had never even *seen* a lightbulb, let alone have one for their own particular use. But Essie had made herself a cozy little den up here on the fourth floor, like a tiny mouse nesting up in the attic, where no one would ever find her.

A window set into the room's roof-slanted wall provided something that Serafina, a denizen of the basement, seldom beheld from this height: a mesmerizing westward view across the Blue Ridge Mountains. The clear sight of Mount Pisgah rising in the distance above the other peaks caught her eye. A few nights after she and Braeden had defeated the Man in the Black Cloak, they had snuck up onto the rooftop to celebrate their victory. She remembered sitting under the stars with him, looking across the mountains, as Braeden explained how that peak was more than nineteen miles away, but it was still on the estate. He had marveled at how it took a day to get there on horseback, following twisting, rocky trails through the mountains, but a hawk soaring on the wind could simply tilt its wing and be there in a moment.

Smiling, Serafina turned and looked around Essie's room as Essie watched her with interest. "I ain't got it too bad, do I, miss?"

"Not too bad at all," Serafina agreed. "I like it here."

Essie pulled a nicely made beige day dress off one of the hooks on the wall. "It's my Sunday best," she said, handing it to over to Serafina. "It ain't nothing fancy compared to what the ladies wear, but—"

"Thank you, Essie," Serafina said, gently taking it from her. "It's perfect."

Essie kept talking as she turned around so Serafina could change.

"I'm a chambermaid now, but I'm fixed on being a lady's maid someday," Essie said. "Maybe serve the lady guests when they come, or even Mrs. Vanderbilt herself. Do you know Mrs. V?"

"Yes," Serafina said as she pulled off her burlap dress. Goose bumps rose up on her bare legs and arms, half chill and half nervousness. It felt so odd to be undressing when there was someone else in the room.

"I thought you must know her, you being you and all," Essie continued.

The fact was that Serafina had become very fond of Mrs. Vanderbilt over the last few weeks and had enjoyed their talks together, but she hadn't seen her around the house in several days.

"My friend's been a-goin' to the girls' school Mrs. V set up, learning how to do her numbers and weave fabric on the loom," Essie said. "Mrs. V wants all the girls to get some kind of education so that they can fend for themselves if they have to."

"I think she's very kind," Serafina agreed as she tried to figure out how to get into the dress. It seemed to have a bewildering array of buttons and drawstrings and other complications.

"Kind as kind can be," Essie continued. "Did you hear about the dairy boy? Two weeks ago, a dairyman and his eldest boy got awful puny, real bad sick, liketa died, so Mrs. V went on over to their cabin with a basket of food to help the family get through for a while. When she saw the boy was on the down-go, she had the menfolk haul him into her carriage, and she carted him all the way to the hospital in Asheville."

"What happened to the boy?" Serafina asked as she finally figured out how to slip into the dress and fasten up the last of the buttons.

"He's still mighty sick," Essie said. "But I hear they're taking good care of him down there."

"You can turn around now," Serafina said.

"Oh, miss!" Essie said. "That's a whole heap better, believe me. Come over to the mirror and take a look while I fix your hair."

Essie didn't seem to care that Serafina was different from everyone else, that her face was scratched, her eyes too large, and the angle of her cheeks unusually severe. She just went straight to work. "This hair of yourn!" she said, and started tugging away at it like it was a bushel of misbehaving ferrets. "We ain't got time for me to do a proper job, but we'll get it wrangled up."

As Essie worked, Serafina found herself looking into the mirror and noticed something odd. There appeared to be chunks of long black hair growing among the rest that she'd never seen before.

"What's wrong, miss?" Essie said, seeing her frown.

"My hair is brown, not black," she said, mystified as she raised her hand slowly up to her head and touched the black strands.

"You want 'em gone, miss? I used to cut my mamaw's gray hairs out all the time. They'd come in all long and wiry like they'd drunk too much moonshine, and we'd cut 'em out quick as they came."

"Just yank 'em," Serafina said.

"That's gonna hurt, miss. There's a lot of 'em."

"Just grab 'em hard and yank 'em out," Serafina insisted. If she'd didn't have enough problems going to the main floor for all to see, now she had strange things growing out of her head. She looked hideous.

Essie selected the strands of black hair and pulled so hard that it tugged Serafina's head back.

"Sorry, miss," Essie said.

"Keep going," she said. As Essie worked, Serafina decided to ask a question about what she'd seen earlier that morning.

"You said you're fixin' to be a lady's maid. Have you served that new girl who's been visiting?"

"The English girl," Essie groaned, making it pretty clear she was none too keen on her.

"You don't like her?" Serafina asked, amused.

"I don't trust that girl any farther than I can throw her, coming in here with all her fancy high-and-mighty airs and puttin' a bead on the young master first thing."

Serafina wasn't sure exactly what she meant by all that, but it occurred to her that someone in Essie's position, working in the rooms on the second and third floors, might see things that she herself did not.

"What about the murder investigator who came in last night?" she asked. "Have you seen him?"

"Not yet, but I heard from one of the footmen that he had all sorts of trunks and cases hauled up to this room, filled with strange instruments of some kind. He's been giving all the servants orders, demanding this and that."

That doesn't sound good, Serafina thought.

Having yanked out several chunks of black strands, Essie picked up her brush and started brushing Serafina's hair in long, pulling strokes. It felt so strange but so oddly pleasant to have someone pull a brush through her hair, the sensation of the drag on her roots, and the detangling of her hair, and the gentle rake of the soft bristles against her scalp. She had to do everything she could to keep from purring.

"Can I ask you a question, miss?" Essie asked as she brushed. "Ya know, Mrs. King keeps tellin' all of us girls to mind our own business, but everyone's been talking about it all the same. We all want to know what's going on."

"Going on with what?" Serafina asked uncertainly.

"With Mrs. V," Essie said. "She didn't come out of her room for breakfast this morning, and she's been feeling so poorly lately that we hardly see her. I'm sure she'll get through it, whatever it is, but I was just wondering if you've heard anything."

"I didn't realize she was down sick," Serafina said as a knot formed slowly in her stomach. That explained why she hadn't seen her.

"She's been sick as a dog some days," Essie continued. "Then other times she perks up for a while. We seen the doctor a-comin' and a-goin'. We all just want to know if she's going to be all right."

"I honestly don't know, Essie. I'm sorry," Serafina said. The news that Mrs. Vanderbilt was sick hung heavy in her heart. "But when I hear something, I'll be sure to tell you."

"I'd be much obliged," Essie said, nodding. "And I'll do likewise."

Finally, Essie set down the hairbrush. She took Serafina's hair in her hands, wrapped it around, and rolled it up into a loose twist on her head. Then she fastened it in place.

"There you go, miss," Essie said. "I think that will do ya for a little while."

When Serafina looked in the mirror, she saw a new girl staring back at her. Her own face was still there, still looking back at herself, but with the dress Essie had lent her and her hair pulled up, she almost looked presentable.

Essie smiled, proud of her handiwork. "You're a right proper girl now," she said, nodding with satisfaction.

"I think I am," Serafina said in astonishment.

Serafina turned toward Essie and, remembering how she had recoiled from her touch when they first met on the stairs, she reached out and slowly put her hand on Essie's arm like she had seen other people sometimes do. The gesture felt unnatural to her, to actually be touching someone in this way, and she wasn't sure it was the right kind of moment for it, but when she did, Essie's face glowed with happiness.

"Aw, miss, it hain't nothin'—just helpin' out another girl, is all."

"I truly appreciate it, Essie," Serafina said.

Then Serafina paused and decided to ask one more question before she went. "A little bit ago, you said everybody's got somethin' that spooks them."

"I think that's about right, don't you?"

"It sounded like you were thinking about something in particular. For you, is it the fear of getting sick like the dairyman's boy?"

"No, miss."

"Then, what is it? What spooks you?"

"Well, I ain't too keen on haints, of course—don't suppose anyone is, people comin' back from the dead and all that—but what sends me a-runnin' are the stories my papaw used to tell round the fire at night to scare us little ones."

"About what?"

"Oh, you know, how when a wind kicks up on a calm day and blows something over, or you find an animal dead in the woods for no good reason, people always say, 'It's just the old man of the forest playing his tricks again.'"

Serafina felt her lips getting dry as she listened to Essie's story. She could hear the fear creeping into the girl's voice. "What old man?" Serafina asked.

"I'm sure you've heard the stories same as me, an old man with a walking stick wandering the shadows of the forest, drifting in and out of the mist, leading folk off the road and getting them lost in the swamps. Sometimes they say he causes mischief around the cabin, curdled milk and dead chickens in the yard. My papaw used to love tellin' stories, but them ones scared me half to death. Still do, truth be told."

"But who is the old man in the stories? Where'd he come from? What's he want?" Serafina asked, mystified.

Essie shook her head and shrugged. "Knock me cold if I know!" She laughed. "It's just some old stupid story, but for some reason it scares the livin' daylights out me like nothin' else. If I find myself out in the woods at night and hear the break of a stick or a gust of wind, half time I just run on home as fast as I can. I'm so bad awful scared of the dark it ain't even funny! That's why I love it here."

"Here? Why?" Serafina asked, unable to fathom the mysterious connection.

"Indoor plumbing," Essie said, laughing. "Ain't gotta go out to the outhouse every night in the dark!"

Serafina smiled. Her new companion was a daytime girl through and through, but there was something about Essie Walker that she was growing mighty fond of.

"But truly, miss," Essie said, turning more serious. "You've gotta get going back downstairs, and I gotta get back to work. If we stay holed up in here like a couple of treed coons much longer, they're gonna send the dogs out for us."

"The dogs?" Serafina said in alarm.

"You know, the bloodhounds, the coon dogs. It's just an expression."

"Yes, of course," Serafina said, realizing that, like Essie, there was maybe more than a few things in the world that spooked her.

As Serafina said good-bye, she was sorry to go, especially to what awaited her downstairs, but she was glad to have made a new friend.

Serafina flew down the stairway, barely touching every fifth step, one flight, two flights, three flights down. Hitting the main floor, she dashed past a startled footman at the butler's pantry door, then headed down the narrow passage through another door, across the Breakfast Room, then another corridor, and finally stopped, took a breath, and stepped calmly into the Winter Garden.

Tall, dangling palms, ficus trees, and other exotic plants filled the room. Sunshine poured down through the arched dome of ornate beams that held the Winter Garden's glass ceiling aloft. Fine pieces of ceramic art were displayed on small viewing stands throughout the tiled room, and French rattan furniture provided places for the fancy folk to lounge.

She'd come here to this central room in the house hoping to meet Braeden before being questioned by the investigator, but she felt so vulnerable walking openly into this grand place where once she had only prowled.

She kept checking for places to hide, her muscles pulsing, first this way, then that, as if she'd need to flee at any moment. Then she spotted Braeden and the English girl standing together. Serafina hesitated. Her body tensed.

The two citizens of the upstairs had changed out of their riding outfits—he into his afternoon black coat, trousers, and tie, and she into a sky-blue dress with a narrow-waist corset, capped puffy sleeves, and silk chiffon covering her forearms. The girl's chestnut-red tresses were piled high on her head, swept back in soft, neat waves, held in place by a twined wooden shawl pin, then spilling down on one side in twisted rolls, sausage curls so tight and perfectly formed they reminded Serafina of coiled springs in her pa's workshop. Whoever they had assigned to be the girl's lady's maid that afternoon must have spent hours curling her hair with a fire-heated curling iron. Serafina had guessed before that the girl was about fourteen years old, but she could see now that she was clearly trying to act older. She wore finely wrought, dangling silver earrings and a black velvet ribbon choker necklace with a cameo pendant. Serafina had to admit that she was an elegant-looking girl, with striking eyes the color of the forest.

As Serafina stepped closer to them, her heart pounded far harder than if she'd been entering a battle with the wolfhounds.

Out of habit, she walked silently. Neither of the humans noticed her. But Gidean's sharply pointed black ears perked up, then dropped down in relief when he recognized her. He wagged his tail nub excitedly. Serafina smiled, warmed by the dog's enthusiasm.

The English girl was facing in Serafina's direction, but she didn't take notice of her until it became quite obvious that Serafina was walking straight toward them. The girl was clearly startled by Serafina's appearance. Her eyes widened and she tilted her head. She looked almost scared. But as Serafina came closer, the girl seemed to compose herself more firmly. She looked at Serafina with a withering gaze, as if to say, *Why in the world is someone dressed like you walking toward someone dressed like me?*

If you don't like this, you should have seen what I was going to wear, Serafina thought.

Pausing just short of them, Serafina stood between the bronze fountain in the center of the room and a beautiful blue-and-white Ming vase on a small wooden table beneath a collection of graceful palms. Serafina remembered overhearing that Mr. Vanderbilt had purchased the vase on his travels to the Orient, that it was over four hundred years old and one of the most valuable works of art in the house. Serafina stood so still and out in the open that for a moment she almost felt like one of the pieces of furniture.

When Braeden finally turned and saw her there, his face lit up, and he smiled. "Hello, Serafina!" he said without hesitation.

Serafina's body filled with a wave of relief and happiness. "Hello, Braeden," she said, hoping she sounded at least somewhat normal.

Even though he should have been expecting her, Braeden seemed so surprised and happy to see her there. Had he been worried about her? Or was it simply because she so seldom visited the main floor in the daytime?

"I . . ." she began, not sure how to say it properly. "I am in receipt of your note," she said, trying to sound as sophisticated as possible but wanting to make it clear she understood the seriousness of the interrogation.

He nodded knowingly, stepped toward her, and spoke to her in a low voice. "I don't know what we're walking into here, but I think we need to be very careful."

"What's the investigator's name?" she asked. "Where does he come from?"

"I don't know," Braeden said. "He came in late last night."

"And what does your uncle say about all this?"

"If the authorities determine that Mr. Thorne was murdered, then the murderer will be hanged."

"He actually said that?" Serafina asked, taken aback, but even as she and Braeden talked, she felt the air bristling around her. When Braeden first saw her and greeted her with such warmth, she had noticed that the English girl stepped back a little, her chin raised and her face tense with uncertainty. Now she was just standing there, waiting quietly. The situation was becoming increasingly awkward for her. Braeden should have been introducing her, but he wasn't. He seemed to have forgotten her. Serafina couldn't imagine that was a pleasant feeling.

It dawned on her that the girl might be as uncomfortable with her surroundings at Biltmore as Serafina was. The girl was a newcomer, still trying to find her place to fit in, and now here was the one boy she knew whispering with some strange, shaggy-haired, tooth-marked vagrant. Despite the sharpness Serafina had felt for the girl the first time she saw her, she almost felt sorry for her.

"Oh yes," Braeden said, seeming to read Serafina's mind and suddenly remember his responsibilities. "Serafina, this is—"

But at that moment, Mrs. Vanderbilt came sweeping down the steps into the Winter Garden. "Ah, I see that you're all here. Good. I'll take you down to the Library to speak with Mr. Vanderbilt and the detective."

The lady of the house wore a handsome afternoon dress, and she was putting on a good front, but Serafina could see she did indeed look a bit peaked. Her cheeks were pale, but her brow was flushed. She seemed to be trying to soldier on through her day with a positive attitude despite her poor health.

"Serafina, before we go down, I would like you to meet someone," Mrs. Vanderbilt said, bringing her with a soft gesture of her hand toward the English girl. "I would like to present Lady Rowena Fox-Pemberton, who is visiting us from very far away. I hope the two of you can become good friends during her time here at Biltmore. We must do all we can to make her feel as if Biltmore is her home."

"It's good to meet you, miss," Serafina said politely to the girl.

"My lady," Lady Rowena said as she looked Serafina up and down in surprise.

"Excuse me?" Serafina asked, genuinely confused.

"You are to address me not as 'miss', but as 'my lady,'" Lady Rowena corrected Serafina, in her formal English accent.

"I see," Serafina said. "Is that how they do it in England? And will you be addressing me as 'my lady' also, then?"

"Of course not!" the girl said in astonishment as color rose to her cheeks.

"All right," Mrs. Vanderbilt said, reaching out and touching each of the girls with an open hand in an attempt to smooth over the situation. "I'm sure we'll get the English-American relations sorted out. . . ."

But as Mrs. Vanderbilt reached gently toward her, Serafina reflexively stepped back and felt the brush of a tall, dangling palm frond against her cheek. The palm leaf seemed to actually move of its own accord and get tangled in her hair. Startled, Serafina reached up and spun quickly to brush it away, thinking that it must be a tree snake or something, for that was exactly how it felt. She snapped around so fast that she bumped into the furniture behind her.

"Oh, do be careful there, Serafina!" Mrs. Vanderbilt cried out in panicked dismay, reaching toward the thing behind Serafina.

That was when Serafina realized that her sudden movement had bumped the small wooden stand that held the Ming vase.

The vase tipped off the stand and fell. Serafina watched in horror as the priceless piece of art plummeted toward the hard tiled floor. She tried to reach for it, but she was too late. It hit the floor with a crash and shattered into a thousand pieces. The sight of the exploding porcelain took Serafina's breath away. The sound of it echoing through the house churned a sickness in her stomach.

Everyone stared at the shattered vase in shock and then looked at her.

Serafina's cheeks burned with heat, and her eyes filled with tears. "I'm so, so sorry, Mrs. Vanderbilt," she said, moving toward her. "I did not mean to do that. I'm so sorry."

"Maybe we can glue it," Braeden said, dropping to his knees and trying to pick up the shards as Lady Rowena Fox-Pemberton stared balefully at Serafina and shook her head as if to say, *I knew you didn't belong in the house.*

"George is going to be heartbroken," Mrs. Vanderbilt muttered to herself, her hand over her mouth as she stared in stunned disbelief at the broken pieces on the floor. "It was one of his favorites. . . ."

"I'm so sorry," Serafina said again, her heart filled with an aching, shameful pain. "I don't know what happened. The plant attacked me." But even as the words slipped out, she knew how immature they sounded. Lady Rowena just stared at her, taking it all in, too smart and well poised to actually smile, but seeming to be on the edge of it. Serafina looked around her at the plants and the other objects in the room. She didn't understand it. She had spent her whole life prowling in this house, ducking and darting, and never once had she ever knocked over or broken anything. And now, just as she was starting to come out into the upstairs world, just as she was wanting to show Mrs. Vanderbilt how much she appreciated her friendship, she did this horrible, stupid, clumsy thing. She wanted to run back down to the basement and cry. It took every ounce of her courage to remain standing there in her shame.

Finally, Mrs. Vanderbilt looked at her nephew kneeling on the floor trying to clean up the mess. "Braeden," she said, "I'm afraid it's not going to work."

Sensing the gravity of his aunt's mood, Braeden slowly stopped his efforts.

"You do not have time for this," Mrs. Vanderbilt said. "You and Serafina are expected to speak with Detective Grathan."

Serafina had never seen Mrs. Vanderbilt act so cold and businesslike to Braeden or anyone else, and it was totally her fault.

"I'll take Lady Rowena for a walk to the Conservatory," Mrs. Vanderbilt said. "You and Serafina go down to the Library immediately."

Mrs. King, the head housekeeper, entered the Winter Garden and spoke directly to Mrs. Vanderbilt. "I've asked a maid to get a broom and dustpan to clean up the broken vase," she said, her voice level and professional. As the highest-ranking servant at Biltmore, the matron possessed a commanding presence. Wearing a practical olive-green dress with mother-of-pearl buttons and a sash around her waist, she kept her hair pulled back in a tightly controlled bun behind her head.

"Thank you, Mrs. King," Mrs. Vanderbilt said appreciatively. "Please take the children to the Library."

When Mrs. Vanderbilt called her and Braeden "children," Serafina saw the satisfaction in Lady Rowena's face.

"Come this way," Mrs. King instructed Braeden and Serafina. It was the kind of voice that was used to being obeyed.

Mrs. King had been running Biltmore for years, even before Mr. Vanderbilt married and Mrs. Vanderbilt arrived. As Serafina followed the matron through the Entrance Hall, she wiped her teary eyes and tried to think about what her pa would tell her at this moment. *Quit yer snifflin' and get your wits about ya, girl,* he'd say, and he'd be right. If she was going to be questioned by an investigator for a murder that she'd been a part of, she had to pull herself together.

Serafina studied Mrs. King as she followed her down the long length of the Tapestry Galley toward the Library, for she had seldom been this close to her.

One of the things that had always mystified Serafina about Mrs. King was that she lived in an area of Biltmore that Serafina had never seen. She was the one and only inhabitant of the mysterious second-and-a-half floor. Serafina couldn't imagine how a whole floor, or even half of one, could exist between two other floors. But she'd learned long ago that all manner of both grand and wicked things were possible at Biltmore. The palm trees, for example, were particularly untrustworthy.

She couldn't help but notice the key ring hanging on Mrs. King's sash. It was a large brass ring with all the keys of the house, for every door, cupboard, and secret hatch, from the basement to the top floor. Serafina had always been mesmerized by the jingling, jangling sound of the hanging keys. But just as she was looking at it, something tiny pulled a key from the ring, darted down Mrs. King's dress, and shot along the floor quicker than two blinks and a sneeze. The brown little creature had been so small and had moved so fast that Serafina barely saw it. And she was quite sure that no one else had. But she'd been C.R.C. long enough to know what it was: a mouse. Sometimes mice move so fast that they're just a flash and then they're gone. Already, she started doubting that she'd actually seen it. How in the world could a live mouse run down Mrs. King's dress? And what was it doing? Stealing a key to the cheese cupboard?

But she had bigger problems to face. As she and Braeden plodded along behind Mrs. King, Serafina looked over at Braeden. His lips were pressed together, his face filled with worry. It felt like Mrs. King was taking her and Braeden to their trial, sentencing, and execution. She had half a mind to turn and run, just get out of there while she still had the chance. She'd be as gone as yesterday's breeze before Mrs. King even noticed she was missing. But she knew she couldn't leave poor Braeden behind, so she trudged glumly along beside him, not knowing what else to do. She felt like she was tied up in a poke sack and was just about to get chucked into the river.

As they entered the Library, Serafina gazed across the familiar room. Thousands of Mr. Vanderbilt's leather-bound books lined the walls of intricately carved wood and sculpted marblework. The books reached all the way up to the angelic Italian painting on the ceiling some thirty-five feet above their heads.

But there was no one in the room. The globes of the brass lamps were lit, and a fire burned in the massive black marble fireplace, but the Library Room was completely empty.

When she glanced at Braeden, it was clear that he was as confused as she was. But the stalwart Mrs. King appeared undeterred. She led them along the bookcases built into the western wall, then turned right and stopped. They were now looking at a section of the room's oak paneling. It took Serafina nearly a second to recognize that it wasn't just a wall. It was a door. And the carving on the door's center panel is what disturbed her: a robed man holding a finger to his mouth as if to say *Shhh!* There was blood dripping down his head and a knife stuck in his back.

"You may step through the door," the matron said. "They are expecting you."

13

Serafina stepped cautiously into the dimly lit room. It was a cramped, closed-in den with leather furniture, shades blocking out the setting sun, and a dark ceiling patterned like the bones of a bat's wing. This was not his usual office, but Mr. Vanderbilt sat behind the desk.

She had been watching the master of Biltmore all her life, but she'd never been able to figure him out. He was a man of immense wealth but quiet word, a refined, bookish gentleman with a slight frame and slender hands. He had shrewd, dark eyes, black hair, and a black mustache.

"Come into the room," he said gravely. He seemed to be in a grim and unforgiving mood.

As she and Braeden stepped slowly forward, she saw

something out of the corner of her eye: a man sitting in the shadows, unmoving, studying her. She couldn't help but pull in a breath. Her heart began to beat heavy in her chest, marking time like a slow, powerful drum.

As her eyes adjusted to the darkness of the room, she began to see the stranger's features. To her surprise, it wasn't the elderly man she'd seen walking into the forest with Mr. Vanderbilt. This man's straggly rat-brown hair fell to his shoulders, and he had a short goatee. He stared at her with intense, unrelenting eyes. He might have been handsome in the past, but so many raised gray scars traced his face that she could see an entire history of battle there, against both blade and claw— it was a wonder that he had survived them. His brown woolen coat and shoulder cape were matted and wind-worn, tattered at the edges, like he'd been on the road for many years.

As the man looked at the scratches on her face and the bite wounds on her hands, it felt like something was crawling up her spine. The muscles in her body twitched and tensed, wanting to fight or flee. He could see too much. Terrifying images flashed through her mind: the gray-bearded man in a wide-brimmed hat stepping onto the road, the snapping jaws of the white-fanged hounds, the black silhouette of a figure sitting in the carriage as it pulled away.

Had this man looked out from the carriage and seen her? If he had seen her at all, he could have only caught a glimpse of her as she ran away. She was wearing different clothes now, and her hair had changed. Whatever it was, he seemed as uncertain about her as she was about him.

In his hand, he held a cane with a spiraling shaft and a curving antler handle. There was something about the cane that made her think it was far more dangerous than it appeared. But it seemed to be a different style than the one she'd seen the night before. It was like there were little flaws in her memory. Had she seen a gnarly stick or a more formal, spiraling cane with a hooked horn handle like this one? Could it change shape?

"Sit down," Mr. Vanderbilt instructed. He pointed to the two small, bare, wooden chairs in the middle of the room. Serafina had seldom heard Mr. Vanderbilt so stern, so sharp of tone, but she couldn't tell if it was because he was angry with her and Braeden or because of this detective's unexpected presence in his home. Mr. Vanderbilt had welcomed all sorts of guests to entertain themselves in the magnificent mansion he had built for that purpose, but he himself had a tendency to withdraw from revelry. He often sat in a quiet room by himself and read rather than imbibe with others. He was a man of his own spirit. And now here was a stranger, a detective, a man of the road, come to call with words of murder, and Mr. Vanderbilt seemed none too pleased about it.

As she and Braeden sat down in the two chairs, she glanced over at her friend. He looked scared and alone. Mrs. King had instructed him to leave Gidean outside the room. He seemed vulnerable without his canine protector at his side, which made Serafina more determined than ever to make sure this Detective Grathan did not get the better of them.

Mr. Vanderbilt looked at her and Braeden. "Detective Grathan is investigating the disappearance of Mr. Thorne. He theorizes that Mr. Thorne did not take his leave of Biltmore of his own accord but encountered foul play while he was here."

"Yes, sir," Braeden said, trying to sound steady, but Serafina could hear the quiver in his voice. There was no doubt in her mind, either, that if they made a mistake here, they might be arrested and charged with conspiring to murder Mr. Thorne. She had led him into the trap. And Braeden owned the dog that helped kill him.

"I recommend that you answer all his questions truthfully," Mr. Vanderbilt said.

Serafina glanced at Mr. Vanderbilt, for the tone in his voice had an unexpected edge to it. On the face of it, he was telling her and Braeden to do the right thing, to cooperate with the detective's investigation. But in another way, it seemed to her that he was signaling them, warning them that they needed to be very careful, like the man might possess the power to discern truth from lie.

"Detective Grathan," Mr. Vanderbilt said as he turned to the man, "everyone at Biltmore will, of course, cooperate with your investigation. This is my nephew Braeden Vanderbilt, my late brother's son, and his friend Serafina. Along with the others you've already spoken to, they were present on the day of Mr. Thorne's disappearance. You are free to ask them any questions you deem necessary to complete your investigation."

The detective nodded, then spoke to Mr. Vanderbilt in a serious tone. "You do not have to be present for this questioning."

Whoa, Serafina thought. He just asked Mr. Vanderbilt to leave the room. *No one* asked Mr. Vanderbilt to leave anywhere.

It was *his* house. Serafina could sense the tension increasing between the two men.

"I will remain," Mr. Vanderbilt said unequivocally.

Detective Grathan looked at him and seemed to decide that for the moment he would not argue with the master of Biltmore. Instead, he pivoted his head slowly toward Serafina. She swore she could hear the sound of ticking cartilage as his head turned. The man studied her for several seconds, seeming to pull every detail of her apart, bit by bit. She noticed his fingers wrapped slowly around the antler handle of his cane. Then he spoke.

"Your name is Serafina, is that correct?" he asked.

"Yes," she said. *And your name is Mr. Grathan,* she wanted to say in return. *Do you and your master own five mangy, over-grown tracking hounds with teeth like daggers?*

"Did you know Mr. Thorne?" he asked.

"Yes, I knew him," she replied truthfully, "but I only spoke to him a few times."

The man studied her. He held his cane—or staff or stick or whatever it was—as he spoke to her. Then he slowly pivoted his head and looked at Braeden. "And did you know Mr. Thorne as well?"

"He was my friend," Braeden said, which was also the truth.

"When did you last see him?"

"At the party on the night of his disappearance," Braeden said. It seemed that he, too, had picked up on his uncle's warning. When Braeden glanced at her with a knowing look, she was sure of it. In that moment, the two friends silently agreed what course they must take: to give the detective no advantage, to speak the careful truth but nothing more.

The detective turned his head slowly back to Serafina. "And when was the last time you saw Mr. Thorne?"

The last time she'd seen him, he'd been lying dead on the ground in the graveyard, his blood leaking out of him, and then his body decomposed before her eyes, his worldly carcass becoming nothing but blood-soaked earth.

"I believe it was the last day we all saw him," she said. "The day he disappeared."

"At what *time* did you last see him?"

"As I recall, it was after dark," she said, but *midnight* would have been more accurate.

"So you were one of the last people to see him here at Biltmore."

"I believe I must have been."

"And what was he doing when you saw him last?"

"The last time I saw him here at Biltmore, he was putting on his cloak and going out the door."

"You saw him leave Biltmore?"

"Yes, very clearly. He was running out the door."

"Running?" the detective asked in surprise.

"Yes. Running." *He was chasing me,* she thought, *and I led him to his death.*

The detective's head pivoted to Braeden.

"And did you see this as well?"

"No," Braeden said. "I went to bed after the party."

The detective's eyes held steady on Braeden for several

seconds as if he did not believe his answer. Then he said, "The black dog is yours." Serafina had no idea how he knew this, because Gidean wasn't even in the room.

"Yes," Braeden replied uncertainly.

"The dog is almost always with you, but you say you went to bed early that night. How and when did the dog suffer a wound to its right shoulder?"

"I . . ." Braeden said, confused and disturbed by the question.

"How was the dog wounded?" the detective pressed.

"I did not see him get hurt," Braeden said truthfully.

"But when did it happen?"

"It was the morning we discovered that another child had gone missing. I sent Gidean out into the woods to track the child," Braeden said.

Serafina thought it was clever the way Braeden said *another child had gone missing*, disguising the fact that it had actually been *she* who had gone missing. She had gone out to trap Mr. Thorne. And she liked the way Braeden described it as *the morning*, which was technically correct because it had been after midnight, but gave the impression that it was the next day.

"And did the dog find the missing child?" the detective asked.

"Yes, he did," Braeden said. Then he looked at Mr. Vanderbilt. "Uncle, why is he asking me all these questions about Gidean? Does he think Gidean and I did something wrong?"

Serafina couldn't tell if Braeden was faking his expression

of fear and bewilderment or whether it was genuine, but either way, it was convincing.

"No, of course not, Braeden," Mr. Vanderbilt said, looking firmly at the detective when he said these words. "He's just doing his job." It was clear that Mr. Vanderbilt would brook little more of this imposition. "Just answer his questions truthfully," he said again, and this time Serafina was sure of it—he was helping them. He was on their side. *Choose your words carefully,* he was telling them. She knew that the key was to avoid and deflect the difficult questions.

The detective turned his head with a sharp scrape of his neck and looked at Serafina. "Do you know what happened to Mr. Thorne on the night about which we speak?"

How in the world was she going to avoid that question without lying through her teeth? She could already see them erecting the gallows and tying the noose for her neck.

"God rest his soul," she said abruptly.

"Then you think that he's not just missing but actually dead?" the man said, leaning forward and peering at her.

"Yes."

"How do you know this?"

"Because he has not returned."

"But do you know *how* he died? Did you see a body? Was there some sort of unnatural force involved?"

In those last few words, the rat betrayed himself. What was he truly looking for? When he said *unnatural force,* did he mean black magic? The man in the forest had instructed his dogs to hunt down what he had called the Black One. This man wasn't just looking for Mr. Thorne's murderer. He was looking for the Black Cloak!

"You haven't answered my question," he pressed her.

"I believe a powerful force must have surprised him and killed him," she said. "Everyone in the mountains knows that the forest is filled with many dangers." And then she remembered the expression that Essie had said always spooked her. "Maybe the old man of the forest is up to his old tricks again."

The detective's expression widened when she said these words. "What kind of powerful force are you talking about?"

"I think there are forces both good and evil in the forest."

"And you believe it was these forces that killed Mr. Thorne?" the detective asked.

"It could be," she said. What she wasn't saying was that it had been the *good* forces rather than the evil ones that had killed Mr. Thorne.

Mr. Vanderbilt leaned forward. "I don't know where your questions are going, Mr. Grathan. I suggest we proceed with the other people on your list."

"I have more questions for these two," the detective said sharply, not looking at Mr. Vanderbilt. Serafina could feel the barely controlled intensity rising within the detective. It was as if he had come in the *disguise* of a civilized person, a police investigator, but now his true character was beginning to show itself.

He thrust his hand into his pocket and brought out a silver

clasp engraved with an intricate design: a tight bundle of twisting vines and thorns.

Serafina's heart began to pound in her chest. Now there was no doubt. The detective had found the remnants of the Black Cloak. That meant he had indeed been out to the area of her mother's den. A flash of new fears flooded her mind. She could feel the heat rising in her body.

"Do you recognize this?" the detective asked her.

The pulse of her blood thumped in her temples. She could barely hear his words.

"Do you recognize this?" he asked again.

"It appears to be a clasp from an article of clothing," she said, trying to keep her voice as flat and undisturbed as possible.

"But you're not answering the question!" he pressed her.

"Mr. Grathan, calm yourself," Mr. Vanderbilt warned him.

"Do you recognize it?" Mr. Grathan asked her, ignoring him.

"It looks as if whatever it once held is now set free," she said.

"But have you seen it before?" he asked again, gripping the handle of his cane like he was going to swing it around and wield it like a weapon at any moment.

She felt a great weight pressing in on her. But as she pretended to examine the clasp, she noticed that something was different: the tiny faces that had been behind the thorns were gone now.

"I have never seen a silver clasp with this design," she said, at last finding a way to hew to the truth.

The detective stared at her for a long time as if he knew she was deceiving him but could not quite frame the words to trap her.

"Detective, we need to move on," Mr. Vanderbilt pushed him.

"I have more questions!" the detective insisted, his voice filled with aggravation, his eyes locked on Serafina. "Do you know which room Mr. Thorne slept in during his stay at Biltmore?"

"It was on the third floor," she said.

"Do you live here at Biltmore?"

"Yes, I do."

"With the female servants on the fourth floor?"

"No."

"Then where do you sleep at night?"

"I do not."

The detective stopped and looked at her in surprise. "You do not sleep?"

"I do not sleep at night."

The man frowned. "Are you a night maid?"

"No."

"Then what are you?"

She looked him straight in the eyes and said, "I'm the Chief Rat Catcher. I track down vermin."

He stared right back at her and said, "Then we have that much in common."

Serafina glanced at Braeden as the two of them quickly left Mr. Vanderbilt's den and crossed through the Library.

"We have to stay away from that man," Braeden whispered to her.

"No, we need to get rid of him!" Serafina said fiercely. She was still breathing heavily from her exchange with him.

"If my uncle hadn't stopped everything and dismissed us, were you going to fight the detective right there?"

Serafina just shook her head. "I don't know," she admitted. As they walked toward the Entrance Hall, Gidean followed at their side.

"Did you see his face? All those scars?" Braeden said. "That man's scary! What's he been fighting?"

"His neck creaked every time he turned his head," Serafina said.

"He was horrible. And he just kept asking question after question. I thought it would never end! What's going to happen if he finds out we were involved in Mr. Thorne's death? Is he going to arrest us?"

"Worse than that, I think," Serafina said. "I'm not sure he is who he says he is."

"What do you mean?" Braeden asked in alarm. Looking at her wounds, he said, "What happened to you last night?"

She desperately wanted to talk to him, but as they reached the Entrance Hall, she heard Mrs. Vanderbilt and Lady Rowena coming in through the Vestibule.

"One of the servants must have notified them that we were done," Braeden muttered. She couldn't be sure, but it almost sounded like there was sadness in his voice.

"Do you have to go?" Serafina asked quietly, glancing at him. She knew he probably did.

"Come on!" he said suddenly, and pulled her in the opposite direction.

Laughing, Serafina ran with Braeden up the Grand Staircase, the wide, magnificent circular stairway that led to the upper floors. She wasn't sure where Braeden was taking her, other than just to escape, but when they reached the third floor, she had an idea where they could go and talk in secret. There was much she had to tell him.

"This way!" she said as they ran through the living hall past several smartly dressed ladies and gentlemen enjoying tea.

"Hello, everybody!" Braeden called cheerfully as they blazed through.

"Oh, good evening, Master Braeden," one of the gentlemen said, as if it weren't unusual at all for two children and a dog to be dashing through the living hall.

"Where are we going?" Braeden asked breathlessly as they darted down a back corridor.

"You'll see," she said.

At the end of the hallway, she stopped just where it dog-legged up toward the North Tower Room. Two small bronze sculptures and a gathering of books sat atop a built-in oak cabinet. The first bronze sculpture depicted a horse being spooked by a rattlesnake. The second was a lean and muscular leopardess, her ears pinned back and her fangs bared as she sank her teeth and claws into some sort of wild beast.

Serafina had noticed over the years that there were sculptures and paintings of great cats everywhere at Biltmore: two bronze lionesses prowled on the mantel above the billiard table, and two rampant lions raised their claws above the fireplace where guests enjoyed their breakfast. She knew it was silly now, but when she was younger, she had always imagined that these were her aunts and uncles, her grandmothers and grandfathers, like family portraits on the wall. An old woodcarving print of a proud, great-grandfatherly lion was displayed in the Library, and there were cousin-like lion faces carved into the decorative corbels in the Banquet Hall. The statues on the house gates depicted the head and upper body of a woman, but if you looked very carefully, which she always did, you could see the lower body of a lion. The one that had always perplexed her the most was the white marble statue leading into the Italian Garden: a woman with a lion draped over her back and a little girl at her side. Even the doorbell at Biltmore's front door depicted a great cat. She had often wondered why Mr. Vanderbilt had collected so many tributes to the feline race. But of all the cats at Biltmore, this small bronze sculpture of a leopardess in the throes of a ferocious attack had always been her favorite.

"What are we doing?" Braeden asked, staring in confusion at the sculptures.

Serafina bent down and opened the cabinet door. Inside were more of Mr. Vanderbilt's books. Getting down on her hands and knees, she moved the volumes aside and gained access to the back of the cabinet. She pushed hard on the wooden panel like she remembered doing before, but it didn't budge.

"What are you doing that for?" Braeden asked.

"Come on, help me," Serafina said, and soon she and Braeden were working shoulder to shoulder. The back panel of the cabinet finally pushed through, opening into a dark hole.

"Follow me," Serafina said, her voice echoing a little as she crawled into the darkness. She hadn't been in here in years, but when she was younger, it had been one of her favorite places.

"I'm not going in there until you . . ." Braeden was saying behind her, but she kept going into the darkness.

"Serafina?" Braeden asked from out in the corridor. "Fine, I'm coming." He must have turned and petted Gidean, because in the next moment his voice became softer. "You wait here, boy," he said. "This doesn't look like a good place for a dog."

Gideon whined a little, not wanting to be left behind again.

Serafina crawled through the cramped, dusty, darkened tunnel until she came to the bottom rungs of a ladder.

"Be careful here, Braeden," she whispered as she heard him coming up behind her on his hands and knees.

"Here we go," she said. She grabbed the first rung and started climbing. The ladder was not straight like a normal ladder. It curved, climbing upward into the darkness. The space around her opened up into a black void: no walls, no ceiling, no floor, just the ladder she was climbing and darkness all around. As she climbed farther and farther, her muscles tensed and her skin tingled. Falling meant certain death.

"Where on earth are we?" Braeden asked as he climbed up the ladder behind her, his voice sounding small in the vast space they were entering. "It's terribly dark in here!"

"We're in the attic above the ceiling of the Banquet Hall."

"Oh my God, do you realize how high that is? That ceiling is seventy feet high!"

"Yes, so don't fall," Serafina advised. "It's open along the sides."

"How do you know about this place?"

"I'm the C.R.C.," she said. "It's my job to know everything there is to know about Biltmore, especially its secret rooms and passages."

As they climbed the ladder into the darkness, it became more and more clear that the ladder was curving up and over the arc of the Banquet Hall's soaring barrel-vaulted ceiling. It felt like they were climbing along one of the rib bones inside the body of a giant wooden whale.

Finally, they reached a lattice of steel girders and joists suspended high above the ceiling. Serafina climbed up onto the top edge of one of the beams, just a few inches wide, and walked along its length. It was a dark and treacherous place. A single misplaced step meant a fatal fall into the darkness. The top side of the Banquet Hall's ceiling hovered below them, but if they fell from the girders, they would hit the ceiling and then tumble along the curve until they disappeared into the black chasm that ran along the side.

"I can't see anything!" Braeden complained as he inched his way slowly and unsteadily along the top of one of the narrow girders. The only light came from a few tiny pinholes in the slate shingles of the roof. It was plenty of light for Serafina, but it left Braeden nearly blind. She reached back and guided him along until they found a good spot and sat on the girder with their legs hanging down into the darkness.

"Well, this is a nice place for evening tea," Braeden said cheerfully. "It's nearly pitch dark, and if I move in any direction, I'll die, but besides that, I love the ambience."

Braeden could not see it, but Serafina smiled. It was good to be at her friend's side again. But then her thoughts turned more serious. After they defeated the Man in the Black Cloak, she had told Braeden about how her pa adopted her and who her mother was, and they'd been sharing with each other the truth of their lives ever since.

"Braeden, I need to tell you what happened," Serafina said.

Over the next half hour, she recounted the night before. She had told some of what happened to her pa earlier that morning, but when she told the story to Braeden, she left nothing out. It felt good to finally tell her friend everything that had happened. Sometimes it felt as if things weren't real, weren't complete, until she shared them with Braeden.

"That sounds terrifying," Braeden said. "You were lucky to get out of there alive, Serafina."

She nodded in agreement. It had been a close call, and she was glad to be home.

"And are you sure Detective Grathan is the second man you saw in the carriage?" Braeden asked.

Serafina shook her head. "I don't know," she admitted. "I think he must be, but I didn't get a good look at him. There are four horses in the Biltmore stables that look like the stallions I saw. Could you find out who they belong to?"

"I'll ask Mr. Rinaldi, the stable master," Braeden said. "Whoever this Detective Grathan is, I don't like him. What are we going to do now? We can't let him find out anything more about us, that's for sure."

It was a good question, and Serafina tried to think it through. "We need to keep low and hidden, and figure out exactly who he is," she said. "We'll watch him very carefully and see what he does."

"Did you see what he had?" Braeden exclaimed. "The Black Cloak's silver clasp!"

"Which probably means he went out to my mother's den. I

saw her just last night, so I think she and the cubs are all right, but he might have come dangerously close to discovering them. Maybe that's why she was so anxious to leave."

"If he discovered your mother's den, it might have been *his* life in danger rather than hers."

"It's those nasty wolfhounds I'm worried about," she said. "They were truly vicious beasts."

"What about that feral boy you described? Do you think he escaped? Who do you think he was? It sounds like he fought very hard."

"I don't know," she said, "but I have to find out. He saved my life."

"We could ask around about him," Braeden suggested. "Maybe one of the mountain folk who work on the estate knows who he is. But why do you think the animals are leaving the mountains? There's been a family of otters living in the river for years, but two days ago, when I was out riding, I saw them leaving, all of them. Yesterday when I checked their holt, they were gone. The den was empty."

"My mother said there were other animals leaving, too, besides the luna moths and the birds I saw, but I couldn't get her to tell me about it."

"Even the ducks that normally live on the pond are gone," Braeden said.

At that moment, Serafina thought she heard something, like a faint scratching noise. She swiveled toward the noise.

"What's wrong?" Braeden asked.

She paused and listened but didn't hear anything.

"Nothing, I guess," she said, realizing that she was still a bit jumpy after her confrontation with Detective Grathan.

"This is a good hiding spot," Braeden said with satisfaction. "We should use it more often. Detective Grathan will never be able to find us in here. But it's probably getting late. They're going to be ringing the bell for dinner soon. I should go."

Serafina remembered that her pa had been excited that the Vanderbilts had sent her a message requesting her presence. But in the end, it hadn't been an invitation to dinner. It had been a summons to an interrogation.

"Yes, you better go," Serafina agreed, a bit too sadly.

"My aunt will be looking for me," Braeden said.

"And Lady Rowena, too, I reckon," she said.

Braeden looked at her and squinted, trying to see her face. "You know, she's not as bad as she seems."

"All right," Serafina said, realizing she had poked her friend a bit too hard.

"Her father sent her here all alone while he travels on business," Braeden continued. "He's some sort of important man, but it seems kind of mean of him to leave her here all by herself where she doesn't know anyone."

"I agree," Serafina said. She could see that the two of them had been talking.

"Rowena's mother passed away when she was seven," Braeden said. "And her father doesn't pay much attention to her. Before coming here, Rowena had barely been outside

London. I know she comes across like she's conceited, and maybe she is—I don't know—but she worries about things just like everyone else."

"What do you mean?" she asked.

"She said she worries that she brought all the wrong kind of clothes to be at a country estate, so she doesn't have anything to wear. She also thinks some of the other guests have been making comments about her accent."

Serafina frowned. It never even occurred to her that *Lady Rowena* would worry about her clothes and the way she spoke.

"I don't know," Braeden said. "I don't think she's a bad person. She's just not used to it here. It seems like she needs our help. My aunt asked me to look after her until her father comes. But that doesn't mean I'm not your friend."

"I understand," Serafina replied finally. And she did. She'd always known Braeden to be a kind person and a gentleman. "Just don't forget about me," she said, smiling a little, then realized again that he couldn't see her smile.

"Serafina . . ." Braeden scolded her.

"I will tell you the truth of it," she said. "Over the last week, sometimes it's felt like you didn't want anything to do with me anymore."

"What about you?" Braeden protested, getting at least as emotional as she was. "What have you been doing? You're always asleep when I'm awake and you go out every night on your own! Sometimes I think that one of these days you're going to turn into a wild creature or something. . . ."

Not likely, Serafina thought glumly.

"So you're not trying to avoid me?" she asked.

"Avoid you?" Braeden said in surprise. "You're just about my only friend."

Serafina smiled to hear him say that. And then she laughed a little. "What are you talking about? You have many friends. Gidean, Cedric, your horses . . ."

Braeden smiled. "And I have a new friend, too."

"Oh, yes?"

"When my uncle and I rode out to Chimney Rock the other day, I found a beautiful peregrine falcon with a broken wing at the base of the cliffs. I don't know what happened to her. Maybe a hunter shot her or she got into some kind of battle, but she was badly hurt. I wrapped her up in my coat and brought her home. Her name is Kess. She's incredible."

Serafina nodded as she felt a gentle and reassuring warmth filling her chest. This was the Braeden she knew. "I can't wait to meet her."

"I bandaged her wing, and I've been trying to help her eat."

"Do you think her wing will heal over time and she'll be able to fly again?"

"No, I'm afraid not," Braeden said sadly. "My uncle gave me a book on birds from his library. It said that if a bird of prey's wing is broken below the bend, it can sometimes heal, but if it's broken above the bend, like Kess's is, then it's impossible. She'll never fly again."

"That's too bad," Serafina said, trying to imagine how

terrible it would be for a falcon not to be able to fly, and for a moment she thought about her own situation, her own limitations. "But at least she'll have you as her friend."

"I'm going to take good care of her," Braeden said. "Peregrine falcons are amazing birds. The book says that they can fly anywhere on earth they want to. The word *peregrine* actually means 'wanderer' or 'traveler.' Sometimes, two peregrine falcons will hunt together. And they're the fastest animal on the planet. Scientists estimate that they dive at over two hundred miles an hour, but it's so fast that no one has ever been able to measure it exactly."

"That's amazing," Serafina said, smiling. She enjoyed listening to Braeden talk about his birds and his other animals. *This is how it should be,* she thought, the two of them sitting in a dark and secret place, just talking. This was the kind of friend she had always dreamed of, someone who was eager to hear her stories and excited to tell her things and content to be with her for a little while.

But she knew it couldn't last. He was right when he said he had to go.

She guided him through the darkness across the beam and over to the top of the ladder. As he began to climb down, he stopped, seeming to wonder why she wasn't climbing down with him.

"Just stay alert tonight," she told him. "Stay well clear of Grathan and don't let him corner you alone. Be safe."

"You too," Braeden said, nodding. "But aren't you coming out?"

"You go on ahead," she said. "I'll stay here awhile."

After he had started down, she wondered why she had let him go without her, why she had decided to stay here in the darkness. She'd accused him of not caring about their friendship, but he'd turned around and accused her right back. Maybe there was more truth in his accusation than hers. Mr. and Mrs. Vanderbilt knew who she was now. She could live openly at Biltmore if she wanted to. She might not have an invitation to dinner, but she could go out there with him into the house. Still, she didn't. Why? She sat in the darkness and thought about it for a long time. She had lived in the darkness all her life. This was where she felt most comfortable.

Her momma had said that she belonged with the folk at Biltmore, and perhaps that was true, but it still didn't change who she was.

Sitting in the darkness for a long while, she barely noticed the time passing. She knew that elsewhere in the house, the Vanderbilts and their guests must have eaten their dinner and gone to bed. The house was quiet and dark.

All her life, she had napped here and there for short periods throughout the day and night, so to her there were no separate, distinct days—time was continuous. She wondered what it would be like to sleep for a long period when the sun went down and wake up new each morning.

It was only the starlight now that filtered down through the pinprick holes in the rooftop, but to her eyes, the starlight-filled holes created a constellation of new stars all their own.

She stood and walked among the rafters in the attic,

hopping across the void from one joist to another, the darkness her domain.

But at that moment, she heard something out of the ordinary and stopped.

She stood in the darkness and waited, listening.

At first, all she could hear was the gentle beat of her own heart. Then she heard it again.

It was a scratching noise, like long claws or fingernails being dragged slowly along the inside of the wall.

She swallowed.

She almost couldn't believe what she had just heard.

She looked all around her, up at the ridge of the roof and along the edges of the walls, but she couldn't see anything that shouldn't be there.

Then she heard a *tick-tick-ticking* sound, followed by a long, raspy hiss. Someone's hot breath touched the back of her neck. She startled wildly and spun around, ready to fight. But there was no one there.

What's going on? she thought desperately, looking around her, but even as she did so, the pinprick stars in the roof above her began to go out.

She frowned in confusion.

It was like the holes were being blocked by something.

What's happening?

There was something . . . or many somethings . . . crawling on the ceiling.

Suddenly it was nearly pitch dark. Even she couldn't see.

Frightened, she ran along the top edge of a girder toward

the ladder. A single misstep and she'd fall to her death, but she had to get out of here.

Some sort of small living creature struck her head with a hard thump. She ducked down, her arms protecting her head, and kept running. Another creature landed in her hair, twisting wildly and screeching. When she tried to grab it with her hands, she felt its razor-sharp bites into her skin. Then a third creature hit her in the face, and she lost her balance and fell. She plummeted into the darkness.

As Serafina fell through midair, she reached out and grabbed desperately. She caught hold of the girder's edge just in time, stopping her fall. She hung down into the darkness above the chasm, clinging to the girder by her fingers. The black void loomed below her like a giant mouth waiting for her to drop into it. The cold, gritty, sharp edge of the steel girder felt like it was going to cut her fingers off, but letting go would be the end of her. All the while, hundreds of creatures flew around her, hissing and clicking, swarming through the attic like a black tornado. Gritting her teeth, she swung her legs and wrapped them around the girder. She hung there upside down. She pulled herself up onto the top edge of the girder, then crouched down to defend herself from the flying creatures.

The hissing grew in intensity. One creature struck the side of her head with a thump, clinging to her scalp and hair, its wings batting. Then another struck her in the face, and she swatted it away. Three more clung to her back. Another struck her neck and bit into her skin. Snarling in pain and anger, Serafina grabbed it against her neck and crushed it in her hand. Then she looked at the dead body she held.

She couldn't believe it. It made no sense. They were chimney swifts! These flying creatures were akin to bats in many ways, but they were actually dark, scaly, hissing little birds. They spent most of their time in the air at dusk, but when they landed, they couldn't perch. Instead they clung to the inside of chimneys and caves with their tiny, sharp feet. Their tails were not feathers but spines. The swifts had filled the attic, thousands of them coating the girders and the walls, like a gray, spiny-feathered, hissing, chattering skin.

Suddenly, the sibilation of the swifts rose into a crescendo of rasping sound, and they all burst into the air inside the attic. A great swirling cloud of them swarmed around her. They hurled their bodies against her, clinging at her with their tiny scaly feet, pecking at her with their sharp beaks, their spiny tails digging into her face, their wings batting and tangling up her hair.

The torrent of swifts was so thick around her that she could not hear or see. She would soon lose track of her position. She wanted to hunker down, curl into a ball, and cover her face and head, but she knew if she did that, she'd never get out. So she kept fighting, flailing her arms, and pulling the creatures off her. Eyes almost closed for protection, she desperately looked around for an escape. Seeing a girder between her and the ladder, she took a leap and managed to just land on it. From there, she pushed her way along the girder through the cloud of birds. She finally came to the ladder and climbed down as fast as she could, fighting the attacking birds all the way.

At last, she pushed her way through the panel at the back of the cabinet and came rolling out, breathless and terrified, into the third-floor corridor. She spun around and slammed the panel shut with her shoulder, closing the swifts behind her.

For several seconds, she just lay there, catching her breath, trying to comprehend what had just happened. Chimney swifts were strange, crepuscular little creatures, but they were normally harmless. She'd seen them flying their cheerful, chirping, mosquito-catching acrobatics above Biltmore's roofs at sunset many times. Why did they now swarm and attack her? She'd been living in this house, crawling in these passages her entire life, and they'd always left her alone. Why was this happening now? Was the house itself turning against her?

She looked around her. The house was dark and quiet. It was well after midnight, and everyone was asleep.

Still feeling scared and shaky from what had happened, she got up onto her feet. She stood unsteadily for a moment, recovering. Then she brushed herself off and pulled the feathers and dead swifts out of her hair.

When she heard a creak in the distance, she stopped, half in a panic that the attack was going to start all over again, but nothing came.

She started walking through the darkness. She followed the

corridor and passed through the living hall with its sofas, chairs, and tables. Earlier, several of the guests had been enjoying their tea here, but now it was eerily dark, empty, and still. It was like they had all disappeared. A terrible chill went down her spine. What if Braeden was gone, and Mr. and Mrs. Vanderbilt, and all the guests? What if they were *all* gone? Maybe she was the last one, the only one to survive the attack. What if everyone else in the house was dead?

She heard another sound. It wasn't a creak this time, but a footstep, and then another. Somewhere in the house, someone was awake. It felt like someone was following her, lingering in the shadows behind her.

When she reached the top of the Grand Staircase, moonlight shone through the rising cascade of slanting, leaded-glass windows, casting silver-blue light across the wide, gently arcing steps and the filigreed railing that spiraled up through Biltmore's floors. Attached to a copper dome at the very top of the staircase, an ornate wrought-iron chandelier hung down through the center of the magnificent spiral. As she headed down the staircase, the black shadow of her body in the moonlight moved along the outer wall like a strange, crawling animal. Then she heard something coming up the stairway toward her.

She stopped, uncertain what she was hearing. Her heart beat faster, and her breaths grew shorter and more intense. It wasn't a small noise or a single step or two. Someone was definitely coming up the stairs. Her muscles jittered, preparing her for battle. Her mind kept telling her to get ahold of herself—it could be one of Biltmore's guests or a servant. But then she realized that her instincts were telling her something: the sound wasn't human. She sucked in a breath and crouched down, ready to leap.

Whatever it was, she could hear the creature's feet clicking and scraping on the limestone steps.

It had four legs.

And claws.

Her chest pulled in air at a steady, rapid race. She could feel every muscle in her body coming alive, ready to fight.

She began backing slowly up the stairs until she reached the upper landing, making as little noise as possible.

But it was coming fast, gaining on her. She could hear it growling now, coming faster.

Its multilegged shadow traveled up the outer wall like a giant spider.

Just when she was about to turn and run, it came up onto the landing and into sight.

But it wasn't a spider.

It was a black dog.

The dog paused and then began to move slowly toward her, stalking her, its head low as it snarled and growled. She backed up as it came toward her.

As it approached, she realized it wasn't one of the wolf-hounds or some other dog. It was her friend Gidean.

Much relieved, she let out a long breath. She smiled and relaxed. "Gidean," she said happily, thinking that he must have mistaken her for an intruder.

But the dog snarled and kept moving toward her, his body

tense and coiled, ready to spring. A new fear grew within her. Her chest tightened.

"Gidean, it's me," she said again, rising desperation in her voice. "Come on, Gidean, it's me."

But Gidean did not recognize her.

Her body flushed with heat.

The large black dog with its pointed ears kept coming slowly toward her, snarling, its teeth bared now, its canines snapping. It was the most terrifying snarl she'd ever heard.

Gidean burst into an attack, growling as he leapt into the air straight at her.

He slammed into her body, biting into her shoulder and knocking her backward off her feet. She hit the stone floor with a painful slam, her head hitting so hard that she nearly blacked out. Then she twisted and spun and punched her way out from under the dog's legs.

"Stop this, Gidean!" she cried as she leapt away. "Gidean, it's me! It's Serafina!"

But the dog leapt again, biting her arm and shaking her as he growled. The only other time she'd ever seen Gidean this fierce was when he was fighting the Man in the Black Cloak. It was like *she* had suddenly become the evil one.

"Gidean, no! Stop!" she cried as she smashed her fists into the dog's face to get him to release her. She kicked and screamed and finally twisted away from him. He immediately pressed the attack, snapping at her legs as she scurried away. She ducked and darted, but wherever she went, he followed. He was incredibly fast. She kept dodging him, but she could not shake him.

She didn't want to fight him, but he just kept coming. He bit her again, his canines clamping onto her leg. With a ferocious tug, he pulled her off her feet, then charged in at her throat. She blocked her neck and rolled away, then leapt to her feet, and he immediately struck her and took her down again.

She didn't want to hurt her friend, but she didn't want to die, either. She couldn't keep going. She couldn't keep fighting him. He was an incredible warrior and filled with a terrific rage, the likes of which she'd never seen. Something had twisted him, deranged him, turned him into a rabid beast that did not recognize her. And he was wearing her down. She could tell that she wasn't going to last much longer.

She fended off one more attack and then turned and fled back toward the top of the stairs as fast as she could.

Outraged by her attempt to escape, the growling Doberman charged after her with shocking speed. Just as she reached the railing, the dog leapt through the air, its fang-filled mouth opened wide for the bite.

16

Gidean slammed into Serafina's body and sent them both somersaulting over the railing, falling, falling, fifty feet to the marble floor below.

As she fell through the open air, the shock of what had happened screamed through her mind, her limbs flailing, nothing to grab onto. She was falling upside down, looking up toward the ceiling. She could see the floors of the house flashing by in the rings of the four-story-high chandelier. The domed ceiling at the top of the Grand Staircase kept getting smaller and smaller as she fell.

She was going to die. When she hit the floor, her bones would break. Her head would crack open. Blood would splash everywhere. And she'd die.

And there was absolutely nothing she could do about it.

She could not jump or bite or run or scream to save herself this time. No clever idea or special trick would save her. Her mother couldn't save her. Her pa couldn't save her. There was no trap she could set to defeat her enemy.

And she didn't even understand who her enemy was or why. Just as she'd feared, the claws of doom had reached down out of the sky and snatched her life away before she even knew they were there.

It felt like it was taking an impossibly long time to fall, like every second was a hundred seconds long. She thought about prowling through the basement at night, and eating chicken and grits with her pa, and looking up at the stars with Braeden. She thought about all the mysteries that would never be solved. Why were the animals leaving? Who was the bearded man? Why had the feral boy helped her? From where would the danger come to Biltmore, and what form would it take?

Then something peculiar happened.

She didn't think about it and *decide* to do it. It just happened. Her body snapped. She tucked in her arms, twisted her spine, and flung out her legs, righting herself in midair. Then she stretched out her arms and pulled in her legs to stop her spin and position her limbs in the direction of her fall. It was an instinct, a split-second reflex, like snatching a rat the instant it tried to run away.

She hit the floor hard but strong, bracing her landing with the bending, crouching muscles of her legs and arms until she was down low on her curled feet and extended hands, her body finally still and unharmed.

She landed on her feet.

But Gidean did not.

His body slammed onto the floor beside her. She didn't just see it and hear it; she felt the crushing blow, the crack of bones, and the whimper of the dog. She knew immediately that the battle was over.

Gidean lay beside her, his head down and bleeding, his body broken in a thousand places. He was nearly dead.

Gidean had been Braeden's constant companion and closest friend since Braeden had lost his family. The dog had walked at Braeden's side wherever he went, ran with him when he rode his horse, and guarded his door at night. There had been a time when she didn't like dogs and dogs didn't like her, but she and this dog had worked together, fought together, and defended each other. Gidean had attacked the Man in the Black Cloak and saved her life. But now Gidean lay dying on the marble floor beside her.

When a shadow moved across the moonlit floor, she thought it must be an owl or some other creature of the night outside the Grand Staircase's windows. She turned and looked up. It was Rowena in a white nightgown, standing on the second floor, looking down at her in shock. Rowena's hair was long, loose, and unbrushed, her eyes wide with fear. She gripped what looked like a pencil in her hand, or perhaps a hairpin, brandishing it in front of her like a weapon.

"Rowena!" Serafina shouted to her. "Go get the veterinarian! Run!"

Rowena did not move. She stared in horrified shock at the sight of Gidean lying on the floor in a pool of blood and Serafina standing over him with blood all over her hands. The girl did not seem to understand Serafina's words. She did not run to get the veterinarian. Instead, she turned and slowly walked in the direction of Braeden's room.

What was she doing? What did she think she saw?

When Rowena returned a few moments later, Serafina heard the rush of frantic footsteps, but it wasn't the veterinarian. Braeden came running down the stairs.

"What's happened?" Braeden screamed as he came. He was beyond distraught.

Braeden ran to Gidean's side and collapsed to his knees at his dog's side. "He's badly hurt!" he cried. "Serafina, what did you do?"

Serafina was too overwhelmed to answer him.

Tears streamed down his face as he hugged his dying dog. In all she and Braeden had been through together, she'd never seen him cry before. "Aw, Gidean, boy, please don't go . . . don't go . . . please, boy . . . no . . . don't leave me. . . ."

Serafina burst into tears. But as she cried, she tilted her head upward and saw Rowena standing there again. Rowena was just staring at her. She hadn't retrieved the veterinarian; she'd gone to Braeden.

Rowena slowly lifted her arm and pointed at Serafina. "I

saw her," she said, her voice filled with trembling. "I saw her do it! She hurled the dog over the railing!"

"That's not true!" Serafina shouted back at her.

Guests and servants flooded down the stairs from the floors above. Mr. and Mrs. Vanderbilt came, utterly shocked by what was happening. The balding, gray-bearded elderly man she'd seen walking in the forest with Mr. Vanderbilt made his way slowly down the steps with his cane, studying the scene. Mrs. King came hurrying into the hall, along with Essie and many of the other maids, but no one seemed to know what to do.

"Get the veterinarian!" Mr. Vanderbilt shouted, and the butler ran to fetch him.

Serafina wiped the tears from her eyes as she looked up at the people of Biltmore. Then she saw the dark figure of Detective Grathan standing on the third floor high above. His long brown hair hung around his head like a dark hood. Holding his spiraling antler cane in his hand, he looked down at her and the crying boy and the bloody dog on the floor between them. She wanted to snarl up at him, to bite him, but he just stared at her, as if it was a scene he'd seen many times before. There wasn't fear in his expression like the others. There was a knowingness in his eyes.

Braeden looked at Serafina, his eyes filled with agony. She knew he could see the fresh blood on her face and the scratches on her body. It was obvious that she and Gidean had fought. "What happened, Serafina?" he cried, tears streaming down his face.

"I don't know, Braeden," Serafina said.

"She's lying," Lady Rowena said as she came down the stairs and stood behind Braeden. "She was fighting the dog and then tricked it so that it jumped over the railing."

"Braeden, please believe me. That's not what happened," Serafina pleaded. "Gidean attacked me. We both fell."

"She didn't fall," Lady Rowena said. "She couldn't have fallen. She's standing right in front of us."

"Gidean would never attack you," Braeden said hopelessly to Serafina as he dropped his head and looked at his wounded dog.

"I—I didn't do this!" Serafina stammered, tears pouring out of her eyes again as she furiously wiped them away. She couldn't understand how this could happen. How could she be in this situation? Braeden had to believe her. She reached out to hold his arm.

"Leave him alone! You have done enough!" Rowena shouted, blocking her. Serafina snarled at the girl, then turned back to her friend.

"I swear to you, Braeden, I did not do this."

Braeden looked desperately at her. "He's hurt bad, Serafina."

"You should leave," Rowena said to Serafina, her voice filled with fear and anger. "You don't belong with civilized people. Look at you! You're like some kind of wild creature! You don't belong here!" Then she looked around at all the frightened onlookers. "How can you live with her in this house? Something's going to happen! It won't just be a dog next time. She's going to hurt someone!"

"Braeden, no . . ." Serafina begged him, clutching his arm.

Out of the corner of her eye, Serafina saw two footmen moving in to protect the young master.

"Braeden, please . . ."

As Mr. Vanderbilt came toward her and Braeden, he gestured for his footmen to take control. She had no idea what Mr. Vanderbilt and the footmen were going to do, but when a footman grabbed her from behind, it startled her badly. In all her anger and confusion, she twisted around hissing and bit him on the hand before she could stop herself. It was pure and utter reflex, an instinct over which she had no control. Her teeth sank into the man's hand, drawing blood. He leapt back, screaming in pain. She could see the horrified faces of everyone around her as they backed away from her. Mr. and Mrs. Vanderbilt stared at her in disbelief, barely able to comprehend what she'd just done. She'd become the very wild beast that Rowena was screaming about.

Filled with shame and anguish, tears streaming down her face, she leapt to her feet. The Vanderbilts and the guests and servants shrank away from her in fear. Gazing around at their horrified faces, she couldn't stand it any longer. She ran. The crowd recoiled in panic as she fled through them across the Entrance Hall. One of the women screamed. Serafina escaped through the front doors and plunged into the darkness outside. It felt like it took forever to run across the open lawn and reach the trees. She kept running, just running, her heart pouring out of her, and still running, into the forest, into the mountains, crying and distraught, more confused than she had ever been in her life. She had bitten a footman and snarled at everyone.

Blood all over her hands, she had snapped and hissed like a trapped animal.

You don't belong here! Rowena's words screamed through her mind as she ran, echoes of her mother's words the night before. She had been cast unwanted from place to place and had nowhere to go.

But worst of all, she'd hurt Gidean terribly bad, and she'd broken Braeden's heart. It felt like she'd betrayed the only two friends she had ever known.

17

Serafina ran into the forest and just kept running, hot tears of anguish pouring from her eyes. Her lungs gasped frantically for breath, her chest filled with shaking emotion. She wasn't running with direction; she was running *away*—away from the injured Gidean, away from the sight of her best friend in anguish, away from the shame of what she'd done.

When she finally slowed to a walk, she sniffled and wiped her nose with the back of her hand and kept walking fast and hard. As she crossed through the great oaks of the forest and Biltmore disappeared farther and farther behind her, her stomach churned. The magnitude of what she was doing began to sink in. She was leaving her pa and Braeden, and Mr. and Mrs.

Vanderbilt, and Essie, and everyone else she knew at Biltmore. She was leaving them all behind.

When she thought about how she hadn't even said good-bye to her pa, she started crying all over again. It broke her heart that he'd hear about this shameful, horrible incident from the servants and from Mr. Vanderbilt, that her pa would hear that she'd hurt the young master's dog and that they'd thrown her out of the house. She could still feel in her teeth the sensation of biting into that footman's hand. She could still see the horrified looks on all their faces when she ran through the crowd of people. Maybe Lady Rowena was right. Maybe she truly was a terrible and wild creature. She didn't belong in a civilized home.

But her mother had told her that she didn't belong in the forest, either. The words still echoed in her mind. She was too human, too slow and weak to fight off attackers. *You don't belong here, Serafina,* her mother had said.

She didn't belong in the forest or at Biltmore. She didn't belong *anywhere.*

She walked for miles, driven by nothing but burning emotion. When she saw a glow of light in a valley below her, she finally slowed down, curious. Tall, rectangular shapes rose up among the trees, some of them dotted with dim points of light, others entirely dark. The sound of a whistle startled her, and then she saw a long, dark chain of boxes curving along the mountainside. The metal snake weaved in and out of the trees, but as it crossed a trestle bridge over a river, a plume of white steam roiled up into the moonlit clouds. *It's a train,* she thought. *A real train.*

She'd learned about locomotives, with their fireboxes and their piston rods, from her pa, and she'd heard tell of Mr. Vanderbilt's grandpa who'd spread his ships and trains across America. Even from this great distance, she could feel the iron beast's rumble in the earth beneath her feet and the pressure of its hurtling movement in her chest. She couldn't even imagine being up close to such a thing. But she wondered fleetingly what it would be like to leap upon such a monster and fly to distant places on long, shining tracks. It was a foreign world down there in the city of Asheville, filled with people and machines and ways of life she did not understand, and from there, an entire country spread out in all directions. What would she become if that was the path she took?

As the sun rose, she kept moving, trekking far up into the Craggy Mountains, mile after mile. She drank from a stream when she was thirsty. She hunted when she hungered. When she was tired, she slept tucked into a crevice of rock. A wild creature she became, full and earnest, if not in body, then in spirit whole.

Later the next evening, as she crossed through a forested cove between two spurs of a mountain ridge, the scent of a campfire drifted on the crisp autumn air. Drawn to it, she came upon a small collection of log cabins where several families gathered around a little fire roasting corn on the cob and grilling trout caught from the nearby stream. She marveled that a boy about her age was playing a gentle melody on a banjo while his younger sister accompanied him on a fiddle. Others were singing soft and dancing slow, like the quiet river by which they lived.

Serafina did not approach the mountain folk, but she sat in the trees on the hillside just above them and, for a little while, listened to their music and let her heart go free.

She watched and listened as the mountain folk played song after song, all of them singing along and dancing in each other's arms. Some of their songs were fast jigs and reels, everyone hooting and hollering, but mostly, as the night wore on, they played the softer songs, songs of the gentle heart and the deepened soul. They drank their white lightning and their autumn cider and rocked in their chairs, telling their stories around the campfire, stories of long-lost loves and heroic deeds, of strange occurrences and dark mysteries. When everyone started drifting off to their beds beneath their cabin roofs or sleeping on the ground beneath the stars, she knew it was time for her to go as well, for this was not her home tonight, this was not her bed. She reluctantly pulled herself up onto her feet and slipped away from the smoldering campfire's glowing light.

She kept traveling, but slower now, less and less anxious to get away from what was behind her. High up into the Black Mountains she climbed, following a ridge of craggy gardens where only rhododendrons and alpine grasses grew. She walked along a stony reach where the moonlit mist fell down the mountains like the waves of a silver sea. She trekked over a highland bald with no trees, just the moonlight, and the geese flying across the dark blue sky. She followed a jagged-edged river and gazed upon a waterfall that fell, and fell, and fell, down one rock after another, splashing and turning, until it disappeared into the misty forest below.

As she was about to carry on, she looked over and saw movement on a ridge that ran parallel to her own. It was a red wolf, long and lean and beautiful, trotting along a path. When the wolf stopped and looked at her, it startled her. But then she realized that she recognized the wolf and the wolf recognized her.

She had seen him a few weeks before along the river, the night she was lost in the forest. So much had happened in her life since then.

She stared at the young wolf for a long time, and the wolf stared at her. He had thick, reddish-brown fur, pointed ears, and incredibly keen eyes. She wondered how he had fared since last they met. The wound he had suffered that night had healed and he looked stronger now.

Then she saw something behind him. Another wolf trotted along the path. Then another. She soon saw that there were many wolves with him, male and female, pups and elders, all traveling with him. But some of them glistened with fresh wounds. Others were limping. She could see that they had fought a great battle against a terrible enemy. Her wolf friend had become one of the leaders of his pack. The pack of wolves wasn't hunting but traveling a long distance. She could see it in the way they moved, the way they held their heads and tails down as they trotted. They were leaving these mountains, like the luna moths and songbirds, and they were leaving them for good.

When she looked at the red wolf again, he seemed to see the sadness in her face, for now she saw it reflected in his.

Something deep down in her began to burn. Her wolf friend had found his kin. He had found his place. The wolves of the pack stuck together. They fought together. That's what a family was. That's what it meant to be kin. You didn't give up on that.

She felt the heat rising in her cheeks against the midnight chill. She thought about Biltmore and her family there. She didn't want to leave them, to be separated from them. She wanted to stick together. She wanted to be a pack of wolves, a pride of lions. She wanted to be a family.

She thought about her mother, and the cubs, and the dark lion, and the feral boy who had saved her life. She wanted to be with them, to hunt with them, to run with them, to be part of their lives in the forest.

They were all her folk. And she was theirs.

Standing there on top of the mountain, she knew what she had to do.

The running would get her to a distant city or to the top of a mountain, but in the end, the running would get her nowhere. There was nowhere to go when you didn't have a family to go home to, to share it with.

As the wolf and his pack disappeared into the trees, she sat down in the gravel right where she had been standing and looked out across the mountains beneath the stars.

Something was wrong. She could feel it.

Why would her mother send her away? That wasn't right.

Why would chimney swifts swarm her?

Why would Gidean attack her?

Why was she running away from Biltmore?

Why were the wolves leaving?

The more questions she asked herself, the fiercer she felt. All these things seemed wildly separate, but maybe all the questions were connected. Maybe they all had the same answer.

She didn't know if Gidean had lived or died after the fall from the railing. She didn't know if Braeden would ever be able to forgive her. But she wasn't going to give up on her family. Families were supposed to stick together no matter what. No argument or terrible event should break them apart. Her pa had shown her time and time again that if something was broken, you fixed it. And the one thing Serafina had learned in the twelve years of her life was that if the rat wasn't dead, then whack it again until it was. You didn't give up. She was going to fight, and she was going to keep fighting until her family understood her.

She was convinced now that something was wrong in the forest. Something was wrong at Biltmore. And she was going to find out what it was and fix it.

She stood, brushed herself off, and headed back down the mountain.

She knew what she must do.

18

Serafina made her way back along the mountain ridge through the thick, scrubby vegetation that grew among the rocks, then down the slopes of Graybeard Mountain into the forest trees of the lower elevations. She rested when she needed to but tried to keep moving. She was determined to find her mother and learn everything she could about the dark force that had invaded the mountains. She had seen the terrifying man in the forest with his dogs, and she had come up against Grathan at Biltmore. She didn't know who or what these men were, or exactly what dark powers they possessed, but she knew she had to fight them.

Her mother and the cubs had abandoned the den at the angel's glade, so the only clue she had to follow was the cryptic words her mother had scratched into the dirt.

"'If you need me, winter, spring, or fall,'" Serafina said, "'come where what you climbed is floor and rain is wall.'"

She imagined it must be a riddle, something she could solve but their enemies could not. But it confused her. Her mother had wanted her to go back to Biltmore, not follow her, so why did she leave any message at all?

As she descended the mountain, she came to a dark stand of decrepit old pine trees with thick, straight trunks coated in black mold, all the lower limbs of the trees withered and rotted, the roots growing along the ground like long, treacherous fingers. The smell of damp earth and rotting wood filled her nostrils. Everything around her was sticky with black pinesap. There were no other plants growing here—no saplings or bushes could survive in the perennial shadow of the blackened pines. Nothing but dark bloodred pine needles covered the ground.

Disturbed by this deadened place, she crouched down and tried to see ahead of her through the murkiness of the night. She wondered if there was a path through it or if she had to find a way around it. She could hear the pinesap dripping from the branches of the trees. A foreboding crept into her. On the ground, beneath the twisted limbs of the pine trees, she saw a dark, unnatural shape.

Her instinct urged her to turn around and go the other direction, put distance between her and whatever this place was. But her curiosity would not let her leave. She crept slowly toward the shape, pulling deep drafts of air into her lungs.

It appeared to be a worn, flat, rectangular stone, and beside it, a low, elongated, heavy iron cage buried in the ground. She took a hard swallow. She studied the cage, trying to understand what it was for. It was no more than a foot or two high. A small door had been fabricated into the end of the cage, with a latch on the outside. *To lock something in,* she thought. It appeared to be a cage for an animal of some kind. Then she found another cage, and then another. As she crept along, low and quiet, she felt a sickening in her stomach. There were hundreds of cages for as far as she could see.

She found a small hut made of twisted branches and gnarly vines. She had seen woodsmen make lean-tos and shelters from branches before, but this shelter did not look like the branches had been cut and gathered, but as if they had grown or slithered into that spot to form walls and roof. The vines and branches interlaced into an unnatural weave, like the hide of a perverse beast. Pinesap dripped from the tree limbs onto the roof of the hut, coating it in a black and stinking ooze. The gray remnants of a campfire smoldered in front of the hut. A black iron pot sat in the smoking ashes. Dozens of dead crows and vultures lay on the ground, their clawed feet cramped into balls.

Serafina's limbs trembled. Her heart pounded. She was frightened by what she was going to find within this dark place. But she had to find out. She had to keep going.

She crept closer to the shelter. She watched and listened. There appeared to be no movement, no sound, other than the constant dripping of the sap.

She crept inside.

There were bundles of wire inside the foul hut but no inhabitant. She found wire cutters, gloves, and other tools, but no indication what all this was for except for a pile of furred animal skins lying on the hut's dirt floor. Black furs and brown, gray and white. She couldn't help but clench her teeth at the sight of it and snarl her nose away from the rancid smell of the dead skin. It felt like spiders were crawling all over her shoulders and neck.

She hurriedly backed out of the hut and scanned the area for danger. This was a deeply disturbing place. She quickly turned to leave. Then she heard a sound that stopped her in her tracks.

A whimper.

Serafina turned.

Back behind the shelter, there were more cages.

She heard the whimper again—a long, pleading, mournful whine.

As she glanced warily around her, her legs buzzed with tension. Her temples pounded. Every sensation in her body was telling her she should not linger here, but her heart was telling her she must go toward the sound.

She crept slowly forward. The other cages had been empty, but to her horror, she found several inhabited cages behind the shelter.

She saw brownish fur inside one of the cages, but she still couldn't tell what the creature was.

She crept closer.

The mound of fur in the cage was a few feet long, and it was shaking.

Then she heard the whimpering sound again.

Serafina tried to stay steady and strong, but she started trembling as badly as the poor animal in the cage. She couldn't help it. She looked behind her, then scanned the forest to make sure no one was near. It felt like a terribly dangerous place. The pine trees grew so close together, and the area beneath the upper limbs was so dark that it was difficult to see any distance at all.

Crawling on her hands and knees, she crept around to the front of the cage.

She peered through the cage's iron bars.

There she saw it.

Serafina looked into the face of one of the most beautiful animals she had ever seen: a young female bobcat. She had large, striking eyes, long whiskers, and a white-marked face with wide ruffs of hair that extended outward from her cheeks and around her head, all the way to her tufted, black-tipped ears. She had grayish-brown black-spotted fur, with black streaks on her body and dark bars on her legs.

But as beautiful as the bobcat was, she was in terrible shape. It was clear that she'd been drooling and clawing, chewing at the metal cage, frantic to escape.

As Serafina approached her, the bobcat became quiet and still, staring at her with big, round eyes. She seemed to understand that Serafina was not her enemy.

Serafina saw that there were other animals in the cages,

too—a woodchuck, a porcupine, even a pair of river otters. One of the saddest of all was a red-tailed hawk with its talons lacerated and bloody, its feathers torn and broken from batting its wings against the wire mesh in its fight to escape.

Serafina quickly glanced around her, frightened that the owner of this camp would arrive at any moment. These terrible cages didn't belong to her, so she had no right to do what she wanted to do. But did she need someone's permission to do what was right?

She looked behind her and then scanned the trees for danger. Her heart began to pound in her chest so hard that she could barely breathe.

She knew she should run, but how could she leave?

She inched closer to the bobcat's cage, unfastened the latch, and opened the door.

"Come on out," she whispered.

The bobcat crept out slowly, afraid of everything around her. Serafina touched the cat's fur with her bare hand. The bobcat looked at her with her huge eyes, then slunk quickly off into the forest. Once the bobcat had escaped the pine trees and was in the safety of the distant undergrowth, she turned and looked at Serafina.

Thank you, she seemed to be thinking. Then the cat finally made its escape, disappearing into the brush.

"Stay bold," Serafina said quietly, remembering the expression the feral boy had used when he had helped her. She didn't know why, but for some reason those two simple words had meant a lot to her.

She quickly released the woodchuck, porcupine, and otters. They all looked strong enough to get home. She was sure the otters would know the way to the nearest river. But the hawk was in a bad way. She thought that he could probably fly, but a red-tailed hawk out at night was in grave danger from its natural enemy, the great horned owl.

She reached into the cage, carefully grabbed the hawk with both hands, and pulled him out. He lifted his wings and tried to pull away, none too happy to be handled. She expected he would hiss and snap at her, but he did not. He stared at her with his powerful raptor eyes and clamped onto her wrist with one of his talons, squeezing so hard that she thought he was going to break her bones. It was as if he somehow understood she wanted to help him, but at the same time, he wasn't going to give up control.

She left the pine forest and the terrible cages behind her, carrying the wounded hawk clutched in her hands.

When she and the hawk had finally escaped the pine trees and entered a better part of the forest, she slowed down. She wished she could carry the hawk all the way back to Biltmore and give it to Braeden to take care of, but she couldn't travel fast enough with a hawk in her hands, and she was pretty sure the hawk wasn't too happy about being carried around by somebody like her. She found a safe thicket of tree brush and stuffed the hawk inside where it could hide from the marauding owls until daylight came. "Rest here, then fly strong, my friend," she whispered.

From there, she tried to move quickly away. She wanted to

put as much distance between her and those terrible cages as she could. She knew that the forest was a wild, untamed place, with all sorts of life-and-death struggles, but what kind of person would trap and capture animals like that? Why would he leave them there, starving and afraid, hidden beneath the darkened trees?

A mist drifted through the branches of the forest and made it difficult for her to find her way, but she kept moving downhill the best she could. She felt a tightness in her stomach. She couldn't escape the feeling that she had just avoided a dark and terrible danger.

Through the mist she saw something out of the corner of her eye. When she looked over, she spotted a figure in the distance walking through the trees. At first she thought it might be the man she'd seen entering the forest with Mr. Vanderbilt. She felt a sudden hope. Maybe she was far closer to Biltmore than she realized. But a heaviness rolled into her chest. She crouched in the underbrush and watched the figure at a distance. He was wearing a long, dark, weather-beaten coat and a wide-brimmed hat. It was the bearded man she'd seen in the forest a few nights before! She hit the dirt in sudden panic.

She tried to stay quiet, but her chest pulled in rapid breaths as she looked toward him. He had a heavy, dark gray beard, not long and scraggly white like many of the mountain men, but thick and wavy like an animal's coat. His face was craggy with cracks and wrinkles, wind-worn like he'd been in the forest for fifty years. She scanned the area, looking for signs of the

wolfhounds, but didn't see them. Nor did he seem to be carrying the walking stick he had before. But she knew it was him.

Staying low and quiet and very still, she watched him. He
seemed to drift into and out of the mist, in and among the
trees, disappearing and then reappearing in the swirls of the
fog. He drifted farther away, then closer, as if the trees themselves were playing tricks on her eyes. He seemed more like a
ghostly haint than a mortal man. As she felt the goose bumps
rising on her arms, she wanted to run, but she was afraid the
sound of her flight would draw his attention.

But she had to get out of here. Just as she started to back
away and go in the opposite direction, the man stopped dead
in his tracks. He pivoted his head toward her with a startling,
inhuman quickness—like an owl spotting prey. His terrible silver eyes peered right at her.

She ducked down to the ground and pressed her back to the
base of a gnarled, old fir tree, hiding. The image of his pivoting
head threw a shiver down her spine.

She heard him moving rapidly toward her.

She had to run, but her chest tightened and her legs clamped.
A sharp pain attacked her throat like someone's fingers had
grabbed hold of her windpipe. Her whole body started shaking
violently with something beyond fear, something beyond her
control. Panic set in. She couldn't get any air into her lungs. She
tried to scream, but she couldn't get sound of any kind to pass
through her constricted throat.

The footsteps came rapidly closer as the man in the long

dark coat came toward her. She could hear his boots sinking into the damp earth as he walked. She became aware of a sudden coldness on the ground beneath her and around her. When she looked down, she saw that the earth had become soaked with blood.

20

Serafina tried to leap up from the ground and flee, but the man had cast some sort of spell on her. Her muscles were rigid. They would not move.

As the man bore down on her, Serafina watched in horrified amazement as the roots of the tree erupted out of the blood-soaked earth, grew rapidly around her wrists, and clamped her hands to the ground. Without her hands to fight, she was completely defenseless.

Like a desperate mink caught in a trap, she bent down and chewed at the roots that held her hands. When another root started slithering like a snake around her ankles, she kicked it angrily away.

Suddenly, the forest that had always been her ally and concealment had become her enemy.

As the man came around the tree, his face was shrouded in darkness save for the silver blaze of his eyes. He grabbed at her with two bony, clutching bare hands, grasping like the talons of an owl. As his long, clawlike fingernails sank into her, she twisted wildly and broke herself free. She thrashed her legs, then darted away.

She ran as fast as she could, until she thought she must have put some distance between herself and her pursuer. But just as she turned her head to look behind her, she heard a *tick-tick-ticking* sound. A terrible, hissing scream erupted a few feet above her left shoulder. The sound scared her so badly that she leapt back and hit a tree. A large, nasty-looking white barn owl flew right over her head, its horrible black eyes peering at her, its mouth open as it let out its bloodcurdling scream.

She dove into a thicket of vine-strangled brambles where the barn owl could not fly. She thought she was very clever. But then the barn owl disappeared and the bearded man began tearing the branches away, pushing into the thicket toward her. She got down on her hands and knees and crawled through the vines into the deepest part of the thicket. She hoped it might provide her some form of protection from the bearded man's spells. But instead, the vines started moving, snaking, twisting themselves around her limbs and neck.

She screamed and thrashed and yanked at the vines as she crawled out the other side of the thicket. From there, she stood up and ran across the open ground.

She wanted to turn, she wanted to fight, she wanted to attack this horrible man, but there was nothing she could do but run for her life. She ran fast through the cover of the forest. She thought she was doing it. She thought she was escaping.

When she glanced back, she saw that the man had not chased her. He was still standing where he had been. He simply flattened his hand to his mouth and blew across his palm in her direction. It was like the cold, corpsy breath of Death himself had struck her. The blood rushed from her head. Her lungs went cold. Her muscles went limp, and her body involuntarily collapsed, somersaulting down a small incline, dead weight and lifeless, until her body came to rest in the dirt.

Her whole body had gone pale and cold. Her lungs had stopped pulling in air. Her heart had stopped pumping blood. She had a few seconds of thought left as the blood drained from her head, but she was a dead girl, a cadaver, lying facedown on the ground.

The man made his way down to her, grabbed her limp body like a rag doll, and pulled her up onto an old stump. But even as he dragged her lifeless body against the cold earth, she could feel the effects of his spell wearing off—like pins and needles in her limbs. She did not understand it, but she was apparently a far tougher creature than he had accounted for in his spell. Her chest tingled with the slip of new air into her lungs. Her heart suddenly thumped to life again, and warm blood flowed through her like waves.

"Now, let's get a good look at you," the man said as he brought her into the moonlight. "Just what kind of little girl are you, sneaking up on me like that?"

When he flipped her limp body around so that he could

see her face, she was terrified, but she kept her eyes closed and pretended to be dead.

"Ah, I see," the man said when he saw her face. "It's you again. I should have known. You've been a nuisance to us already, haven't you? And I've seen enough of your kith and kin to know that it's only going to get worse if I let you grow up."

As Serafina felt her strength coming back into her muscles and the saliva wetting her mouth, she knew she only had one chance. The old rat trick. Bursting alive, she twisted around and bit the man's right hand as deeply and fiercely as she could.

The man reflexively yanked back his hand. But she didn't let go at first. His arm's yanking motion pulled her entire body up. At that moment, she released her bite and went flying through the air. She landed on the ground, rolled to her feet, and ran.

21

Serafina ran for miles, and then walked, and then ran some more, traveling as far from that place as she could.

She tried to think through everything she had seen. She knew it had been the same bearded man she had encountered in the forest a few nights before. He had seemed to be drifting in and out of the trees with an almost specter-like quality, like an apparition in the mist. Was he the old man of the forest that the mountain folk spoke of? He seemed to know her. He had said that she was a nuisance, like she was getting in his way. But in the way of what? What was his goal? Was it truly to find the Black Cloak? Or was it more than that? She thought about the stallions pulling the driverless carriage, and the swifts swarming her in the attack, and Gidean attacking her on the stairs. . . . Was he somehow controlling these animals? Who-ever he was, he could use his hands to throw deathly spells that Serafina never wanted to experience again.

When she had come down from the craggy gardens, she'd intended to find her mother and make her tell her everything she knew, and then from there, go on to Biltmore. But what if the bearded man had already found her mother and the cubs? What if he had killed them? It was too terrible to think about. She ran faster. Now more than ever, she had to find them.

As the sun rose and she traveled through the forest, she tried to think about where her mother might have gone. But other questions crept into her mind, too. Did her mother know this intruder was invading her territory? Had her mother sent her away to keep her safe?

Serafina thought again about the message her mother had left for her.

It didn't seem to make any sense.

"What you climbed is floor"?

She racked her brain. "What did I climb?" she asked herself.

Was it a tree of some kind? A floor of wood?

She thought about her battle against the wolfhounds. She had leapt into a tree, then ran along a branch, then fought the dogs on the ground until they backed her against the rock face at the bottom of the cliff.

And then she got it.

She had climbed up the rock wall.

So maybe she was looking for something that had a rock floor.

What kind of room has a rock floor?

Then she smiled. Not a room. "A cave," she said.

But there were many caves in the mountains. She thought about the next line of the riddle.

"What does 'rain is wall' mean? That makes no sense."

As she walked through the forest, she kept repeating "where rain is wall."

"How could rain be a wall?" she said to herself. "Rain is water. . . . You drink water. You wash with water. You swim in water. . . ." The possibilities were endless.

And pointless.

There was water everywhere. She looked at the clouds. There was even water up there. Water started out in a cloud, and then fell as rain, and then flowed across the earth into the rivers. She thought about rivers.

When is a river a wall?

Walls are vertical.

Then it came to her.

"A waterfall," she said with satisfaction. A wall of water, a wall of rain.

There were no lakes or ponds in these mountains, but there were plenty of waterfalls. The mountains were alive with moving water. The mountains had been *carved* by moving water, in all its forms and spirits: great rivers that roared headlong over cliffs, and tiny streamlets that trickled through the deepest woods. There were triple-tiered falls that slipped across cascading stone and falls that poured over sliding rocks to icy-cold pools below. There were tall, narrow falls that plummeted from jagged heights and low, quiet falls that smoothed their boulders round.

But what she needed was a waterfall with a cave. She knew of several. But one was far too wet. The other far too easy to find. Her mind settled on a waterfall she knew of that was hidden in a small, protected cove. Is that where her mother had gone?

There was only one way to find out, so she headed for it.

"What you climb is floor and rain is wall," she said as she walked. It made sense. It made perfect sense. And it felt good that something in the world finally did.

When she arrived at the waterfall several hours later, late in the morning, she studied it from a distance, wary of the danger it might contain. The water flowed smooth and straight over the edge of rock. She could smell the crash of the clear blue water into the pool below, and feel the droplets floating on the breeze as the mist touched her cheeks.

She didn't want to go right inside the cave, because she wasn't sure what was in there, but she crept slowly, carefully, toward the entrance, staying low to the ground and very quiet.

"I was hoping you'd come," said a loud male voice immediately behind her.

Startled beyond her wits, she arched her back and jumped straight up, hissing and spinning around to defend herself.

22

Serafina landed on all fours on a tree limb and looked down at her attacker.

She stared for a moment and then blinked, unsure of what she was seeing.

The feral boy was sitting casually on the ground just a few feet behind where she had been.

"Do you want to climb trees?" he asked, smiling. "Or are you hungry?"

Still feeling the jolt of fear tingling through her body, she studied the boy. He had an uncanny stealth to him. She had not heard him or sensed him in any way.

He was a thin, well-muscled boy with light brown skin and dark shaggy hair just the way she remembered him. His chest was bare, as were his feet; he wore nothing but a simple pair of worn trousers.

"Come on, let's eat," he said matter-of-factly, standing up and walking along a barely discernible path toward the waterfall. She noticed the taut muscles of his back as he moved.

"Wait," she said.

The boy stopped and looked at her. His eyes were chestnut brown with traces of gold. "I'm Waysa," he said. "And you're Serafina."

"How do you—" she began to ask, in confusion.

"We'll be safe here, at least for now," he said. "We're pretty sure he doesn't know about this spot."

She looked at him in amazement. How did he know so much about her and her situation? And who was the "we"?

Her brow furrowed. "So you were the one who left the message for me?"

"Of course," he said with the slightest hint of a shrug.

"And you were the one who saved my life against the wolfhounds. . . ."

"You weren't doing too bad yourself," he said, smiling. "You're very bold. You might have made it."

"Thank you kindly for what you did," she said seriously, remembering his bravery and how close she had come to death.

"You're more than welcome," he said. "Come on, we have to get out of sight."

Although she knew she should be cautious, she felt comfortable and at home with this boy in a way that she had never felt at home with anyone in her life.

She climbed down onto the ground, looked around her, and then followed him into the cave behind the waterfall.

She'd seen such caves where the river came down in a deafening roar of churning whitewater, but here, the water poured down in a smooth, even flow, with sunlight passing through it, creating a shimmering silver wall.

Sometimes it seemed to her as if the whole world was made of light: the shine of moonlight through the clouds, the green glow of luna moths, the silver light of midnight on a river, the blue light of dawn—and now the blaze of a sunlit wall made of rain. And, of course, there could be no light without darkness, no waterfall without stone.

As she stepped farther into the cave, she saw that the back wall was encrusted with dark purple amethysts. When she turned in the direction she had come, and looked out through the opening beneath the waterfall, she saw a most magnificent phenomenon. The sunlight shining through the mist rising from the falls cast a collage of rainbows across the opening. She couldn't help but smile.

"You don't see that every day," she said in awe.

Her mind was bursting with a hundred questions for this boy, but there was a part of her that felt a gentle calmness to be here, to be someplace that felt safe and protected, and finally rest for a moment.

As she turned back around and cast her gaze across the sandy rock floor, she saw that there wasn't much inside the cave, but it looked dry and comfortable, and the boy did have several blankets, some food, and a small campfire.

"You want your meat cooked?" he asked, glancing toward her as he squatted near the fire.

"Yes, please," she said. She hadn't answered him earlier, but the truth was that she was as hungry as a spring bear, and very tired.

As Waysa cupped his hands around his mouth and blew into the fire, the embers came to life with his breath, then he added a few more sticks.

Once he had the fire going strong, he lifted up two choices from the night's hunting. "I've got a rabbit and a drummer."

The brownish chickenlike bird he was calling a drummer looked like what the folks at Biltmore called a grouse, a game bird known for thumping its chest with its wings. "The drummer looks good," she said.

"Good choice," he agreed. "Tastes even better than chicken."

She looked around the cave and wondered exactly where and how this boy lived. Was he one of the mountain folk or was he wild?

"So you've eaten chicken, then. . . ." she said.

"I tend to stay clear of cabins, but I'm not above the occasional snatch, if that's what you're asking."

"And this is your home?" she asked.

"No. Your mother wouldn't let me live here even if I wanted to. This isn't my territory. It's hers, or at least it was. I'm in between."

"My mother?" she asked, turning toward him.

"She's all right. Don't worry. We all survived."

A wave of relief passed through her, and she could feel herself relaxing.

"Your mother is scouting ahead, looking for new territory," Waysa said.

He pulled his lips back from his teeth and uttered three guttural sounds.

Something rustled behind her. When she turned, she noticed for the first time a small, jagged hole in the rock at the back of the cave. And something was crawling out of it.

The small, spotted, furry head of Serafina's half brother popped from the hole and meowed. He pushed his way out, and his whole body emerged. He came trundling toward her, all proud of himself and happy to see her, purring and meowing. She knelt down and pulled him into her chest and purred with him as he rubbed his body against her.

When Waysa gave another call, Serafina's half sister came running out at full blast and crashed into Serafina with joy. Serafina laughed, swept her half sister up into her arms, rolled onto the rock floor of the cave, and let the cubs leap upon her.

"You're here! You're all right!" she said, her chest filling with happiness.

The cubs swatted her with their soft paws, tackled her,

pretended to bite her arms, and wrestled with her. Then they turned on each other, and a whole new mock battle began.

Waysa soon had the grouse cooked, and the two of them ate it around the campfire. The food was delicious, and she enjoyed sharing pieces with the cubs.

"You're a fine cook," she said, looking at Waysa. He was at home in the forest, hunting his food, living in a cave. She remembered how fiercely he had fought, how brave he had been, how silently he had moved through the forest when he snuck up behind her. She had sensed it all along, but she hadn't been allowing herself to hope—Waysa wasn't just the feral boy who had saved her from the wolfhounds. He didn't just disappear. He had gone to get her mother. He had come back for her, found her lying at the edge of the river, nudged her onto her mother's back, and run with her through the forest. He was the dark lion! He was the one her mother had warned to leave her alone. This meant that her mother wasn't the only catamount in the world. There were others!

"You said that you're in between, that you're just passing through," she said. "So where do you come from?"

"Cherokee, southwest of here."

"Are your kinfolk from there?"

"Originally, but not anymore," he said bitterly. He rose and turned his back to her, and for a moment she was frightened that he was going to leave the cave completely.

"I'm right sorry," she said, realizing that something terrible must have happened. Waysa had been so casual, so bold, so full of life, but now a darkness clouded his spirit.

He paused and shook his head, unable to continue for a moment, then began to speak in a slow and serious tone. "It was three weeks ago. We had just completed a hunt together. We were happy and safe, and soon my brothers and sister and I would be going out to find territories of our own. But then the conjurer came upon us. He killed my older brother first, before any of us even knew he was attacking. My father fought him with every muscle in his body, but finally fell. My mother was killed as well, and then my two younger brothers. I was almost able to save my young sister." Waysa stopped, his hand covering his face as he shook his head and turned away. "We all fought him," he said, his voice ragged with emotion. "But his spells were far too strong."

"I'm sorry, Waysa," Serafina said softly, tears brimming in her eyes. She tried to stay fierce and strong, for his benefit if not her own, but seeing Waysa's pain cleaved a fissure in her heart as deep as wounds of old.

"I fled," he said, his voice quivering with shame. "When I saw my sister die, I didn't know what else to do. There was no one left. There was no one else to fight for. I felt like I just wanted to die. I ran and kept running and didn't stop for days. Then I entered your mother's territory, and she nearly killed me."

Serafina nodded, remembering how her mother had attacked her the first she met her. "She's like that," she said. "She defends her territory somethin' fierce."

He nodded. "As it should be. My mother had her own

territory, and my father his. And soon my brothers and sister would have had theirs, too. My sister was . . ."

Waysa's words drifted off. He didn't want to continue whatever he was going to say.

"So my mother ran you off the first time you came into her territory," Serafina said, standing and trying to change the subject. "But now you're looking after her cubs."

"She saw that I helped you against the conjurer's dogs. And when he attacked the cubs last night, I fought at her side to defend them. We've decided to work together now, come what may. This is the safest place we know, so I agreed to hide here and protect the cubs while she scouts ahead. She hated to leave them, but she can travel so much faster without them, and she wasn't sure what she'd find where she's going."

As more questions flooded Serafina's mind, she looked over at her half brother and half sister. They were her family, so close to her in so many ways, and yet so different from her as well. They were forever mountain lions. And she was forever human. They shared the same affliction: to always be what they were born.

"You look exhausted," Waysa said, "and like you've been dragged through a mud pit. You need to rest. But before you do, we should get you cleaned up."

"What do you mean?" she asked, turning toward him.

But in one quick moment, he rushed her and tackled her headlong through the waterfall. The shock of the icy-cold water hit her first, then she felt herself tumbling downward.

24

Serafina felt a swoop in her stomach as she fell through the rush of the waterfall, her body plummeting toward the rocks and water below. Her mind exploded with fear of what was going to happen when she hit the bottom.

She had tried to cross that one river at its most shallow point to escape the wolfhounds, and it had nearly killed her. She'd never swum in deep water. She wasn't even sure she could. And she certainly didn't want to find out like this.

But at that instant, her whole body plunged with a great, enveloping crash into an ice-cold pool of deep blue. The biting cold was the most immediate shock she felt. But the force of her fall sank her down, down, down into the churning water, surrounded by clouds of swirling bubbles. She tried to flail her arms and legs, but she just kept sinking. Her lungs were going to burst, desperate to take a breath.

A hand grabbed her wrist and pulled her up.

As soon as her face broke the surface, she heaved in a great, gasping breath of air and started flailing and splashing.

Waysa held her to keep her afloat. "Don't panic! I've got you!"

"I can't swim!" she sputtered.

"Paddle your legs," Waysa told her, and she started pushing her legs rapidly against the water. "All right, good. Now paddle your arms in front of you, close to your chest, like this. Good. You see, you paddle your arms and your legs together, like you're crawling as fast as you possibly can."

Serafina had no choice but to listen to everything he was telling her to do. "Keep paddling!" he ordered. "Good. Now I'm going to let you go."

"Don't let me go!" she screamed.

"I'm letting go. . . ."

When Waysa released her, she paddled furiously and kicked her legs and held her head above the water in front of her, terrified at every breath that it would be her last. But she soon found herself holding her own. She wasn't immediately sinking! She could swim. She could actually swim!

"That's it! You've got it!" Waysa shouted.

It turned out that swimming was like falling and landing on her feet without getting hurt. For her and her kind, it was a reflex. It wasn't something she would have ever chosen to do, but now that she had to do it, she could do it almost instinctively. She paddled around in the pool, filled with joy. She could actually swim!

"It's so cold!" she complained, half angry and half laughing.

"Just keep paddling. You'll get used to it," Waysa said, swimming beside her.

Serafina swam one way and then another. She tried turning her body this way and that, feeling the water rush over her skin. It felt like she was flying slowly through soft, thickened, ice-cold air.

When they were done, Waysa climbed out of the pool onto the rocks and boulders at the edge of the river. Then he turned and put out his hand.

She grabbed hold and he hoisted her up onto a boulder. From there, they climbed together, hand over hand, back up to the cave. They threw more sticks onto the fire, gathered the warm, fuzzy cubs into their arms, and huddled around the flames.

"You could have given me a warning!" she said.

"Would you have done it if I had?" he said, laughing.

"No!"

"You see," he said, gloating. "You're going to find swimming useful for crossing rivers on long journeys."

It felt good to be warm and clean again, her hair lying around her shoulders, and her body strong. The icy water seemed to have a powerful and rejuvenating effect.

For a little while, as they sat by the fire, she and Waysa talked about their lives. She knew she should ask him about the bearded man he had called the conjurer, and where her mother had gone, and all the other questions on her mind. But she'd been running and fighting for so long that, for a little while, she just wanted to feel like things were going to be all right. In the cave, it was like it was just the two of them in the world, and the world was good. She asked him questions about his sister and the other members of his family, and he seemed grateful to have a chance to talk about them. He asked her about her life at Biltmore, about her pa and her younger days. She told him about Braeden, and what had happened to Gidean, and how she'd fled in shame. Talking to Waysa was easy. It felt like a salve on the wounds of her heart.

When she and Waysa curled up in their blankets on opposite sides of the campfire, she was relieved to finally sleep for a few moments. She dreamed of forests—of tall, beautiful trees and flowing water, rocky slopes and deep ravines. And she dreamed of swimming.

A short time later, she awoke curled up in a little ball with the two sleeping cubs. They were warm and soft, breathing quietly with little purring sounds, their heads tucked into her chest and legs.

Waysa was awake as well, gazing at her from across the fire. For a long time, she did not speak, and neither did he.

When she finally did say something, her words were soft. "You fled your home from far away. You've been running. When you came here, you could have kept running. What kept you here, Waysa?"

Waysa turned away from her and gazed at the waterfall.

"Why did you stay?" she asked, her voice low and gentle.

"I've been waiting for you," he said softly.

She felt her brows furrow as she looked at him. "I don't understand."

"I would have passed through and kept going days ago, but after I saw you in the forest that night . . ."

"What?" she urged him. "After you saw me in the forest, what happened?"

"I wanted to wait for you," he said.

"What do you mean, wait for me?" she asked gently, narrowing her eyes at him.

"I thought we could leave here together."

Serafina could hear the seriousness in his voice.

"You don't truly know me," she said.

"You're right," he said. "I don't. I don't know anyone anymore, not a single living soul other than you, and your mother, and the cubs."

Serafina didn't know what to say. It was the way of a young mountain lion to leave his mother and find a territory of his own, but it was the way of a human to want a friend and a family.

As Serafina stared at Waysa, she realized that there was far more to this boy than she thought. He was asking her to leave this place with him, to go live in the forest and run through the ferns and hunt drummers and swim in pools together. He'd been hoping to find her again. He'd been waiting for her.

She watched him for a long moment, just holding his gaze, and then she said, "You realize I can't change."

"Of course you can," he said.

"I've tried. I can't do it."

"You're just not seeing what you want to be."

"I don't understand."

"Once you envision what you want to be, then you'll find a way to get there."

"I don't think so," she said.

"I'll teach you," he said, and his voice had such confidence, such kindness, that it was almost impossible not to believe him.

As she turned away from him and cuddled with the cubs, she thought about what Waysa had said. She slowly realized that there was a new path opening up in front of her now. It awed her to think about it. One path would take her home to Biltmore like she'd planned, to people she knew and loved, but to conflict and pain and uncertainty as well. But this other path, with Waysa, would take her away, maybe forever. She knew she would miss her pa and Braeden, but she wondered what starting over would be like. Would she come to know Waysa in the way she knew them? Would she go on to see new mountains and new waterfalls? Were there different kinds of trees and animals in those distant places? Would she finally find a place to belong? What would become of her? With Waysa's help, could she truly learn to change?

As she tried to envision her future, she realized there were many paths, many different ways to go, and part of growing up, part of *living*, was choosing which paths to follow. Two main paths lay before her, leading to two very different lives.

She slowly got up to her feet and tried to think it through. She knew that she had to be smart and she had to be bold. But more than anything, she knew she had to follow the path of her heart.

Standing in the cave with Waysa, Serafina tried to imagine all that had happened when the conjurer attacked her mother and the cubs—the bearded man casting his spells and twisting vines. The cubs must have been terrified.

"Is that why he attacked?" she asked Waysa. "Did he want the cubs?"

"He's been capturing animals of all kinds," he said. "That's why they're fleeing. They sense the coming danger. And that's why you and I must take the cubs and leave this place, Serafina. As soon as you are rested enough to travel at speed, we must follow your mother's path and join her."

Waysa's words were a shock to her. She longed to see her mother again, but her heart ached painfully at the thought of leaving.

"We can't fight this darkness, Serafina," Waysa warned, seeming to sense what she was thinking. "We must flee these mountains."

"But I don't understand," Serafina said. "Tell me what's going on. Why is all this happening? Why did my mother send me back to Biltmore?"

"Your mother loves you and her cubs more than anything in the world. She thought you'd be safe at Biltmore. But she was wrong."

"Is Biltmore in danger?" Serafina asked in alarm.

"Everything's in danger. Especially Biltmore."

"What?" Serafina said. "Then we need to help them, Waysa."

"We can't," he said, shaking his head. "He's far stronger than we realized. He's even stronger than when he killed my family three weeks ago. He's gathering more and more power as he comes this way. His power is tied to the land, to the forest and the people and animals he controls within it. But Vanderbilt and his vast estate stand in his way of controlling this region for himself."

"But who is he? Who is this man?" she asked, panic building up inside her.

"He's a shifter, like the catamounts. He can shift into a white-faced owl at will. But he uses his power for evil, to try to control the forest, to steal from it, to take its animals and its trees and the magic within it and bend them to his will. My people call him the Darkness, for he is a future through which they cannot see. Shifters inherit their gift, pass it down from one generation to the next, but he has taken his power further.

He has spent years learning to twist the world we know, to throw curses and cast spells. He wants to control this forest, to make slaves of us all, from the smallest mouse to the largest bear, and everything in between. He hates the catamounts most of all because he cannot control us. We stand against him. He will destroy anything in these mountains that gets in his way."

"Are you saying that he's going to attack Biltmore?"

"I don't know by what path or trickery he will come," Waysa said. "He's a conjurer of the dark arts. He does not fight with tooth and claw like you and me. He does not fight straight on. He uses subterfuge and deceit to weave his way. He flies silent. He watches like an owl and keeps himself hidden at a safe distance. He concentrates his power into weapons and then sends in his demons to do his bidding."

Serafina tried to understand. "Do you mean . . . a weapon like the Black Cloak?"

Waysa nodded. "The Black Cloak was a collector of souls, one of the first concentrators of dark power that he ever created. I do not know all the different spells he will cast this time, but the tearing of the Black Cloak wrought a terrible new fury in him. That's what started all this. That's what brought him here."

"Are you saying the creator of the Black Cloak has come alive? Not Mr. Thorne, but the cloak's actual *creator*?"

"He's never been dead," Waysa said.

"I don't understand. Where does he come from?"

"My father told me that the old man of the forest lived in these mountains long ago. He was born with unusual powers, but he yearned to develop and control the powers he possessed.

He traveled to the Old World, where he learned the dark arts from the necromancers there. By the time he returned, he had become a powerful conjurer. He found a shadowed cave in which to live, like a spider building a nest. He cast spells on the people in the nearby village and enslaved the animals of the forest. He—"

"Why didn't anyone try to stop him?" Serafina interrupted.

"They did. The catamounts rose up against him and fought him in a great battle. They nearly defeated him. He lost his strength and became but a ghost of what he was. He's been far away from here, gathering new skills and powers in foreign lands, but now he's come back, more powerful than ever. Even as we speak, he's hiding like a rattlesnake beneath a log, letting his venom build up within him, biding his time before he strikes again."

"Then we need to fight him!" Serafina said.

Waysa grabbed her by the shoulders so quickly it startled her. "Listen to me, Serafina," he said, looking into her face. "He's made a staff of twisted purpose to focus his power. It allows its wielder to control animals, to do his bidding against their will. And not only that, he has a new ally, a conjurer with power frighteningly similar to his own. The two of them working together will be unstoppable. They see this as their land—their forest and their mountains—and they plan to take it all back. And the more they take, the more powerful they become. We cannot fight them!"

"My mother will beat them!" Serafina blurted out before she could stop herself. But even as she said it, her chest filled with a dreadful realization. "My mother already fought the conjurer before, didn't she . . ."

Waysa nodded slowly.

"That's why she won't fight him again. . . ." Serafina said.

"That's right," Waysa said, but then hesitated.

She looked at him. "What is it? Tell me."

Waysa lifted his eyes and met her gaze. "Twelve years ago, the conjurer killed your father," Waysa said softly.

"My father?" Serafina asked in astonishment. "My true father?" She couldn't even imagine this. "But how? Why? How do you know about my father?"

"Your father was a catamount like us. All the catamounts knew him. Your mother hid it from you because she didn't want you to follow in his footsteps, but he was a great warrior, the fiercest fighter and strongest leader the catamounts have ever seen. My mother and father and all the creatures of the forest fought at his side against the conjurer twelve years ago. That was when the conjurer was nearly defeated. Your father led the fight against him. He was the one who taught my father the expression that my father taught me."

"The expression?" Serafina asked in confusion. "What expression?"

" 'Stay bold!' your father used to say when the others lost heart. It has been the mantra of the catamounts ever since. 'Stay bold!' "

"My father started that?" Serafina asked in bewilderment. "But what happened to him?"

Waysa shook his head in regret. "Your mother and father

rallied all the allies of the forest and led an attack against the conjurer. They weakened him severely, draining nearly all of his power. They almost destroyed him entirely. But it is the way of his kind that even when he seems to be dead, he is not. His spirit lives on. He hides in a darkness the rest of us cannot see. At the very last moment of the battle, your mother was absorbed into the Black Cloak and your father was struck down. Your father stayed bold to the very end. He saved the catamounts and the other creatures of the forest in that battle. But he lost his own life."

"What?" Serafina said. "How could all this be true? My mother did not tell me any of this."

"Your mother wanted to protect you, Serafina. She didn't want you to fight battles that you couldn't win. She thought you would be hidden and safe within Biltmore's walls. But it's clear now that all is lost there, too. We cannot win this war."

"But who is he, Waysa?" she asked again. "Who is the old man of the forest? And who is this Mr. Grathan? Is that the other conjurer you spoke of? Or is it one of his demons?"

"I do not know by what names or forms he and his allies come this time," Waysa said, "but I know the conjurer has returned. And he will kill anyone who resists him. As fiercely as your mother has always defended her territory, she knew that no matter how dangerous it was, she must leave this place behind, that she must go forth as quickly as she could to search out a new territory for her and her cubs. She has gone deep into the Smoky Mountains, scouting ahead into unknown forests, talking with the catamounts there, looking for a new place for us to live. We shall find new territory in those distant mountains, a place bright and free, and we shall guard it well. The Great Smoky Mountains will be the last bastion of our kindred, Serafina, the last homeland for those few of us who have survived."

Serafina listened to Waysa's words in amazement. She knew the danger he was talking about. She'd experienced the conjurer's spells firsthand. She remembered what it felt like to have the air pulled from her lungs. And she'd witnessed his staff of power at work. But as tantalizing as it was to go with Waysa and the cubs to join her mother in the mountains far away, the path with them was like the city she'd seen in the valley, and the train on the mountainside, and the wolves traveling the ridge to distant peaks: even as these new paths opened up to her, she knew they were not the paths of her heart. She wanted to go back to her pa and Braeden, and to Essie and Mr. and Mrs. Vanderbilt. Biltmore was her home. If the old man of the forest could steal breath and control animals, there was no end to the harm he could do. He could force Cedric to turn on Braeden. He could kill Mr. Vanderbilt with the bite of a wolf. His spy, Mr. Grathan, had already squirmed his way into the house like a rat through a sewer pipe. Maybe it was Grathan who wielded the staff of power that Waysa spoke of, like Mr. Thorne had wielded the Black Cloak. She didn't know exactly what their plan was, but she had to stop them.

"Somehow, we must figure out a way to fight," she said fiercely. "I will not turn my back on the people of Biltmore."

"Serafina, you've seen his spells and his demons," Waysa

argued. "We cannot fight that. I saw the very breath pulled from my sister's lungs even as she tried to say good-bye to me. Come with me and the cubs to find your mother. We'll go up into the Smoky Mountains, and we'll be safe there. There are trees and valleys and rivers for hundreds of miles."

"I'm sorry, Waysa," Serafina said, shaking her head. "I have to go back."

"You told me that the people of Biltmore said you don't belong with them," Waysa said. "You told me that you ran away from there. You're a catamount, Serafina. You have *us* now. You don't need them anymore!"

Waysa's words crashed into her, but she tried not to listen. She *couldn't* listen. She knelt down and hugged her little siblings. "Go without me," she told Waysa. "Take care of the cubs. Follow my mother's path like you planned."

"Serafina," Waysa said, his voice strong, "you don't need them!"

Serafina felt the emotion welling up inside her, almost too much to bear. She stood and embraced Waysa. She held him tight for a long moment. And then she let him go, knowing that it might be the last time she ever saw him. "But I *do* need them," she said. "And more than that, they need me."

She looked at her catamount kin one last time, then turned and headed toward Biltmore.

"You can't save Biltmore all by yourself!" Waysa shouted after her as she slipped into the underbrush.

"I won't be alone," she said.

26

Just before dawn, Serafina crept through the darkened forest that surrounded Biltmore. In the morning's slow change from darkness to light, there was no breeze, no sound, just a stillness in the cold air and the breathing of the earth. The mist floated like long-stretching gray clouds among the branches of the trees. She was eager to find her way up to the house. But then she spotted the silhouette of what looked like a robed, hooded figure in the haze. She ducked down, squinting through the morning fog, trying to figure out who or what she was seeing. Was she too late? Was the conjurer already here?

The figure appeared to be a gray-bearded man with a walking stick moving slowly through the trees. As she studied him, he seemed to drift in and out of the mist, disappearing for several beats of her heart, then reemerging again. Was it the old man of the forest? Then she saw him poke his walking stick into the ground, take something small out of his satchel, kneel down, and bury it.

As she crept closer, she saw that he wasn't wearing the robes that she thought she'd seen before, but a long, lightweight coat against the morning chill. It was the elderly stranger she'd seen walking into the forest with Mr. Vanderbilt. And she'd seen him again standing with the other guests the night she fled.

She watched him, trying to understand what he was doing. He walked another twenty feet, then looked around, seemed to make a decision, and then knelt down again. It took her several seconds to realize that the small things he was pulling out of his satchel were acorns. He was planting trees.

Memories flooded into her brain like water that had been blocked behind a dam for many years. He wasn't a stranger at all. She had watched this man years before. His name was Mr. Frederick Law Olmsted. He was the landscape architect who had designed the grounds of Biltmore Estate, and he was one of Mr. Vanderbilt's closest friends and mentors. Biltmore had been his last and most ambitious project before he retired. She tried to remember the last time she'd seen him. Was it three years ago? Four? Mr. Olmsted's face was far older than she remembered, and his body more frail, like something had happened to him while he was gone.

When she was just learning to prowl the grounds, she had

seen Mr. Olmsted supervising hundreds of men constructing the gardens and the grounds according to his design. But there had been other times, quieter moments like this, when she saw him by himself, when he didn't think anyone else was watching, walking alone with his knobby cane in his hand and his leather satchel over his shoulder, seeming to wander the fields and woodlands, planting tree after tree after tree, as if shaping the very future of the forest. It was as if he could envision in his mind what it would look like a hundred years hence. And while he was a famous man who worked on a grand scale with hundreds of workers at his command, sometimes, secretly, he still liked to plant certain seeds and saplings himself, as if to touch the soil for touching's sake. A hickory here. A rhododendron bush there. Somehow, he could see the future.

It was hard to imagine now, years later, with Mr. Olmsted's young forest flourishing all around them, but when Mr. Vanderbilt and Mr. Olmsted first came to this area, most of the trees had been cut down, the farms had been spoiled, and the terrain had been what her pa called a *scald*—treeless, ruined land. Her pa had told her that it was Mr. Olmsted and Mr. Vanderbilt who had decided to change all that.

As Mr. Olmsted made his way through the forest, she realized that he must be heading out toward the Squatter's Clearing, one of the few remaining areas of the estate that had not yet been planted with either garden, farm, or forest. She was relieved that the elderly wanderer was Mr. Olmsted, but she wondered why he had come back to visit Biltmore again after all his years away. And what was this normally peaceful man so determined to do that it got him up in the morning before the sun even rose?

Leaving Mr. Olmsted behind her, Serafina slipped quietly through the darkness into the Biltmore gardens, past the pond, along the azalea path, and to the Conservatory, its thousands of steamed glass panes glistening in the morning starlight. She remembered one time, when she was eight years old, her pa had come over to repair the hothouse's boiler and she had prowled among the exotic plants, pretending to be a jaguar in the jungles of South America.

Making her way up into the shrub garden with its meandering, crisscrossing paths, she smelled the winter bloom of the Carolina jessamine. Coming with the season's crisp air, and the explosion of green and red holly and mistletoe in the surrounding woods, the yellow flower of the jessamine always reminded her that Christmas would soon arrive. But never mind gentle Mr. Olmsted, and the mistletoe, and Christmas, she thought, catching herself. There'd be no Biltmore at all if she didn't stop Mr. Grathan and the dark forces she'd seen in the forest.

She crawled through the air shaft at the rear foundation of Biltmore House and climbed up through the metal grate. After being away for several nights, the dark, quiet, secluded corridors of the basement were a welcoming home.

The smell of the pastry kitchen and the warm sheets in the laundry and all the other things she'd grown up with brought a swirl of fond memories back into her heart.

She made her way to the workshop, past the benches and tools, and back into the supply racks, where she found her pa sleeping on his mattress, gently snoring. She thought about going to her own mattress to sleep, but she didn't. Without making a sound or disturbing him in any way, she curled up beside her pa. She'd never been so happy to be home in her life.

She did not wake him, because she still felt ashamed of the incident that had caused her to run away. She didn't know how he would react to her when he woke. But she was sure that as he slept, he somehow knew that she was there, curled up beside him, that she was still alive, still prowling the shadows of the house and forest, and that she still loved him with all her heart.

When her pa opened his eyes, he roused himself from his cot and looked at her as if to be sure that he wasn't dreaming.

"Pa . . ." she said softly.

He swept her up into his arms and pulled her into his great chest and swooshed her around the room, as if to capture her and never let her go. "I was so worried about you," he said, relief flowing through his words. As she felt her heart breaking free with joy, she knew she was finally home.

When they settled down, she explained to her pa everything that had caused her to leave, that she never meant to hurt anyone. And as her pa started making their breakfast, he gave her a bit of a gentle talking-to.

"When somethin' bad happens, Sera, no matter how foul and painful it is, ya don't go runnin' off," he told her. "Ya come home, girl. Ya come to me and we talk about it, whatever it is. That's what kin are for. You got it?"

She nodded. She knew he was right. "I got it, Pa."

As they ate their breakfast, Serafina turned to darker

thoughts. "Tell me what's been happening here, Pa. Is everyone all right? How is Braeden?"

Her pa shook his head. "I'm afraid the boy's been having a hard time of it."

"Did Gideon die?" she asked, her voice quivering.

"The dog was terribly wounded, beyond the veterinarian's help. I don't know if they finally decided to put him outten his misery."

A flash of heat seared Serafina's face. She pressed her lips tight together to keep the hot tears from bursting into her eyes. She took in a breath and covered her face with her hands, and then, after several seconds, she tried to continue. "Is everyone else all right?"

"No, there's other bad news," he said. "Unfortunately, the stable master, Mr. Rinaldi, passed away while you were gone."

"What happened to him?" Serafina asked. "Was he sick?"

Her pa shook his head like he still couldn't believe it. "He was kicked by a horse and killed."

Serafina looked at him in alarm. "Was it one of those stallions?"

"I don't know which horse it was, but it was the darnedest thing. Everyone was shocked by it."

"I'm sorry about Mr. Rinaldi," Serafina said.

"But other than that, more guests have arrived for the Christmas jubilee, and Mr. Vanderbilt has been very busy."

"What about Mrs. Vanderbilt? Is she feeling better?"

"She's been up and around on some days, but other days I don't see her at all."

"Is Detective Grathan still here?" Serafina asked.

"He came down here yesterday a-looking for you," her pa said.

"What did you say to him?" Serafina asked in surprise.

"I told him you were good and gone and that I didn't know where you were, which was the truth."

"Good," she said. That was the best thing her pa could have said. The less Grathan knew about her the better. "Whatever he says, whatever he does, do not trust that man, Pa."

She glanced around the room to see what her pa was working on. "Were you able to get the elevator gears fixed like you wanted to?"

Her pa nodded with satisfaction. "Them gears are fit as a fiddle now, working well and fine, just like I knew they could. But your vermin have been mommucking again."

"What do you mean?" Serafina asked, confused.

He stepped over to one of his benches and showed her a bundle of black-coated wire.

"What's that?" she asked, moving toward him.

"The house is protected by a fire alarm system that's all tied in to a central point by these here wires, but take a look. . . ."

At first, Serafina thought he was showing her a wire that had been cut by snippers, but when she looked at it more closely, she saw tiny tooth marks. The wire had been *chewed*.

"I guess, when you're away, the rats will play," her pa said. "Them darn varmints chewed the insulation clean off, then bit right through the copper core. Never seen anything like it. If I hadn't noticed this and fixed it, the whole system woulda been useless. We might woulda had a fire start up and get total out-ten hand before we had time to put out the flames. And worse yet, people wouldn't have had time to get out."

"I'll see to them rats, Pa," Serafina promised, furious that she'd only been off the job for a short time and the rats were already back.

As she and her pa caught up on things, she realized how foolish she'd been to feel ashamed to see him. He had no reproach, no anger, nothing but love and concern for her.

"You were gone for a few long days," he said, seeming to sense what was on her mind. "How far'd ya go?"

"Up into the Black Mountains," she said.

"The Blacks?" he said in surprise. "That's way back up in through there to them rocks. Musta been awful bad cold this time a year."

"Not too bad," she said. "Did Superintendent McNamee and his men go out into the forest to look for that poacher?"

He pa nodded. "They went out, came back, didn't see nothin', but they found all manner of tracks out there."

"There's something bad comin', Pa," she told him.

"What are you talking about?" he asked, looking at her with a seriousness in his eyes. There had been a time when he didn't have ears for her stories, but that time had passed.

But even as he laid out the question before her, she realized how difficult it was going to be to explain everything she'd learned. "I got a glimpse of something nasty in the forest, and it's comin' this way," she said. "Just be careful, Pa. And tell me if you see anything unusual, all right?"

Her pa stared at her, silent and unblinking, not liking her answer one bit. She'd gotten his attention full and earnest now. "You're acting like you saw a haint or some such," he said quietly.

"I did, Pa," she said. "I did."

She didn't mean that she had literally seen a ghost, but it was the only way she could get to the gist of it. A man, a haint, a demon, a spirit—she had no idea what he truly was, but she knew he would come. And Grathan was already crawling beneath their very noses. The first thing she needed to do was to somehow gain Braeden's trust again, warn him about what she'd learned, and develop a plan of attack. It made her all qualmish in her gut whenever she tried to think about what she was going to say to Braeden about what had happened with Gidean, but she knew she had to do it.

When they heard the first sounds of the servants down the hall, she and her pa realized it was time for them to start their day.

She said good-bye to him and went down the corridor.

As she passed the open door of the servants' washroom, she saw her reflection in the little mirror above the basin. She gave it nothing but a glance as she walked by, but then she stopped, backed up, and looked again, surprised by what she saw.

Given how she'd occupied herself while she was away, it didn't surprise her that the dress that Essie had lent her was torn and stained. She'd need to apologize to Essie and somehow replace it. And she saw, too, that her face had been marked by a rather gruesome variety of cuts and scratches to go along with the vicious scar from the neck wound she'd suffered a few weeks before. She was not a pretty sight. But what truly gave her pause were her eyes. All her life, her eyes had been a soft golden amber color, but now they looked bright yellow. She frowned and growled a little in frustration. She seemed to be evolving from merely peculiar-looking to positively hideous.

She went up the back stairs to the main floor, ducked into a heating register, then shimmied her way up a vertical metal shaft to the second floor. Crawling through the air shaft down to Braeden's end of the house reminded her of their adventures a few weeks before. She came to the register that supplied Braeden's bedroom and peered through the decorative metal wall grate beneath his desk and into his room.

Her heart swelled when she saw that Braeden was there. She so desperately wanted to push open the grate and speak with him, explain what had happened, and try to convince him one more time that she never meant to hurt Gidean. But then she saw something that shocked her. Gidean was lying on the floor next to Braeden. He was alive! She didn't know how that was possible, but she was so glad and relieved. Gidean lay in a soft bed of pillows that Braeden had made for him, his eyes shut as Braeden stroked his head. He was clearly gravely wounded, but he was alive!

"I'm here with you, boy," Braeden said to his dog as he gently petted his ears.

When the tears seeped out of Serafina's eyes, she quickly pulled back from the grate and crawled down the shaft a few feet. Sitting alone in the darkness, she hugged her knees to her body and covered her face. If she watched Braeden and Gideon any longer, she'd start sobbing—from sadness, but mostly from relief that he was still alive—and no one wanted to hear sobbing in their heating register.

Serafina heard the faint sound of approaching footsteps. She crawled to the adjacent register, which looked into the hallway.

Whoever it was had stopped walking. He was just standing there outside Braeden's door. What was he doing?

She could see his shoes and trousers, but she couldn't see his face because of her low position. She knew it wasn't Mr. Vanderbilt, for she knew his shoes well. She pressed herself to the floor and tried to look upward. Now she could see that the man standing outside Braeden's door was holding a spiraling wooden cane with a hooked antler handle and he had straggly rat-brown hair.

Suddenly, she felt the closeness of the shaft she was hiding in, the dusty air moving in and out of her lungs. She tried to stay calm, but her chest rose and fell more and more heavily as she waited and watched.

She expected the man to knock, but he did not.

He leaned forward, pressed his ear against the door, and listened.

The rat was spying on Braeden.

Serafina watched, her heart beating strong and steady in her chest, marking time. When Braeden came out of his room, the spy stepped back into the shadow of an alcove and hid from him.

Serafina sucked in a breath and readied herself to push open the register cover and leap into action, but as Braeden walked by, the man remained hidden. He did not attack.

To Serafina's astonishment, Gidean walked at Braeden's side. The dog moved slowly, carefully, but he was walking on his own. Serafina couldn't believe it. How was this possible? She'd only been gone a few days. How could the dog's broken bones have healed so quickly?

The spy waited until Braeden was gone, then quietly slipped into his room.

That dirty rotten rat, Serafina thought as she crawled back to the other register to watch him.

The intruder rummaged hurriedly through Braeden's desk and opened his dresser drawers. She worried that he'd pull back the register cover and see her there, or maybe hear her breathing, but she had to stay and see what he was doing. As he bent down to look under Braeden's bed, she saw the side of his scarred face. Just as she'd suspected, it was Grathan.

She felt the fear rising up in her stomach.

Why was he rummaging through Braeden's belongings? Was he truly looking for evidence of Mr. Thorne's murder? Or was he looking for clues to the whereabouts of the Black Cloak?

Or did Braeden have some other connection to all this that she didn't understand?

Grathan found a small map of the riding trails that Braeden had been working on, but seemed frustrated that he couldn't find anything else. When he finally left Braeden's room, Serafina breathed a sigh of relief, but she couldn't rest.

She dropped down through the vent shaft to the main floor and looked through a register just in time to see Gidean lying down in the morning sun in the Entrance Hall with the master's huge Saint Bernard, Cedric. That meant Braeden couldn't be too far away. But finding him and staying undetected wasn't going to be easy.

Many of the fancy-dressed guests were taking their strolls. Servants bustled about the house attending to their various duties upstairs and down. Several families of Vanderbilts were arriving from New York to spend the holidays. Serafina prowled from spot to spot, avoiding a gaggle of housemaids and then sneaking past a pair of footmen, one of whom had a bandaged hand from her bite a few days before.

By afternoon, the house was so busy that she had to take refuge in the hidden compartment beneath the stairway on the south side of the second floor. When she overheard two chambermaids saying that the young master had gone out to the South Terrace, she ran for it.

Slipping out a side door, she darted along the columns at the front of the house, beneath the strange creatures carved into the tops of the columns and the gargoyles mounted along the edge of the roof. Few people seemed to notice them, but she had always been fascinated by the menagerie of Gothic carvings that adorned the house—weird dragons and chimeras, sea horses and sea serpents, bearded men and fanged beasts, strange girls with wings, mysterious figures in cloak and hood, and a hundred other fantastical creatures of the imagination. She had always wondered where Biltmore's stone carvers had come up with their ideas.

She ran down the steps to the long, wisteria-covered Pergola that bordered the South Terrace, a flat, open, grass-covered courtyard with a picturesque view of the river valley and the mountains beyond. Braeden and Lady Rowena stood on the terrace alone, gazing out at the scenery. Serafina had been hoping that Lady Rowena's father had finally arrived and taken her away, but clearly that hadn't happened.

Serafina desperately wanted to talk to Braeden, to warn him about what she'd learned in the mountains, but she couldn't do it with Lady Rowena there. She ran down the length of the Pergola, came up the steps that approached from the other side, and then peeked across the terrace.

Lady Rowena wore a peacock-blue walking dress with an elaborate triple lapel, a black-laced throat, and a collar that stood high around the back of her neck, as if holding the tumble of her red hair. She carried a matching parasol casually over her shoulder to protect herself from the sun. She reminded Serafina of the girls depicted in the hand-colored fashion plates of the ladies' magazines. She seemed to have a new dress or outfit for every activity and time of day.

But the sight of Braeden and Lady Rowena together wasn't the most startling thing. What surprised Serafina was that Braeden was carrying a large bird of prey on his leather-gloved left hand. *That must be Kess, Braeden's peregrine falcon with the broken wing.*

Kess was a strikingly handsome bird, with blue-gray wings and back, and a pale breast streaked with dark bars. Her throat was pure white, but much of her head was black, like she was wearing a helmet and mask, ready for aerial battle. But what Serafina loved most of all were Kess's powerful yellow talons with long, curving black claws, perfect for raking her prey from the sky.

"It's a rather menacing-looking creature, isn't it?" Lady Rowena remarked to Braeden.

When Serafina heard Lady Rowena say this about such a

beautiful bird of prey, she struggled to keep herself calm. She wanted to yell *That's the stupidest thing I've ever heard!* but she was pretty sure that at least one of them would figure out who it was hiding in the bushes.

"I think she's beautiful," Braeden said calmly.

There was something about his tone that caught Serafina. He didn't seem angry or annoyed like she thought he should be. If anything, he seemed a bit distant, like he had other things on his mind. But then he seemed to slowly bring himself around and focus on the moment at hand.

"Well," he said, "let's see what she can do today. . . ."

Braeden had told her that the falcon would never be able to fly again. She thought it was kind of him to bring Kess out into the sunlight, at least so that she could look around and remember better days. But then, to Serafina's amazement, Braeden lowered his arm and threw the falcon up into the sky. Kess didn't just fly; she flapped up into the breeze and soared, calling out in pure joy. Serafina could see the smile on Braeden's face as he pointed to the bird and talked to Lady Rowena, excitedly sharing all the different facts he knew about hawks and falcons. Kess's flight had changed his mood entirely.

The flying peregrine had long, pointed wings that pumped her through the sky, and a long tail that she used for steering and braking. Serafina could tell that she was still favoring her damaged wing, but she seemed so happy to be in the sky even for a little while. But it bewildered her. How did Braeden fix a broken wing that could not be fixed?

Lady Rowena watched the flying falcon in silence as if

nothing she was seeing impressed her. Serafina wanted to scratch her eyes out more than ever. But right at that moment, something extraordinary happened. A red fox ran up the steps, brushed past Serafina, and trotted across the South Terrace toward Braeden and Lady Rowena. The fox had a beautiful red-and-silver coat, with black legs, a white underside, and a huge, puffy red tail. Its ears were perked up, its nose pointed, and its eyes alert.

When Lady Rowena saw the fox coming toward her and Braeden, she screamed, "An animal!"

The startled fox paused and sat a few yards away from them as if he was sorry that he had scared the girl in the fancy dress.

But Braeden squatted down and faced the fox. "Come on, little guy. We won't hurt you," he said, stretching out his hand. "You're welcome to join us. How's your paw doing?"

The fox walked up to Braeden and sat at his feet.

Serafina watched in amazement. A dog or a horse was one thing, but how could Braeden befriend a wild fox?

Keeping low, she crawled up a few more steps to get a closer look.

The falcon continued to circle in the open air out beyond the wall where Braeden and Lady Rowena were standing. When Braeden whistled, the bird tilted her wing and looked at him.

Braeden smiled. "Did you see that? Did you see how she looked over at us? She's so happy!"

"Well, I must say, it does seem to like you," Lady Rowena said with a smile, finally giving in to Braeden's enthusiasm as she watched the bird fly around them.

"She's a girl," Braeden said gently. "Her name is Kess."

He seemed to be so willing to teach Lady Rowena about animals and show her a better way of thinking, like he understood that she was from the city and didn't understand animals the way he did. Serafina thought he was far more patient than she could ever be.

"Can you get her to do whatever you tell her to do?" Lady Rowena asked. "Does it follow your commands?"

"No," Braeden said. "She's my friend. I do things for her and she does things for me."

"I see. . . ." Lady Rowena said thoughtfully, looking up at the bird. Suddenly, this interested her. She turned and pointed toward the ridge of the house. "Can you have it kill one of those pigeons up there?"

"Actually, those are mourning doves, not pigeons," Braeden said, but he looked toward the doves and then looked toward the falcon. "I suppose," he said uncertainly, "but I don't want her to stress her wing. And I don't think she's hungry. I fed her some chicken à la crème this afternoon, and she seemed to like that very much."

Serafina smiled. Classic Braeden. Stealing gourmet meals from under the nose of Biltmore's French chef to feed to his animal friends. When Serafina's stomach growled, she realized she wouldn't have minded some of that chicken something-something herself.

"So she can't actually do anything useful, then," Lady Rowena said. "You haven't taught her any tricks."

Braeden quietly knelt down and petted the fox's head and

ears. He finally seemed a little discouraged by Lady Rowena's words. "I have an idea," he said, standing once more. "Let's try this. . . ." He walked a few feet and picked up a stick.

"What are you going to do with that?" Lady Rowena asked.

"Kess's wing is still on the mend, but let's see if she wants to play a little."

Braeden hurled the stick up into the sky, then gave a long, whistling call.

The whistle and the flashing, somersaulting stick caught the falcon's attention immediately. She rolled, tucked her wings, and plunged into a stoop. She dove, plummeting at high speed through the air. At the last second, she pulled back her wings, thrust out her talons, and grabbed the stick.

"She got it!" Braeden exclaimed.

Serafina's heart leapt with the thrill of seeing the bird in action.

"Well, look at that," Lady Rowena said.

Even Miss Hoity-Toity is impressed, Serafina thought with a smile.

But then the falcon came gliding toward Lady Rowena at head level.

"What is it doing?" Lady Rowena asked, cowering back and shielding herself with her parasol. "Why is it flying at me? Tell it to stop!"

The falcon flew over her head and dropped the stick on her. "Help! It's attacking me!" Lady Rowena screamed as the stick bounced harmlessly off her parasol and fell to the ground. The fox darted in, grabbed it, and trotted over to Braeden as if they were all playing a grand game of fetch.

"They're just playing with you," Braeden assured Lady Rowena.

As he knelt down and petted the fox again, he gazed up at the flying falcon. "She's such a wonderful bird," he said. Serafina could hear the admiration in his voice, and maybe a little sadness. "Once her wing has healed all the way, she'll be ready to fly long distances again, and she'll continue her migration to South America. Can you imagine flying all the way to the jungles of Peru?"

"Well, I have to say, it seems a shame to let it go after all the work you've put into it," Lady Rowena said. "You don't want to lose it. Perhaps you can use a rope to tie it to a branch so it can't get away."

"If you tied her with a rope, she couldn't fly," Braeden said, horrified by the thought.

"A string, then, or a steel wire, something to control it. A steel wire would definitely work."

As Serafina fumed over Lady Rowena's horrible suggestion, Braeden whistled a low warbling call.

The falcon turned and flew toward him.

"Watch out!" Lady Rowena cried.

But the bird came in for a nearly perfect landing on his arm.

"Kess is my friend," Braeden said. "Friendship is more powerful than the strongest wire."

As the fox trotted into the woods, and Braeden and Lady

Rowena walked back toward the house, Braeden carried Kess on his arm. "Would you like to come to the stables with me while I put Kess away?"

"Of course not," Lady Rowena said, wrinkling her nose.

"Come with me," Braeden urged her. "I'll show you the mew we built for Kess."

"I don't go into stables of any kind. I might get my clothes dirty," Lady Rowena said haughtily. "I shall go upstairs and change for our stroll." With this, Lady Rowena separated from Braeden and went into the house.

Serafina quickly followed Braeden as he walked toward the stables. She hoped she could talk to him alone. But as she came up behind him, her stomach felt like it was spinning. What could she say that would make any difference to him? How could she explain what happened? Before she could work up the courage to say something, the stablemen came into view and she lost her chance.

A few minutes later, as the sun was beginning to set, Braeden met Lady Rowena out in front of the house again.

Serafina was surprised to see that the English girl had completely changed her appearance in a short amount of time. Her hair, her clothing, and her accoutrements were all different. Apparently, going for a walk on the wooded paths of the estate required a completely different outfit from what she'd had on while standing on the terrace.

Lady Rowena now wore what looked like a girl's hiking outfit from a grand shop in London, with a formfitting buttoned jacket, a long dark skirt, and jaunty leather ankle boots.

And, of course, the outfit came complete with a matching hat, a small pair of opera glasses, presumably to better enjoy the natural scenery, and a fancy, obviously useless feather-adorned hiking staff.

Braeden and Lady Rowena walked side by side down the estate's wide, perfectly manicured paths. These were just the type of fancy folk that Mr. Olmsted had designed the paths for, to give them the feeling that they were in nature, that they were in the deep parts of the forest, but without the inconvenience or discomfort. Serafina followed at a safe distance, trying to figure out what to do. She needed to talk to Braeden, but here Lady Rowena was again, blocking her way! As they passed through a grove of hemlock, oak, and maple trees, she couldn't quite manage to hear what they were saying, but they seemed to be deep in conversation about something.

As Braeden continued to talk with Lady Rowena, Serafina felt an itch creeping up her spine. At first she thought it might be the aggravating tone of Lady Rowena's high and mighty accent or the annoying tilt of her overly stylish hat, but she slowly realized that it was something far more serious than that.

Serafina scanned the forest. She spotted a dark shape on a branch, high up in a nearby tree. The sight of it put a lump in her throat and she became very still, not wanting to move another inch lest it notice her. It was deep in the cover of branches and difficult to see, but from its silhouette, it appeared it might be an owl or some other type of large bird. She couldn't make out the details or colors of the creature, but she could see that it had a rounded head and no ear tufts. Owls normally slept in the day, of course, but as night came on, this one seemed to be perched there in the canopy of the trees, silently watching Braeden and Rowena on the forest floor below.

Serafina decided that she could wait no longer, whether Rowena was there or not. She had to talk to Braeden.

As she rose to approach him, she remembered Braeden on his knees crying in anguish in a pool of blood at Gidean's side and Rowena screaming at her to get out of Biltmore. She remembered biting the footman and running away in shame. A hot flash flushed through her body. Her legs wobbled beneath her. But she pushed herself on. She stepped out of the bushes, walked up behind Braeden and Rowena, and spoke.

"Braeden, it's me. . . ."

28

"Serafina . . ." Braeden said gently. He did not move toward her or say more. It was as if he was gazing upon some sort of rare animal in the forest and he didn't want to scare her off.

She did not move. "Hello, Braeden . . ." she said, her voice trembling. All the emotions she was feeling were in those two simple words—the sadness for what had happened to Gideon, the sorriness for her part in it, and the fear of his reaction.

"You've come back. . . ." Braeden said. When she heard the faint, uncertain trace of surprise and hope in his voice, she realized that he did not hate her; he had *missed* her, and that was far more than she had hoped for.

She nodded to let him know, that yes, it was her intention

to come back. "I'm right sorry about everything that happened," she said.

Just as Braeden started to move toward her, Serafina noticed Lady Rowena again, standing behind him. Serafina expected the girl to be angry, maybe even start yelling at her to go back to the forest where she belonged, but she didn't. Rowena's face was white with fear. "What are you doing here?" she asked warily. "Why have you come back here after what you did?"

"Rowena," Braeden said, lifting his hand to assuage her.

"You are not wanted here," Rowena said to Serafina.

"Rowena, stop," Braeden said, touching her arm. "You're wrong. She *is* wanted here."

"Thank you," Serafina said softly to Braeden. She knew she didn't deserve his loyalty, but she was relieved to have it. "I think I know what happened to Gidean, why he attacked me."

Braeden did not seem to absorb her words. "Did you hear what happened to Mr. Rinaldi?" he asked her, his voice trembling with misery and confusion.

"My pa told me that he was kicked by a horse. Was it one of those stallions?"

"No . . ." Braeden said, the shame in his voice so heartbreaking that she wanted to hug him. "It was one of *my* horses," he said.

"It wasn't your fault, Braeden," Serafina said emphatically.

"But I was the one who trained them," he said, lowering his head. "I never thought one of my horses would ever do something like that."

"That's exactly what I'm saying," Serafina said. "It wasn't

your horse's fault. And it wasn't Gidean who attacked me. Those animals were under someone else's control."

Braeden raised his head. "What do you mean?"

Rowena suddenly stepped between them. "She's talking about witchcraft. She's trying to trick us!"

"She's not trying to trick us," Braeden said.

"You can't possibly want this creature here," Rowena said.

"Yes, I do want her here," Braeden said. "She's my friend."

"But you saw her," Rowena said. "She bites!"

"Many of my friends do when they're cornered," Braeden said.

Serafina smiled. But Rowena stopped and looked at Braeden, confused, her brows furrowed. Serafina could see by the expression on her face that Rowena was truly struggling to understand what was going on. But how could she? So many awful, incomprehensible things were happening at Biltmore.

Serafina turned toward her. "I know this must all seem very strange, Rowena," she said. "But I didn't mean to hurt Gidean. I would never do anything to harm him or Braeden, or anyone else at Biltmore, including you."

Rowena looked at her and seemed to take in what she said, but she was still suspicious. She looked uncertainly at Braeden. "What she's telling you about the animals can't be true," she said. "Black magic isn't real."

"Trust me," Braeden said firmly. "Sometimes it is."

"Are you saying you actually believe her?" Rowena asked. It wasn't anger but genuine astonishment.

"I do," he said. "It all fits."

"This all makes sense to you?" Lady Rowena said in disbelief, shaking her head.

"Braeden and I have been through this together before, Lady Rowena," Serafina said. "We've learned to trust each other."

"And we've learned to trust what we see even when what we see seems impossible," Braeden said.

Rowena looked at Braeden. "But is this truly what you want, Braeden? You want to be around this ragged girl?"

"Yes, I do," Braeden said. "I should have never doubted her. She's my closest friend, Rowena. But that doesn't mean Serafina and I can't be your friend as well."

Rowena's face roiled in dismay, and she turned away. She took several steps down the path. For a moment, Serafina thought she was going to walk back to Biltmore on her own even as night fell.

But then Rowena hesitated.

Serafina had disliked Rowena from the first moment she'd seen her horseback riding with Braeden, and she hated the way Rowena was frightened of the things she didn't understand, and the girl had definitely jumped to all the wrong conclusions about *her*. But as Serafina watched Rowena standing there in the path, she thought maybe Rowena was far smarter and tougher than she first appeared. Maybe she wasn't the only one who had jumped to conclusions. Rowena seemed to be thinking everything through now, trying to understand the situation she was in.

Serafina watched as Rowena exhaled a long, uneven breath, then turned and looked at her and Braeden.

The aloofness and disdain that had always been Rowena's armor had broken down a little bit and molded into something else. There was a seriousness in her eyes that Serafina hadn't seen before. She looked like a girl who wasn't going to give up, who was determined to figure out where she fit in, where she belonged. And that was a girl Serafina could relate to.

Serafina stepped slowly toward her.

"I know that you and I are very different," Serafina said, "but I am not your enemy."

Lady Rowena did not reply, but for the first time she was looking at her and truly listening to her.

"We have both said things and done things around each other that we shouldn't have," Serafina said, "but there's a danger at Biltmore far more important than any of that. Black magic, evil spells, whatever you want to call it. But it's very real. And we've got to stop it."

Rowena studied her without saying a word for several seconds. Serafina could not tell if it was suspicion or wariness or fear, or if somehow she'd managed to get through to her. But then Rowena spoke.

"You know," Lady Rowena said to her, "you're a rather fierce person."

"And you're altogether too well dressed," Serafina said. "We all have our faults."

As Lady Rowena looked at Serafina, the edge of her mouth curled into a little smile. "We do indeed," she said finally.

While they were talking, the setting sun had been gradually withdrawing its light from the trees, slowly pulling the colors from the world around them, and bringing the details of the forest to life in the way that Serafina was used to.

"Now, tell us what you found out, Serafina," Braeden said. "What's going on with the animals?"

"First, tell me about Gidean," Serafina said. "How is it possible that he's walking?"

"Gidean is still weak, but he's healing very quickly," Braeden answered Serafina's question.

"I've never seen anything like it," Rowena said.

"That's such good news," Serafina said, relieved, but she sensed Braeden's confusion.

"When I saw Gidean lying there on the floor in all that blood," Braeden said, "I swear he was dead—or just about to die. His body was broken. His eyes were closed. I got down on my knees, and I leaned forward to say my last words to him. When I put my hands on him, his body was so still, so lifeless. I thought I was too late, he would never hear my words to him, he was already gone. But then I felt his heart start beating. And a few seconds later, he opened his eyes and looked at me with such emotion in his eyes."

Serafina swallowed hard. "How is that possible?"

"I don't know," Braeden admitted.

Feeling a shiver run down her spine, Serafina glanced up into the trees just in time to see the owl open its wings and disappear into the darkness.

"Do you remember what happened before, Braeden, with the Black Cloak . . ." she said. "I think it's happening again— not the cloak itself, but something else like it. I encountered the bearded man again. He's some sort of conjurer. The mountain folk call him the old man of the forest. The Cherokee call him the Darkness. I think that Grathan is his spy here at Biltmore. Or maybe one of his demons or his apprentice. I'm not sure. But they're working together. We need to watch Grathan and figure out how we can defeat him."

Braeden nodded. "We should find out what room he's staying in, and when we're sure he's not there, we should search it."

"Are you talking about Detective Grathan?" Lady Rowena said. "He's staying in the Van Dyck Room on the third floor."

Serafina and Braeden both looked at Lady Rowena, surprised that she knew something about their enemy that they did not.

"I overhead him telling the staff that he'd be going out this evening and he wouldn't be back until the morning," Rowena said.

Braeden smiled, obviously impressed.

"I could be much more useful if I actually understood what we're talking about," Rowena said.

"If what you say is true, then you've already been useful," Braeden said.

"But hold on," Serafina said doubtfully. "You said he was going out *tonight*?"

"Yes," Lady Rowena said confidently.

"But why?" Serafina asked. "What reason did he give for going out at night? The house is surrounded by nothing but gardens and forest for miles."

"He told the staff that he would be taking his carriage into town," she said. "But of course I knew he was lying."

"You did?" Serafina asked in surprise. "How?"

"He had the wrong kind of shoes. He had his old, cracked muddy boots on. Positively dreadful. No one in their right mind would wear such hideous things into town."

Serafina smiled. She was liking Rowena more and more. "Tell us what else you noticed."

"Well, he's an extremely poorly dressed person—that I can tell you without hesitation. His coat is badly worn and altogether of the wrong season. Someone needs to tell that man that it's 1899."

Serafina nodded. The fashion critique was expected, but then Lady Rowena continued.

"Yesterday, the nasty man followed me through the Rose Garden. He probably thought I didn't know he was there, but a lady knows when a man is following her, whether he's a proper gentleman or a commoner like Mr. Grathan. He's been watching Braeden very carefully as well. And he's been looking for you, Serafina. Did you know that? He asked me at dinner two nights ago if I knew if you had truly left Biltmore. He stays well clear of Mr. Vanderbilt and Mrs. King, but he's been cornering the servants and asking questions about somebody called Mr. Thorne and something about a sculpture of a stone angel in the forest. I don't know what it all means, but at dinner every night, he pulls guests aside and practically interrogates them."

Serafina stared at Lady Rowena in stunned disbelief. The girl was a walking encyclopedia of house gossip and intrigue.

"Well," Lady Rowena said in response to Serafina's look of surprise, "I've been rather bored here all alone. I had to take up *some* sort of hobby, didn't I?"

"What about Mr. Olmsted?" Serafina prompted her.

"What does he have to do with any of this?" Braeden asked.

"What have you seen, Rowena?" Serafina persisted.

"He lurks in his gardens late in the afternoon. After dinner, he spends endless hours in the library looking over old sketches and photographs as if he's pining for the bygone days. But every morning at breakfast, Mr. Vanderbilt asks where he's going for a walk that day, and he says he's just wandering, going wherever the wind takes him. But he's lying, just like Mr. Grathan."

"Lying?" Braeden asked.

"Mr. Olmsted is lying to Mr. Vanderbilt?" Serafina asked.

"Oh, yes. Definitely. He says he's going for a leisurely stroll, but he goes straight out like a shot in the same direction every day, like he's on some sort of mission out there in the woods."

"She seems to be a fount of observations," Braeden said, amused by this sudden turn.

Serafina took in everything Rowena had said, then focused on the next step. "Braeden, do you remember the four stallions I told you about?"

Braeden nodded. "I went to the stables and checked into it, but the stallions were gone. The stablemen told me that they were only here for a short time, and they hadn't seen them since."

Serafina frowned. "Can you find out exactly who they belonged to?"

"Normally, I would ask Mr. Rinaldi, may he rest in peace. But I could go back and see if he registered the horses' owners in his logbook."

"Good, please do that," Serafina said. "It might provide us more clues about how all this fits together."

"And what about me?" Lady Rowena asked. "If Braeden has a job, then so should I."

Serafina studied her. It was hard to believe that this was the same Rowena as before, but she truly did seem like she wanted to help and be part of their group.

"If there's spying to be done, then I'm your girl," Rowena said. "What do you want me to find out?"

Serafina wasn't sure how far she could trust Rowena, but she'd give her an assignment as a test.

"I want you to get a list of all the guests staying at Biltmore and what rooms they're in. Every bedroom has a name, so learn them, just like you did with Mr. Grathan's room. And if any-one new arrives, we definitely need to know that. We also need to know everything that's talked about at dinner, especially involving Mr. Grathan."

"Absolutely," Rowena said. "I'm chuffed about this. This is so much more interesting than sitting around with the old ladies, sipping tea. Are we going to have a secret handshake?"

"A what?" Serafina asked in confusion.

"You know, like real spies."

"I don't understand," Serafina said.

"What about secret code names?"

Amused, Braeden looked at Serafina and smiled. "Yes, what about secret code names, Serafina?"

"Look," Serafina said. "If anyone sees anything unusual, like the arrival of a new stranger or an unexplained shadow in the garden, anything like that, then you need to find me and tell me right away."

"Got it," Braeden agreed.

"You can count on me," Rowena said.

"And, Lady Rowena," Serafina said, "this is important. You can't tell anyone else about what we're doing. No one. Do you understand?"

"Yes."

"Do you swear?"

"I swear," Rowena said.

"For any of us, at any time, if something happens and it's an emergency, then stop the master clock and the other two will see it."

Braeden nodded, liking the plan.

"For heaven's sake, how are we supposed to do that?" Rowena asked in bewilderment.

"There's a large clock in the carriage house courtyard," Braeden explained. "It runs on gears. It controls fourteen other clocks throughout the house so that every room is on Standard Time, just like in my great-grandpa's train stations."

"What a marvelous way to make sure the servants don't have any excuses for being late!" Lady Rowena exclaimed.

Serafina shook her head.

"So, how do I set this signal?" Rowena asked.

"On the third floor of the carriage house, there's a small room with the clock's gear mechanism inside," Braeden explained. "Simply pull the lever to stop the clock. But don't break anything or there'll be hell to pay from Serafina's pa."

"Not to mention your uncle," Serafina added. "If anyone sets the signal, then we'll all meet out on the roof right away. But only use the signal in case of extreme emergency."

"On the roof?" Lady Rowena exclaimed. "How do I get on the roof?"

"Take the stairs up to the fourth floor, cross through the hall, go down the corridor on the left, and climb out the second window," Braeden said, as if this was the simplest thing in the world.

"Remember, don't stop the clock unless it's an extreme emerg—" Serafina began, but before she could finish her sentence, she heard someone coming up the darkened path. The hairs on the back of her neck stood on end.

"Get down!" she said, pulling Lady Rowena and Braeden into the bushes.

"What are you doing?" Lady Rowena complained. "My dress might get snagged on a thistle!"

"Sssshh!" Serafina said as she dragged the girl to the ground and covered her mouth with her hand.

Serafina spotted the flicker of approaching torchlight on the leaves of the surrounding trees. She heard the sound of coming footsteps, heavy boots treading across the ground.

A dark figure came toward them up the path. Her chest tightened when she saw the man's long, weathered coat. Then she saw his spiraling cane and his dark hair. Her heart pounded. It was him! It was the rat-fiend Grathan. Rowena had been right. He wasn't going into town for the evening. He was coming right toward them!

As he strode rapidly up the path, a murderous determination clenched Grathan's scarred face. It was as if he'd uncovered some new piece of information. He was no longer going to investigate, interrogate, or spy. He was going to *kill*. He gripped his cane in his hand as if he could transform it into a savage weapon at any moment.

Serafina glanced at Braeden as he hunched low to the ground, his eyes fixed on their enemy. Lady Rowena began to squirm in panic, her chest rising and falling in her corset, but Serafina held her tight. She tried to keep them all quiet, but *her* chest was pulling in air, too, now, fast and hard, preparing her body for battle. Her muscles buzzed, ready to explode.

Grathan was thirty feet away, moving quickly. She could

hear the shift of his clothes along with the pounding of his feet.

Twenty feet away now . . .

If it came to it, she thought she could run fast enough to escape him, but Rowena couldn't in her long dress.

Ten feet away now . . .

Serafina decided that if Grathan spotted any one of them, she must immediately attack.

He was right on top of them now. She crouched down, poised for the lunge.

For a moment, nothing happened. She thought he was going to pass them right by without ever seeing them hiding in the bushes just a few feet off the path. But then a beast howled in the distance.

Braeden and Lady Rowena both startled, their eyes flaring wide. Serafina grabbed their arms and held them in place.

Do.

Not.

Move.

Hearing the howl, Grathan stopped abruptly on the path. All Serafina could hear now was the sound of his breathing and the flame of his torch. Peering up through the ferns at him, she slowed her breaths until she was perfectly quiet, not moving in any way. But around her, her companions shifted nervously. Even their rustling clothes made too much noise.

Grathan gazed up the path in the direction of the howl. The scars on his face looked like the claw marks of a wild animal. When she saw the glisten of the torch's flame reflected in his eyes, she felt a twist of fear coiling through her body.

Serafina watched Grathan as he stood on the path. He tilted his head as if listening for the sound of another howl. Then, after several long seconds, he hurried up the path with new urgency.

When Grathan finally went around a bend in the path and disappeared, Serafina held her position. She sensed that Braeden and Rowena were anxious to move. They weren't used to long periods of stillness like she was, but she kept them there, her hands holding them in place for several minutes longer, until she was sure it was truly safe.

Finally, she looked at her companions, lifted her finger to her lips, and then pointed toward Biltmore. The three of them ran home without saying a word.

Serafina could easily run faster than both of them, but she took up the rear, watching behind them to make sure Grathan hadn't doubled back. She knew there would come a point in the near future when she would have to fight him, but the last thing she wanted was to confront him now, unprepared, in the darkened forest with her two companions. She had to find a way to gain an advantage over him.

As they reached the outer edge of the gardens, she was glad to see the faint lights of Biltmore in the distance.

"Did you see that?" Lady Rowena said proudly as they hurried toward the mansion's side door. "He walked right past us and didn't even see us!" She crouched down and moved her hands in front of her like she was a master of stealth. "I was totally invisible! I was like a thief in the night!"

Serafina smiled, but Braeden looked confused. "Where was he going?" he asked. "What's out there in the woods?"

"I told you we can't trust that man," Rowena said.

"Let's hurry back to the house," Serafina said as they crossed the lawn.

"There's a formal dinner tonight," Braeden said, seeming to sense what she was thinking, "so the house is going to be very busy."

"As soon as things quiet down, after dinner is over and everyone goes to bed," Serafina said, "I'll sneak up to the third floor and search Grathan's room."

Serafina took them through the side door, and then they hid in the shadows beneath the Grand Staircase and gazed out across the Entrance Hall.

The house was softly lit with candles placed here and there on the mantels and tables, which gave the rooms an almost ethereal feeling. It was very quiet, save for the gentle music of violins and cellos playing in the Banquet Hall. It was good to see the Vanderbilt families and all their friends celebrating together. Serafina loved all the ladies' sparkling dresses. Christmas Eve was just a few nights away.

A beautiful, formally dressed young lady in her early twenties and a handsome young gentleman slowly descended the Grand Staircase arm in arm. The young man wore black tails, a white tie, and white gloves. Serafina loved the way the silver buttons on his shirt and vest glinted in the candlelight and matched the watch chain dangling from his pocket. The young lady on his arm wore a voluminous silvery dress with capped shoulders, a taut corset, and a long train that swished as it dropped from step to step as she came majestically down the stairs. She wore graceful white satin gloves and carried a silvery folding fan that matched her dress. A ring of shimmering pearls encircled her neck. Her dark hair had been swept up and arranged into the most elaborate coiffure Serafina had ever seen.

"Who's that?" Lady Rowena asked, entranced.

"Her Grace Consuelo Vanderbilt, Duchess of Marlborough," Braeden said quietly. "And her husband, Charles Richard John Spencer-Churchill, the ninth Duke of Marlborough. My cousins."

Serafina smiled. She had no idea how he remembered

names like that, but the girl sure was pretty. She loved the way Duchess Consuelo lilted her fan as she walked.

Serafina watched breathlessly as the young couple sauntered through the Entrance Hall and around the Winter Garden on their way to the evening meal.

In the Banquet Hall, the servants were preparing the forty-foot-long main table for the eight o'clock dinner as all the gentlemen in their black tails and white ties escorted their ladies in their long, formal dinner gowns. The shine of silver platters and the sparkle of crystal glasses in the candlelight seemed bright compared to the darkness from which she and Braeden and Lady Rowena had just come.

"Y'all better go on upstairs and get changed for dinner," Serafina whispered to her companions. "When you go to bed tonight, stay safe. Lock your doors. Tomorrow, get that information we talked about. And keep your eyes peeled for new clues."

"Got it," Braeden said.

"Will do," Lady Rowena agreed.

As Lady Rowena split off and went up the Grand Staircase, Serafina couldn't help but feel surprised by the girl. She was not at all what Serafina had expected.

"What are you going to do now, Serafina?" Braeden asked when Lady Rowena was gone.

"I'm going to keep watch," she said.

"I'll watch with you," he said.

Serafina looked at him. "You don't have to do that, Braeden.

Go to dinner with your family and then go on to bed. Get some sleep. I'm just glad I'm home."

"I couldn't sleep when you were gone, and I'm sure not going to sleep now that you're back," he said.

She looked at him and felt the warmth of his words moving through her. "Thank you, Braeden," she said. "It was the same way for me. I'm none too eager to run away again—believe me."

Smiling, Braeden said, "Let me go tell my uncle that I'm back, and then I'll meet you here."

"What about your dinner?" she asked, gesturing toward the glittering folk gathering in the Banquet Hall in the distance.

"What about yours?" he asked, moving his hand in an inviting way toward the gathering. "I'm sure we can find a gown for you to wear."

Serafina smiled uncomfortably, feeling a new kind of fear roiling up inside her. "Thank you," she said hesitantly, "but I'm not quite ready for that."

He nodded, understanding. "Then where are you going to eat your dinner?"

"My pa grills chicken on the cookstove in the workshop," she said.

"Sounds good, if you and your pa wouldn't mind another mouth to feed," he said.

"Um . . . yes . . . that would be . . . fine," she stammered, surprised and a little scared of the idea of Braeden eating supper with her and her pa. "What about Lady Rowena—won't she miss you at dinner?"

"Oh, Lady Rowena may need us in the woods, but she

doesn't need us at a dinner party. That's her home territory, and she'll do fine without us. Let me just go ask my uncle to excuse me from joining the dinner tonight, and I'll send a message on to Rowena so that she doesn't think I got absorbed into a black cloak or something."

Serafina smiled, and before she could stop him, he walked away and did exactly what he said he would. He spoke briefly to his uncle and, to Serafina's amazement, walked right back to her. There was no conflict or argument.

"Lead the way," he said, grinning. "I'm starving."

When she walked into the workshop with Braeden at her side, her pa nearly dropped dead from shock, but he made the best of the situation as quickly as he could. He pulled up a bench stool and wiped it off for Braeden to sit on. He gave Braeden his sharpest pocketknife to cut his chicken with. And he even managed to cobble together what looked impressively similar to a napkin for Braeden's lap. Serafina just sat back, ate her chicken, and smiled at the sight of the two of them sitting together and trying to chat.

Braeden used such refined English and her pa used such mountain talk that sometimes she had to help them understand each other. For the first time in her life, she felt like she didn't just *belong*, but like she was the glue that held the world together.

After dinner, Serafina invited Braeden to do what she imagined friends all over America did after a good meal together. They went rat catching.

"My pa told me that some sort of rodent has been chewing at the wires," Serafina explained.

"Then let's get to it," Braeden agreed.

As the last of the gilded ladies and gentlemen upstairs retired to their bedrooms for the evening, and as the servants cleaned up the Banquet Hall, Serafina led Braeden through the back rooms of the basement. In an hour or so, when everyone was asleep, she'd sneak up to Grathan's room on the third floor and search it, but until then, the hunt was afoot. They prowled the darkened corridors and shadowed storage rooms of her old domain, bringing back memories of her life in the world below.

After all that had happened to her over the last few weeks, she thought catching a couple of wire-chewing rats would make for easy pickings. But she and Braeden searched and searched and they couldn't find them. As the night wore on, it became more and more perplexing. She used her eyes and her ears and her nose just as she always did, but the rats were nowhere to be found. Her pa had said there were rats in the house. And she was the Chief Rat Catcher. She always found her rats. But for some reason, she could not find them tonight.

"Is it me?" Braeden asked. "Am I making too much noise?"

"No, I don't think that's it," Serafina said. "We're checking all their favorite hiding spots. If they're down here, we should at least be seeing them."

"What about upstairs?"

She shook her head. "There aren't any rats upstairs. I never let them get that far." She frowned, not sure what to do.

"Maybe your pa was mistaken about the rats," Braeden said.

"It's possible," she said, "but I saw the wires, and they definitely looked like they'd been chewed."

Just after midnight, she and Braeden gave up the hunt and went back upstairs to the main floor. There was no one there. All the lights were off and the candles had been extinguished. The servants had gone to their rooms upstairs and down. The musicians had closed up their cases and gone home for the night. The Banquet Hall and all the other rooms on the main floor were dark and empty.

"Come on," she said, waving for him to follow her as she crept up the darkened Grand Staircase. "We'll search Grathan's room."

At the top of the second floor, they hunkered down and looked upward to make sure the stairs were clear, then padded quietly up to the next level.

When they reached the third floor, they crouched down once more, protected by nothing but darkness and the sweep of the staircase. At that moment, Serafina realized they were in the exact location where she and Gidean had gone over the railing. She looked over into the dark, empty living hall. The moon shone in through the windows, casting the room in an eerie silver light.

A shiver ran through her.

She heard something on the other side of the living hall.

When she looked at Braeden, she could tell by his expression that he had heard it, too.

It was faint and difficult to make it out. She cupped her hands behind her ears to amplify the sound.

Then she heard it again.

A faint slithering just ahead.

The scrabbling of tiny feet on bare floor.

She touched Braeden rather than use her voice, and together they crept forward along the wall.

When the sound stopped, they stopped as well. When the sound resumed, they crept forward once more.

Now she could hear the creatures breathing, the scratching of their toenails on the floor, and the dragging of their tails. She felt the familiar trembling in her fingers and the tightness in her legs.

"It's the rats," she whispered to Braeden.

They crept slowly and quietly across the darkened living hall until they reached the corridor between the North Tower and the South. When she peeked around the corner, a dark fear boomed in her chest. At the end of this corridor was the cabinet with the hidden door that led to the attic where the chimney swifts had attacked her.

Were the rats in there?

She stepped slowly forward, still listening, still trying to figure out exactly where the rodents were. She heard what sounded like the grinding teeth of a hundred rats.

She was now standing in the exact spot where Gidean had attacked her that night.

"Serafina . . ." Braeden whispered, his voice filled with terror, as his trembling hand searched for and then touched her arm.

And then she saw it. Attached to the wall was a large wooden fire alarm box with a glass front and brass instrumentation inside. It had been there for years. But crammed inside the box tonight was a mass of roiling dark fur and scaly tails.

Their gnawing teeth clicked like the sound of a thousand cockroaches. The rats were chewing on the electrical wires.

She watched the rats in horror, too shocked to move. Braeden clutched her arm tighter.

Then the sound stopped abruptly.

All at once, all the rats craned their necks and looked at her.

A large, grisly looking rat crawled out of the box. Then another followed it. The rats, seemingly half out of their minds, rose up onto their back legs and stared at Serafina. Then they all started moving toward her.

She couldn't believe what she was seeing. She wasn't hunting them—they were hunting her!

Filled with fierceness, she charged toward them, wondering how she was going to catch them all. But they weren't moving like normal rats moved. They weren't scurrying away in fear at the sight of her. They ran *toward* her.

"Serafina!" Braeden whispered in terror, looking around them.

When Serafina looked down, she saw what he was seeing: hundreds of spiders and centipedes crawling out of the woodwork.

"Serafina!" Braeden cried again as he frantically wiped the spiders off his legs.

Serafina heard a terrible *tick-tick-ticking* sound and a long, raspy hiss. She felt the hot air of a breath on the back of her neck. She spun around in panic, but there was nothing there except a darkened corridor.

"Braeden, run!" she shouted.

They turned and ran. They tore through the living hall and down the Grand Staircase. She glanced over her shoulder. A brown slithering carpet of hundreds of rats flooded down the staircase behind her. It was like a waterfall of rats. She burst forward with speed, but Braeden couldn't run nearly as fast as she could. The rats were going to eat him alive.

But just as she slowed down to wait for him, something flashed by her.

"Come on, slowpoke!" Braeden shouted as he slid at incredible speed down the endless, smooth wooden railing of the spiral staircase.

The wave of rats slammed into her feet and scratched their way up her bare legs. She tried to tear them away, but it was no use—there were too many of them. She took a flying leap onto the rail, grabbed on, and went sliding down behind Braeden.

It felt like she'd been dropped off the edge of a cliff. The swoosh of her spinning descent made her insides float. She and Braeden slid down, down, spiraling down to the next level, then ran and leapt, and slid again, following the great curve of the railing all the way down to the main floor. When they reached the bottom, they leapt off the rail and ran down into the basement.

Serafina knew she shouldn't, but at the bottom of the basement stairs, she turned and looked behind her.

31

The rats were gone.

Those dirty, awful, insane creatures had chased her three floors down and then simply disappeared.

Had they vanished into thin air, or had they slunk back into the walls? Had the rats been some sort of conjuration?

She growled in frustration, angered by what had just happened. She was the Chief Rat Catcher! There weren't supposed to be rats in Biltmore House. She had made sure of it for years. And now all of a sudden there were hundreds of huge vicious ones, the likes of which she'd never seen before!

And since when did spiders crawl out of walls and attack? It was as if the animals' only purpose was to scare her off the third floor.

Braeden sat on the floor beside her, panting, his back against the wall as he tried desperately to catch his breath.

"Good night!" he exclaimed, shaking his head. "If this is what rat catching is like, you can count me out next time!"

"Come on," she said, touching his shoulder.

"Tell me where we're going," he said as he got up off the floor.

"We're going back up there."

"What?" he said, holding his ground. "Please say we're not."

"Don't you want to see if they're still up there? That was Biltmore's Grand Staircase! How can there be rats on it?"

"I swear, your curiosity is going to get you killed one of these days, Serafina. And me, too, I think."

"Come on," she said. "We've got to see."

Gathering their courage, they crept up the basement stairs to the main floor, then came slowly and carefully around, and looked up the Grand Staircase. There were no rats or spiders or centipedes. There was no sign of them at all. They were gone.

The moonlight lit the Grand Staircase in a silver glow, as if inviting them to ascend once more. But as they stared at the foreboding threat of the empty staircase and felt the hairs on the backs of their necks tingling, they both knew there was no way they were going to try to get back up to the third floor tonight. That was just about the last place on earth they wanted to go.

"There shouldn't be that many rats in the house," Braeden whispered.

"There shouldn't be *any* rats in the house!" Serafina said

fiercely, smoothing down the back of her neck with her hand. "Something isn't right, Braeden."

"A lot of four-legged nasty somethings," Braeden agreed. "Come on, let's find someplace safe to rest."

Avoiding the Grand Staircase, they used the back stairs to reach the second floor, then padded quietly to Braeden's room.

Gidean greeted Braeden happily at the door, then came over to Serafina, his tail nub wagging. She knelt down. Her eyes closed, she hugged him and petted his head, feeling a warmth in her heart. She was so glad that he seemed to have no memory or confusion about the battle they'd fought against each other that terrible night.

While Braeden slept in his bed, Serafina was happy to curl up with Gidean in the warm glow of the fireplace and try not to have nightmares of rats that didn't flee.

She awoke a few hours later, just before dawn. She had reconnected with Braeden and her pa, and even Lady Rowena now, but after everything that had happened—breaking the Ming vase, her fight with Gidean, biting the footman, terrifying the guests, and all the rest—she wasn't sure if everyone in the house would be glad to see her, so she had stayed low and quiet. But there was one more person she thought she could trust. And it might be a perfect, sneaky way to get safely into Detective Grathan's room when he wasn't there.

She quickly ran up the back stairs to the fourth floor, snuck down the hall, and slipped into the third room on the right.

"Oh, miss, it's you!" Essie said, smiling in surprise. Freshly dressed in her maid's uniform and getting ready to start her workday, Essie set down her hairbrush and went to Serafina. "I heard tell about everything that happened. I've been so worried about you! Where'd ya go?"

"I ran away up into the mountains," Serafina said.

"Oh, miss, you shouldn't have done that," Essie said. "That's far too dangerous for a little thing like you. There are panthers up there!"

Serafina smiled. "Those were the least of my problems."

"What? What happened?" Essie said, clutching her arm.

"I'm all right," Serafina said. But then she stepped back and presented her sorry state. "I'm sorry about ruining your nice dress, Essie."

"Oh, you never mind about that, miss," Essie said, pulling her back toward her. "Come sit down here on the bed. I can see you're mulling over somethin'."

"Do you know that man Detective Grathan?"

"Yes, I've seen him," Essie said. "He's been asking all sorts of questions about Mr. Vanderbilt and Mr. Olmsted, and about you, too, and Master Braeden, and the dogs."

"He asked about Gidean and Cedric?"

"Oh, yes! He's been asking after the young master's dog in particular. I can tell you one thing for sure: everyone is mighty tired of that man."

The night before, Serafina hadn't known for sure if she should trust Lady Rowena, but so far what the girl had said about Detective Grathan had turned out to be true.

"Do you clean Detective Grathan's room?" Serafina asked, finally coming to the purpose of her visit.

Essie scowled. "Maggie and me are supposed to be cleaning it, but he ain't been givin' us the chance."

"What do you mean?"

"He always locks his door, and he's given us strict instructions to never enter his room. He could have a dead cat in there for all we know, and there'd be nothin' we could do about it."

"A dead cat?" Serafina asked in alarm.

"It's just an expression," Essie said.

"Do you have a master key or anything like that?"

"Oh, no, miss, I ain't got permission for that. Most guests don't lock their doors. No reason to. But Mrs. King says if a guest wants privacy, then we should give it to them."

Serafina shook her head in frustration. This seemed like another dead end.

"So what's the big interest in Detective Grathan?" Essie asked.

"I think he's up to no good, and I want to catch him at it," Serafina said, which was the God's honest truth.

"Well, you be careful," Essie warned gravely. "He strikes me as a bad awful man."

Serafina nodded. Remembering the rats the night before, she said, "I'll do my best." Then one more thought came into her mind.

"Which room is Detective Grathan in?" she asked Essie. She thought it would be good to double-check what she'd learned from Rowena.

"Well, when he first arrived, Mrs. Vanderbilt told us to put him in the Sheraton Room, which is a very nice room, but Detective Grathan had some sort of problem with it."

"What did he say?"

"No one could understand what he was yammering on about, but he complained high and low about it so much that they finally just give in and put him where he wanted to be. I mean, how rude, to be a guest in someone's house and then to demand a particular room!"

"What room did he demand?" she asked.

"The Van Dyck Room at the top of the stairs on the third floor."

This was the same room that Lady Rowena had named, so this wasn't new information in itself, but when Serafina heard Essie say these words, her heart began to thump. *The room at the top of the stairs on the third floor.* That was right where she and Braeden had encountered the rats, and right where Gidean had attacked her, and before that, the chimney swifts. Then she remembered that the black-cloaked Mr. Thorne had used the same room.

"On my way back from the water closet this mornin'," Essie continued, "I heard the other girls talkin' about Detective Grathan."

"What did they say?"

"Well, you know he missed dinner last night, which was extremely rude to Mr. and Mrs. Vanderbilt. He came in late, went straight up to his room, tracking mud all the way, which poor Betsy had to clean up before Mrs. King saw it in the morning, and then he rang his bell. He had the gall to demand his dinner be brought up to him in his room. The cook had to get hisself out of bed, reopen the kitchen, warm up a plate for him, and send a footman all the way up there. That would have been no problem at all if he'd showed a speck of gratitude, but he wouldn't even let the footman in his room. He shouted at him to set the tray on the floor outside the door and go away."

Serafina listened with fascination. "So Detective Grathan is back in the house. . . ."

"Oh, yes, he's back, but I wouldn't cry none if Mr. Vanderbilt kicked him right on out again. All the other guests are so friendly and appreciative, especially round the holidays, but he's just a very rude and demanding man."

"Thank you for all the information, Essie," Serafina said, clutching her arm. "You've been a good friend to me. I'll pay you back for your dress as soon as I can."

"I know you will, miss," Essie said. "I've got a few minutes before I have to go. Do you want me to do your hair? It looks like you've been through a right lot of trouble."

Serafina smiled and nodded appreciatively. "Yes, that would be nice."

"How would you like me to do it?" Essie said, standing behind Serafina and gathering her hair up into her hands.

"Have you seen Consuelo Vanderbilt, the Duchess of Marlborough?" Serafina asked with a twinkle in her eye.

"Oh, miss, that would take an hour!" Essie said. "I'm a-fixing to get to work!"

"All right, a roll and a twist it is," Serafina said, laughing.

After talking with Essie, Serafina ventured down to the

lower floors. Moving from one hiding spot to another, she watched the comings and goings of the bustling house for the rest of the morning, but she didn't see anything suspicious or out of the ordinary. There was no sign of Detective Grathan. The rat seemed to have gone to ground. She wondered if her two allies had spotted anything. Somehow, they had to come up with a plan to defeat Grathan once and for all. They couldn't keep dodging him. But so far, they hadn't even been able to get into his room. Something terrible happened every time she tried. She felt like she needed some sort of trap.

That afternoon, she went outside to patrol the perimeter of the grounds. She wondered if there was a point at which the old man of the forest would attack head-on. From what direction and in what form would he come? Or would the attack come from Grathan himself, within the house?

She spotted Mr. Vanderbilt and Mr. Olmsted walking down a path together in the gardens, and hurried to listen in on their conversation.

"Have you checked in on the planting crews working down along the river?" Mr. Vanderbilt asked Mr. Olmsted.

"They're making good progress," Mr. Olmsted said. "Mr. Schenck has a good eye for the land." Serafina recognized the name of the chief forester they had hired to manage Biltmore's woodlands.

"All we need now are a few more decades, and we'll have a lovely forest again," Mr. Olmsted said.

The two men laughed a little, but Serafina could see a seriousness in Mr. Olmsted's expression, in the wrinkles around his eyes. The old man was hiding something from Mr. Vanderbilt, just as Lady Rowena had said.

"I just want to keep making progress," Mr. Vanderbilt said to Mr. Olmsted as the two friends walked together.

"Don't worry, George. We'll keep at it," Mr. Olmsted assured him. "We're going to make it so beautiful at Biltmore that no one will ever know what it was like before. You and your family and your guests will be able to enjoy the bounty of nature for years to come."

"I appreciate that, Frederick," Mr. Vanderbilt said.

"I learned long ago," Mr. Olmsted continued, "that whether it's a delicate tea rose or a three-foot oak, planting and growing requires an immeasurable amount of patience."

"I don't always have it," Mr. Vanderbilt said.

"Neither do I," Mr. Olmsted admitted.

Serafina thought that Mr. Olmsted should have chuckled or smiled when he said that, but he didn't. There was a darkness in him that she did not understand. There were thoughts on his mind that he was not sharing with Mr. Vanderbilt. She wondered again why he'd come back to Biltmore now, at this particular time.

As she watched and listened to these two men, she thought about her own life. Years ago, she had often seen these two friends together, walking and planting, talking about what species of trees would grow in each area, how they could bring in more water here or protect an area from the wind there, like shepherds of the forest. She had never thought about it before, but lately she had started to realize that all the comforts, buildings, and machines around her were once nothing more than someone's dream. In the not-too-distant past, these things had just been an idea in someone's head. When Mr. Vanderbilt's grandfather grew up, people had to walk or ride horses to travel great distances, but he'd imagined trains crisscrossing America. It was only by those trains that his grandson was able to venture from New York to the wilds of western North Carolina. And then his grandson had dreams of his own and built a great house in the mountains. Mr. Edison had imagined a lightbulb that would bring light to the darkest nights. Other people had imagined the elevator, and the dynamo, and all the other inventions her pa worked on every day. But unlike the men of iron, Mr. Olmsted had dreamed of vast gardens and endless forests. Those were the things he'd brought into the world. Thinking back in time, she wondered if the mountains, and the rivers, and the clouds, and even human beings, had been *God's* dream a million years before.

As she thought about all this, she couldn't help but wonder about herself. *Envision what you want to be, then you'll find a way to get there,* Waysa had told her in the cave behind the waterfall. She knew she wasn't going to invent a machine or build a great building, but she had to figure out who and what she wanted to be. She had to envision her future, and then she had to get there.

When she snuck back into the house that evening, she hunkered down in the second-floor air shaft and tried to think about what she could do. What trick could she use to trap Grathan? She had tried to get into his room and failed. She could barely keep track of where he was. But he had to have some kind of weakness.

Restless for some sort of plan, she crawled through the shaft and checked Braeden's room, which was empty. So she made her way down to the Library. As usual, she entered through the vent near the ceiling. Just as she began climbing down the bookshelves to the Library's second-floor walkway, Serafina heard footsteps approaching. She scurried into a hiding spot, crouched down, and waited for someone to enter the room.

But no one did.

She kept waiting, curious. She was sure she had heard something. It was like the person had paused just outside the door and wasn't coming in. The longer it went on, the more curious she became. Was she mistaken?

Suddenly, a figure appeared in the room, but not through the main door like she'd expected. Someone stepped out from behind the upper portion of the room's massive fireplace mantel. It was Lady Rowena! Serafina realized she must have used the hidden passageway that led from the house's second floor directly into the top level of the Library.

Serafina thought she should reveal herself to Rowena, but there was something furtive about the girl's movements, so she crouched down and watched her.

Rowena quickly ran down the finely wrought spiral staircase to the Library's main floor, her lavish, dusky-rose dress billowing behind her. She looked around as if to make sure no one else was in the room, then darted over to the walnut wall panels just to the left of the fireplace.

Serafina crept along the railing, but before she could get to a better vantage point, she heard a faint metallic ratcheting, a turning sound, and then a distinct *click*. This was followed by the squeak of what sounded like a hinge. Rowena must have found some sort of small hidden compartment in the wall. There was a rustling of paper and then a long sliding sound.

Rowena came back into view with a bundle of rolled documents in her hands. She took them over to one of the tables and opened them up. It was hard to tell from a distance what the rolls contained, but they seemed to be architectural drawings of some kind.

What was Rowena looking for? Was she studying a diagram of the house so that she would know it as well as Serafina and Braeden did? Or maybe she'd found the list of guests and was now matching them to the various rooms of the house like Serafina had told her to. It seemed wrong for Rowena to be snooping around in the Library when no one else was there, but then Serafina realized that she herself was doing the exact same thing. Maybe Rowena had some theory she was pursuing about Detective Grathan. When Serafina asked Rowena to join her and Braeden, she had no idea the girl would be so committed. She seemed to truly enjoy playing spy. Serafina was eager to hear what she had learned.

Just as she thought about revealing herself to Rowena, Serafina heard the sound of footsteps walking down the Tapestry Gallery toward the main door of the Library. Lady Rowena quickly stuffed the drawings back into the hidden compartment in the wall, sat down on the sofa in front of the fire, and pretended to read a book.

This girl is good, Serafina thought as she watched with a smile. That was a trick she'd never thought of before. The old act-like-everything-is-fine-here trick.

A footman came into the room. "I beg your pardon, my lady," the footman said, bowing slightly. "Dinner will be served at the normal hour of eight o'clock this evening, but please be advised that most of the clocks in the house have stopped, so we are letting our guests know that it's currently seven o'clock and they may wish to start getting dressed for dinner at this time. Thank you."

Serafina's body jolted when she heard the footman's words. The clocks had stopped! Lady Rowena was here in the Library, so that meant Braeden had sounded the alarm! He was in trouble!

Rowena seemed to understand this as well, for she immediately brushed past the footman and hurried out of the room.

Serafina darted from her hiding spot and ran for the rooftop.

32

$\mathcal{S}$erafina climbed through the fourth-floor window onto the roof of Biltmore House and hurried along the top side of the Grand Staircase's copper dome. She made her way between the slanting slate roofs, rising chimneys, pointed towers, and sculpted stone gargoyles of Biltmore's rooftop realm. The ridges of the roof were capped with ornate copper trim embossed with patterns of oak leaves, acorns, and George Vanderbilt's gold-gilded initials burning bright in the moonlit night.

As she came to the edge of the roof, she had a nighthawk's view of the Winter Garden's glass rooftop and the estate's many courtyards and gardens far below her. With the glistening stars above and the forested mountains rolling into the distance, the roof provided her a breathtaking view of her world.

She heard a tremendous racket coming her way and spun around.

"The clocks have all stopped!" Lady Rowena said breathlessly as she tried to climb through the window out onto the roof in her fancy dress.

Serafina went over to help her. Lady Rowena's dress, which was decorated with a profusion of silk taffeta roses, was so long and cumbersome that when she tried to clamber through the opening, her legs became entangled. The two of them worked together to push the fabric aside, avoid stepping on the flower-encrusted skirt hem, and pull her through the small window without tearing anything.

"We've almost got it," Lady Rowena groaned. "Just a little more."

Finally, she popped through the opening and fell onto the rooftop.

"I'm here," she said, gathering herself up like a soldier standing at attention. "Someone stopped the clock!"

"I stopped it," Braeden said as he stepped easily through the window and onto the roof.

"What's happened?" Serafina asked him. "Did you see something?"

"Gidean and Cedric are missing," Braeden said, his voice cracking.

"What do you mean, they're missing?" Serafina asked. Some dogs were natural wanderers, but losing track of a wounded Doberman and a giant Saint Bernard seemed almost impossible to her.

"We've searched all over the house and the grounds. Cedric seldom leaves my uncle's side and Gidean has never gone missing before, but no one can find either of them," Braeden said in dismay.

Serafina tried to think it through. She walked to the edge of the roof and looked down, first at the gardens, with their many statues and paths, and then outward, across the forest.

She remembered what she had seen in the dark shadows of the pines the last time she'd gone out there.

She didn't want to think about it.

She didn't want it to be true.

But the memory kept rising up in her mind.

"I think I may know where they are. . . ." she said, feeling a sickness in her stomach even as she said it. It was the last place on earth she wanted to go.

33

"Thank you for meeting with us, sir," Serafina said as Mr. Vanderbilt walked into the Library.

"Braeden told me that you had important information regarding the disappearance of the dogs," Mr. Vanderbilt said, his voice grave. She could not tell whether he was angry with her for what had happened a few nights before, when Gidean was injured, but he was obviously deeply worried about Cedric's disappearance.

"Serafina can help us, Uncle," Braeden said. "I trust her with my life, and with Gidean's and Cedric's, too. The strange things that have been happening at Biltmore, the way Gidean attacked Serafina, Mr. Rinaldi's death, Cedric and Gidean's disappearance . . . they're all related."

"In what way?" he asked.

"Mr. Vanderbilt," Serafina began, "you met me for the first time a few weeks ago when the children disappeared."

Mr. Vanderbilt's face turned even darker than it already was. "Yes," he said, looking at her. "Is this the same?"

"No, not exactly," she said. "But you saw then that you could trust me."

"Yes, I remember," he said, studying her.

Serafina looked at Mr. Vanderbilt and held his eyes. "I never meant to hurt Gidean. And I don't believe he ever meant to hurt me. I'm not sure, but I think I might know where the dogs are. They're in the forest. But I don't want to go there alone. I think we should form a hunting party with men and horses and weapons, and I'll lead us there. Whatever this turns out to be, we'll fight it together this time."

Mr. Vanderbilt looked at her for a long time, clearly taken aback by what she was saying. He seemed to fathom how frightened she was. "This is *that* dangerous. . . ." he said quietly, thinking it through.

Still looking at him, she slowly nodded.

Mr. Vanderbilt contemplated everything she'd said, then looked over at Braeden.

"We need to go get the dogs, Uncle," he said. "And Serafina is the only one who can take us to them."

"What will we encounter when we get to this place you speak of?" Mr. Vanderbilt asked her.

"I do not know for sure," she said, "but I think there will be animals in cages."

"Cages . . ." he repeated, his face clouding with dismay as he tried to imagine it. "When would you want to do this?"

Serafina swallowed. "Now, sir," she said, feeling sick to her stomach even as she said it.

"It's pitch dark," he said.

"I don't think we have time to wait, sir. If my suspicions are right, then the dogs are in terrible danger. I think he's going to kill them, sir. We have to go tonight. And one more thing: it should only be yourself and your most trusted men."

"There are many men here who will want to help," Mr. Vanderbilt said. "And if there is something criminal going on, Detective Grathan will insist on coming."

Serafina pursed her lips. "He's the main one who should *not* come, sir. I believe Mr. Grathan to be a grave danger to us."

Mr. Vanderbilt stared at her with his penetrating dark eyes for several long seconds, seeming to take in everything she'd told him. She held his gaze, waiting for him to reply.

"I understand," he said, slowly nodding. "We'll do it exactly as you say."

A half hour later, Mr. Vanderbilt had assembled the rescue party in the courtyard just as he'd promised, including eleven handpicked men on horseback, and Serafina on foot along with two trackers and their dogs. Many of the men carried torches, the flames snapping and flickering in the darkness. When Serafina saw Braeden enter the courtyard on his thoroughbred, her heart sank, but she could tell by the determined look on his face that she couldn't prevent him from coming. And Lady Rowena rode beside him, seeming just as determined. She no longer rode sidesaddle, but astride, the pretense of courtly daintiness set aside. Her cheeks were flush in the chill air. She wore a fashionable riding coat, but it was dark and heavy and well suited to the task. She had pulled her red hair back and tucked it into the coat's hood. Her hands were covered in leather gloves, and she carried a riding stick, like many of the men. She looked the part. Serafina wasn't surprised that the girl had insisted on coming—she just hoped Lady Rowena wouldn't be sorry when they got there.

Mr. Vanderbilt and the hunt master called everyone forward, and the horses set off at a trot. The hunting party rode out of Biltmore just after midnight under the dying glow of a clouded moon.

34

As Serafina walked through the forest with the mounted hunting party all around her, she felt like a general leading an invading army into battle. But the thudding hooves, shifting saddles, jangling bridles, and breathing men made so much noise that it was impossible for her to hear anything else. She split off from the others and traveled ahead of them through the trees so she could better hear the forest around them.

She knew she shouldn't get too far ahead of the others. A swirling mist floated in the low areas of the land and in the boughs of the trees, moving through the forest like waves of ghosts, one after the other, dancing among the rocks and the trunks of the trees, sometimes blocking her view of the horses and the men.

She glanced back at Braeden, Rowena, and Mr. Vanderbilt riding on their horses with the men in a loose wedge formation. She knew that the master of Biltmore had always loved the beauty of the outdoors, but he was not a hunter, in spirit or experience, and he had asked the estate's hunt master to lead the horsemen and the trackers during the search. The hunt master rode in front of the two Vanderbilts and all the other riders. He was a large, commanding man with a gruff voice and stout demeanor, and looked like he had spent most of his life in a saddle. She could see the hunt master watching her with steady eyes, following her movement through the brush ahead of them. She was the only one who knew the way.

The trackers—two rugged-looking men in heavy coats—traveled on foot like she did, holding a pack of six Plott hounds: large and lanky black and brindled dogs that had been bred for hunting bear in these mountains since the seventeen hundreds.

But as she led the search party up the mountain toward the stand of pines where the cages were located, the trackers looked confounded. Their dogs had their noses to the ground but seemed confused, barking and agitated, and sniffing all around. Rather than picking up a distinct scent that they could follow, the Plotts started growling.

"Steady the hounds!" the hunt master ordered the trackers sternly.

"Jesse there is acting like he's on a wildcat," one of the trackers said as he gestured at the dogs on their leashes. "Bax is lookin' like he's on a bear. And old Roamer is snarling like there's somethin' over yonder hill that he's never smelled before."

The hunt master glanced at Serafina.

They had finally come to the stand of pines that she was looking for, but the trees were so thick and the limbs so low that there was no way for them to get their horses through. And she knew enough about hunting to know that there was nothing the hunt master liked less than ordering his riders to get off their horses. He'd rather go around something than dismount, but she was certain that the cages were *through* the pines.

"Straight through these trees," she said, signaling with her hand.

She had no authority to be telling the man how to manage his hunt, but she had to tell him what she knew. She glanced toward Mr. Vanderbilt, who had reined his horse up beside the hunt master.

But before the hunt master could give the call to dismount, an explosion of strange howls erupted from the trees. The barking, yipping, screaming howls put a shiver down Serafina's spine. They weren't the howls of wolfhounds or wolves, but something else. The men looked all around, their eyes white with fear as their horses shifted and turned, crashing into one another.

Pairs of glowing eyes came at them through the darkness, at least fifty, moving this way and that.

The Plott hounds barked and snarled, ready to fight.

"Hold steady, men!" the hunt master shouted, trying to bring order to the rapidly deteriorating situation. "Keep your seat beneath you!"

A snarling, twisting wolflike creature lunged out of the

darkness and attacked the hunt master's horse. The panicked horse went screaming onto its hind legs, rearing and striking.

"Pull back!" the hunt master shouted as more of the wolflike creatures came charging in, biting at the horses' legs, leaping onto the riders and pulling them from their saddles.

Fear exploded in Serafina. These weren't dogs or wolves. They were *coyotes*, a massive band of them, brought into the mountains by an unnatural force. Coyotes didn't normally come to these forests, for the wolves were their enemies.

Filled with panic, she sprinted toward Braeden, Rowena, and Mr. Vanderbilt through kicking horses, snarling coyotes, and screaming men. Her legs burst her forward, propelling her into the mayhem. She ducked and dove, dodging the vicious lunges of the coyotes as she ran.

The coyotes took down the two trackers even as the Plott hounds tore into the coyotes, but there were far too many of the coyotes for the hounds to battle them all.

Braeden and Mr. Vanderbilt were expert riders and had been alert to danger, so neither of them had fallen from their saddles in the initial surprise of the attack. But Mr. Vanderbilt's horse was bucking and shifting and throwing itself around, smashing into tree limbs, nearly knocking poor Mr. Vanderbilt from its back. It seemed as if even their horses had become their enemies now.

"Pull back!" the hunt master shouted as he struck a coyote in the snout with his torch.

"Braeden, come on!" Rowena called, shouting for them to retreat as she struggled to rein in her terrified, thrashing horse.

"We have to keep going!" Braeden screamed, desperately determined to help Cedric and Gidean, but finally even he was forced to pull back with the others.

Many of the men who had been thrown from their horses fled in terror on foot. Those who managed to stay in their saddles yanked their reins around and charged away. But the coyotes pursued them, snapping at their horses' legs and haunches, trying to corner and trap the lumbering horses in the heavy brush.

As the hunting party retreated in disarray back toward Biltmore, Serafina hunkered down to the ground at the base of a tree. She didn't know what to do. She found herself in a dark, quiet patch of the forest, all alone. She watched and listened to the chaos as it receded into the cloak of the forest's mist. A bout of hopelessness swirled through her. She couldn't fight off an entire band of coyotes. She couldn't settle the spirits of those panicked horses or bring calm to those struggling men. A lump formed in her throat as she caught one last glimpse of Braeden, Rowena, and Mr. Vanderbilt as they pulled away. She desperately wanted to follow them home. The thought of being left behind in this place terrified her.

But she did not move.

A dark and frightening thought crept into her mind. The only way she could save Gidean and Cedric was if she carried on alone, sneaking and crawling beneath the black limbs of the pitch-covered trees while the men battled the coyotes in the distance. Her only hope was to creep unseen and unheard into the dark lair of her enemy.

SERAFINA and the TWISTED STAFF

As she developed her plan in her mind, she heard something moving slowly toward her. At first she thought she heard four feet on the ground, but then she realized it wasn't a stalking coyote or wolfhound. The front two legs were softer of foot, more careful. The back two trudged along, sounding heavier. It wasn't *four feet*. It was two hands and two knees.

35

Braeden's head poked through the underbrush.

"Aw, Braeden, you shouldn't have come back!" Serafina said in exasperation. "What did you do?"

"I fell off my horse," he said, trying to sound innocent.

"You liar," she said. "You never fall off your horse!"

"But coyotes were attacking!"

She shook her head. "No, that wasn't it. I saw you, Braeden. You didn't fall off your horse!"

"Fine," he admitted finally. "I broke off from the main party, but my horse was too scared to come back up here. I couldn't convince him to go any farther, but I didn't want to leave you out here, so I slipped off and let him go back with the others. He'll be all right."

"It's not the horse I'm worried about!" she said, perturbed. "You should've stayed with the others."

"I didn't want to leave you alone out here in this terrible place in the dark."

"The darkness is where I belong," she said. "But you don't."

Braeden gestured toward the stand of pines. "I may not be able to see in the dark like you, Serafina, but if our dogs are in there, then I have to help them."

"What happened to Lady Rowena and your uncle? Are they all right?"

"Yes. They stayed with the rest of the hunting party."

"And that's where you should be." She stared at him, angry at his stubbornness. He had no idea what he was getting himself into. But she knew there was no talking him out of it.

"All right," she said finally, and crawled over to him. "We'll go in together, but you must stay close to me, and you must be absolutely quiet."

The two of them ducked below the lowest limbs and crept together into the thick stand of pines. The trunks and the branches and the ground itself were coated with sticky black sap that exuded like dark blood from the bark of the trees. The sap permeated everything with a reeking, sickeningly sweet smell. The upper boughs of the trees blocked the moon and the stars, cloaking the area beneath into a murky black world. Even she had trouble seeing.

She had to put her hand out in front of her to keep from running into dead hanging branches, but each time her fingers touched something in the darkness, the viscid pitch stuck to her fingertips, slowly coating her hands with an oily mucus. Her feet and hands kept sticking to the ground, making little sucking and snapping noises as she moved.

She knew that Braeden must be utterly blind, so she took his hand and put it on her shoulder. "Just hold on to me as we go through," she whispered. She could feel his hand trembling even as he held her. She couldn't imagine how terrifying it must be for him to creep blindly into this terrible place.

As they crept forward, moving from tree trunk to tree trunk along the pitch-coated ground, her nostrils wrinkled at a foul smell. At first she thought it must be the smell of rotting pinesap, but then she realized that it was the smell of animals, of animal waste. Then the smell got much worse.

She heard a hissing, gurgling, boiling sound just ahead and saw the orange flickering light of some sort of cooking fire in the distance.

"What is that?" Braeden whispered uncertainly, finally able to see something.

"That's where we're going," she said.

As they crawled forward into the smoky haze of the fire, Serafina's hand inadvertently touched a cold, flat, slimy surface that she thought was a rock. Looking down, it took her several seconds to realize that it wasn't. It was a gravestone, flat in the ground, so old that the letters and numbers had worn off and nothing was left but a blank surface.

In front of the gravestone, in the area of ground where the body lay below, there was an old mortsafe—a heavy, bolted iron cage, sunk low into the ground, long and narrow like the proportions of a body. She didn't know whether mortsafes were intended to keep grave robbers out or dead bodies in, but it was now being used for an even more horrifying purpose. A small door had been constructed at the end of the iron cage. Inside the cage lay a doe and two spotted fawns, staring out at her, crumpled down so low that they couldn't even stand.

Looking to the right and to the left, she saw that there were many of these old gravestones and iron cages, hundreds of them for as far as she could see. She had encountered the cages here a few nights before, but she hadn't realized they'd been constructed from the iron mortsafes of an old graveyard. There was an entire cemetery beneath the thick forest of pine trees. The graveyard had been abandoned long ago, and the forest of pines had grown on top of it. She looked around her. The cages were filled with animals of all kinds. In the next cage over, a mink ran back and forth, back and forth, desperately looking for a way out. The cage near Braeden held a friend of his: a small red fox, curled up tight and trembling in fear, its eyes staring at Braeden pleadingly.

"We have to let them go!" Braeden said, his voice shaking.

"Wait," she whispered. Seeing all these caged animals, she knew her enemy must be near. They had only so much time to do what they'd come to do. As they crept through the cages toward the fire, they passed a weasel and a family of raccoons. She could feel her pulse starting to pound in her temples, and her limbs starting to shake. She looked all around her, scanning the cages. Somewhere out there in the swirling mist, trapped in the cages beneath the low, dripping limbs of the pine trees, she knew that Gidean and Cedric lay helpless.

Suddenly, Braeden's hand gripped her shoulder so tightly that it hurt. She caught her breath when she saw the silhouette of the man walking in the distance. It was the gray-bearded man of the forest in his boots and his long, weather-beaten coat. He moved with strength and purpose, focused on his work. As he pushed handfuls of branches into the fire, swirls of sparks roiled upward. The blaze snapped and hissed with the new supply of burning sap. Then she saw the source of the terrible smell: the man was boiling something in the black iron pot resting in the fire.

Serafina's muscles jumped and buzzed. She wanted to run away. But at that moment, she heard a *tick-tick-ticking* sound, and then the terrible hissing scream as a barn owl flew in. She shoved Braeden flat to the ground, cowering in fear beneath the searching eyes of the owl as it flew low beneath the branches of the pines, right past them, and over to the fire and the bearded man. The owl dropped a crooked twig at the man's feet and then kept flying.

In response to the passing owl, the bearded man raised his chin and chattered a frightening cry, uttering the *tick-tick-ticking* sound followed by a low, self-satisfied hiss. She saw now that the owl wasn't just his familiar, or a servant under his command. There was alliance in that hiss, a dark and horrible love.

"We shall burn that place down!" he shouted to the owl. She could see his leathery, craggy face. He was a man possessed by a hatred and insanity more murderous than she had ever seen.

Braeden trembled beside her, his face as white as a ghost, his mouth gasping for breath. She clutched him to give him courage.

The man bent down and picked up the twig the owl had dropped. She thought he was going to throw it into the fire with the rest, but in the next moment, there was a trick in her eye, she flinched, and the small twig became as long and stout as a walking stick. It was the staff of power that Waysa had told her about. The Twisted Staff was blackish, thorned, and deeply gnarled, with what looked like a slithering snake or vine curling around and twisting along its length. And at this moment, the staff seemed to possess a seething, pulsing, demonic power, as if it sensed that soon it would gain even more.

At the man's feet lay a dark pile of skinned fur, black and brown and white, the remnants of animals that he had used in his terrible concoction. She couldn't imagine what horrible thing he was doing, but then he raised the Twisted Staff upward and dipped it into the pot, coating it over and over again with the thick, viscous liquid as he mumbled words she could not understand.

Then he drew the dripping staff from the putrid mixture and went over to one of the nearby cages. Serafina looked over and saw with horror what was inside. It was Gidean! Her friend crumpled down onto his haunches, his teeth snarling with anger, but his eyes filled with fear as the man approached the cage. The man pointed the staff at the cage. The cage door flung open. Gidean, his whole body trembling, crawled out of the cage toward the man. *Bite him, Gidean!* she wanted to scream. *Bite him and run!* But Gidean could not. The man was using the Twisted Staff to control him.

As she reached back to clamp her hand over Braeden's mouth, she knew it was too late. Seeing Gidean under the staff's control, Braeden made a sound of anguish. The bearded man's neck snapped around, and he looked straight at Braeden, his silver eyes blazing.

Serafina sprang into attack. She charged straight at him, knowing that her only chance was to take him down before he could lift his hand and throw a spell.

But the man raised his hand to his lips and blew across his open palm.

She felt the breath of death shoot through her. Her body went cold. Her muscles went limp. And she collapsed to the ground.

Braeden collapsed behind her.

Lying on the ground with her breath stolen and her heart stopped, the side of her face in the dirt, she gazed out through unblinking eyes. Braeden lay flat out on the ground beside her, just a few inches away, his eyes wide open, glazed and unmoving, staring at her in terror. She could not turn her head, but on the trunks of the pitch-blackened trees, she saw the flickering shadow of the bearded man moving toward them.

36

Serafina slowly became aware that she was awake, but she could not open her eyes, and she could not move. She could feel the cold earth beneath her and air moving ever so slowly into and out of her lungs, but she could not utter a sound.

She smelled dead pine needles and the sap-covered earth where her face lay against the ground. She tasted dirt in her mouth.

She was lying on her side, her right arm up by her head, her left arm bent beneath her body, twisted behind her at an unnatural angle, her legs crumpled up close to her. She sensed the crawling sensation of the wet sticky pitch on the bare skin of her legs, her arms, and her face, but she could not lift herself from it.

She could hear nothing but the faint and desolate sound of wind in the trees.

Is this how I'm going to die? she thought. And then she thought that it must be. She felt herself sinking down into darkness.

"Serafina!" someone whispered urgently to her, as if determined not to let her lose hope. The voice had no body, no face. It was not Braeden's voice, nor her pa's. And soon her certainty that she had heard the voice drifted away with the wind.

She lost consciousness again and then came back. Time went by. She wasn't sure how long. It could have been a few seconds, or a few minutes or a few hours.

When she was finally able to open her eyes, she still couldn't lift her head. She saw mostly blackened ground, and just above that, a crisscross of bolted iron bars and wire mesh, and through the cage to another cage that contained one of the white swans she had seen on Biltmore's lagoon a few nights before.

"Serafina!" the voice called again.

The sound was coming from the other side of the swan.

She slowly managed to lift her head.

It broke her heart to see a brown-skinned boy with long, shaggy dark hair in the cage there. He looked so small and weak in the cage that she almost didn't recognize him, but his brown eyes were looking back at her, his spirit fierce and unbroken, like a caged feral cat.

"Stay bold, Serafina!" he said, his voice filled with ragged emotion.

"Waysa . . ." she tried to say, but she barely heard her own dry, croaking voice. As she tried to get up, her head bumped against iron bars that held her to the ground. The bearded man had caged her to a grave in an iron mortsafe like all the other animals.

Craning her neck and peering between the iron bars, she looked out of her cage. She could see the bearded man working in his camp a short distance away. Her body jolted with fear at the sight of him, but the cage held her. She could not escape. The hissing, crackling fire glowed with flickering orange light, the sparks rising upward in a swirl and the haze of smoke drifting through the crooked branches of the trees.

The man moved around the fire, slowly feeding it fuel as he tended the iron pot. Splinters of scattered images poured into her mind as she remembered everything she had seen: the owl, the staff, the wolfhounds, the carriage, the horses, the rats, the coyotes. What did it all mean? The man dipped the Twisted Staff into the mixture over and over again, infusing it with its terrible power.

"What happened to you, Waysa?" she whispered. "How did you get here?"

"I had to save the cubs," he said, his voice grave. Serafina imagined that when the bearded man attacked, Waysa had turned to fight him rather than run from him, giving her mother and the cubs the split second they needed to escape.

A fierce wave of emotion filled her muscles with a little bit of strength. She tried to turn her body.

The eyes of a wolf peered at her through the iron bars of one of the adjacent cages. It was her old companion that she'd seen on the mountain ridge. Despite his valiant efforts to lead his pack to the safety of the highlands, they never made it out of the forest. As the wolf gazed at her from behind the bars, her heart sank. There was nothing she could do for him, nor he for her.

She was both relieved and heartbroken that Braeden lay in the cage next to her, his body facedown and outstretched beneath the iron bars of the mortsafe. He looked like the corpse of a boy who had crawled out of his grave but could get no farther, trapped beneath the bars. His body looked utterly lifeless, his skin pale and clammy, but his eyes were open, staring out in bewilderment.

"It's me, Braeden," she whispered over to him, trying to bring him around. She was pretty sure he was alive, but the conjurer's spell had hit him hard. "Wake up! It's me! It's Serafina!"

But even as she tried to rouse him, she wondered what they would do. What would come next? She was surrounded by caged animals. She *was* a caged animal. The bolted iron bars and the wire mesh in between were far too strong for her to break through. She pushed and pulled against the cage. She kicked at it and rammed it with her shoulder. But it made no difference. She could not get out.

37

Serafina tried digging down into the ground, past the pine needles into the dirt. She dug until her fingers bled, but it was no use. The mortsafe went deep into the ground. If she dug down deep enough, she'd find nothing but rotted boards, bones, and body.

The iron bars of the mortsafes were close enough together to keep an adult human from getting through, but on many of the cages, including the one she was in, the bearded man had installed wire mesh to make sure smaller animals could not fit between the iron bars and escape.

"I've tried to get through the wire," Waysa said as she examined the mesh on her cage. He started kicking the wire mesh with all his strength. It barely moved, but as Serafina saw the wire mesh flexing from the pressure of his kicks, she had an idea.

She pressed herself close up against the lower side of her cage. The wire mesh consisted of squares just big enough to fit several fingers through. She grabbed one strand of the mesh tightly in her fingers and bent it. Then she bent it back. She bent it again. And then back again. Over and over again.

"What are you doing?" Waysa whispered.

Serafina did not answer, she just kept bending that one strand of wire back and forth, back and forth. Her fingers were getting raw and her muscles ached. But finally, she felt the wire heating up. She kept bending and bending as fast as she could. Then it snapped! She'd broken the strand!

She couldn't help but smile when she saw the astonished look on Waysa's face. She had just broken metal with her bare hands. She was *magic*.

She immediately started on the next wire, bending, bending, bending, until it snapped in her fingers. "Thank you, Pa!" she whispered to herself as she moved on to the next wire. Working on one strand at a time, she slowly peeled back an area of the wire mesh close to the ground where the space between the iron bars was largest. She tried to crawl through the hole, but it was very tight. She couldn't get through.

"Get down, Serafina!" Waysa whispered a warning.

Serafina froze where she was, clinging to the dirt like a frightened animal as she heard the *tick-tick-ticking* sound and the raspy scream of the owl. It flew right over their heads as it came into the camp. The man hurled the staff up into the sky. It blurred into a twig. The owl caught it in midair with its claws, then disappeared into the trees.

Serafina didn't understand what was happening, but she was more determined than ever to get out. She pressed her face into the dirt and shoved her head into the hole. Buttressing her feet against the other side of the mortsafe, she used the strength of her legs and torso to push her head through the hole, scraping her ears so close that they tore and bled. She shifted her neck, bent in her shoulder blade at her detached collarbone, and wriggled herself into the hole. Once she got some of her head, shoulder, and arm through the hole, she reached out for something to grab onto so she could pull her whole body though, but there was nothing to grab, nothing to pull on. She clawed at the earth, but she found no purchase. Now she was stuck, wedged in the hole. She could move neither back nor forward.

When she looked around for a branch or a rock or something to hold on to, she saw Braeden in the cage next to her working furiously to bend the strands of the wire mesh like she had.

"Hold on, Serafina!" Braeden whispered, but she knew it was no use. His body was larger than hers. Even if he got through the mesh, he couldn't fit between the bars.

Nothing was working. Feeling the panic of entrapment, Serafina started gasping for air. Her heart pounded. She tried to keep her wits about her, but she breathed faster and faster. She looked toward the fire in the distance. How much time did they have before the bearded man came for them?

Finally, Braeden managed to break a small hole through the wire mesh of his cage. Just as she'd suspected, he couldn't fit his body through the narrow gap between the iron bars. But he put his hand through the hole and stretched his arm out toward her. At first, Serafina didn't understand what he was doing, but then she got it. She pressed herself up against the bars of her cage and stretched her arm out toward him. She pushed and pushed, her fingers outstretched. Reaching across the space between the cages, their hands finally clamped together in the middle. "Gotcha!" he said as he grabbed her hand. Then he pulled her toward him.

Now, with Braeden pulling on her arm and her pushing with her legs, she found the leverage she needed. She managed to wriggle herself all the way through the hole and crawled out on the other side. She made it through! She had escaped!

She quickly crawled over to Braeden's cage and tried to open the latch from the outside.

"He's coming!" Waysa whispered frantically.

Serafina heard the thrashing sound of the bearded man's footsteps heading in their direction.

She finally got Braeden's cage open and pulled him out. "Go free the dogs!" she whispered to him. Then she hurried over to Waysa's cage and unlatched it.

The bearded man would be here in a matter of seconds.

As Waysa crawled free, Serafina glanced over. Gidean and Cedric were down on their haunches, excitedly looking at Braeden as he opened their cages. Serafina used the last moment to quickly unlatch the wolf's cage. Her young wolf friend looked at her with gratefulness in his eyes. Then she raced away, knowing that the bearded man was just steps behind her.

She and Braeden and the others fled the cages, ducking low beneath the limbs of the pines as they ran.

Behind her, she heard the snarling attack of the freed wolf as it leapt from its cage at the bearded man. She had no idea what would happen next, but at least the wolf had a fighting chance.

Serafina, Braeden, Waysa, and the two dogs fled into the cover of the pines. Waysa led the way, often scouting ahead for danger. Serafina didn't know how it was possible, but Gidean seemed to have regained some of his old strength and speed. Cedric was a heavy dog, unused to running long distances, but he was determined to keep up. Serafina ran at Braeden's side, making sure he didn't fall behind. They finally escaped the blackened pines and entered the oaks, but they did not slow down. Their fear pushed them onward. They ran for miles.

But partway back to Biltmore, Braeden collapsed, too tired to continue. She let him rest for ten seconds, but then pulled him back up onto his feet. "Get up, Braeden!" she told him. "We've got to get home!"

They ran some more, but Braeden finally crumpled in exhaustion. Too tired to run any farther, he did not give up or ask the others to slow down. He called Cedric over to him. "I need your help, my friend," he said as he climbed onto the Saint Bernard's back and held on.

"Come on, Cedric! Come on, boy! Let's go!" Serafina called the dog, and together they ran. Coming from a long line of rescue dogs, Cedric seemed to understand exactly what they wanted. He charged forward with new speed and purpose, carrying the young master along with him.

They ran through the hickory and the hemlock, through the alder and the elm. They crossed thickets and meadows, streams and ravines, pushed by a fear darker than they had ever known.

As the faint light of Biltmore House finally came into view near dawn, Serafina sensed that they had escaped the horror behind them. She slowed and looked over at Waysa. They breathed heavily as they walked beside each other.

"I have to go back to Biltmore," she said.

Waysa nodded. "I'll go find your mother and the cubs and make sure they're safe." Then he stopped her with his hand and looked at her with new ferocity in his eyes. "You were right. We can't run from this fight. I will rejoin you later. Stay bold, Serafina."

"Stay bold, Waysa," she said in return as they quickly embraced, and then Waysa dove into the underbrush and disappeared.

Braeden watched her say good-bye to Waysa, and then said, "I see you found the boy from the forest."

"He joined with my mother and the cubs. His name is Waysa."

"He reminds me of you," Braeden said, his voice weak and tired, but filled with a kindness that she did not expect.

"Me too," she agreed.

"Do you want to go with him?" Braeden asked uncertainly. He looked toward the house in the distance. "The dogs and I can make it to Biltmore on our own from here."

"No," she said. "I want to go home with you."

Braeden nodded, and they continued on together toward Biltmore with Gidean and Cedric at their sides.

"Look," Serafina said when she saw a rider galloping at high speed across the large lawn in front of the house. The rider was up on her stirrups, leaning forward in the saddle, galloping at incredible speed, her long red hair flowing behind her. It was Lady Rowena!

Rowena rode into the stable courtyard.

When Serafina and Braeden and the two dogs walked into the courtyard a few moments later, a force of thirty men were gathering, some on foot, some with horses.

"Mount up, men," Mr. Vanderbilt shouted from atop his horse. "We're going back out."

Serafina and Braeden looked around at the ragged group. Many of the men from the original hunting party were wounded and exhausted. They had been fighting the coyotes in the forest all night. The horses had suffered the worst, and the trackers had lost all but one of the Plott hounds. The badly shaken hunt master, who had dismounted from his sweating, terrified horse and now sat collapsed on the ground, appeared too shocked by what they'd been through to even rouse himself. But most of the men were mounting fresh horses, and new men were joining the effort.

Rowena was right there with Mr. Vanderbilt, on a new horse and ready to ride. Her hair was hanging down, her face was scratched, and she looked exhausted, but she seemed determined to help in the search.

"Come on, hurry," Rowena was calling to the others as she wheeled her horse around. "We have to go and look for them!"

Serafina's pa, several of the stablemen, and a dozen other servants were also joining the group.

But when Mr. Vanderbilt pulled his horse around, he saw Braeden and Serafina and the dogs coming toward him.

"Thank God," Mr. Vanderbilt said. He dismounted, dropped his reins, and took the exhausted Braeden into his arms.

"Serafina," her pa said, relieved, as he came toward her and pulled her into his chest.

"I'm all right, Pa," she said. "I'm not hurt."

As she hugged her pa, Serafina saw Rowena dismount and

embrace Braeden, obviously relieved that he was still alive. The other men were patting the young master's back and welcoming him home.

Mr. Vanderbilt knelt down and scruffed Cedric's neck. "It's good to see you, boy," he said as he petted his dog. Then Mr. Vanderbilt's dark eyes rose up and looked at Serafina.

"I'm sorry, sir," she said, her voice shaking, fearful that he'd be angry at her for leading them into such a catastrophe. As she and her pa turned toward Mr. Vanderbilt, she said, "I had no idea that was going to happen."

"None of us have ever seen anything like that," he said. He wasn't angry with her. His voice was filled with a sense of common purpose. They were a pack. They were in this together.

"Could the coyotes have been infected with rabies?" her pa asked.

"I hope to God not," the veterinarian said, overhearing their conversation as he tended to the slashed leg of a nearby horse. "If it's rabies, then all the men, horses, and dogs who were bitten last night will be dead within days, and there's nothing we can do about it."

"It didn't look like rabies to me," Mr. Vanderbilt said, shaking his head. "There had to be fifty coyotes, and they had a deliberateness in their eyes."

The hunt master shook his head. "Those animals were possessed," he mumbled, his eyes glazed with disbelief.

"We need to go back, Uncle," Braeden said.

"Go back?" Mr. Vanderbilt said in surprise.

"There are still animals up there that need our help."

Mr. Vanderbilt shook his head. "I'm sorry, Braeden. We're not going back out right now. We can't risk it. Everyone is exhausted. We need to rest and regroup."

"It was awful, Uncle," Braeden said, and then proceeded to describe the bearded man and the animals in the cages. "Serafina got me and the dogs out of there, and then we ran."

When Mr. Vanderbilt looked at Serafina, she could see the gratitude in his expression, but she knew the fight wasn't over. "We need to find Mr. Grathan, sir," she said. "He's involved in this."

"I was suspicious of him from the start," Mr. Vanderbilt said. "He represented himself as an officer of the law, so I didn't think I should interfere with his investigation, but I hired a private detective to check into his credentials."

"What did you find out?" Braeden asked.

"Mr. Grathan has no association with any city or state agency. He's a fraud."

"What are we going to do, Uncle?" Braeden asked.

"I've sent word for the Asheville police to come at once. They'll arrest him."

"But where is Grathan now?" Serafina asked.

"We've searched for him. He's not in the house," Mr. Vanderbilt said. "But he may still be on the grounds."

"I think Grathan is far more dangerous than he seems, sir," Serafina said. "And I fear that the police will be coming on horseback or carriage and will run into the same type of problem we did."

Mr. Vanderbilt nodded. "We'll arm several groups of men

and start looking for Grathan on the grounds. If and when the police arrive, we'll go back up into that area, free those animals, and destroy the cages. Until then, I want all of you to stay in the house and stay safe."

As the men continued talking, Serafina, Braeden, and Rowena huddled beneath the arch of the Porte Cochere, the carriage entrance that led into the house.

"What happened?" Rowena asked, her voice quivering.

"We're all right," Braeden said. "We got the dogs. That's the important thing."

"I was so worried about you," she said, looking at both Braeden and Serafina. Serafina realized that danger and death seemed to erase the lines of class. Suddenly, everyone was the same, fighting to hold on to their lives and the people around them. She saw it in Mr. Vanderbilt, her pa, the hunt master, the trackers, and the men on their horses willing to go out into fearsome dangers to rescue her and Braeden. And now she saw it in Lady Rowena.

"Thank you for helping us, Rowena," Braeden said.

"When my father sent me here to Biltmore, he told me to make friends," Lady Rowena said, looking at the two of them and smiling wanly. "I think maybe I have."

"You definitely have," Braeden said.

"Will your father be coming to Biltmore soon?" Braeden asked.

"I believe he'll be here rather sooner than we all expect," Rowena said. "He's coming for Christmas."

Serafina thought she sensed something strange in Rowena

when she said this. Was it sadness? Worry? She couldn't quite place it.

"Are you eager to see him?" Serafina asked.

"The truth is," Rowena said, "my father thinks I am a rather silly little girl."

"I'm sure that's not true," Braeden said.

Rowena shook her head. "No, it's true. I'm afraid my father has never thought too much of me. But pretty soon, one way or another, he's going to have to start."

"He'd be very proud of you if he knew how brave you were last night," Serafina said, trying to encourage her.

But as they were talking, Rowena looked like she was going to keel over right where she stood. Exhaustion had finally begun to catch up with the poor girl. Braeden reached out to steady her.

"If you will excuse me," Lady Rowena said finally, touching Braeden's arm and closing her eyes for a moment like she was going to faint, "I'm feeling rather tired. I'm going to my room to take a bath and change into some clean clothes."

Braeden nodded. "Get some rest and we'll do the same. My uncle and the men will take care of things now."

As two of the maids helped the bedraggled, mud-splattered Lady Rowena limp slowly back to the house, Serafina heard her mutter in bewildered shock, "Oh dear, I think I may have gotten dirt on my dress." She was so exhausted she was nearly delirious.

Serafina stayed with Braeden. As she looked over at Mr. Vanderbilt talking to her pa and the other men, she knew they were making sensible decisions, but she couldn't get over the feeling that it wasn't enough, that everyone, including her, was missing something. It was as if they were putting together a puzzle, and they thought they were almost done, but there was a whole other box of pieces that they didn't even know about.

She watched as the stablemen washed the blood from the courtyard bricks and the maids cleaned the mud from the steps that led into the house.

"Come on," Serafina said to Braeden, and they began to walk along the front of the house. "We need to figure this out."

"Whoever that man was last night, he seemed insane," Braeden said.

"Like he was consumed by some sort of feud or blood vengeance."

"He said he was going to burn the place down," Braeden said.

Serafina remembered the chilling words.

"What do you think he was talking about?" Braeden asked.

"I'm not sure," she said.

"Do you think he was talking about Biltmore?" Braeden asked.

As they reached the front entrance of the house, Serafina glanced up at the carved stone archway above the front door. It depicted a strange-looking bearded man brandishing a long spear or staff of some kind.

"I don't know. It's definitely possible. Does the Vanderbilt family have enemies?" she asked. "What about your uncle? Does anyone hate him or want to do him harm?"

"No, I don't think so," Braeden said. "He's a good man."

"I know he is," Serafina said. "But is there something from his past that we don't know? What do we know about his life back in New York before he came here? Or all his trips to Europe and all over the world? Could it be that he came to the remote mountains of North Carolina for a reason?"

"You think he was trying to escape something?"

"Or maybe *someone*? I don't know," she said.

"Come on," Braeden said, leading her into the house. "I have an idea."

The two of them were tired, dirty, and hungry, but they were too intent on solving the mystery to stop now. Serafina followed Braeden down the gallery and into the Library.

"What are we looking for?" Serafina asked as they entered, not sure how Mr. Vanderbilt's collection of books could help them.

"My uncle keeps his travel records here," Braeden said as he went over to one of the cabinets. "Maybe we'll find something."

Serafina went to Braeden's side and tried to help him look. But she wasn't sure what they were looking for.

She found a set of black leather-bound journals entitled *Books I Have Read—G.W.V.* As she flipped through the pages, she saw that Mr. Vanderbilt had been recording the title and author of every book he'd read since 1875, when he was twelve years old. There were thousands of entries over the years, in English, French, and other languages.

Braeden found evidence of his uncle's many trips throughout the United States and abroad, to England, France, Italy,

China, Japan, and many other countries. And she knew that the house was full of art, sculpture, and artifacts from his travels. In fact, she'd just shattered one of them. Any one of those artifacts could have been haunted or cursed in some way, which might explain a blood vengeance against Mr. Vanderbilt.

But the more she thought about it, the more one particular thought came to her mind. The man she'd seen on the road that first night hadn't struck her as a New Yorker or any other kind of northerner or foreigner. His skin was craggy with the weathered cracks of these mountain winds, his mustache and beard were long and gray like many of the local elders', and his voice was tinged with the sound of the mountain folk. She could not be sure from their brief and terrifying encounters, but he seemed like an Appalachian man.

She remembered the disturbing words he'd screamed to the owl: "We shall burn that place down!"

"Let's look into the records of Biltmore House," she said.

"Not my uncle's travels?"

"No, let's focus on Biltmore," she said, more confident now.

"Those are over here," he said, leading her to a different set of boxes.

As they dug through the papers, it was hard to imagine finding any answers there, but when Braeden opened a box of scratchy old photographs, she leaned in closer.

The first photograph she examined showed a vast stretch of clear-cut land with nothing but stumps and weeds, a team of twenty or thirty mules, a couple of wagons piled with firewood, and a score of scroungers with axes. It was hard to imagine, but judging by the view of the mountains in the background, it appeared to be the hilltop on which Biltmore was constructed. The clearing was so open and bare and treeless. There were no gardens, no woods, just scarred and empty land. This was how it had looked when Mr. Vanderbilt bought the land years before.

The next photograph showed hundreds of stonemasons, bricklayers, carpenters, and other craftsmen building the lower floors of Biltmore House. There were men and women, white folk and black folk, Americans and foreigners, northerners and southerners, and many mountain folk. Her heart warmed when she spotted her pa in one of the photographs, working on a geared crane system among many other men. She smiled, for in her mind, she'd always imagined her pa working alone, building Biltmore almost by himself, for that was how she'd always seen him working. She realized how foolish she had been. He had been but one of thousands of men who had worked for six years. It was amazing to see the scaffolded walls of Biltmore rising from nothingness in photograph after photograph.

A while later, as she searched through the documents of Biltmore trying to find the clues they needed, Serafina looked over at Braeden. Exhausted, he had fallen asleep in one of the cushioned chairs. Serafina let him sleep, but she kept looking.

"I'm starving," Braeden announced when he awoke. They quickly retrieved some food from the kitchen. But as soon as they'd eaten and washed up, they went back to work.

Later that afternoon, as Braeden was digging through yet another box, he handed her a photograph. "Look at this one."

Something about it caught Serafina's eye. Like the other photographs, this one was filled with men and wooden scaffolding, and the half-built Biltmore rising in the background. She wasn't even sure what the photographer had been trying to make a picture of, other than the construction site itself. Some of the men in the picture were working, some talking, some looking at the camera, others not. When she studied the photograph more closely, one of the men drew her attention. The image was so small it was difficult to tell, but he had a heavily wrinkled face and a long gray mustache and beard. He was not wearing a long coat or carrying a walking stick, but he was gazing into the camera and his eyes looked like dots of silver. It was their enemy—the man she'd seen in the forest. This was him. She was sure of it. That meant he wasn't a forest haint or nightmarish specter, but a real person. At least, he had been years before.

"Braeden, look at this," Serafina said, showing him the photograph. "We need to know who this man is."

"Then we need to talk to Mr. Olmsted," Braeden said.

As Braeden led Mr. Olmsted into the Library, Serafina watched the balding, gray-bearded old man carefully.

"How can I help the two of you?" he asked as he made his way into the room, using his wooden cane for balance. "Sounds like it was a bad business all around last night, especially for you two."

A little startled that Mr. Olmsted was so aware of what was going on, Braeden looked over at Serafina, who was standing by the giant globe.

Serafina shook her head slowly to Braeden. *Don't talk about it. Just get on with our question.*

"Sir," Braeden said, "since you were in charge of many of

the work crews during Biltmore's construction, we were wondering if you could help us with some photographs we found."

"I can certainly try, Master Braeden," he said as he settled onto the sofa in front of the fireplace. "This looks like a nice, warm spot."

"So here is the photograph that we—"

"Perhaps we should have a nice hot cup of tea before we get started," Mr. Olmsted said, seeming not to hear that Braeden had already started talking.

"Uhhh . . ." Braeden hesitated, glancing again at Serafina. "Certainly, of course," he said as he went over to the wall and pressed the button for the butler's pantry.

"While we're waiting for the tea, perhaps we can look at this photograph," Serafina said, taking the photo from Braeden and walking over to Mr. Olmsted.

"We certainly can, Serafina," Mr. Olmsted said. It startled her when Mr. Olmsted used her name. She didn't even realize that he knew she existed. But then he patted the cushion next to him and invited her to sit beside him. Surprised, she sat on the sofa with him and put the photograph in his hands.

"Oh, this is an old one. . . ." Mr. Olmsted said, studying the photograph with interest. His hands trembled as he held it.

"Do you recognize this man here?" Serafina asked, pointing.

"You rang, sir?" the footman said as he came into the Library in his black-and-white livery.

"Mr. Olmsted would like a cup of tea, please," Braeden said.

"Right away, sir," the footman said, and exited.

Serafina watched as Mr. Olmsted studied the face in the photograph. His expression started out mildly curious, as if he was remembering the fond days of old when he was designing the gardens, sculpting the land, and supervising the crews as they planted thousands upon thousands of trees, bushes, and flowers. But then his expression shifted. He narrowed his eyes and brought the photograph up close to his face.

"Maybe this will help, sir," Braeden said, handing him a magnifying glass he'd pulled from a nearby table.

"Oh, yes, thank you, Master Braeden," Mr. Olmsted said, and studied the photograph. "Yes, I remember this fellow," he said finally.

"Who was he?" Serafina asked.

For several seconds, Mr. Olmsted seemed lost in thought, as if he was trying to figure out how to answer her question. "Well, I will tell you a story about a piece of land not too far from here," he said finally. "Years ago, George Vanderbilt was traveling the country with his mother. He was still a young man, just twenty-six years old. He went out riding his horse one day in the mountains, and he drew rein at the top of a hill. He thought the prospect of the distant scenery very fine. It occurred to him that one day he would like to build a house in that location. He bid his lawyer to see if it was possible to purchase that particular parcel of land. Finding the price to be cheap and the owner anxious to sell, he instructed his lawyer to buy that land and all around it. After securing many thousands of acres, George finally invited me to the location and took me out to that spot on the hill. He said to me, 'Now, I have brought you here to examine this land and tell me if I have been doing anything very foolish.'"

Mr. Olmsted smiled as he remembered his friend's words.

"What did you tell him?" Braeden asked. "Was it foolish?"

"Well, I told him the hard truth of it. The site had a good distant outlook, but the land itself had been abused by scavengers and subsistence farming for many years, the soil was depleted, and the woods were miserable, the very hillsides eroding for lack of trees and undergrowth. The squatters who occupied the area didn't own the land, but they had cut down the trees for their cabins and fuel, and most especially to sell the wood in the city. I watched as these squatters drew jags of hickory cordwood to the city in their carts, selling the wood to the highest bidder. You see, back then, wood was almost a form of currency, and these men were stealing it right out of the forest until there was no forest left, and then they'd go on to the next mountain. They had chopped and burned most of the forest in the area."

"Burned?" Braeden asked in dismay.

Mr. Olmsted nodded. "After cutting down all the trees, they made grazing fields for their cattle and hogs. The native cherry, tulip, black walnut, locust, and birch that were so vital to these mountains had all been destroyed. Corn, grain, and tobacco had been grown year after year until the soil was worn out. This was not unusual for the cotton states after the war. Much of the land had been ravaged and lay in a most desperate state."

"So my uncle had made a terrible mistake just like he

feared," Braeden said in astonishment. "Did he abandon that property and come and find the Biltmore land with all its beautiful trees?"

Mr. Olmsted smiled a slight but devilish grin beneath his mustache, as if Braeden's words had pleased him. "Not exactly. I told your uncle that the hilltop on which he hoped to build a house did indeed have a lovely view, and the distant acres had potential. I explained that with extensive planting, I thought we could rebuild the natural environment that had been lost. It would take time and money, thousands upon thousands of plantings, and years to grow. It had never been done on this scale before, but if we could do it, then it would set an example for reforestation throughout the South and, indeed, throughout all of America. We would show the way to conserve and build our forests, rather than just cut them down."

"Wait," Braeden said. "I don't understand. Are you saying that was *Biltmore*?"

Mr. Olmsted smiled. "You are currently standing in the exact spot on which your uncle sat on his horse, looked across the mountain view, and decided he wanted to build a house."

"But all the beautiful trees and the gardens . . ." Braeden said.

"We planted them," Mr. Olmsted said simply.

Serafina sat mesmerized, listening to Mr. Olmsted. Unlike Braeden, who was a relative newcomer to the estate, she had grown up here from the very beginning with her pa, so she knew the story, but she still enjoyed hearing it. It amazed her the way Mr. Olmsted thought about things on such a vast scale, across the mountains and the whole country, and over decades of time. It seemed like she spent most of her time trying to survive the next few seconds. She couldn't even imagine what it must be like to envision the landscape decades in advance.

But her thoughts soon turned to the dark business that had brought them to this moment.

"But who is the man in the photograph, Mr. Olmsted?" she asked.

"Ah, yes," Mr. Olmsted said, turning more serious. "That's where our story continues. That same year, as we began the reclamation work, we soon learned that the clear-cutting and selling of the wood wasn't just happenstance. It wasn't just individual scavengers passing through. There was a depraved and conniving man named Uriah organizing it all. He didn't have any more right to this land than the other squatters, but he was a trickster, a deceiver. He did favors for people and then held them accountable. He lent money on ill terms. Most of the squatters in the area were obligated to him in some way or another, and the others feared him, for those who opposed him met with violent ends. By the time we arrived, he controlled them all. I think he must have been an old slaver or something because he seemed to relish having power over other people. He seemed obsessed with controlling *everything*."

"But my uncle had bought the land," Braeden said, confused.

"That's right, he had. Over a hundred twenty-five thousand acres, covering four counties. He had bought it lawfully from its original owners, but these marauders of the forest did not care who legally owned the land, and neither did Uriah. They had been cutting these trees for years and no one was going to stop them. To Uriah, this land was his domain and his alone."

His domain and his alone, Serafina thought.

"None of us realized when we started the reclamation of the land and the construction of the house that we'd have to deal with this Uriah fellow. Despite the power he had held over the local squatters for many years, it was obvious to us that Uriah's better days were behind him. I think he might have been injured in the war or weakened by a devastating disease. He was in bad shape. He seemed desperate in his dealings with us, like he was barely hanging on to the last vestiges of the corrupted empire he'd built here. We couldn't figure out why he didn't just give up his illegal claims and go away. It was like his very life depended on it. In any case, he obviously wasn't the type of man to go easily. He started putting up a serious fight."

"What did my uncle do?" Braeden asked.

"Well, we wouldn't let a man like Uriah get anywhere near your uncle, of course. But Mr. McNamee, the estate superintendent, had plenty of run-ins with the wretch, as did Mr. Hunt, the house's architect, and I. One confrontation after another. We began bypassing Uriah and dealing with the squatters directly. We gave them jobs and farmland to work. We needed the help and they were happy to join us. Many of them settled into cabins on the property or found homes in town. But Uriah hated us, challenged us constantly, telling us what we could and couldn't do, what boundaries we could and couldn't cross, as if he himself owned the land. We were in the right by morals and the law, so it would have been easy to discount the man, but I tried to deal with him fairly. I never trusted him, but I sensed that he was far more sinister than he seemed, and I was loath to make him too sharp an enemy. There's nothing more dangerous than a desperate man. But Mr. Hunt didn't share my trepidation of Uriah. He treated him with all the respect he deserved. Which is to say, none at all. And Uriah despised Mr. Hunt for it."

"But Uriah didn't know Mr. Vanderbilt?" Serafina asked, confused.

"Not personally, no, but he definitely knew *of* him. Uriah hated George Vanderbilt most of all, for he saw George as the master of all his misfortune."

"But it wasn't my uncle's fault!" Braeden insisted.

"No, it wasn't," Mr. Olmsted agreed. "But Uriah didn't see it that way."

Serafina and Braeden remained quiet as the footman entered the room with a silver tray of fine Biltmore-monogrammed china, and then proceeded to serve Mr. Olmsted his tea. Slowly, one by one, he set out a finely decorated saucer, a teacup, a tea-pot, a bowl of sugar, a teaspoon, and a creamer, and then he slowly poured the steaming tea while they all waited in silence. It seemed like it was taking forever. When the footman was finally gone, Serafina jumped right back into the conversation.

"What happened to Uriah in the end?" Serafina asked.

Mr. Olmsted took a sip of his tea and then set the cup down on its saucer with a light *tink*. "Well, he confronted us one too many times, and we all lost our patience. I'm afraid we had a most violent exchange of words. Finally, Mr. McNamee

Search

ordered his security men, more than twenty armed men on horseback, to tie his hands and take Uriah away by force."

"What did they do to him?" Braeden asked.

"They took him by train to the coast. I believe they mentioned something about putting him on a ship bound for foreign lands. In any case, we were glad to see the back of him."

"Uriah must have been very angry about that," Serafina said.

"Anger doesn't begin to describe his state of mind. I won't repeat all the obscenities he cast at us, but he cursed us up and down and vowed he'd return and kill us all. 'Even if it takes me a hundred years,' he screamed, 'I'm going to come back here and burn your house to the ground!'"

"Wait," Serafina said. "Is that actually what he said, those exact words?" A lump formed in her throat, for she already knew the answer. She could just imagine hearing him scream those words. In fact, she was pretty sure she already had.

She sucked in a breath. At long last, she had finally marked her enemy. This man, Uriah, was a shifter and a conjurer like Waysa had said, kin to the white-faced owl, sorcerer of the dark arts, his power tied to the land. He was the old man of the forest that the mountain folk told stories about around their fires at night. He was the deceiver and master of the tree-killing squatters that Mr. Olmsted had seen. And he was the enemy that her mother and father and the other catamounts had fought against and weakened twelve years before. By the time of Biltmore's construction, Uriah could no longer hold on to his malicious realm. But when he was cast out into the world, he began regathering his strength, finding new dark arts to wield, turning his pain and his hatred into a black and sinister magic more powerful than ever before—all so that one day he could come back to these mountains, burn Biltmore to the ground, and reclaim his dark domain.

She knew now that when she put on the Black Cloak, it had deceived her, tried to convince her that it had been created for good, but it hadn't. Uriah had pulled Mr. Thorne into his web of deceit and sent him into Biltmore to gather souls, to gather power. And now Uriah was making the Twisted Staff to give him control over the animals. Uriah wanted the people, and the animals, and the forest, and the land, and he was going to use his demons and his devices to do it. He wanted to control it all.

"Are you all right?" Braeden asked, touching her arm.

She blinked and pulled herself out of her thoughts and looked at him. "Yes, I'm all right, I'm sorry, go ahead."

"Mr. Olmsted," Braeden asked, "would it truly be possible for someone to burn down Biltmore?"

"I'm not the architect, but I can tell you what I know."

"Pardon me, Mr. Olmsted," Serafina interjected suddenly as a thought came into her mind. "What happened to Mr. Hunt?"

"In the last year of the house's construction, just a few months before the greatest work of his life was completed, our friend Mr. Hunt sadly passed away."

"He died?" Braeden asked.

"Yes, I'm afraid so. We were all very shocked and devastated by the terrible turn of events."

"How did he die?" Serafina asked.

"He got a cold first, and then a bad cough, and then his gout flared up. The doctors weren't sure, but in the end, it appeared that he died of heart failure."

"A cold?" Braeden said, shocked. "It started with a cold?"

This news seized Serafina with new fear. No one died from a cold. Was this what was happening to Mrs. Vanderbilt? Was it the same sickness? Had Uriah cast a spell on the mistress of Biltmore?

"You were going to tell us about the possibility of fire," Braeden urged Mr. Olmsted.

"As you can imagine, Mr. Hunt was very concerned about fire at Biltmore, and being a shrewd man, he incorporated many defenses against it. First, he built the entire underlying structure of the house from steel girders, brick walls, and stone, rather than wood. Second, the house is divided into six separate sections so that if a fire did start, it could not spread. And third, there are fire detectors throughout the house—all tied together by an electric alarm system."

When Mr. Olmsted said these words, Serafina looked at Braeden and Braeden looked at her. *The rats . . .*

"It was all beyond me, of course," Mr. Olmsted continued. "I'm a planter of trees, not an electrical engineer, but I remember that it was all very advanced."

"But what if someone lit the fire on purpose?" Serafina asked.

Mr. Olmsted shook his head. "They might try, but thanks to Mr. Hunt, it would be difficult to succeed. First, they would need to defeat the fire alarm, and second, they would need to know the internal details of the house's six sections to know exactly where to light the fires."

"Did Uriah see all that when the house was being built?" Braeden asked.

"Oh, no, he had no access to such information."

"Is there a way someone could find out about it?" Braeden asked.

"Well, I suppose. The details of Mr. Hunt's construction are described in his drawings."

"Where are those?" Serafina asked.

"Don't worry," Mr. Olmsted said. "No one could ever reach those plans. They are kept hidden and protected under lock and key in this very room."

After Mr. Olmsted left the Library, Braeden looked at Serafina. "What are we going to do?"

"First, you need to tell your uncle about what we've learned. I'll go ask my pa to make sure the fire alarm system is working. But before I do that, do you remember the night we were attacked by the horde of rats?"

"We were going to search Grathan's room."

"But the rats stopped us," she said. "Then the dogs went missing. I don't know where Grathan has gone to, but I'm going to sneak into his room and search it."

"You be careful," Braeden said as he nodded his agreement. He glanced out the window toward the setting sun. "When I talk to my uncle, I'll also find Rowena. She'll be wondering where we are."

"Lady Rowena was very brave last night," Serafina said. "You go find her. Let's meet on the back Loggia in half an hour."

"Got it," Braeden said.

As she headed up the back stairs to the third floor, she tried to think everything through. It was clear that Uriah had conjured the Twisted Staff to help him destroy Biltmore and the Vanderbilts. But just as Waysa had said, Uriah didn't fight straight on. He wasn't wielding the staff himself. He had sent in Grathan, his apprentice and spy. When she came to the hallway that led to the Van Dyck Room, she paused and took a deep breath. She'd tried to get into this room multiple times before and failed, but this time she was determined to do it.

She crept down the hallway and pressed her ear to the door, listening for movement within. When she didn't hear anything, she slowly turned the doorknob. It was locked. She wished she had Mrs. King's master key ring, but she didn't.

She ran down the corridor, slipped into a heating vent, and climbed through the wall. It took her a while to find her way through the shafts, but she finally found the brass register she was looking for and pushed into Mr. Grathan's room.

She felt like she was crawling into a dragon's lair. But she found herself in an elegantly attired chamber, with goldenrod damask wallpaper, a parquet wood floor, a Persian rug, a small fireplace, and chestnut furniture. The walls were adorned with Van Dyck prints hanging on the wall by long steel wires. It surprised her, but there was nothing obviously wrong or out of place about the room. *I guess there's no dead cat,* she thought, remembering Essie's expression.

But the room wasn't entirely empty, either. A worn shirt and a wrinkled pair of trousers lay draped over one of the chairs. Three leather suitcases sat on the floor. It made her palms sweat to think about it, but Mr. Grathan could come back at any moment.

She searched the room as fast as she could, looking for shoes and clothing stained with pinesap or the black smudges of fire coals. It crossed her mind that she might even find incriminating containers of the highly flammable sap itself. She reckoned the pine forest wasn't just a way for Uriah and Grathan to conceal themselves, but part of their plan to destroy Biltmore. Her pa had told her once that there was nothing hotter than a forest fire burning through a stand of pines, that the trunks of the trees actually exploded when the sap boiled. It would be an ideal way to start a fire inside a house, even one that was designed not to burn.

When she didn't find what she was looking for, she opened one of his leather suitcases and rummaged through it. Nothing but clothes. She opened up the next suitcase. Still nothing. After checking the third, she finally stopped. She gazed around the room, frustrated.

There's nothing here. . . .

From what she could find, Mr. Grathan appeared to be a normal, everyday man. She pursed her lips and breathed through her nose, perturbed.

This doesn't make sense. . . .

Where were the fire matches and containers of pinesap? Where were the books filled with pentagrams, runes, and evil spells? Grathan had been so determined to make sure no one entered his room, but what had he been doing? Hiding his stupid toothbrush?

There has to be something here. . . .

She went back and double-checked the leather suitcases. She searched them more thoroughly this time, looking for unusual seams or details that seemed out of place. Then she found it. There was a small hidden compartment in the lining of one of the cases.

Now, this is interesting. . . .

Inside, she found newspaper clippings—some tattered, going back years, others more recent—but they were all articles about hauntings, strange disappearances, and gruesome murders. Many of the names and cities in the articles were underlined.

What are you doing, Mr. Grathan?

Along with the clippings, she found an old, tattered map of the United States. Each of the locations mentioned in the various articles was circled and also marked with what looked like a small *X*. But then she realized they weren't *X*'s. They were little crosses. And even more disturbing, some of the locations were marked with more than one.

Her first thought was that he was obsessed with following reports of occult and supernatural phenomenon. But then she realized that maybe he wasn't just a follower. Maybe he was the *cause* of these events.

Wherever he goes, people die.

Her heart began to pound. She dug through the clippings again, checking the date on each one. The headline of the most recent one read, *The Mysterious Disappearance of Montgomery Thorne.*

Grathan truly had come to investigate Mr. Thorne's disappearance, but he wasn't a police detective. Why had he come?

Besides Mr. Thorne, three names were mentioned in the article, the known residents of Biltmore Estate: George, Edith, and Braeden Vanderbilt.

This isn't good. . . .

Most of the circles on the map were worn and faded, but there was one that stood out: the circle that marked the location of Biltmore Estate. There was no cross beside it.

After going to all these other places, he's come here. . . .

She gazed around the room, trying to think.

The room is so empty, so few clues. But there has to be a way . . .

She stood and she turned.

How can I see what can't be seen?

She noticed a slight discoloration on the floor in front of one of the upholstered chairs. She got down on her hands and knees and put her nose to that area of the carpet.

It's dirt from a shoe. . . . It's a scuff mark. . . . Mr. Grathan sat in this chair. . . .

She moved upward and ran her nose slowly along the arm of the chair, sniffing for scents. At first she couldn't pick up anything other than the fabric itself. Then she caught a faint but extremely distinct smell.

I've smelled this before. . . .

It was the scent of some kind of powdery stone. And she could smell the lingering trace of metal. It seemed so familiar. She could picture it in her mind, but she couldn't think of its name. It was a small, rectangular, smooth gray stone.

It's a whetstone! That's what my pa called it.

She'd seen her pa use a whetstone in the workshop to scrape a steel blade until its gleaming edges were razor sharp.

She swallowed.

Grathan sat in this chair and sharpened a bladed weapon. . . .

Her chest began to rise and fall more heavily, her lungs wanting more air. She tried to think it through.

Uriah summoned Grathan here. But Grathan isn't just a spy. . . . He's an assassin!

He isn't just a murder investigator. He's the murderer!

She couldn't help but look around the room, but she'd already searched it. There was no weapon to be found.

How does he carry the weapon and conceal it?

And more important, who has he come to kill?

She remembered that Essie and Rowena had told her that Grathan had asked many questions about Mr. Thorne, Gidean, and Braeden. One was already dead. One was a dog.

There was only one name remaining. . . .

When she heard a noise outside the room, she hit the floor and slid under the bed.

She waited and listened, her chest rapidly pulling air into her lungs.

She heard the muffled sounds.

There was some sort of commotion out in the corridor, people talking, a sense of alarm.

Her chest filled with panic. She sniffed the air for the smell of smoke, but didn't detect any.

She quickly crawled out from under the bed and went over to the door. When she heard Essie's voice, she quickly stepped out of the room.

"Oh, miss, it's you!" Essie said in surprise. "What are you doing here?"

"Is there a fire?" Serafina asked. "What's happening?"

"We came up lookin' for *you*, miss," Essie said.

"Me? Why me?"

"Someone told Master Braeden that you were seen in the gardens badly injured. Master Braeden was all a-jumble about where you were, so he sent us up here to look for you while he searched outside."

"Injured?" Serafina said in bewilderment. "I'm not injured. Who told him that?"

At that moment, Serafina remembered the night she'd caught the wood rat: every time it tried to run away, her reflex had been to snatch it up again. When she fell from the Grand Staircase, her reflex had landed her on her feet. Reflexes were a powerful and useful force. But they could be used against you. She knew it because she'd done it. A few weeks ago, she had walked the corridors of Biltmore dressed as a defenseless victim in a fancy red dress. She had used Mr. Thorne's reflex against him and lured him to his demise.

But now here she was.

Someone was in control and it wasn't her.

If she was suddenly discovered to be missing and thought to be injured, who was the first person at Biltmore who would react? Who would immediately jump onto his horse and ride blindly out into the darkness of the night all by himself to save her?

She imagined running out into the gardens and finding Braeden's lifeless body lying on the ground, ambushed and stabbed to death by a man with a sharpened blade.

She grabbed Essie's arm. "I'm going to go out and find Braeden and bring him back. But you need to do something very important. Run downstairs as fast as you can and get my pa, Mr. Olmsted, and Mr. Vanderbilt. I want you to tell them to check the plans of the house and find the places it's most vulnerable to fire. Go to those places and look for pinesap on the floor and walls, or any kind of flammable material. They should station guards to protect those areas. Make sure no one can light a fire."

"I'll do it. I'll do it right away!" Essie said.

Serafina touched Essie one last time and then she ran. She didn't care who saw her or heard her now. She ran frantically through the house and down the stairs, her lungs gasping for air.

As she sprinted through the Entrance Hall, she heard the hooves of Braeden's horse clattering across the courtyard in front of the house. She burst out the front door just in time to see Braeden gallop by. He was leaning forward on the horse, filled with panicked urgency. She'd never seen him go so fast. But he was riding headlong into darkness toward the gardens.

"Braeden!" she shouted after him. "Come back! I'm here! I'm alive!" But he didn't hear her.

Serafina ran after him. As she went out into the night, she heard the loud, bloodcurdling howl of a wolfhound in the nearby trees. A flood of dread poured into her mind. It sounded like a wolfhound sentinel in the woods had spotted Braeden and was sounding the call for his white-fanged brothers to join him.

Then she heard the long, yipping, yelping, snapping howl of a single coyote. The howling answer of a hundred other coyotes rose up from all around Biltmore's grounds.

A terrible thought struck her mind. All this deception and disguise wasn't just about finding the Black Cloak and burning down Biltmore. Now they wanted *Braeden*. Braeden in particular. And soon they would have the boy in their jaws.

She heard another sound in the distance. She knew the wraithy racket all too well: the clatter of four horses and a carriage on the road to Biltmore.

They were coming. They were all coming.

Then she spotted movement ahead at the edge of the gardens. She sucked in a breath. The black silhouette of a figure lurked in the shadows, hunched and slinking in a long dark coat. It was Grathan. He was wielding his cane like a weapon.

"Braeden!" Serafina screamed as he and his horse disappeared into Biltmore's vast gardens, but he was too far away to hear her.

As Grathan ducked into the gardens behind Braeden, he

gripped his cane in two hands and drew out a long, pointed, swordlike dagger. There it was. The weapon he had been hiding had finally come forth! The freshly sharpened edges of the blade shone in the moonlight with gleaming power. Brandishing the blade in front of him, Grathan followed Braeden down the path into the gardens. He was going to kill him!

Serafina burst forward with new speed. When she finally reached the path, she caught something out of the corner of her eye: A white-faced owl glided low across the courtyard and then disappeared into the garden trees.

Her chest tightened with fear.

Grathan, the wolfhounds, the coyotes, the stallions, the owl—everything was coming together.

The trap had sprung. And she and Braeden were the mice.

Serafina raced down the path that Braeden and Grathan had taken, but as she rounded a bend, she came upon an unexpected sight.

Grathan stood frozen in the path. His back was to her as he stared at the ground in front of him. Whatever it was, it had stopped him dead in his tracks.

"Don't move," he said, his voice trembling, as he glanced back at her.

Serafina didn't understand what was happening until she saw the timber rattlesnake coiled up on the path in front of him. It was a thick, dangerous-looking snake, nearly five feet long, brown and patterned with jagged bars. Its nasty wedge-shaped head was raised up off the ground, its yellow eyes staring at him, and its black tongue flicking.

She felt so confused. Why had he warned her?

"Just don't move, Serafina," he said again as the snake began to rattle.

Then Serafina saw that it wasn't just one rattlesnake. There were many of them, lying all over the path and the surrounding grass. One of the loathsome pit vipers coiled mere inches from her bare legs, its head moving back and forth as if it was angling for an attack.

Grathan gripped his cane in one hand and his dagger in the other.

He tried to step backward, but as soon as his legs moved, the closest rattlesnake struck like the snap of a whip, leaving two bleeding holes in his leg, so fast that even Serafina barely saw it. Grathan tried to leap back from the terrifying strike, but he landed off the path, right onto a second rattlesnake. That rattlesnake lunged forward, its mouth spread, and sank its venomous fangs deep into his calf. As he cried out and tried to jerk away, a third snake struck his thigh. Grathan screamed in pain and tripped backward, dropping his dagger. The other snakes converged upon him, striking him in the face and throat and chest. Their fangs pumped venom into his bloodstream. Grathan's arms and legs and his entire body were shaking. Serafina had no idea whether she should fight the snakes or run. There was nothing she could do but stand there in horror and watch.

Grathan lay flat on the ground now, faceup, with his limbs splayed, the snakes draping and coiling around him. The man's face was dark and swollen with poison, but his eyes were open and he looked at her.

"She's . . . not . . . who . . . she . . . seems. . . ." he gasped in a weak, raspy voice, barely able to speak.

"What?" Serafina asked in confusion. "I don't understand!"

"Run!" he gasped.

"Tell me what you're talking about!" she cried. She wanted to get closer to the man and hear what he was trying to tell her, but she had to keep her distance from the snakes. She knew she was in danger, but she had to have to answers. "Who are you? Who are talking about?" she asked him.

But Grathan's eyes closed and he was gone. He died right before her eyes.

Serafina stepped back, then stepped back again, aghast with what she saw.

She had thought that Grathan was her mortal enemy, the second occupant of the carriage, Uriah's spy and assassin. But she suddenly felt a strange sadness that something had just happened that shouldn't have happened and that it was all her fault. She looked down at the poor dead man on the ground. Had she made a terrible mistake about him? It seemed like he was trying to help her at the end, like he was trying to tell her something.

The silver clasp of the Black Cloak lay in his open, dead hand. She wanted to grab it, but the snakes coiled around his arm.

As horrified as she was by what she'd just seen, she tried to tell herself that what had happened was good, that these snakes had just killed her enemy. It was over! Her enemy was dead.

But she shook her head and growled. There weren't rattlesnakes in Biltmore's gardens. Vipers didn't hunt in groups and attack people on paths in the shrub garden. They'd been brought here by an unnatural power. But if he was evil, Grathan should have been *controlling* these snakes, not getting killed by them! The puzzle wasn't *solved*. There were just more pieces!

At that moment, she heard a *tick-tick-ticking* sound behind her, followed by a long, raspy hiss, not a rattle like a snake's, but the clicking sound of a barn owl. She felt the hot air of a breath on the back of her neck.

"I thought I got rid of you," said a voice behind her.

42

Serafina spun, ready to fight.

But it was Lady Rowena standing a few feet behind her. Serafina's first thought was that she must have been mistaken in what she had heard and felt. Lady Rowena stood before her holding a twig in her hand, as if to defend herself with it. Serafina was just about to ask her what she was doing there, when Rowena spoke.

"I see . . . the Black One is here," Rowena said in a peculiar voice. When she said the words, Serafina couldn't help but glance at the Black Cloak's silver clasp, which still lay in Grathan's dead hand.

Following her glance, Rowena's eyes opened wide. Then she smiled. "Oh. Thank you. We'd misplaced that."

Rowena moved toward Grathan's body, seemingly undisturbed by the fact that he was lying dead on the ground and that he was draped with rattlesnakes. She stepped among the snakes as they coiled and raised their heads and watched her with their searing yellow eyes, but they did not rattle or bite her. She bent down and picked up the silver clasp. "I'll take that off your hand," she said to Grathan's dead, swollen face.

As Rowena spoke, Serafina realized that she sounded different than she had before. Her snobbish English accent seemed to have decayed into a casual, snarling tone, as if she'd grown weary of the ruse.

"I'm afraid Detective Grathan here had been doing a bit too much detecting," Rowena said, "and he was getting dangerously close to telling Vanderbilt his theories. I guess the poor, lost soul saw himself as some sort of demon-killer, a fighter against evil. The fool thought he was going to kill me with a dagger."

A loud and sudden howl erupted from the woods, the call of a wolfhound, so close that it startled Serafina into pivoting toward it. But Rowena didn't seem bothered by the howl at all.

When Serafina looked back at her, the small stick in her hand had become a gnarled and twisted wooden staff. In that moment, Serafina remembered Lady Rowena's riding crop, and the wooden pin in her hair, and the parasol on the South Terrace, and the hiking staff in the woods. *It goes with my outfit!* she had insisted in her snobby tone. Every time she'd seen Rowena, the girl had been in different clothes, but she'd always been carrying something long and wooden.

Serafina realized now that Mr. Grathan hadn't snuck into

the garden to kill Braeden with his dagger, but to kill Rowena. He wasn't a police detective like he was pretending to be, but an occultist, a hunter of the strange and unusual. And he'd found it.

"There and there," Rowena said, pointing the staff to two positions along the garden path and the snakes slithered to where she pointed.

Finally, Rowena turned and looked at Serafina. "Yes, I thought I got rid of you."

"When was that, exactly?" Serafina said, trying to stay bold despite her confusion and her fear.

"When you and the dog went over the stair rail."

"Eight to go, I guess," Serafina said, her eyes locked on Rowena.

"I was none too pleased, believe me."

"Actually, you looked scared."

"Don't flatter yourself." Rowena scowled. "I was just surprised. You're a tougher little creature than you look. But I should have known with your kind."

As they spoke, Serafina couldn't help glancing toward the house to make sure there were no signs of smoke or flame, but she immediately regretted it.

"What are you looking for?" Rowena asked her. "It's too late, you know. I already lit the fires. There's nothing you can do to stop it now. Your precious house is going to burn. I told you I was going to finally do something to make my father proud."

Serafina tried to leap away and run, but she couldn't move

her feet. She looked down at the ground. To her astonishment, vines of ivy were growing rapidly around her ankles and up her legs.

Before she could tear the ivy away, she heard the sound of a single horse coming swiftly down the path.

The image of Biltmore's bronze statue of a rattlesnake-spooked horse flashed in her mind.

Rowena turned toward the sound of the horse.

Braeden came around the corner on horseback. "Serafina, I've been looking all—"

"Braeden, run!" Serafina screamed as loud as she could as Rowena raised the Twisted Staff.

43

The rattlesnakes struck out and sank their fangs into the horse's legs. The horse squealed as it went up rearing and striking, its head thrashing and its eyes wild with panic. Braeden fell from the horse, making a horrible cracking sound when he hit the ground.

Serafina tried to leap to Braeden's defense, but she immediately fell headlong, the ivy tentacles clamping her feet to the ground.

As she frantically ripped the ivy away, a snake rose up in front of her face, hissing and rattling, preparing to strike. With a quick flash of her hand, she whapped it on the head so fast that it never knew what hit it. Rattlesnakes were fast, but she was faster. When a second snake lashed at her with its fanged strike, she leapt straight up into the air to dodge it, then pounced on it and crushed its head.

But even as she killed the snakes, the ivy grew around her feet again, entrapping her. As Serafina tried to tear the vines away, she glanced up to see thick plumes of dark smoke roiling up from the walls of the house. Biltmore was on fire!

Serafina saw Braeden squirming out of the way of the rearing, stomping horse. The horse wasn't just frightened of the rattlesnakes. Suddenly, it wanted to kill him. The earth shook every time it hit the ground with its huge black hooves, Braeden frantically rolling this way and that, barely escaping being crushed. One stomp and Braeden would die. There was nothing she could do to save him.

But at that moment, a lean, dark mountain lion leapt out of the darkness and tackled the horse in a tumbling, screaming collision of wild beasts. Waysa had arrived. The catamount wasn't large compared to the massive size of the horse, but he fought with a lion's speed and power, moving so fast that sometimes he was nothing but a brown blur.

The five wolfhounds came running into the battle. Rowena pointed the Twisted Staff at Braeden, who was trying to get himself up onto his feet. The dogs attacked him, easily bringing him down. They clamped onto him with their fangs and dragged him screaming across the ground.

Serafina snarled and hissed in frustration as she tore the twisting ivy from her legs. Waysa's arrival gave her new hope. The second she was free, she ran toward Braeden, grabbed one of the wolfhounds by its haunches, and yanked it away. When the angry dog spun around and lunged at her with its snapping jaws, she dodged the strike and struck its head.

"Get her staff!" she screamed to Braeden, but he was on the ground, kicking and screaming, fighting for his life. One wolfhound had hold of his right hand. Another, his left wrist. And a third had hold of his leg. They weren't just biting him, or trying to kill him, they were dragging him away. Serafina knew that Braeden had barely even seen Rowena, let alone understood the complexity of what was happening. Serafina had seen the whole thing, and even she didn't understand what was going on. The snakes could strike him. The dogs could rip out his throat. But they weren't. The dogs were dragging him away.

It wasn't until Serafina heard the terrible clatter of the four stallions' hooves in Biltmore's courtyard that she began to understand. The wolfhounds, the Twisted Staff, the stallions and the carriage. Uriah and Rowena wanted Serafina dead and out of the way. But they wanted Braeden *alive*!

Waysa charged out of the bushes at the staff-wielding Rowena. When she pointed her weapon at two of the wolfhounds, they hurled themselves into the lion's charge. The catamount and the two wolfhounds exploded into a vicious battle of tearing fangs and ripping claws.

Rowena slashed the staff out into the forest and shouted something Serafina didn't understand. Sensing that she was bringing in more animals twisted to her command, Serafina rushed toward her. The only way she was going to defeat Rowena was to get the staff.

A massive bear came charging out of the trees. Serafina

gasped, barely able to believe her eyes. Black bears were normally such quiet, unaggressive creatures of the forest. She had no idea how she could fight the snarling five-hundred-pound beast.

The bear hurled itself at her with its great maw of teeth. She dodged its first attack, but the animal spun around with startling agility and lunged again, roaring with anger, swiping at her with its massive paws, its teeth clacking. She dodged again, and then again, surprising even herself with how fast she could move when her life depended on it. She knew if the bear got hold of her, it'd be the end of her. She darted this way and that, beneath it and around it, so close to it that she could smell its fur. Even when its claws missed her, the force of its bruising shoulders against her chest shot lightning bolts through her ribs.

As she kicked and screamed and thrashed and dodged the bear, the wolfhounds dragged Braeden's body up to the carriage with the four dark stallions waiting at Rowena's command. Serafina didn't understand what was happening, but she knew she had to help him or she was going to lose him forever. But she couldn't save him. She couldn't even save herself!

Rowena and the wolfhounds pulled Braeden's now limp, unconscious body into the black carriage and disappeared inside. The stallions reared up with terrifying neighs, like they'd been prodded by a painful goad. Gusts of steam poured from their mouths and nostrils. The horses burst into a run, pulling the carriage behind them. And in the distance, great clouds of smoke filled the sky.

Serafina scurried and rolled, dodged and darted between the swipes of the bear's slashing paws and the snaps of its deadly teeth, but she could not escape.

She caught a glimpse of Waysa battling the wolfhounds. Rowena could control many things, but she could not control *him*. His soul was still half human, which made the catamounts a particularly dangerous enemy to Rowena and her Twisted Staff.

The bear threw itself into its next attack. Serafina ducked to the side and tried to dart away. When it spun around and lunged at her with a mighty swipe of its paw, she leapt up a steep incline. Bears could run much faster than humans, so she couldn't outrun it. They climbed trees with great speed, so that was no good, either. Playing dead was certain death. Nor did she have the strength or claws to damage the bear, or a weapon to fight it with. All she had was her agility and her mind. She darted into the sticks of a bush, thinking that the steep incline and dense thicket would give her a chance to escape. But that meant nothing to the bear. It charged up the slope and crashed through the brush like it wasn't even there, roaring and swiping as it came.

Serafina knew that she was outmatched by the bear in almost every way, but then an idea sprang into her mind. There were still a few things she could do better than a bear.

She turned and she ran. Just as she knew it would, the bear dropped down onto all fours and chased after her. She knew she only had so many steps before the bear caught up with her and attacked her from behind. It would drag her to the ground and maul her with its teeth and claws until she was dead. She heard the pound of its running feet and the bellows of its breath coming up behind her. Terrified, she glanced over her shoulder as she ran. There it was, charging toward her at full speed, its muscles rolling beneath its heavy black fur. Her short, frantic breaths exploded through her. She was running as fast as she could, but it would overtake her in half a second.

Finally, she came to what she was running for and jumped. *Thank God for Mr. Olmsted,* she thought as she fell through the air. She landed in the crushed stone of the long, formal, rectangular Italian Garden, which was sunk deep into the natural terrain and surrounded by a twelve-foot-high stone wall.

The moment she hit the ground, she turned around and looked up. The bear did not stop. It came barreling over the drop-off and leapt into the Italian Garden right behind her, determined to catch her and kill her. She scrambled out of the way just as its huge form hit the ground with a great crash beside her, shaking the earth. It immediately swiped at her with a mighty swing of its paw, then lunged with snapping jaws. She scurried up the white marble statue of a Greek goddess next to the garden's wall, climbed to the top of its head, and then leapt.

"It's not an Italian Garden, Mr. Olmsted," she said as she landed on the top edge of the wall, clinging to it with her hands and feet. "It's a bear pit!"

The bear roared and charged forward to follow her, but as it tried to climb the statue, its flailing paws and massive weight broke the Greek goddess into pieces, and the beast came tumbling down. The bear sprang to its feet and looked up at her and roared again, but it could not climb the stone wall or leap to the top. The bear could jump *into* the walled garden, but not *out* of it.

She'd done it. She'd escaped.

Serafina quickly ran along the top edge of the wall and disappeared into the bushes before the bear found its way out on the other side. Leaving the Italian Garden behind her, she ran through the shrubs and came to the road. But it was empty. The carriage was long gone. Serafina's mind had been filled with confusion since the moment Rowena had appeared. Who was she? And where was Uriah?

She looked toward the rooftops of Biltmore in the distance, and her heart sank in dread. Dark smoke and mist roiled across the hilltop, blurring her view of the house. It looked as if the towers and the rooftops were being enveloped by a conjurer's spell. Rowena's fires were burning! Serafina wanted to run to the house and scream for help, but she couldn't. She had to put her faith in Essie and go save Braeden.

Pulling herself away, she ran down the road in the direction that Rowena had taken him. But even as she ran, she knew it was no use. The stallions pulling the carriage were fast. She'd never catch up with them. She could hear the sound of their hooves receding in the distance.

Once again, she needed far more speed than her lousy two feet could give her. As she ran down the road and the immediate fear of the bear began to wear off, she couldn't believe how foolish she'd been to not know that Rowena wasn't who she had pretended to be. She felt angry and disgusted with herself. She was stupid. She was weak. She was slow. It felt like her feet were heavy, like she was plodding down the road.

But, somehow, she had to save Braeden!

I want to be fast, she thought in frustration as she ran. *I want to be strong! I want to be fierce!*

Waysa's words came into her mind. *Once you envision what you want to be, then you'll find a way to get there.*

She had envisioned her mother in her lion form many, many times, and it never did her any good, but as she ran desperately down the road to catch up with the carriage carrying her friend away, a flash of memories splintered through her mind.

She remembered Uriah saying *Find the Black One!* as he offered the wolfhounds a scrap of cloth.

She remembered the black strands that Essie had cut out of her hair.

As she ran after the carriage, she could feel her feet hitting the ground and her lungs gasping for more air.

She remembered seeing the reflection of her yellow eyes in the mirror.

She remembered Rowena saying *the Black One is here,* then moving her eyes to what was in Grathan's hand only *after* Serafina had looked there.

A fierce emotion poured through her. She had to run and run and keep running, driving all her anguish and her pain down into her muscles, pumping her chest, pulling air into her lungs, pounding blood through her heart, and driving strength into her legs.

She had been trying to envision her mother in her mind all this time, but she realized now that it wasn't her mother she had to see.

She felt her speed doubling, then tripling, her muscles rippling with sudden power. She leapt off the road and tore through the forest. She bounded a ravine and burst into new speed on the other side.

As she came around a bend in the road, she saw the carriage in the distance, pulled by the raging stallions, their shoulders and haunches bunching and bulging as their hooves clattered across the road. Their steel horseshoes threw flashes of sparks beneath their feet as they ran.

She found herself catching up. She heard herself growling. She felt the length and sharpness of her fangs. She felt her claws ripping across the earth. The powerful bellows of her lungs pumped in air.

And even as she ran full tilt, her eyes and ears sensed everything around her, behind her, and ahead of her.

She saw flashes of gray and brown coming toward her from the left and the right. They were fast runners. Long tails. The flash of snarling teeth. Dozens of coyotes charged in at her, biting at her sides.

Serafina wanted to turn and fight them, but she knew that if she did, she'd lose the carriage. She'd lose Braeden. So she kept running, blazing through the forest. Two of the coyotes dove in and clamped onto her sides. Then a third bit her haunch, holding on to her with its teeth. She stumbled and regained her balance and kept running, but then another coyote clamped onto her.

Suddenly, a tan-colored flash burst beside her, and a half-dozen coyotes went tumbling away, whining in pain and fear, many of them bleeding as they went down. Serafina's mother ran beside her, fighting her way through, clearing her path. Her mother had returned! The lioness leapt onto the closest coyote, sank in her claws, and took it down in a whining, snapping, somersaulting ball. Serafina kept on running, driving through, gaining speed now. Her mother reappeared and took down another coyote, and then another. Soon she and her mother were running side by side unopposed, two catamounts at full speed through the forest, the coyotes well behind them.

Just as the carriage crossed a stone bridge, Serafina leapt onto the backs of the four stallions, her claws ripping into their bodies as they tried to rear up and fight her. They bent their necks in their leather harnesses and snapped at her with their crushing teeth, but they were no match for her saber-toothed fangs and razor-sharp claws. Their panicked, flailing struggles pulled the four horses wildly off-kilter. The carriage careened off the road and went tumbling down, Serafina and the stallions battling all the way, until it finally crashed into the bottom of the ravine.

She could only become what she could envision.

And finally she had envisioned it.

Find the Black One! Uriah had told his dogs. But it wasn't the Black Cloak he had been searching for.

It was *her.*

He knew she was going to get in his way.

She realized as she leapt upon the backs of the stallions and tumbled down into the ravine that her father hadn't been a mountain lion like her mother.

He had been a *black panther.*

And now, so was she.

It all came together in her mind. Her mother and father had fought Uriah twelve years before. Her father had been the Black One, the warrior-leader of the forest who had almost defeated Uriah and whose descendants could never be allowed to rise again.

But now his daughter—the new Black One—had come into her own. And her name was Serafina.

45

Serafina clawed her way out of the wreckage. She leapt easily up onto a large rock and looked down at the pieces of the broken carriage, desperately searching for Braeden.

She was relieved when he crawled slowly out of the debris, battered and disoriented but still alive. When he glanced up at Serafina, his eyes widened in surprise. He was startled for a moment, but then Serafina saw the recognition flood through his expression and he smiled. He knew exactly who she was.

But he did not take the time to speak or approach her. He immediately dug through the debris and found the Twisted Staff.

"Braeden, give that to me. . . ." Rowena said, her voice seething as she clambered from beneath the broken boards of the carriage. "We don't have to fight each other," she said. "Just like you said, we're friends. Join me and all this will be over."

Braeden gripped the staff at each end and slammed it over his knee, but it did not bend or break.

"You aren't strong enough to destroy it," Rowena said. She stepped toward him and slowly put out her hand. "Just give the staff to me, Braeden, and we'll work together. I'll show you how to use it. We'll combine your powers with my powers, and we'll control everything in these mountains. No one will be able to stop us, not even the catamounts."

Braeden looked at her silently.

"These aren't your people, Braeden. You know that," Rowena said. "Haven't you felt the pull I'm talking about? You came to these mountains two years ago and you've been searching ever since, but you won't find the home you're looking for at Biltmore." Rowena's lip curled a little bit. "It's filled with nothing but humans."

Finally, Braeden turned. It looked like he was going to simply walk away from her.

"Braeden, I'm warning you one last time. . . ." Rowena said, her voice rising.

But at that moment, Braeden stopped. Now it seemed as if he was going to turn toward her. But he lowered his arm and then hurled the staff way up into the sky.

Rowena frowned, looking both annoyed and perplexed by his action. "You know it's going to come back down," she said condescendingly.

But Braeden just smiled and gave a long whistling call. "Not necessarily," he said.

At that moment, something came swooping in across the darkened sky.

"What is that?" Rowena snapped in surprise. "What are you doing?"

"Just a friend of mine," Braeden said. "No wire."

The peregrine falcon came in high, but then tilted and rolled. She reached out and grabbed the Twisted Staff out of midair with her talons. Then, with several quick flaps of her wings, Kess propelled herself upward. She seemed to drift across the moonlit sky almost effortlessly.

"Bring that bird back here right now, Braeden!" Rowena shouted. "Do you know what you've done?"

"Yes, I think I do," Braeden said, nodding as he turned from the falcon and looked at Rowena. "I want to make this very clear: I will never join you, Rowena."

"You're going to wish you had," Rowena spat.

But as the staff became more and more distant in the talons of the falcon, two of the wolfhounds emerged slowly from the trees, their hearts no longer twisted by its controlling power. The wolfhounds stalked toward Rowena, their heads low and their eyes filled with menace as they bared their teeth and growled.

"No," she ordered them, facing them uncertainly, thrusting her bare hands toward them. "No! Stop! Get out of here!"

But they did not go. And they did not stop.

"You're free now! Go!" she shouted at them.

Beasts of their own will, they continued to move toward her. They were indeed free.

The dogs leapt upon her. Her shouts turned to screams. She writhed and fought. One bit her leg. The other her side. Serafina leapt into the battle to help the wolfhounds fight her. But at that very instant, there was a blur of sight and sound, and Rowena disappeared from between the two dogs.

A barn owl flapped up into the sky. Serafina pulled back in surprise, startled by what she'd just seen.

She suddenly remembered the first night she saw Uriah in the forest. She had assumed that the owl had been his familiar, his eyes and ears of the forest, but it had been Rowena! He had passed her the shape-shifting staff that very night.

And now Rowena was flying straight toward the peregrine falcon.

Serafina thought it was strange that Kess wasn't flying high and fast like a falcon could. She was flying low and slow, down the length of the French Broad River, along an edge of jagged cliffs. Was the weight of the staff too much for her to carry, or did she have something else on her mind?

Then Serafina saw something that turned her heart cold. The gray-bearded man in the long, weather-beaten coat emerged from the trees at the top of a distant rocky hill. She could see his black silhouette in the moonlight. Serafina felt the hackles on the back of her neck rise up, the air pulling into her chest. It was Uriah. He'd finally come. The conjurer saw the peregrine falcon carrying his Twisted Staff away and the barn owl coming up behind the falcon in close pursuit.

Suddenly, Serafina understood.

She burst into a run, sprinting as fast as she could through the forest toward the cliffs that ran along the river. She knew exactly what Uriah was going to do next and where she needed to be when it happened.

Waysa had told her that Uriah had learned the dark arts during his travels in the Old World. And she remembered thinking that Uriah's call to the owl a few nights before had been filled not just with the sense of alliance she expected, but a dark and horrible love. And now she'd seen Rowena turn into an owl, just like Uriah. Rowena wasn't just the demon he'd sent into Biltmore to find its weaknesses. She wasn't just the conjurer's apprentice and the wielder of the Twisted Staff. Rowena was his *daughter*.

46

Serafina tore through the forest up the hill, straight for the rocky, hundred-foot-high cliff edge where Uriah was standing. As her black shape sprinted invisibly through the night, she kept her eyes fixed on the elusive conjurer. Just as she'd hoped, the man disappeared with a startling blur and turned into an owl. Uriah flew toward Rowena and Kess. It was the reflex she'd been counting on, that Uriah couldn't help but fight at his daughter's side and take back the stolen staff. Serafina knew that she couldn't defeat Uriah when he was in human form and able to use his hands to throw his spells. But as he flew down the length of the river along the jagged edge of the cliffs in pursuit of the falcon, she ran like she'd never run before, her yellow eyes locked onto Uriah as he flew. The flurry of her powerful legs pulled her rapidly across the terrain. Seeing the edge of the cliff in front of her, she drove forward with one last burst of power. And then she leapt.

Her timing was perfect. She sailed thirty feet off the edge of the cliff. As she soared through the air, she pulled back her paw, then slammed it forward with a mighty strike into Uriah as he flew by. Her deadly claws raked through the bird. Feathers exploded. The ravaged owl spun end over end from the force of the blow.

She'd done it.

She had defeated the man of the forest.

She had killed her enemy.

Her chest filled with relief and happiness, but then the momentum of her leap gave way to a different sensation. Free fall. She felt herself being pulled toward the earth, her fall picking up more and more speed. As she twisted her spine and righted herself, she caught a glimpse of a breathless Braeden reaching the rocky edge and looking out in terror as he realized she had jumped off the cliff.

She fell and fell. A hundred feet was too high for even her to survive, whether she landed on her feet or not. She had but one hope: that she had leapt out far enough.

She hit the water and it exploded all around her. She felt the great crash of it, and then it enveloped her. Her huge black body plunged deep into the river's dark currents. The force of the rapids immediately began to sweep her away.

Knowing what she had to do, she quickly started paddling. She rose to the surface in a flurry of bubbles, took a deep breath, shook off her whiskers, and then paddled steadily for the shore, using her long black tail to steer.

She spotted Uriah's bloodied white-feathered body floating down the river. She wanted to bite the owl, crush it, make sure it was dead, dead, dead, but the rapids took him away before she could catch him. She'd have to be satisfied with the havoc she had wrought.

She swam out of the rapids and hauled herself up onto the rocky shore. Waysa came trundling down the shoreline to meet her in mountain lion form, his jaunty steps making it clear that he was pretty pleased with himself, as if he was saying, *I knew that swimming lesson would save your life one day.*

The two catamounts quickly ran back up the path to the top of the cliff, where Braeden waited. He smiled in relief when he saw Serafina, but then he pointed.

Serafina looked into the distance. Rowena, still in owl form, was attacking the peregrine falcon with her talons, hitting Kess's body with strike after strike. Serafina didn't know if Rowena had seen her father die, but there was a new fierceness in the owl's attacks.

Normally, a falcon would flip claws-up to meet an incoming dive, but because Kess was carrying the staff, she could not, so she took the hits and flew on the best she could. But Rowena was relentless, striking again and again. Then Rowena finally grasped the Twisted Staff in her talons and tried to yank it away. The two intertwined raptors locked together, clawing and screeching, tumbling down through the air, fighting as they fell. But then suddenly the falcon flew upward again, pulling with powerful strokes toward the clouds, dragging the staff and the owl with her.

"What is Kess doing?" Braeden asked as he peered up into the sky.

Kess flew higher and higher, ignoring the owl's clawing talons, pecking beak, and battering wings.

The two birds went so high they disappeared, even to Serafina's eyes.

"What happened?" Braeden asked in astonishment. "Where'd they go?"

But Serafina could not reply.

Serafina could hear the two birds battling up in the sky. She heard the screeching and hissing noises of the owl, and the long *kak-kak-kak* of the peregrine, and then everything went quiet.

She peered up at the sky and took a breath. One of the birds finally came into view. It was flying alone, carrying the Twisted Staff in its talons. Serafina's heart sank when she saw that it was the owl. It was Rowena. Serafina kept looking, but there was no sign of Kess. It appeared the falcon had lost the battle.

The owl flew toward them now. Serafina dreaded what was going to happen next. Once Rowena changed back, she could use her staff to start the battle all over again, hurling god knows what kinds of animals at Serafina and her allies. And it was clear that Uriah had taught his daughter well. He might not have thought too much of her, but Rowena had become a powerful young conjurer in her own right.

"What happened?" Braeden asked as he looked all around,

his voice frantic and confused. "Is Kess dead? Did Rowena kill her?"

Serafina thought she must have. But then she spotted a tiny dot way up in the sky, hundreds of feet above the forest. It was Kess, flying strong, far higher than a barn owl could ever fly. Serafina wondered what she was doing way up there. Then Kess tipped into a barrel roll and dove.

Serafina watched as Kess dove through the sky toward the unsuspecting Rowena. The falcon tucked her wings close to her body and shot through the air in a striking stoop, moving faster than anything Serafina had ever seen in her entire life.

"There she is!" Braeden gasped at the last second, just as Kess came slashing into view.

The falcon struck the owl so hard that it popped with an explosion of feathers. Serafina could feel the force of the hit in her chest, like two stones striking against each other in mid-air. Then Kess pinwheeled around and raked Rowena with her talons in a second attack. The burst of white owl feathers swirled in the air. The stunned owl somersaulted lifelessly, falling toward the ground.

At the instant of the strike, the owl released the staff. It fell end over end through the air for a hundred feet. Then the falcon swooped down and grasped it in midair.

Serafina watched the body of the owl fall, dead weight all the way down, and then disappear into the trees on the other side of the river. After what had just happened, it seemed like Rowena had to be dead, but Serafina watched and waited to see if the owl flew back up again. It did not.

"Look!" Braeden said, pointing up into the sky.

It was Kess. The falcon was flying toward them. She came in low and steady. Serafina could see her black mask and her bold white chest with its black bars. She was flecked with her enemy's blood, but she looked healthy and strong. She gave a call, a cheerful *kak-kak-kak,* as she passed overhead, still carrying the Twisted Staff.

Kess flew out past the edge of the cliff and over the river. With a few strong pumps of her pointed wings, she rose higher.

Braeden whistled triumphantly to her. At first, Serafina thought he was calling her back to him to bring him the staff, but then she realized that he wasn't. He was calling his farewell.

"Good-bye, Kess," Braeden said softly. His dream that Kess would someday fly the world again was coming true. "Have a safe journey, my friend."

Serafina watched as the falcon flew across the valley of the great river, and then up and over the rising forest toward the peaks of the mountains in the distance. Kess pumped her wings and tilted her tail, and a few moments later, she disappeared, gliding over Mount Pisgah nineteen miles away.

Unlike the owls of the night and the hawks of the day, Kess flew and hunted both night and day. She was a peregrine, which meant she was the great wanderer of the sky. She could fly wherever and whenever she wanted to.

Tonight she would follow the rocky ridgelines of the southern mountains and the glint of the stars and find her way southward, continuing her long journey to the jungles of Peru. Along the way, she could drop the Twisted Staff into a blazing volcano or use it to build a nest on a cliff in the Andean clouds. But whatever she decided to do with it, it was gone.

"I couldn't figure out at first why Kess was flying so low down the length of the river," Braeden said. "But then I remembered that peregrine falcons sometimes hunt in pairs, cooperating with each other to bring down their prey. She must have known that you were on her side, Serafina."

Serafina took a long breath into her lungs and felt her heart swelling with wonder and hope.

She lifted her head and sniffed the air. There was no smell of smoke drifting through the forest. When she looked toward the house in the far distance, she didn't see the glow of flames rising up from its walls. Essie must have warned Mr. Vanderbilt and the others in time so they could put out the fires before the house was badly damaged. Essie had done it! Biltmore was saved.

It was over.

She and her allies had won.

Her enemies were finally dead.

Her mother emerged from the underbrush, bloodied and

limping from her war with the coyotes. But she had defeated them. She had cleared them from what was once again her territory. She carried Serafina's wriggling half sister by the scruff of her neck, while her half brother walked at his mother's side. The two cubs were muddy, matted, and stained with blood, but they were bold with life.

Relieved and exhausted, Serafina finally lay on the ground to rest, draping her long, lean black body in the grass. Her mother set down her half sister and came over to her. Serafina could see the love and admiration in her mother's eyes as she came toward her. Her mother brushed up against her and purred with happiness and pride. Serafina had finally done it. She'd finally become a full-whiskered catamount. Waysa sat down beside her, batting her playfully with his paws, as if to say *I told you that you could do it!* The catamounts were united. And they were here to stay.

Serafina gazed around her at the trees and the mighty river and the wreckage of the carriage, and tried to comprehend all that had happened. She remembered being so frustrated by her limitations, by what she could and couldn't do at that particular point in her life. She realized now that her life wasn't just about who she was, but about who she would become.

She looked at Braeden. He smiled and lay down on the ground with her and the other catamounts. He obviously felt quite at home with them, among the kith and kin of his heart.

Finally, he leaned his back against the long length of her panther body. He wiped the blood from a cut at his mouth, and then he shut his eyes, tilted his head back, and rested his head against her thick black fur.

"I don't know about you, Serafina," he said with a smile, "but I think we're getting rather good at this."

She could not smile in return, but she felt a warm and powerful gladness in her heart, and she swished her tail and gazed toward Biltmore Estate and the distant mountains. She had finally done it. She had finally envisioned what she wanted to be. And became it.

48

The next morning, when Serafina woke up in the workshop in her human form and walked outside onto the grounds, she looked out across the mountains and came to a realization. It was through the darkness of the blackest night that she had come to love the brightness of the rising sun.

That morning, Mr. Vanderbilt and Braeden formed a work crew with nearly a hundred men from the estate's stables, farms, and fields, and they went out to the animal cages. Serafina and her pa went with them.

The troop of men and horses encountered no difficulties on the way.

When they arrived at the pine forest, Mr. Vanderbilt and the other riders dismounted and entered by foot.

They found the animals still in the cages, but the campsite had been abandoned, the fire cold, nothing but gray ash. Serafina couldn't help but carefully scan the forest, looking for any evidence that Uriah might have somehow survived the battle the night before, but saw nothing. He appeared to be truly gone.

Braeden knelt down in front of one of the cages, opened it up, and helped the red fox crawl out of it. Recognizing him, the fox came to him immediately and crawled up into his lap. He held the fox in his arms and soothed it with strokes of his hands.

"Everything's all right now," Braeden said as he petted the fox. After a few moments, the fox seemed stronger of both body and spirit and trotted off into the forest.

Braeden went to the next cage and freed a beaver from its imprisonment. As he opened the cages, some of the animals immediately ran into the forest. Others needed his care. He knelt down with them and held them until they were strong enough to be on their way. He freed the raccoons and the bobcats, the otters and the deer, the swans and the geese, and the weasels and the wolves.

It filled Serafina with joy to see the animals running free and running strong. "Stay bold," she told them in a whisper.

As Braeden freed the animals one by one, Serafina's pa and the other workers in the crew used their crowbars, chisels, and hammers to tear out and destroy the cages so they could never be used again.

At the end of the day, as they traveled back to Biltmore

through the oaks and chestnuts, the elms and the spruce, Serafina thought that the character and spirit of the forest through which they traveled had changed.

Scurries of flying squirrels ran up and down the trunks and glided from tree to tree. Otters played in the streams.

"Look up there, Serafina!" Braeden said, grabbing her arm in excitement.

She gazed upward and saw thousands of birds, streams and streams of them flooding across the clear blue sky. There were skeins of geese flying in echelons of V's, swans and ducks in long lines, and clouds of fluttering waxwings, cardinals, and jays.

"Isn't it magnificent, Serafina?" Braeden asked her, his voice filled with wonder. "I'm so glad you're here to see this with me because I would have never been able to describe it. Did you ever think you would see something like this in your whole life?"

Serafina stood with Braeden watching the birds and she smiled. "Not like this," she said.

Serafina sat in a red damask-upholstered gold chair in front of a French-style vanity table and mirror in the Louis XVI Room on the second floor of Biltmore House. Light poured into the beautiful oval-shaped room, with its curving white walls, red draperies, and golden-brown wood floor. Essie stood behind her, brushing Serafina's long, silky black hair.

"I don't know what happened to your hair, miss, but it's beautiful," Essie said as she brushed it.

"Thank you," Serafina said, looking at herself in the mirror. All traces of the brown were gone. Only the black remained. And it wasn't shaggy and streaked like before, like a spotted cub's camouflage, but smooth and shiny and entirely black.

Her clean, bare neck and shoulders showed the scars of

her past, the jagged wound she'd taken to her neck when she destroyed the Black Cloak, the bites of wolfhounds on her arms and upper shoulders, and a new cut she'd suffered fighting Rowena and her animals: a long scratch across her cheek just below her eye. The appearance of the wounds did not bother her. They were the scars of battles fought and battles won.

But she still had one worry. "How has Mrs. Vanderbilt been?" she asked.

"She's been down sick on some days, but then she perks up. No one expects it of her this year, but ya know she likes to give Christmas presents to all the children of the estate workers. She's been sendin' me and the other girls hither and yon for all sorts of gifts. She and I spent the entire mornin' wrapping the presents and puttin' them under the tree."

"You must be excited about the Christmas jubilee tonight," Serafina said, smiling. It was good to hear that maybe Mrs. Vanderbilt was feeling a little better.

"Oh, yes, miss. I can't wait. But after all the ruckus last night, I hope it's quieter tonight, or old St. Nick might just look down on Biltmore's rooftop and keep on flyin'."

"Thank you again for everything you did, Essie," Serafina said. "You saved a lot of people's lives, and you saved the house, too."

"You should have seen the look on Mr. Vanderbilt's face when I told him everything you said. I've never seen him move so fast! He gathered up your pa and all the men, and the guests, and all the maids and cooks. We went to all the places in the basement and kitchen and pantries and the stables, and just like you said, there was pinesap and kerosene already aflame. Somebody had lit all those fires. It was so frightening! Your pa said someone cut the wires on the alarm boxes, so he sounded the alarm himself. Then he got the fire hoses throwing water, which was truly something to behold. Mr. Vanderbilt got the bucket brigades going real quick like. Everybody chipped in and worked together, and we put those fires out in no time at all. But it coulda been a disaster!"

Serafina smiled as she listened to Essie tell her story. "You're right," she agreed. "It could have been a disaster. But it wasn't. You saved us."

"It wasn't me. It was *everybody*—everybody working together."

Serafina nodded in agreement.

"But what about you, miss?" Essie said. "A lot of strange happenings last night."

"Strange happenings?"

"Oh, all the cats were a-caterwauling, and the coyotes were a-howlin', and the horses racing the moon. Noises, screams in the night, all sorts of commotion. Somebody actually crashed a carriage off the bridge by the river, smashed it to smithereens."

"Truly?" Serafina said.

"I heard that Mr. Vanderbilt checked into that peculiar Mr. Grathan. Turns out he was some sort of shady character who goes around the country investigating ghost stories and ever what. He was a complete charlatan. Maggie and me thinks he and that English girl tried to run off in the carriage together, that's what we think. No one's seen hide nor hair of either of 'em since last night, and I bet ya we're not a-gonna!"

"I bet you're right," Serafina said.

But deep down she felt a pang of sadness for poor Mr. Grathan. She remembered the scars on his face. They were not unlike her own. There were just many more of them. Mr. Grathan had been a demon killer, just like she was. But this time the demon had killed him first. Serafina realized that she had made a mistake in her judgment of both Mr. Grathan and Rowena in different ways, in part because of how they looked and dressed, and she vowed to be far more careful next time.

"You want to know what?" Essie said, leaning down to her and speaking in a low, conspiratorial tone. "You're not gonna believe this, but Maggie said she looked out her window last night and saw a black panther."

"Do you believe her?"

"Oh, sure. I saw one once, years ago."

"You did?" Serafina asked in surprise.

"I wasn't but five or six at the time, but I recall it like it was yestermorn. One of the clearest memories of my entire life. I was walking down the road with my nanny and my papaw, and this big old black panther crosses the road right in front of us. He stopped and turned and looked right at us. He had the most beautiful yellow eyes you ever did see. But I was afeared. I thought that panther was gonna eat us for sure, and he probably woulda done if it weren't for my pa. I wanted to take off a-runnin' and I woulda been halfway outta Madison County, but my papaw gripped my shoulder and held me in place and we just stared at that big cat. That panther stared right back at us, eyes keen like he was as knowin' as you and me. And then he turned and continued on his way. My pa said that them kind are very rare, that there can only be one black one at a time. So, if Maggie saw one last night, I guess a black one has returned to these parts. Don't want to get et, of course, but I sure would love to see him."

As Essie told her story, tears streamed down Serafina's cheeks, and then she began to sob. Essie had seen her father.

"Aw, miss, I'm sorry," Essie said. "What'd I say? I didn't mean to scare you! The panther ain't gonna hurt us none. You're such a delicate creature, aren't you?"

Serafina looked at Essie in the mirror, shook her head, and wiped her eyes. "I'm not scared," she said.

"Never mind about all that commotion last night. I'm sure it was nothin'. My papaw would say it was just the old man of the forest up to his tricks again, nothing to mind."

Serafina smiled and nodded and blew her nose into a silk handkerchief from the table.

"Don't fret none. We're gonna fix you up real nice for tonight," Essie said as she stood behind Serafina and worked on her hair. "We have plenty of time now. Do you want me to put your hair up into a fancy coiffure like Consuelo Vanderbilt's was the other night? It's very popular these days."

Serafina smiled and imagined it in her mind, but then she said, "Actually, I have another idea," and explained to Essie what she wanted.

She liked talking with Essie and spending time with her. There was something soothing about it that brought her home. But then Serafina saw Essie's expression change, maybe as she thought back on the unexplained happenings and the strange sounds she'd heard in the night.

"Do you believe in haints and spirits, miss?" Essie asked her.

"I believe in *everything*," Serafina said very seriously, remembering all that she had seen.

"Me, too," Essie said as she stroked Serafina's hair.

"Essie, do you remember when we first met a while back, you were fixed on becoming a lady's maid to Mrs. V's guests?" Serafina asked.

"Well, that's right," Essie said. "But ya know what I reckon?"

"What's that?" Serafina said.

"On special nights like this, at least, I reckon I'm *your* lady's maid, miss."

"I reckon you are." Serafina nodded and smiled, and reached up and touched Essie's hands with her own. "But you know what I want more than that, Essie? I want you as my friend."

"Aw, now," Essie complained, "you're gonna start me a-cryin' if we keep this up!"

At that moment, there came a gentle knocking.

"Who could that be?" Essie asked as she went over to the door. "Don't they know us girls are busy in—" As Essie opened the door and saw the young master standing there, she ran out of air to speak.

Serafina rose and went over to Braeden as the shocked Essie moved quietly backward into the room.

Braeden held in his arms two large white boxes with ribbons.

"What's this?" Serafina asked, studying the boxes as Braeden smiled.

"A Christmas present for each of you," Braeden said as he handed the first one to her. "Open it up."

"Truly?" Serafina said.

But she didn't wait for an answer. Inside the box, Serafina found a gorgeous creamy satin winter ball gown.

"It's beautiful, Braeden," Serafina said. "Thank you."

"Essie, you, too," Braeden said, handing the second box to her. "This is to cover Serafina's debt to you."

"Oh, my, will you look at that!" Essie said, beaming as she opened the box and saw the gown within.

"They're both beautiful," Serafina said, watching Essie.

Braeden stepped closer to them and spoke in a facetiously conspiratorial tone. "Now, between me, my aunt, and Essie, this is the third dress we've given you, Serafina. Perhaps you could try to be just a little bit more careful and not ruin this one right away."

"I'll do my best," Serafina said, smiling, and gave Braeden a hug as Essie wiped tears of joy from her eyes.

50

As Serafina and Braeden walked together through the house to the Christmas party, Braeden took her down several corridors to the Smoking Room. It was a richly appointed hideaway, with dark blue velvet chairs, fine blue wallpaper, and shelves of gold-leafed leather-bound books, where the gentlemen would retreat after dinner to smoke their cigars and talk in private. The room was empty at the moment, but Serafina could tell that Braeden had paused for a reason.

"I want to show you something I think you'll find interesting," he said. He took her by the arm and led her into the room. "One of the groundskeepers found something in the woods. He wasn't sure what to do with it, so he gave it to the taxidermist."

As Serafina walked into the room, she looked around her.

On the sculpted marble fireplace mantel sat a stuffed animal on a stand. There were other stuffed animals in the house, so this in itself wasn't unusual. But it wasn't just a pheasant or a grouse. It was a barn owl with its sharp talons clinging wishfully to a crooked stick and its wings splayed upward as if in sudden alarm. The owl seemed to have a particularly shocked look on its face.

"Ah," Serafina said, admiring the owl. She wasn't sure if it was a male or a female, wasn't even sure how to tell the difference, but she decided it looked like her old friend and nemesis. She gave the owl a slow and solemn nod. "Good evening, Rowena. Excuse me, I'm so sorry . . . *Lady* Rowena."

"Well," Braeden said, "my aunt Edith asked us to make her feel at home."

Serafina smiled and looked at the owl. "Rowena, you will always have a home here at Biltmore."

Serafina was pleased that she and Braeden and their allies had defeated Rowena, but the truth was that in some ways her father had twisted Rowena's heart as malevolently as his staff had twisted the minds of those poor animals. Serafina couldn't help but wonder what would have happened if Rowena had seen past her need to impress her father, had turned away from her father's vengeance, and had taken a different path.

After studying the owl for a moment, Serafina asked Braeden, "Did the groundskeeper find only one?"

"I'm afraid so," Braeden said. "But I asked him to gather some of the other men and go back out and keep looking, both in the forest and along the shore of the river, just in case."

"Good," Serafina said. "I would feel a lot better if we had two owls on the mantel rather than one," she said.

Leaving the room, Serafina and Braeden walked over to the Banquet Hall.

Before going in, Braeden paused at the door and looked at Serafina.

Serafina gazed into the soft glow of the candlelit Christmas party in the opulent room. Glittering ladies in their long, formal gowns and handsome gentlemen in their black jackets mingled about the room, talking and laughing warmly, holding their champagne in long crystal flutes. Along with the sparkling folk, most of the house servants were there as well, filled with a relaxed cheer and looking so different in their best day-off clothes, the formalities of work put aside for this special evening.

Many of the children of the servants were hovering by the Christmas tree, waiting excitedly to open their presents. Serafina remembered being a little child curled up in a ball in the darkness at the bottom of the basement stairway listening to the Christmas party above, longing to see and to share in the smiling faces of the other children. And here she was tonight, her first Christmas upstairs. As familiar as all this was to her, and as strange and foreign as well, this was the society she lived in. This was her home. These were her people, her kin, both distant and close.

Standing with Braeden in the doorway, Serafina could see their reflection in one of the mirrors on the wall. It was mesmerizing to see themselves there. Braeden wore the black jacket, white tie, and white gloves that were customary of a young gentleman of his station. His scrapes and bruises had been attended to, and his hair had been neatly combed. His face was lit up with happiness and his brown eyes sparkled with the reflection of the room's light.

Serafina wore the beautiful golden-cream satin gown that Braeden had given her for Christmas, with its magnificently embroidered pearl- and braid-trimmed corset and its long cascading train. As was customary of a young lady, she wore matching satin opera gloves, and glistening shoes adorned her feet. But unlike the other girls in the room, who wore their hair up and arranged, curled into tightly wound coiffures, she had decided to let her silky jet-black hair lie long and smooth over her shoulders, and her eyes were as yellow as a panther's.

A few nights before, Braeden had invited her to join the dinner party, and she had said that she wasn't quite ready, but now he posed the question to her again.

"Ready to go in?" he asked softly.

"I am," she said, and they stepped into the room together.

51

Serafina had spent all the Christmases of her life in the darkness of the basement. When she stepped into the grand room, it glowed with the soft light of hundreds of candles, bathing everyone's faces and their smiles in a golden hue. The women's silver-threaded dresses seemed to scintillate in the light of the Christmas tree. Everything in the room had been decorated with holly and mistletoe and poinsettias. Stockings hung on the mantels of the crackling fireplaces.

A score of foresters had used a wagon and a team of Belgian draft horses to pull the massive, thirty-five-foot Fraser fir tree up to Biltmore's front door. Then a crew of men, including her pa, had worked together with ropes, pulleys, and poles to erect the giant tree in the Banquet Hall. There, it had been decorated over days on end by servants and guests alike who stood on ladders, adorning it with velvet ribbons, sparkling orbs, and splendorous ornaments until its glow filled the entire room. Now beneath the tree lay a heap of Christmas presents for the children of the estate workers: dolls and balls, horns and chimes, trains and bicycles, harps and drums, wagons and pocket knives, and other toys of all kinds.

Serafina and Braeden made their way over to the Christmas tree and stood beside it. They watched with a smile as Mr. Vanderbilt called for everyone's attention and quieted the room. "Good evening, everyone, good evening. Merry Christmas to you all!"

"Merry Christmas!" everyone shouted in return.

"As you all know," Mr. Vanderbilt continued, "here at Biltmore, we pride ourselves on staying up to date with the latest advancements in science and technology. And tonight, on Christmas 1899, I would like to introduce to you what may in fact be the coming new century's most important invention."

With a mischievous look in his eyes, he waved in a dozen smiling maids, including Essie, carrying baskets full of candy canes, which they handed out to all the children and adults in attendance. But they weren't just normal all-white candy canes like they had all seen before. They were striped with a magnificent red spiral that brought loud cheers and laughter of delight from everyone in the room.

As the night slipped on, the servants laid out all sorts of food: ham and roast turkey, dressing and cranberries, and much more—all the bounty of the estate. For dessert they had plum pudding and fancy cakes, ice cream from the estate's dairies, and apple tarts from the estate's orchards.

Soon, Mr. Vanderbilt persuaded Mr. Olmsted to collect the children around the fireplace and read them a poem that began " 'Twas the night before Christmas . . ."

Serafina and Braeden gathered with the other children and listened to the poem with rapt attention.

She loved the part that said "when all through the house, not a creature was stirring, not even a mouse." She had felt that way many times as she prowled through Biltmore at night. And she loved the line "The moon on the breast of the new-fallen snow . . ." The author of the poem had finally found a way to use daytime words to capture nighttime beauty.

Halfway through the story, she looked over and saw her pa gazing at her. She remembered how he had found her in the forest when she was little. All he'd ever wanted in his life was to have a family, for her to be his daughter, and tonight he was filled with a happiness and a relief she had never seen in him before.

She rose and walked over to him. "At least there wasn't any salad tonight, Pa," she said.

"And none of them forks to learn on, thank goodness," he said, winking at her, and took her into his arms.

A few moments later, she overheard Mr. Vanderbilt, Mr. Olmsted, and the chief forester, Mr. Schenck, gathered around the fireplace talking about the Biltmore School of Forestry that they'd set up. Her pa told her that it was the first school like it in all of America, to share the knowledge of rebuilding and managing forests. From what she could tell, it sounded like the men of Biltmore were hatching grand plans for the future.

"Thank you so much, Frederick," Mr. Vanderbilt said warmly to Mr. Olmsted. "What a delightful Christmas present it was to go out to Squatter's Clearing with you this morning and see all the work you've been doing. I must say, you're very good at keeping a secret! I had no idea that you and the crews had made such good progress. You've planted the entire clearing! It's marvelous!"

"You're welcome, George," Mr. Olmsted said, smiling broadly beneath his gray beard. The deceit she'd seen in Mr. Olmsted's eyes days before was the surprise Christmas present that he'd been planning for his old friend.

And seeing his smiling face, she realized now that the seriousness she'd sensed in Mr. Olmsted since his arrival wasn't some nefarious plan, but an elderly man's awareness that he only had so much more time on this earth to finish his work. He was determined to make good on his promise to Mr. Vanderbilt to build him a property and a forest that people would cherish for generations to come. The expression she saw in the wrinkles around his eyes and his mouth was the realization that he had probably come to his favorite place on earth for the last time in his life, that this would be his last Christmas at Biltmore, and one of his last years in a world he so dearly loved.

As Serafina stepped away from the men by the fireplace, Mrs. Vanderbilt came over to her, and with a smile, handed her a small, wrapped present with a red bow.

"You forgot to open yours, Serafina," Mrs. Vanderbilt said gently.

"For me?" Serafina said in surprise. She tore away the wrapping paper and lifted the lid on a small wooden box. Inside, she found a finely painted porcelain miniature of a beautiful spotted jaguar. It was one of Biltmore's very own cats.

"Thank you, Mrs. Vanderbilt," she said, looking up at her as she wiped a tear from the corner of her eye. "I'll be very careful with it."

"It's just my way of saying thank you for everything you've done," Mrs. Vanderbilt said.

Hoping she wasn't being too forward, Serafina asked, "How have you been feeling, Mrs. Vanderbilt?"

"You needn't worry about me," Mrs. Vanderbilt said, touching her gently on the shoulder. "I'm going to be all right." But even as she said the words, Serafina sensed that there was something that Mrs. Vanderbilt wasn't saying.

At the end of the evening, Serafina stood with Braeden by the Christmas tree. She could feel that everything was good and right between them.

"Merry Christmas, Braeden," Serafina said.

"Merry Christmas to you as well, Serafina," Braeden said. "I'm glad we're finally home."

After a few seconds, her curiosity got the best of her, and she asked him the question that was on her mind.

"You know what you did for Gidean and Kess . . ." she began. "Has it always been that way?"

"I've loved animals all my life," he said, "but . . . I don't

know. . . . When I was little, I found a meadowlark with a broken leg. I fed it and took care of it, and a few days later, its leg
healed and the bird flew off. I just thought that was how it was
supposed to work. . . . But when I helped the peregrine falcon
and then Gideon, I began to realize . . . that maybe I was different. Kess's wing should not have healed."

"But it did," Serafina said, looking at him. "I need to ask
you something else, Braeden. Do you think it might work on
people?"

"I'm not sure," he said.

She paused and then finally asked the real question she
wanted to ask. "Do you think you could help your aunt Edith?"

"I don't think that's something I can heal," he said.

"I understand," Serafina said glumly, lowering her head.

But then Braeden smiled. "My uncle just told me that my
aunt isn't ill. She's with child."

Serafina looked at him in surprise. A wave of shock and
relief passed through Serafina. Mrs. Vanderbilt was going to be
all right—more than all right. She was going to have a baby!
That was such tremendous news.

But even as Serafina smiled, she could see that Braeden was
thinking about her earlier question, about everything that had
happened with Rowena and Gideon and the falcon.

"Honestly," Braeden said, "I don't truly understand what
power I have."

Serafina smiled. "None of us do."

52

Serafina lay on the front balcony of the Louis XV Room of Biltmore House, swishing her tail and looking out across the open grass of the Esplanade as the moon rose, casting its silver light over the tops of the distant trees. No one could see her there, for she was as black as the night itself. The daytime folk were in the house behind her, sleeping soundly in their beds.

Serafina could see the silhouette of the wolves passing through the moon's light on a distant hill. They were returning. And in the spring, the songbirds would come, just as they had for a million years. The dark spell on the forest had been broken. The Twisted Staff was gone.

A beautiful green luna moth fluttered by with its long tails streaming behind. She watched as it flew up past the balcony, then headed for the gardens. It was late in the year for luna moths, but the animals were coming home.

In the room behind her, Mrs. Vanderbilt and the baby within her lay sleeping. Serafina could sense their calm and steady heartbeats. She did not know why her mistress had decided to sleep this evening in the room they planned on turning into the nursery. It was as if she and her baby were eager for their meeting day to come.

Serafina gazed out across the lawn of the Esplanade to the hilltops, looking for unusual shapes in the mist, or a silhouette among the trees, or the silent passing of an owl.

She watched and she listened. She was the black sentinel in the night.

She did not know when, or in what form, but she knew that one day more demons would come.

She vowed to be watchful.

She vowed to be ready.

For the night was her domain and hers alone.

Just a few days before, she had thought that she had to decide between one path or the other, between the forest and the house, between the mountains and the gardens.

But now she knew she did not have to decide whether she was a creature of the night or the day, whether she was catamount or human, wild or tame. She was all these things. She could be whatever she wished to be. Like the peregrine falcon that flies both night and day, she would do whatever she wished to do. The C.R.C. and the Guardian. The human and the panther. She was all these things and more.

But just as she felt a dark and lovely peacefulness finally beginning to flow into her soul, she saw a black-cloaked figure moving through the trees in the distance. She couldn't make out the identity of the figure, couldn't even be sure it was entirely human, but whatever it was, it stopped, and turned, and looked at her with glowing eyes.

Serafina's heart pounded in her powerful chest as she stared back at the figure. She could feel her muscles beginning to bunch beneath her and her lungs filling with air.

As she rose to her four feet, she glanced behind her to make sure Mrs. Vanderbilt was still safe in the bedroom.

But when Serafina turned back to look at the figure in the distance once more, the figure was gone.

An Invitation to Biltmore

If you'd like to see and experience Serafina's world, I invite you and your family to visit Biltmore Estate, a wonderful real-life place nestled in the forested mountains of Asheville, North Carolina. My family and I live nearby and have been exploring it for years.

This story is fictional, but I've done my best to describe the house and other historical details accurately. When you visit Biltmore, you'll see the sunlit Winter Garden, the magnificent Grand Staircase, Mr. Vanderbilt's spectacular Library, and all the other main rooms featured in the book. You'll walk through the estate just as Serafina, Braeden, and Lady Rowena did. If you come at Christmastime, you'll be awed by the giant Christmas tree in the grand Banquet Hall. And if you know which one of Biltmore's 250 rooms to check, you may even spot a certain owl on the fireplace mantel.

I can also assure you from personal experience that the darkened attics, hidden doors, and secret passages described in the book are real. These aren't for visitors (they are *hidden* doors after all!), but you may be able to spot one or two!

Here and there in the story, I have used artistic license for reasons of pacing (I figure you didn't want to read an encyclopedia), but in general I've tried to stay true to the spirit and detail of the house.

If you enjoy the outdoors, you should explore the forests and mountains that surround Asheville. You can venture up past the Craggy Gardens to the tallest mountain in the eastern United States just as Serafina did during her journey. You can see the same waterfalls and swim in the same rivers.

Many of the characters depicted in the story were real-life people, including George and Edith Vanderbilt, the housekeeper Emily Rand King, and Frederick Law Olmsted, the father of landscape architecture in America. Even Cedric the Saint Bernard was real.

My goal in depicting Mr. Olmsted the way I did, including showing him planting trees, was to capture the spirit of his and George Vanderbilt's original vision for rebuilding and protecting the forest surrounding Biltmore, which would go on to become the birthplace of forest conservation in America. The conversation I depicted between the two men was inspired by Olmsted's personal letters. But I did use artistic license to bring him back to Biltmore for a visit in 1899, a few years after he retired. Given more room, I would have also liked to have described the roles of Gifford Pinchot, Carl Schenck, and others. Years later, after George Vanderbilt passed away unexpectedly, his wife, Edith, fulfilled his vision for the forest by selling the vast majority of their forested land to the government so that it would be protected by the public trust. It became what is today the Pisgah National Forest, one of America's first and finest national forests.

Whenever I see the unique beauty of Biltmore House and its surrounding gardens and trees, I can't help but marvel at the vision and power of the human spirit when it aspires to good purpose.

—Robert Beatty

Acknowledgments

First, I would like to thank you, the readers, for helping to spread the word about *Serafina and the Black Cloak*. It is because of your support on Book One that I was provided the opportunity to continue Serafina's story.

My deep thanks go to Laura Schreiber and Emily Meehan, my editors at Disney Hyperion, for their insight into storytelling and their commitment to the Serafina Series. And thank you to the rest of the wonderful team at Disney Hyperion in New York and LA.

Thank you to the middle-grade students and teachers of Carolina Day School, the ladies of the LLL Book Club, and all my other beta readers.

I would also like to thank the freelance editors who provided invaluable feedback on the manuscript: Jodie Renner, Sam Severn, Jenny Bowman, Kira Freed, Sheila Trask, Dianne Purdie, John Harten, and Misty Stiles.

Thank you to Dr. Bridget Anderson, an expert in turn-of-the-century southern mountain dialect. Having always enjoyed the different way people speak in our diverse country, I appreciate her assistance, helping me to honor the traditions of southern mountain talk.

Thank you to my Serafina home team in Asheville, including Scott Fowler and Lydia Carrington at Brucemont Communications, Robin McCollough for helping to spread the word, Paul Bonesteel and the talented team at Bonesteel Films, and everyone else in Asheville who helped make the book a success.

Thank you to Deborah Sloan and M.J. Rose for helping me to get the word out. And thank you to my agent, Bill Contardi, and my foreign-rights agent, Marianne Merola, at Brandt & Hochman in New York. And thank you to Egmont UK and my other foreign publishers.

I would also like to thank all the kind and supportive folks at Barnes & Noble in Asheville and throughout the southeastern region, and Malaprop's Bookstore, and all the other bookstores throughout the country who have believed in me, supported me, and been such gracious hosts. And thank you to all the teachers and librarians throughout the country who have used *Serafina and the Black Cloak* in their classrooms and work tirelessly every day to inspire reading in young people.

Thank you to my friends Dini Pickering, Chase Pickering,

and Ryan Cecil, fourth- and fifth-generation family members of George Vanderbilt. I am honored by your support and encouragement. And thank you to all the staff members and management at Biltmore Company, especially Ellen Rickman, Tim Rosebrock, and Kathleen Mosher.

Finally, I would like to thank my family, including my two brothers and my Jankowski in-laws, but most especially my wife and three daughters, who not only inspired this story, but helped create it, develop it, and bring it to the world. In the words of W. H. Auden, you are "my working week and my Sunday rest, my noon, my midnight, my talk, my song."

SERAFINA and the SPLINTERED HEART

ROBERT BEATTY

Don't miss Serafina's next adventure!
Turn the page to start reading.

$\mathcal{S}$erafina opened her eyes and saw nothing but black. It was as if she hadn't opened her eyes at all.

She had been deep in the darkened void of a swirling, half-dreaming world when she awoke to the sound of a muffled voice, but now there was no voice, no sound, no movement of any kind.

With her feline eyes she had always been able to see, even in the dimmest, most shadowed places, but here she was blind. She searched for the faintest glint of light in the gloom, but there was no moonlight coming in through a window, no faint flicker of a distant lantern down a corridor.

Just black.

She closed her eyes and reopened them. But it made no difference. It was still pitch-dark.

Have I actually gone blind? she wondered.

Confused, she tried to listen out into the darkness as she had done when she hunted rats deep in the corridors of Biltmore's sprawling basement. But there was no creak of the house, no servants working in distant rooms, no father snoring in a nearby cot, no machinery whirring, no clocks ticking or footsteps. It was cold, still, and quiet in a way she had never known. She was no longer at Biltmore.

Remembering the voice that had woken her, she listened for it again, but whether it had been real or part of a dream, it was gone now.

Where am I? she thought in bewilderment. *How did I get here?*

Then a sound finally came, as if in answer to her question.

Thump-thump.

For a moment that was all there was.

Thump-thump, thump-thump.

The beat of her heart and the pulse of her blood.

Thump-thump, thump-thump, thump-thump.

As she slowly moved her tongue to moisten her cracked, dry lips, she sensed the faint taste of metal in her mouth.

But it wasn't metal.

It was blood—her own blood flowing through her veins into her tongue and her lips.

She tried to clear her throat, but then all at once she took in a sudden, violent, jerking breath and sucked in a great gasp of air, as if it were the very first breath she had ever taken. As her blood flowed, a tingling feeling flooded into her arms and legs and all through her body.

What is going on? she thought. *What happened to me? Why am I waking up like this?*

Thinking back through her life, she remembered living with her pa in the workshop, and battling the Black Cloak and the Twisted Staff with her best friend, Braeden. She'd finally come out into the grand rooms and daylight world of the fancy folk. But when she tried to remember what happened next, it was like trying to recall the fleeting details of a powerful dream that drifts away the moment you wake. It left her disoriented and confused, as if she was grasping for the tattered remnants of a previous life.

She had not yet moved her body, but she felt herself lying on her back on a long, flat surface. Her legs were straight, her hands neatly lying one over the other on her chest, like someone had laid her there with respect and care.

She slowly separated her hands and moved them down on either side of her body to feel the surface beneath her.

It felt hard, like rough wooden boards, but the boards felt strangely *cold*. *The boards shouldn't be cold,* she thought. *Not like this. Not cold.*

Her heart began to pound in her chest. A wild panic rose inside her.

She tried to sit up, but immediately slammed her forehead into a hard surface a few inches above her, and she crashed down again, wincing in pain.

She pressed her hands against the boards above her. Her probing fingers were her only eyes. There were no breaks or openings in the boards. Her palms began to sweat. Her breaths got shorter. A desperate surge of fear poured through her as she craned her body and pushed to the side, but there were boards there, too, just inches away. She kicked her feet. She pounded her fists. But the boards surrounded her, closing her in on all sides.

Serafina growled in frustration, fear, and anger. She scratched and she scurried, she twisted and she pried, but she could not escape. She had been enclosed in a long, flat wooden box.

She pressed her face frantically into the corner of the box and sniffed, like a trapped little animal, hoping to catch a scent from the outside world through the thin cracks between the boards. She tried one corner, and then the next, but the smell was the same all around her.

Dirt, she thought. *I'm surrounded by damp, rotting dirt. I've been buried alive!*

Serafina lay in the cold black space of the coffin buried underground. Her mind flooded with terror.

I need to get out of here, she kept thinking. *I need to breathe. I'm not dead!*

But she could not see. She could not move. She could not hear anything other than the sound of her own ragged breathing. How much air would she have down here? She felt a tight constriction in her lungs. Her chest gripped her. She wanted her pa! She wanted her mother to come and dig her out. Someone had to save her! She frantically pressed her hands against the coffin lid above her head and pushed with all her strength, but she couldn't lift it. The sound of her screeching voice hurt her ears in this terrible, closed-in, black place.

Then she thought about what her pa would say if he was here. "Get your wits about ya, girl. Figure out what ya need to do and get on with doin' it."

She sucked in another long breath, and then steadied herself and tried to think it through. She couldn't see with her eyes, but she traced her fingers along the skirt and sleeves of her dress. They were badly torn. It seemed like if she had died and there had been a funeral, then they would have put her in a nice dress. Whoever had buried her had been in a hurry. Had they thought she was dead? Or did they want her to suffer the most horrible of deaths?

At that moment, she heard the faint, muffled sound of movement above her. Her heart filled with hope. *Footsteps!*

"Help!" she screamed as loud as she possibly could. "Help me! Please help me!"

She screamed and screamed. She pounded the wood above her head. She flailed her legs. But the sound of the footsteps drifted away, then disappeared and left a silence so complete that she wasn't sure she'd heard the sound at all.

Had it been the person who buried her? Had he heaved the last shovel of dirt onto her grave and left her here? Or was it a passerby who had no idea she was here? She slammed her fists against the boards and screamed, "Please! I need your help! I'm down here!"

But it was no use.

She was alone.

She felt a dark wave of hopelessness pour through her soul.

She could not escape.

She could not survive this . . .

No, she thought, gritting her teeth. *I'm not gonna let myself die down here. I'm not gonna give up. I'm going to stay bold! I'm going to find a way out . . .*

She slid herself down toward the end of the coffin and kicked. The coffin's rough boards felt thin and crudely made, not like a proper solid casket, but like a ramshackle box nailed together from discarded apple crates. But the earth behind the rickety wood braced the boards so firmly that it was impossible for her to break them.

Then she had an idea.

"Six feet under." That was what her had pa told her years ago when she asked him what they did with dead people. "'Round here they bury folk six feet under," he'd said.

She squirmed inside the dark, cramped space, bending her body up like a little kitten in a lady's shoe box, and positioned herself so that she could put her hands on the top center of the coffin's lid. She figured that six feet of dirt must weigh an awful lot. And her pa had taught her that the center of a board was its weakest point.

Remembering something else he'd taught her, she knocked on the board above her and listened. *Tap-tap-tap.* Then she moved down a few inches and knocked again. *Tap-tap-tap.* She kept knocking until she found a place with a slightly deeper, more hollow sound where the dirt was packed a little less firmly behind it. "That's the spot."

But now what? Even if she managed to crack the board, the dirt above would come crashing down on her. Her mouth and nose would fill with dirt and she'd suffocate. "That's not gonna work. . . ."

Suddenly an idea sprang into her mind. She buttoned her dress tight up to her neck and then pulled the lower part of the dress up over her head, inside out, so that the fabric covered her face, especially her mouth and nose. It was cramped in the coffin and difficult to move, but she managed to get the dress bundled around her head and then wriggled her arms out of the sleeves so that her hands were free. If she was lucky, the fabric over her face would give her the seconds she needed.

Knowing that her hands alone weren't strong enough to break the boards, she rolled onto her stomach and positioned her shoulder at the top center of the coffin.

Bracing herself, she pushed upward with her arms and legs and the strength of her whole body. There wasn't enough space inside the coffin to get herself all the way up onto her hands and knees. But she bent herself into a coil and pushed the best she could, slamming her shoulder against the coffin's lid over and over again. She knew that one strong blow wasn't going to do it. And slow pressure wasn't, either. She needed to get a good, hard, forceful rhythm going. *Bang, bang, bang.* She could feel the long boards of the coffin's lid flexing. "That's it, that's what we need," she said. *Bang, bang, bang* she slammed. "Come on!" she growled. Then she heard the center board cracking beneath the weight of the earth above. "Come on!" She kept pushing. *Bang, bang, bang.* The board began to split. Then she felt something cold hit her bare shoulders. She should have been filled with joy that her plan was actually working, but her mind filled with fear. The lid had cracked! The coffin was caving in! Cold, clammy, heavy dirt dumped all over her, pushing her down to the coffin floor. If she hadn't tied her dress over her head, her mouth and nose would have filled with dirt at that very moment and she would have been dead.

Working blind, with nothing but her grasping hands to guide her, she grabbed great handfuls of the incoming dirt and chucked them into the corners of the coffin, packing the dirt away as fast as it poured down through the hole, but it just kept coming, coming, coming. The terrible weight of the dirt surrounded her legs and shoulders and head. It was getting more and more difficult to move. She sucked in breaths through the fabric of her dress as fast and hard as she could. Her chest heaved in panic. She couldn't get enough air!

Finally, when there was no more space in the coffin to push the dirt, she tried to make her escape. She jammed her head straight up through the hole, pushed with her legs, and started digging toward the surface. But the dirt came down so fast, and pushed in so hard, she never had a chance. Even as she dug, the dirt began to suffocate her. Its crushing weight pushed against her chest, driving one last scream from her lungs.

Loose earth poured down around her head and shoulders, collapsing onto her faster than she could dig it away. She felt the pressing weight of it all around her, closing in on her, trapping her legs, but she kept clawing, kicking, squirming her way blindly up through the darkness, desperately trying to pull gasps of air through the fabric covering her face. She felt the material pushing deeper and deeper into her mouth as the dirt pressed in, gagging her, shutting off the flow of air to her aching lungs.

Then she heard a fast scratching sound above her, like the frenzied digging of an animal. She hoped that Gidean, Braeden's dog, was trying to rescue her, but a terrible, low growling sound told her it wasn't her canine friend. Whatever kind of creature it was, the beast's claws tore at the earth, ripping it away with terrific power. Was it a bear digging up its supper? It didn't matter. She had to keep climbing. She had to breathe!

Sharp claws raked across her upstretched hands. Serafina shrieked in pain, but she grabbed hold of the beast's paw. *Gotcha!* She held on for dear life. The force of the paw yanked her body up through the ground.

The snarling beast jerked its paw again, trying to free itself of her, yanking and pulling, but Serafina held on tight.

When her head finally broke the surface of the ground, she sucked in a mighty gasp of air, flooding her lungs with new life. Air! She finally had air!

She lost her grip on the beast's paw and it pulled away, but she clambered out of the dirt until her shoulders and arms were free.

Hope filled her heart. She'd made it! She'd escaped! But as she reached up and pulled the fabric from her head, she heard a loud roaring snarl, and the claws came down at her again, raking across her scalp just as she tried to duck away. Clutching wildly at the earth with her hands, she quickly scrambled out of the grave and got up onto her hands and knees to defend herself.

She had crawled out of the ground into a moonlit graveyard, overgrown by a dense forest of trees and vines. A large stone angel, with her wings raised up around her, stood on a pedestal in the center of the small clearing. Serafina had no idea how she'd gotten here, but she knew this place. It was the angel's glade. But before she could take it all in, she heard something behind her and spun around.

A black panther was coming straight toward her, crouched low for the lunge, its ears pinned back, its face quivering with fierceness as it opened its mouth and hissed with its long fangs bared and gleaming, ready to bite.